THE

KREMLIN BETRAYAL

THE
KREMLIN BETRAYAL

Leon Berger

A LOON IN BALLOON BOOK

THE KREMLIN BETRAYAL
© 2008 Leon Berger

Library and Archives Canada Cataloguing in Publication

Berger, Leon, 1949-
    The Kremlin betrayal / Leon Berger. -- 1st ed.

ISBN 978-0-9737497-5-5

    I. Title.

PS8553.E672K74 2008   C813'.54   C2008-903502-X

Published by: Loon in Balloon Inc.
                  Suite #3-513
                  133 Weber Street North
                  Waterloo, Ontario
                  Canada   N2J 3G9

Cover design by Leon Berger and Jef Burnard
Interior design by Jef Burnard

Printed and bound in Canada by
Friesens Corporation
Altona, Manitoba, Canada

FIRST EDITION
987654321

ACKNOWLEDGMENTS

While historical facts can be researched through articles, biographies and archives, the real flavour of an era only comes from the people who lived it. I'm therefore grateful to everyone who took the time to recall their personal memories of London and elsewhere from the days of the early Cold War.

In particular, I'd like to offer special thanks to Pauline Sawadsky of Lachine, Québec, who related numerous anecdotes of her remarkable life. Her formative years were spent in Ukraine under the oppression of Stalin. When Hitler invaded in 1941, her small town came under Nazi authority and she was consigned to work as a slave labourer. She spent the post-war years as a refugee in England, before finally arriving in Canada.

I should also mention a Moscow businessman called Sergei, who I met by chance in the bar of the Budapest Kempinski, not long after the Soviet Union fell. He told me he'd been a member of his country's diplomatic service during the post-war years, and his rambling tales of poverty and scarcity in the former East Berlin formed the basis of my descriptions in this novel. I recall buying several rounds of expensive scotch but I never did learn his family name.

KEY INTELLIGENCE AGENCIES OF THE COLD WAR: 1952/53

USSR
MGB: *Ministerstvo Gosudarstvennoi Bezopasnosti -*
Ministry for State Security
MVD: *Ministerstvo Vnutrennikh Del -*
Ministry for Internal Affairs
(Later, both organizations were merged into the KGB)

East Germany
MfS: *Ministerium für Staatssicherheit,* a.k.a. Stasi -
Ministry for State Security

USA
CIA: Central Intelligence Agency (formerly OSS)
FBI: Federal Bureau of Investigation -
domestic counter-intelligence
NSA: National Security Agency -
cryptology and communications analysis

UK
SIS: Secret Intelligence Service a.k.a. MI6
MI5: counter-intelligence
Special Branch: police division responsible for national security

West Germany
Gehlen Organization: CIA-sponsored, known to employ many
ex-Nazi SS
(Later became BND, the state Federal Intelligence Service)

"I trust no one, not even myself."
Joseph Stalin

PROLOGUE

London: Autumn, 1953

Even now, six months after Stalin's death, I'm still hearing the whispers.

What they're saying is that the 74-year-old dictator didn't die of natural causes, as officially reported by *Pravda, Izvestia, Tass* and the rest of the Soviet media apparatus, but that he was assassinated during dinner on the night of February 28th, his fatal hemorrhage having been deliberately induced by the ingestion of warfarin, a flavourless compound often used as rat poison.

If such a case could ever be made, the prime suspects would have to be the four members of the Kremlin Politburo who were with him at his Blizhnyaya *dacha* on that particular evening. All of them gained considerably from his parting. They were Georgi Malenkov, Nikolai Bulganin, Nikita Khrushchev and, perhaps most sinister of all, Stalin's close friend and fellow Georgian, Lavrenti Beria, the balding, bespectacled Minister for Internal Affairs, who probably had the best motive of any of them. He was about to be purged. This meant either a quick death by firing squad, or a slow death behind barbed wire in a frozen Siberian gulag. It all depended on Stalin's whim.

As for me, I'm neither confirming nor denying the assassination rumour. But if, for the sake of argument, there were indeed some legitimacy to the notion, I might just be in a position to offer some fairly damning evidence. That's right, me, a complete nonentity, a total nothing in the great scheme of things: Edmund Albert Schaeffer - itinerant journalist, world-weary traveller and occasional dupe.

I'm also fully aware that harbouring such knowledge might be extremely prejudicial to my well-being, which is why I'm spending this wet Wednesday afternoon at the Kardomah coffee house on Oxford Street, a location that's reassuringly public. My aim is to set down as much as I can, as soon as I can, just in case something untoward should happen in the near future: perhaps a stray brick from an overhead construction site; or maybe a slight shove in the back just as the Central Line eastbound comes rattling into Holborn station. There's no end to the creative possibilities a Soviet *razvedchik* might dream up.

As can be imagined, this situation is not doing much for my state of health, either. I appear considerably older than my half-century on this earth would suggest and, on certain days, I don't even recognize myself when shaving. My gray eyes seem to have sunken ever deeper into their sockets, my face has taken on the texture of faded leather and my hair, once a rich sheen of umber, is now the same colour as a racoon. I'm still reasonably robust, I suppose, but I can't seem to do anything about my elevated blood pressure or clogged arteries: the kind of chronic symptoms that result from high stress and snatched food.

Worse, my entire life seems to have left me like a stranded refugee. I grew up in Berlin, Ontario, only child of a German-Irish union, but my parents died in an accident during my last year of school. Eventually, after wandering the world aimlessly for a while, I washed up as a freelance correspondent in that other Berlin, the slightly more famous one in Germany. Thanks to my father, I spoke the language fluently and, during my decade there, I made a lot of friends. But then, of course, along came Hitler and most of them perished too. As if that weren't enough, the only woman I ever really loved, Katharina, was forced out of my life when the Third Reich finally deported me in 1938.

So, today, here I am in this brave, post-war world, physically present but spiritually lost, with history repeating itself before my eyes. Instead of the Nazis, we now have the Soviets to worry about but, if you ask me, there's really not much to choose between them. Fascists, Communists - they're supposed to be at opposite ends of the ideological spectrum but the result is the same: tyranny, coercion and mass murder, all justified by endless tracts of propaganda.

In fact, the only real difference this time around is that the

Soviets have managed to steal the secrets of the atomic warhead from right under our Western noses. It means that, even as I sit here in civilized London, the megaton payloads are within striking distance. Yes, that's right. The hell-fires of Armageddon can arrive with just a few minutes' warning and the best advice Her Majesty's Government can offer is to suggest that, when the sirens wail and the mushroom clouds threaten, factory workers should crouch beneath their benches, housewives should descend to their basements, and schoolchildren should crawl under their desks. It's true. It's all printed in the leaflets the ministry hands out.

But is anyone here worried? It sure doesn't seem like it to me.

As I glance around from my table, I see the same solid citizens who survived the Blitz, except they're now a little older and more prosperous. To my left, for example, are a couple of salesmen taking a break, their sample cases on the floor next to them. One is older, a shrewd veteran of his trade, while the other is a fresh-faced apprentice in his new Tweed jacket. Over to my right are three prim ladies with their latest Doris Day hair-do's, surrounded by packages from their lunch-hour shopping expedition at Selfridges. Beyond, near the back wall, there's a crowd of pimply undergrads with striped varsity scarves, joking around in order to get a rise out of a dour, thin-lipped waitress from Lancashire. The aroma of the foamy espresso she's serving seems to percolate its way through the thick, clingy atmosphere of damp raincoats and Player's cigarettes.

It's an intriguing portrait of a society in change, with all the makings of an in-depth article I could perhaps sell to some of the more serious magazines; or at least I would, if only I could apply myself. The problem for me right now is that I'm just a little distracted by the necessities of my own survival.

The grim fact is that any one of the nice people who wander in here might be a Soviet agent and I have to be continually on my guard. Am I being watched or followed? Are my most innocuous movements being observed, noted and analyzed? Are my letters and phone calls being intercepted and transcribed? This is no mere paranoia on my part, I assure you. After the series of recent spy scandals, I have good reason to be concerned. The names seem to crowd the headlines: Rosenberg, Sarant, Barr, Fuchs, Burgess, Maclean, Cairncross and so many others; all those painfully naive denizens of the West who, for their own convoluted idealism, chose to betray their native lands. What it all goes to prove is that, in this new lunacy we call the Cold War, the Soviet threat is all too real and I fear I've become just another of their many targets.

How the hell did I get into this mess?

That's an excellent question and it deserves an answer, if only to myself. That's why I've been working on this account of how it happened, following the trail to Stalin's death, and trying to place the many factors into some kind of sequence, as well as into perspective. The information comes from myriad sources, both classified and off-the-record. But, to the best of my knowledge, this is how the chain of events linked itself together and how, for a brief time, I became an intelligence agent; a secret operative at the very centre of a geopolitical fiasco.

To begin, we must go back a year and a half - long before my own personal involvement - to that first Soviet incursion into Western territory. Risk was inherent to the operation, as it would be with any such paramilitary action, but nobody at the Kremlin could have possibly envisaged the full extent of the debacle, or its far-reaching consequences.

1952

We open this blood-stained chronicle during the pre-dawn hours of Saturday, April 12th, when a submarine of the Soviet Navy left its supply dock at the grimy Polish port of Gdansk and slipped unobtrusively into the cold, black swell of the Baltic Sea. On board was a full complement of fifty-two maritime personnel, plus a four-man *spetznaz*, a special ops combat unit of the MGB, the Ministry for State Security.

Due to the importance of the mission, the vessel assigned was not one of the captured ex-Nazi U-boats, of which there were over a dozen still active in the Soviet fleet, but the newly designed Whiskey class S-80, first of the Project 613 series, laid down in 1950 at the Gorky yards and launched for sea trials later that year. It was an efficient craft, powered by quiet, diesel-electric engines and well-armed with a comprehensive arsenal of torpedoes, mines and cannon. For the current operation, however, it had one major flaw. The S-80 was designed primarily for coastal patrol, not for long-range operation.

After the vessel had cleared the harbour perimeter, the *spetznaz* gathered privately in the cramped galley behind closed doors. That's when the leader of the unit, a humourless 41-year-old called Vladimir Petrov, unlocked a scratched metal briefcase and pulled out a thick folder containing the mission orders. He was slightly taller than average, with cropped, rust-coloured hair and a raw-boned face that had been wiped of expression by his experience during that last battle for Berlin in the spring of '45, when he'd been obliged to fire on boys of ten and eleven who'd been drafted to defend the dying Nazi regime. It was primarily for that reason that he loathed everything to do with Germany and the Germans with a special, personal bitterness. They'd turned him into a child-killer and the involuntary shame was seared into his soul.

His big hands were ingrained with grease, more used to the hardware of war than the sheaves of a written briefing, and he unclipped the various papers as if he were disassembling a Kalashnikov. The first item he opened was a nautical map of the Baltic region. He spread it out on the table, then stabbed a forefinger at their target location: a small West German island situated in the narrow straits between the north coast of Schleswig-Holstein and the southernmost Danish territory of Lolland.

"Fehmarn," he said succinctly. "Quiet, rural, mostly flat. The good news is that it's a night mission under covert conditions. If all goes well, there should be no need for weapons discharge."

"What's the bad news?" This was the youngest of the team, Pavel Filshin, from Rostov near the Russian-Ukrainian border. He had the brash confidence of youth and was invariably quick with a remark: sometimes too quick for his own good. It occasionally landed him in trouble.

Petrov stared at him for a long moment before voicing the reprimand: "You looked at the map but you didn't *see* it." Then he turned to his second-in-command, a sergeant by the name of Mischa Borovik, a broad-shouldered man with a pockmarked face and a temperament to match. "Mischa, what's the bad news?"

Borovik's voice was low and hoarse, the throaty sound of a heavy smoker. "The bad news is that this tub can't make it that far. We don't have the range."

Petrov gave a single nod of confirmation. "More accurately, we don't have the range *submerged*. But this is the best we've got, so we'll make it work."

"How?" This was Filshin again. "By swimming the rest of the way?" His instant grin revealed the empty space where he lost one of his front molars in an inter-service hockey game.

From Petrov, not even the flicker of a smile. "No," he replied, as if it had been a serious question. "We'll do it by surface-running as much we can. That way, we'll have the range and we can also make better speed."

"How much?" Filshin asked.

"How much what?"

"How much time will we spend surface-running?"

"Close to seventy per cent." Petrov paused to let the communal groan take its course. "But most of that will be in darkness," he continued. "Any risk will be at first and last light. If you want a positive assessment, the navy says they expect no opposition in the area, which means no British, no Americans. The Scandinavians have nothing that can track us."

"How about the Germans?" This was the fourth member of the unit, the taciturn Likhachev from Krasnoyarsk, east of the Urals. He was, of course, talking about the West Germans, not the new "comrades" to the east. They had no military resources, banned since 1945, but it was their home territory and there might be all manner of police and civilian activity along the coastline, from authorized rescue services to simple fishing boats, any of which could lead to a submarine sighting.

"Screw the Germans," rumbled Petrov, not really caring too much if the vitriol of his memories affected his judgment. He felt he was entitled to his own realities.

In response, he received a murmur of agreement from his sergeant, Mischa Borovik, who'd also fought in the war. The two younger men, Filshin and Likhachev, glanced at each other but, this time, they chose to remain silent. So far, they weren't too impressed, either with the tone of the briefing, or with the odds of success.

The Fehmarn plan was certainly audacious, perhaps even reck-less, yet I believe it might well have succeeded had it not been for Moscow's written directive, which fell unexpectedly into the wrong hands. As obsessive as the Soviets can be on such matters, it's reasonable to state that nobody at the Kremlin could have possibly predicted this eventuality.

The document in question originated on the executive third floor of the Lubyanka, the notorious centre for state security, and was dispatched in the form of a DKS, a numerically coded file. It was classified at the highest security level, OV, or *Osoboy Vazhnosti* (special importance) and, then, just to emphasize its priority status, the envelope was sealed with the imprint of the Minister for Internal Affairs himself, Lavrenti Beria. As a result, it caused something of a flurry when it finally arrived at the Soviet Control Commission in the Lichtenberg district of East Berlin.

The instant it cleared the delivery pouch, it was hand-carried through the building by the ranking duty officer. According to inter-nal procedure, any dispatch with that classification had first to be delivered to the desk of the Commission chairman, Vasily Chuikov, the stern, unyielding peasant-soldier who'd earned his reputation at the brutal siege of Stalingrad. However, since his office fell under the auspices of the GSFG, the Soviet military occupation authority, he was under no obligation to acknowledge its receipt. He didn't care for clandestine activity and he especially didn't like Beria. He therefore refused to open it and handed it immediately back to the duty officer, instructing him in barrack-room language to get the damn thing directly to its intended destination, as shown clearly on the address label: Department B-1 of the MGB at Karlshorst, local headquarters of the First Directorate, responsible for all covert intelligence in the territory of West Germany.

When the highly classified envelope finally arrived at the MGB, the acceptance docket was reluctantly signed off by the head of station, a saggy-jowled, deeply-lined Muscovite of middle age by the name of Alexei Mikhailov, code name "Axel." He had wavy hair and heavy black eyebrows which shifted according to his expression.

Once upon a time, Mikhailov had been a typical young recruit, fresh from the Chekist academy and willing enough to advance the Bolshevik cause wherever it might take him. During the "Great Patriotic War," as the struggle against Hitler was known, he'd actually been based in New York, at the consulate on the Upper East Side, where he became one of a team of Soviet operatives trying to pry loose the most precious nuclear secrets from the heart of Los Alamos.

But, after 1945, everything changed and there was a long period of organizational flux. The NKVD, which had achieved such spectacular espionage success in both the US and the UK, underwent several transmutations. First, it was split into the MGB, responsible for state intelligence, and the MVD, which had jurisdiction over internal security. Then, various functions of both were briefly amalgamated with GRU, military intelligence, to form the ungainly KI under Molotov. When that proved unworkable, the military withdrew the GRU, leaving most aspects of clandestine activity to the enlarged MGB.

Any of these changes might have provided Mikhailov with an opportunity to return to Moscow, perhaps even to a hero's welcome, but he was shrewd enough to know that the farther he stayed from the machinations and purges of his home city, the safer he would remain. So, he volunteered for yet another foreign posting, this time in Berlin, divided capital of the newly formed *Deutsche Demokratische Republik*, known in English as the GDR, the official nomenclature for the Soviet puppet state of East Germany.

Fortunately, he was well-equipped for the role. Although his waistline had become a little thicker than it was in his prime, he'd replaced his physical stamina with an even more important asset for someone of his profession: patience. Over the years, he'd become a great deal more cautious and had, by his own conscious efforts, developed a remarkable instinct for his specialized trade. In Mikhailov's own marginal world, he was judged to be one of the great survivors and he didn't want to ruin his record at this late stage of his career.

For a few moments, he sat with the envelope in his hands and considered what to do. He, too, would have liked to ignore it but, unlike Comrade Chairman Chuikov, he didn't have the luxury of that option. He was expected to deal with it and he knew it meant a long night ahead, so the first thing he did was order fresh tea from his secretary. Then, with something of a sigh, he closed the door to his office, unlocked the cipher books from his personal safe and tried to focus on the task at hand. Decryption was a mundane job normally left to department technicians but, in this case, the unusually high classification required him to handle it himself. He was a little out of practice, so the task took longer than he thought but, once he was done, he knew for certain that he, and he alone, was aware of its contents.

Outside, the sky was lightening towards another sullen morning and he could already make out the sad, gray buildings of Karlshorst. No bright neon or inviting storefronts here, not like in the western sectors of Berlin. Not like New York either, he thought, where the energy and enterprise just seemed to continue unabated, even during the war.

In many ways, he regretted leaving the US. He wasn't a true Marxist ideologue, never had been: just a loyal, faithful servant of the Soviet Union who tried to do his best. Like many others in his position, his only aim in procuring military secrets was to help his country "even out the odds," to use his favourite phrase, first in the fight against Nazi Germany and then, after the war, to ensure a world balance-of-power with the almighty Americans. In his view, his actions in this regard were both reasonable and justified. Although his work here in East Germany could be seen as a continuation of that same effort, he found the country here to be cold and depressing, much more severe than he ever expected. Despite a higher position with more responsibility, the daily hardships made his existence seem monotonous and his life lethargic. He found himself longing for the hectic pace of Manhattan and the vibrancy of his old Washington Square neighbourhood, with its multitude of ethnic restaurants: Chinese, Italian and Jewish - small, informal places, where he and his wife could sit and talk and laugh.

More and more, these days, he was indulging in these small bouts of nostalgia and it was out of such thoughts that the idea originally formed itself, an idea he just couldn't seem to shake. On the contrary, the longer he considered it, the more the pieces began to fit into place. The notion had lain dormant in the alcoves of his brain for many years and all it needed was the right moment to shake loose. Suddenly, today, here it was. The directive that had just fallen into his hands was so highly classified that, within the entire Soviet framework of East Germany, he was the only one who knew about it. This was the opportunity he'd been waiting for.

Still, he hesitated.

For an hour, two hours, he sat there, gazing out at nothing at all. Finally, he took a deep breath and simply placed the decrypted file into his worn black briefcase. It was as easy as that. Then he pulled on his overcoat, turned out the light, locked his office door and descended to the car park. If he returned the document within a few hours, no-one would be any the wiser and no harm would be done. If not, he'd be committing the most serious crime of all under Soviet law: treason against the state.

By my calculation, it was just as Alexei Mikhailov was driving home through the early-morning streets of East Berlin that, three hundred kilometres to the north, the Soviet Navy S-80 encountered the enemy frigate. As far as I can tell, the dates and times pretty much coincide.

At that hour, the submarine was still surface-running through the murky Baltic tides, trying to eke out as much distance as possible before the emerging daylight made it vulnerable to observation.

The course it was following had been pre-determined as the best compromise under difficult circumstances. While a route that hugged the Polish shoreline would have been safer, it was less direct; on the other hand, a passage closer to the Danish island of Bornholm would have meant a shorter journey but it left them far too exposed to casual observation. The only choice was to thread the gap between the two extremes, chart a course down the centre and hope that the springtime ocean swell would hide them, at least as far as Rügen. After that, it was all or nothing. They'd have to make a run for it, adjusting to a southwest heading for the final approach through the straits known as the Mecklenburger Bucht to the island of Fehmarn.

It was a bold maneuver and the navy planning committee knew in advance it would require a certain measure of good fortune to succeed. This morning, however, such fortune seemed to be in short supply.

At approximately 05:45, the watch officer spotted the silhouette of a frigate on the bright eastern horizon. It appeared to be changing course, circling around towards them, as if tracking. Potentially, such vessels have lethal capability against submarines and the order was immediately issued to dive to periscope depth. Had the S-80 been detected? There was no way to tell at this range. If the oncoming ship was of recent design, it would no doubt be equipped with the newer sensoring systems but the captain of the S-80 couldn't yet make that kind of visual identification.

Down below, the *spetznaz* gathered in Petrov's claustrophobic cabin and waited, their anxiety multiplied by their own feelings of helplessness. Under these conditions, locked away inside this steel cigar tube, what could they possibly do? They were fighting men with no way to fight.

The frigate steamed closer on what seemed like an obvious intercept course until it was less than a kilometre away. That's when word came down to Petrov that it was sailing under a Danish flag: good news that brought a general sigh of relief. The only frigates currently in service for that nation were obsolete as fighting ships: the River class "Holder Danske" and "Niels Ebbesen," both purchased from Britain at the end of the war and refitted solely for training purposes. However, just to be safe, the S-80 descended to a depth of twenty metres and came to a full stop, holding position until the Danish ship steamed past, totally unaware of what lay directly beneath.

As far as Petrov could make out, the encounter was by pure chance and the intercepting vectors the kind of random occurrence that can happen at sea. Nevertheless, it had been a close call. If he believed in destiny, he might have perceived it as some kind of omen but, being of a pragmatic nature, he simply dismissed the incident from his mind and sat down with his men to breakfast.

Home for Alexei Mikhailov of the MGB First Directorate, Berlin, offered no respite from his bleak surroundings: just a drab apartment block in Marzahn, east of Lichtenberg.

I knew that area from before the war and, even back then, it was depressed: an ailing district which hardly deserved the designation "working-class" because work so was hard to come by. When the Soviets took over, they installed some limited social facilities on behalf of the Party and even tried to initiate several trade associations but, with a moribund economy and a scarcity of resources, most of these efforts floundered.

Due to the covert nature of his occupation, Mikhailov took no part in such neighbourhood activities. His wife, Irina, had at least managed to make limited contact with a few of the building residents so as to appear friendly and not arouse suspicion but he, himself, was only on nodding acquaintance and he normally tried to cause as little disturbance as possible as he went about his business. This morning was no exception and he did his best to tread softly on the cold, cracked concrete as he hauled himself wearily up to his fourth-floor apartment in the early light. There was once a working elevator but it had been out of service for three months and nobody had yet been to inspect the thing, never mind fix it.

The problem was that he couldn't just select his own place to live. This was East Germany and accommodations were officially assigned. But every time he complained to the Soviet Control Commission, they said the same thing. They told him to relax, that the situation was just temporary; except that he and his wife had been living here for over a year now with no hint of anything better coming up any time soon. He understood the irony - it was his own

Red Army that had destroyed most of the local infrastructure during the last few weeks of the Third Reich - but that didn't fully explain the situation. If the West was successfully rebuilding, why couldn't the East? In Moscow, Foreign Minister Molotov had rejected the Marshall Plan concept as "dollar imperialism" but cynics replied that it was only because the Soviet Union lacked dollars.

Out of breath as usual, Mikhailov paused on his landing to sort the right key from his ring. Even now, at daybreak, the stairwell smelled of boiled cabbage. He thought Irina would still be asleep but, when he entered, he found her in the kitchen on her hands and knees, with her head under the sink and an outsized wrench in her hands.

"There's a leak," she told him by way of a greeting. "I think it's dripping through downstairs. Any minute now, we'll have that old *babushka* up here, yelling and banging on the door."

"Did you call the janitor?"

"Janitor? What Janitor? Have you ever seen a janitor around here? Me, I think the whole idea of a janitor is just a bad joke."

Gently, he helped her to her feet. Then he stood back as she made an unconscious attempt to tidy her messy hair. She'd tied it back with a clip but long strands had made their escape and now hung down over her cheek. She was a slim, sandy-haired woman, with delicate, almost pixie-like features and narrow hands that were now sore from having scraped them.

Despite her fragile appearance, Irina Mikhailov had a practical nature, having trained as a seamstress back in Yaroslavsky, an ordinary working class district within the Severo-Vostochny *okrug*, the north-eastern administrative district of Moscow. By her own admission, she wasn't as attractive as she used to be - her eyes, for example, looked listless and hollowed out - but she liked to think she made up for it with her supportive attitude. Yet even that seemed to be getting harder here in Berlin and her good-natured tolerance had given way to a kind of long-suffering perseverance.

Alexei Mikhailov understood and wasn't unsympathetic. In fact, truth be told, he was surprised his marriage had lasted this long, after all he'd put her through over the years.

"I thought you'd be still asleep," he said to her quietly.

She looked about ready to cry from the frustration, so he lifted one of her hands to his lips and kissed it, enjoying the slightly embarrassed look on her face at this irresponsibly romantic gesture.

"This place..." she said, not even bothering to complete the sentence.

"I know, I know."

He took a cursory glance around, at the chipped porcelain, the warped cupboards, and the scratched and scraped linoleum on the floor that might have once been blue. Beyond was the cramped living room, with old wallpaper covering the cracks and worn curtains doing their best to prevent drafts from the badly-fitting windows. The bedroom was no better but at least they had their own bathroom and toilet which, according to the Soviet Control Commission's bureaucracy, qualified the place as a "luxury" apartment.

When he looked back at her, he could see that a tear had already begun to form. It was no more than a bead of moisture in the corner of her eye, but it was unmistakable - and this was the moment he made his final decision.

"What if I told you," he said, "that you'll never have to spend another night here?"

She raised her face up to his, neither understanding nor believing what he was saying to her, and she immediately assumed the worst. "Why? What happened? You're being transferred? You're being sent back to Moscow? Oh my God, I knew this would happen, I knew that one day..."

He placed his finger to her lips to calm her down. "None of the above," he said.

For a few moments she waited until she couldn't take it any more. "What?" she demanded. Then she reached out and shook him by the arms. "Alexei, *what*?"

Yet another second or two passed. "How would you like to go back to the West?"

"To the West? Where? New York?"

"I was thinking somewhere like London."

"London? You *are* being transferred."

"No, I'm not."

There was a silence but it was only to absorb the full scope of what he was telling her. She was no fool and didn't need to have it spelled out. From the little he'd said, she could work it out only too well and her reply came almost as a whisper, as if uttering the words out loud would be too rash, even here in the privacy of their own apartment.

"You're going to defect," she said. It was less a question than a statement.

"Only if you agree."

It was almost too much for her to contemplate. "I don't know... I mean, you always said... What I mean is, what would you have to do? You always told me that if it meant, you know, giving up names and so on... You said you'd never do that."

This was difficult for him. In all the years they'd been married, he'd never quite figured out just how much to tell his wife and had, invariably, settled his internal struggle by sharing just enough that she could feel included in his life but not enough that she would be imperilled by knowing too much. "I won't be giving up any names," he said.

"You won't? Then why... Why would they take you?"

"Because I've got something else they might want."

"Like what?"

Too many questions, he thought, and too much responsibility if he told her. "It's a document. Just a document."

"What sort of document?"

It wasn't suspicion in her voice as much as the need to know all the details of this enormous step they were about to take. Still, he was reluctant to reveal too much of the truth. The last thing he wanted was to blurt out that this so-called document was, in fact, a highly classified directive that had come straight from Beria himself, no doubt on Stalin's personal orders, and that it concerned a raid by armed combat agents into Western territory. Leaking information like that could mean a ticket, not to London, but to a Siberian gulag.

Mikhailov tempered his reply. "I think it's something the British might find of value," he said gently.

"It would still make you..." She came to a halt, not wishing to say such a terrible word to her husband.

"What? A traitor? Yes, you're right, it would."

"It wasn't an accusation, Alexei. I didn't mean it that way. I just want you to be sure..."

"Sure?"

"That you'll be able to live with yourself afterwards."

That's when it all came bubbling to the surface, all the frustrations, all the doubts. "Why, you think I haven't done enough for my country? Do you know what I gave them over the years? Do you have any idea? The secrets I stole for them? The plans I delivered? The risks I took? I just about gave them the entire atomic bomb, for heaven's sake."

"I know," she said softly, "I know."

"You think buying a new life with some lousy piece of paper even begins to compensate for what I've done? Don't we deserve a new life, Irina? Don't we deserve more than..." He indicated the apartment around them. "More than this?"

She sat down wearily at the small wooden table where they normally ate breakfast together: usually just a little salted fish, some yogurt and a slice of black bread. This morning, however, there was nothing prepared. She'd been too busy with the sink. She put her head in her hands and tried hard to concentrate, to get it all together in her mind, all the implications and possibilities. Then, after a while, she looked up at him slowly. "When? When do we go?"

He shrugged. "This morning. Now, if you like. The sooner, the better."

Then all at once, the realization set in and her face opened up. She leapt from the chair and, with a beaming smile and a girlish shriek, she threw her arms around his neck.

MGB manuals are crammed with even the most trivial of logistics data. I know, because I've met senior counter-intelligence analysts who spend their days poring over purloined copies; anything to gain a slight edge in this endless game they all play.

That's how I happened to learn, for example, that Department B-1 in Berlin was allowed the permanent use of five automobiles, all locally-built Sachsenrings. Of these, four were decrepit F8's, which must have taken the solitary motor pool mechanic all his time just to keep them on the road. The other car in the fleet was a more recent three-cylinder F9, which Alexei Mikhailov used in his capacity as head of station. It seems that this vehicle was maintained exclusively for him, one of his few worthwhile perks, and he drove it for both department business and whatever minimal pleasure he could salvage from his few spare weekends.

This morning's trip would fit into neither category, yet he had absolutely no guilt about taking the vehicle, even though he knew it would never again see the MGB compound at Karlshorst. Add car theft, he thought, to the list of crimes he was about to commit.

It took longer than they expected to decide what to pack, so it was just after 09:30 on Saturday, April 19th, that Alexei and Irina Mikhailov left their dump of an apartment for the last time. Neither of them was sorry to be leaving and they didn't even bother to take a last look around. They placed their suitcases in the back of the car - the matching set they bought at Macy's in New York - complete with the Moscow directive quickly stitched inside one of the linings by Irina, the ex-seamstress. It was her contribution, she told him.

On leaving the Marzahn tenement, they simply drove through the divided city, passing from the Mitte district in the East to the

Tiergarten in the West. In the spring of 1952, such a crossing was still comparatively painless, with few of the barriers and roadblocks that began going up just a few months later. From that point of view, their timing was fortuitous.

Once they were safely through the city core, they just kept going. While the Eastern half of the city was controlled by the Soviets, the Western sectors had been governed since 1945 by the three other occupying powers: American, British and French. In theory, Mikhailov could have chosen any of them to claim asylum but, in practice, the choice was more limited. Having worked undercover in the US, his relations with that nation were suspect. As for the French, he wasn't too impressed by their wartime complicity and nor did he speak their language. He therefore continued driving all the way across to the other side of town, to the 365-acre sports complex in Charlottenburg, which had originally been built for Hitler's showcase Olympics but which now housed the British military administration.

Mikhailov drove in under the shadow of Speer's stone stadium, its bombastic statues having emerged remarkably unscathed from the conflict, and came to a halt at the guardhouse barrier. With a friendly smile, he rolled down his window to address the fresh-faced soldier who stepped forward: a corporal, no more than nineteen or twenty. The uniform the young man wore was of heavy brown cloth, with polished black boots and, perched on the side of his head, a black beret. Not being a military man, Mikhailov didn't recognize the regimental badge but he certainly knew about guns and immediately identified the standard Lee-Enfield rifle that was slung almost casually over the corporal's shoulder.

"Good morning," said Mikhailov in fluent but accented English, a smooth amalgam of Soviet syntax with American pronunciation.

"Papers..." demanded the soldier in heavy Cockney. He made the word sound like "pipers."

"No... no, I don't have any papers. My name is Colonel Alexei Mikhailov, commander of the MGB First Directorate, Berlin."

The young man didn't seem too impressed and, in reply, just repeated his request, this time slower and louder to make sure the visitor understood: "I need to see your papers."

"No, I'm afraid you don't understand. I'm head of Soviet intelligence and I... we... that is, me and my wife here... would like to claim political asylum." Mikhailov waited but all he received was a blank look, so he just smiled gently. "Look, son, no offense, but maybe you should just fetch your boss, okay?"

Alexei Mikhailov gazed across the table at the officer who had introduced himself as Major Thomas Gallagher of British military intelligence: an angular, awkward man, with a mousy blond mustache to match his hair and pale blue eyes that seemed to squint in permanent suspicion. For Mikhailov, it was something of an insult, being obliged to answer accusatory questions by an inferior rank, almost like one of Stalin's *troika* inquisitions. Nevertheless, he was prepared to be civil, if that's what it would take.

"You see," Gallagher was saying amiably, "the problem for me is that, well, to be honest, it's just a little too good to be true. I mean, put yourself in my shoes. Here I am, working in a bit of overtime on a quiet weekend, minding my own business you might say, when all of a sudden, in walks... well, what some might consider the definitive prize. Rather convenient, don't you think? I mean, what are the chances?"

Mikhailov rubbed his hand across his face. He'd already been here an hour and, apart from the corporal on the gate and the sergeant who escorted him up here, this Major Gallagher was the only person he'd seen. Mikhailov decided to ignore the comment. There was no way he could alleviate the man's doubts anyway, so he just shrugged and looked around, as if noticing the environment for the first time. It was not an office but a small meeting room. On one side were a couple of windows that looked out on the bland wall of the stadium. On the other was a wide metal cabinet on top of which stood a large globe, the kind used in classrooms, with a flat dent in the Atlantic Ocean where it had been dropped. In the centre of the room, where they were sitting, was a scratched metal table with six vacant chairs. Quietly, he asked: "Are we expecting someone else?"

"Oh, yes, I expect so. I'm sure that, once the word's out, they'll be thick as flies wanting to meet you... all the merry men, each one hoping you're the real thing and that they can finally earn themselves a ticket out of here."

"You don't like Berlin, Major?"

"Why? Do you?"

Mikhailov surrendered the point. "I understand your doubts about me," he said. "In your place, I'd be the same."

"Oh, I'm sure you'd be a lot worse."

A half-smile from Mikhailov. "Yes, you're probably right."

"You say you were in New York during the war?"

"Attached to the consulate, yes."

"What street?"

"You're slipping, Major. You asked me that twenty minutes ago."

Gallagher gave it a little more emphasis. "What street?"

"East 61st."

"And what's around there?"

"Around there?"

"What's in the area, the vicinity?"

"Are you trying to catch me out, Major?"

"Just answer the question... if you can."

"All right, what's in the vicinity of East 61st Street? Now let me think... To the south, I believe there was East 60th and to the north? Ah, yes, that would have been East 62nd."

"Very droll," replied Gallagher. His face remained deadpan. "The point is, Colonel, if you're so chummy with our American friends, might I ask why you drove all the way across town to us? Why do *we* deserve such an honour?"

Mikhailov shrugged. "My wife would like to live in London."

"Ah, yes, I see. Shopping at Harrod's and so forth."

"Something like that."

"Well, that's understandable. And how about yourself? Wait, don't tell me. You love our way of life, right? A day at the races followed by an evening at the pub. You a drinking man, Colonel? Pint of bitter with the lads on a Friday night? Game of darts? Is that your style?"

"Actually, it's the climate," said Mikhailov, matching the sarcasm. "Rain down the back of my neck, runny nose… I'm looking forward to it."

Again, not even a flicker of a smile. "Yes, quite. So I suppose I'd be wrong in assuming it's because you wouldn't exactly be welcome back in the good ol' US of A."

"Now why would you assume that?"

"Just a guess."

Mikhailov sat back in his chair. He certainly wasn't about to admit to being on the FBI's most wanted list, or that J. Edgar Hoover himself had once personally sworn to get his hands on "that son-of-a-bitch Commie spy."

Mikhailov sat back and decided on another angle. "I like you, Major, you know that? You don't trust anybody. A man after my own heart. But what I'm wondering is why you're still at that rank. What are you, forty-four, forty-five? Well educated... obviously from a good family. Tell me, just who did you upset? Must have been somebody high up the ladder, otherwise you'd have made brigadier by now at the very least. Was it back in London, perhaps? Was that it? Some screwball operation got fouled up and you got nailed as the fall-guy?" Mikhailov saw no reaction from the other side of the desk but knew he'd touched a nerve. "As a result, you missed your promotion and got posted out here in the wilderness, am I right?"

Gallagher was obviously riled and, when he chose to strike back, his natural instinct was to revert to the time-honoured tradition of the schoolyard, by simply the flipping the question around. "Is that what happened to *you*, Colonel? Is that why *you're* here in Berlin? You got passed over when they were giving out those big shiny medals up at the Kremlin?"

"As a matter of fact, that's not at all why I'm here."

"No?"

"You want to know the truth? Okay, why not? The truth is that I volunteered for this posting."

"You volunteered? Really? You a masochist, Colonel?"

"No, just a realist."

"And why, pray, would you volunteer for East Berlin when you could be back home in Moscow? Didn't you tell me that's your home town?"

Mikhailov's face turned serious. "If you'd ever lived in Moscow, you wouldn't ask such a question." Then he decided he'd said enough and changed the topic: "Some tea would be appreciated, Major. With lemon, if it's not too much trouble."

"Yes, of course, no problem. Just as soon as we've made a little headway, all right? Then we can share a nice pot of tea together like the best of pals."

Once again, Mikhailov sighed, this time out loud. "Is this some kind of torture, Major? Is that what you're putting me through?"

"Headway, Colonel. Let's just focus on that, shall we? Now, how about divulging some of your secrets. What do you say? They don't have to be big ones, not yet anyway. Just a few tidbits will do for the time being."

"I'm not here to divulge any secrets," replied Mikhailov.

"So why *are* you here?"

"To *negotiate* my secrets."

"Negotiate! Excellent!"

"I just didn't think I'd be interviewed by the military."

"No? And who did you think would be here at British military headquarters? Princess Margaret?"

"I thought you might bring in MI5."

"The spy boys? Oh, good heavens, now why on earth would we do that?"

"I don't know. Perhaps because I'm MGB?"

"Yes, so you keep saying. The problem is, you offer me nothing to prove it."

"You have my service book."

Gallagher fingered the worn, olive green document that sat forlornly on the table in front of him and stared at it for a moment. The cover was printed with the letters "CCCP," Russian initials for the USSR, plus the sword-and-shield crest of the MGB. "Well, yes, it seems real enough, I'll give you that. But, of course, I could buy one of these down at the Spittelmarkt and it would look just as authentic." He tossed the book down on the table and sat back in his chair. "The point is, Comrade, I'm not here to decide how big a fish you are. I'm just here to see if you're really a fish at all and not some piece of flotsam that got caught in the net."

"And if you decide the latter, then you'll just throw me back?"

Gallagher didn't answer. He just took a long breath, as if he, too, was becoming bored with it all. "Well, we've just about exhausted that metaphor, don't you think? Now look, you say you're here to negotiate? Fine, so let's negotiate. You know what I'm after. So what do you want in return?"

"Not much, in the great scheme of things."

"No, of course not, you're a modest fellow. You don't really want much at all. Just a whole new identity for yourself and your wife, some shiny new passports, perhaps a furnished flat in a good part of town. How does Mayfair sound? Then, of course, there'd be the pension, the health plan, the expense account... What kind of car would you like, by the way?"

"I haven't decided yet," said Mikhailov with equal sarcasm. "I was thinking a Rolls but a Bentley would do at a pinch. Depends how much I can get for the F9." It was funny, a worthy reply, but Mikhailov refused to acknowledge his own humour. Instead, he just shook his head as if to say that he, too, was tired of the game, that it was all a waste of time, this entire conversation. "Look, Major, let's stop all this nonsense, shall we? I'm getting a cramp just sitting here. The bottom line is this. You don't trust me at all, yet you're asking me to trust you completely. Is that fair?"

"Fair? Why should I be fair? *You* came to *me*, remember? Just waltzed in to this concrete toilet bowl from out of nowhere, expecting me to believe every word you say." A pause. "All right, Colonel, you want an answer? I'll give you an answer. You actually *don't* need to trust me, not for our current purposes. All you need to do is give me a brief rundown of what we can expect from you so that I can pass the message along. That way, it looks like I've done my job and all the people yet to join us can decide whether it's even worth making the effort, you get my drift? So why don't you just be a good little defector and give me something I can take to them, then we can all get on with our lives, all right? What do you say? Does that sound reasonable?"

Mikhailov hesitated a few moments but, finally, he decided the man was right. Somebody had to make the first move. "What I'm offering," he said, "is full disclosure about an operation that's just getting underway. If you move fast enough, you can take action."

"An operation! Well now, that's more like it. Very exciting. But can you be just a bit more specific, Colonel? What kind of operation? Where? When? How? And exactly why would we wish to take action?"

"I'm not prepared to tell you that."

"Oh, really? What a pity. And we were doing so well."

"What I *can* tell you is that I was copied on a highly classified directive that came from... Let's just say it came from the top."

"The top. I see. And are we talking about the top here in Berlin... or the top all the way up there in Moscow?"

"Moscow."

"Ah, the *very* top. Well, that puts it in a whole new light." Gallagher sat back and stretched out his long, thin legs. "So why would a mere Colonel in Berlin be copied on a directive from the very top in Moscow?"

"Procedure."

"Which means?"

"Which means, Major, that the target location is here in West Germany."

"Is that right?"

"And since I'm in charge of covert operations in this territory, MGB procedure requires that they release an advisory."

"And why would that be?"

"Isn't it obvious?"

"Tell me anyway."

A sigh. "To make sure we stay out of whatever it is they're doing."

"Left hand, right hand, so to speak. Well, that makes sense. And what exactly *are* they doing?"

"They're looking for something."

"Something? Just... something? With all due respect, Colonel, that means nothing at all."

Mikhailov grunted his agreement, then relented. "Okay, okay. So this much I'll tell you. It came from your old friend, Uncle Joe, and now he wants it back."

"Stalin? He was the one who issued the directive?"

"No, it came from Beria but it must have been on Stalin's orders."

"Really? Stalin himself? And what might it be, this certain something?"

"I don't know, exactly."

"So what is it, *approximately*?"

Mikhailov took a long breath. "I only know what I'm required to know. You're military, you should understand that."

"What I understand, Colonel, is that you're not really telling me anything. Why should I believe you?"

"Because I have proof."

"You do? Show me."

"I will. All in good time."

"You have it with you, this proof? In your pocket perhaps?"

"No, not in my pocket."

"And what form would this proof take?"

"I can give you the directive itself."

"The original?"

"No, of course not," said Mikhailov, speaking slowly and deliberately, as if to a wayward child. "The original is a numeric cipher. If I gave you that, you'd want me to translate it word for word and, from that, you'd be able to work out the code structure."

"Yes, well, thank you for explaining that. It hadn't occurred to me."

Mikhailov dismissed the remark with a vague wave of his hand. For a while, the exchange with Gallagher had been mildly entertaining but now it was just getting on his nerves. "What I *can* give you is the decrypted version. It's very accurate, I promise you. I did it myself."

"You don't have people to do that for you?"

"I told you, it's highly classified."

"Classified, right. You see, that's the problem, Colonel. We've already examined this directive of yours and I'm afraid it's just not that convincing."

Mikhailov just stared at him. Then a deep fury spread visibly across his face. "You have it already?" he fumed. "You ripped open my bags like I'm some common criminal? What kind of game are we playing here? I thought you British were civilized. That's one of the reasons I came here. Now I find you're nothing but a bunch of goons."

Gallagher let him rant, just so he could get it out of his system. Then he said quietly: "Pot calling the kettle black, Colonel?"

"What's that supposed to mean?"

"What it means is that it's a bit hypocritical, don't you think? From someone who says he works for the MGB."

Mikhailov didn't answer, too disgusted with himself. It was stupid of him to think they wouldn't just seize his luggage from the car and tear it apart. For some reason, all he could think of was how upset Irina would be when she found out that her matching set from Macy's had been destroyed.

"You really must think we're totally incompetent," Gallagher was saying. "Or maybe you're starting to believe your own propaganda... The idiotic British with their open society, letting all those home-grown spies steal their precious secrets. You must laugh yourself silly."

"Yes, you're right, sometimes we do."

"I don't see you laughing now."

"You know what, Major? I'm starting to think I don't like you, after all."

"Do you really think I give a damn?"

"No, you're right, it's not important. And nor are you. So will you be passing along my document or not? Can you tell me that, at least?"

"Oh, yes, don't trouble yourself about that. I'll be passing it along... but I doubt it's worth a whole new life. Not by a long way. We'll be wanting much more than that, I can assure you. Bentleys are quite expensive, you know."

It was not even noon but Mikhailov felt exceedingly tired. He'd worked all night decrypting the document, then had all his remaining adrenaline pumping just to drive his way over here and now he'd just wasted the rest of the morning talking to an idiot like Gallagher. But it was even more than that. He was simply weary of it all: his life, his career, the whole thing. What was it all for? What was the result? Where was the joy? He was also annoyed at the lack of respect they were showing him. Wasn't he entitled to that much at least? He shook his head again, almost imperceptibly this time, and shifted position in his chair, facing slightly away from Gallagher, his body language underlining the fact that he was done with this conversation. Let them send in someone else.

All this time, Irina Mikhailov had been waiting in a small side room, no more than four metres by three. She had nothing to do or to read. Worse, she had no idea how long this would last - a day, a week, a year - and she was starting to get the uncomfortable feeling that it might never end.

Unlike her husband, she was offered tea and a sandwich by a pleasant female officer from the Women's Royal Army Corps, known as a "WRAC." The young woman was pretty, in a prim sort of way, with taupe-brown hair, broad shoulders like a swimmer, and small, firm breasts which strained at her green army blouse. She reminded Irina of their only child, Olga, who was about the same age and who was now on assignment as a nurse with the Bethune Clinic in Mao's new Red China - but that just led to a fresh bout of anxiety.

The immediate excitement of leaving had already worn off and a nagging, doubt-filled fear was beginning to set in. What would the MGB do when they discovered her husband had gone? Would they send assassins? Would they persecute her family? Her former friends? There was a good chance that Olga was out of harm's way for the moment but she wasn't beyond Moscow's ultimate reach and that was the problem. Nobody was.

★ ★ ★

The second British official who came in to see Alexei Mikhailov was a civilian: a short, dapper individual wearing a dark suit, with a striped tie in bottle green and burgundy. Mikhailov assumed the colours must be from some school or other but he knew as little about that as he did about regimental badges. He'd definitely have to brush up on British tradition if he was going to be living there.

"Morning," said the man, as he sat down in the same chair that Gallagher had vacated. He seemed a lot more cheerful than the dour Major. "How are we today?"

He placed a manila file down in front of him, which he opened and began reading, his brow furrowed with concentration. His dark eyes seemed watery, either from fatigue or perhaps some myopic condition, and he occasionally lifted a hand to massage them with thumb and forefinger, a subconscious affectation.

"And who are *you*?" said Mikhailov bluntly. By this point, he was beyond niceties.

"Sorry, " said the man, in the same jovial tone. "Forgetting my manners. Malcolm Davies, Foreign Office. And you are..." He read from his notes: "Alexei Ivanovich Mikhailov, head of Department B-1 of the First Directorate, MGB, Berlin... Would that be right?"

"Yes."

"Always a good start, getting the name right. And do they call you Alexei or Alex?"

Mikhailov looked at him, not sure which way this would be going. "It doesn't matter what you call me. What matters is whether you believe me."

"Excuse me?"

"Do you believe my name is Alexei Mikhailov? Do you believe I'm a colonel with the MGB?"

"What? Oh, gracious me, yes. All checked out, no doubt about that. Pleased to make your acquaintance, actually. Very pleased indeed."

"That wasn't Gallagher's reaction."

"No, well, don't mind him. The military, you understand. I'm sure it's the same with your lot."

Mikhailov could hardly argue with that. "So... we're making progress," he muttered.

"Anybody offered you anything, by the way? Something to eat or drink?"

"Do you have a hot dog by any chance? I miss a good hot dog."

"Sorry, no can do, I'm afraid. You're confusing us with the Yanks."

"Then how about tea, do you have that?"

"Yes, of course, absolutely."

"With lemon, if you don't mind."

Davies reached over to a black phone on the side cabinet and gave the necessary request, just overflowing with his own politeness. Then he turned back to the file in front of him and pulled out what looked to be the decrypted directive. "What I'm really interested in, Colonel, is this operation you're telling us about. I see it's classified 'OV'... *Osoboy Vazhnosti*... Must be tremendously important."

Mikhailov was a little surprised to hear good Russian coming from the man's mouth. It showed a certain amount of professionalism, which was a nice change, but he decided not to comment. "Important? Yes, you could say that. To some people, anyway."

"I presume you're talking about Comrades Stalin and Beria. Isn't that what you told Major Gallagher?"

"Orders from Stalin, directive from Beria."

"The objective being what?"

"You have the document. You know as much as I do."

"Fair enough, but it says the mission is to retrieve a manuscript and we're just wondering if that's the correct word. You see, after decryption and translation..."

"Yes, the word is 'manuscript.'"

"As in a book manuscript?"

"That's right."

"A little strange, don't you think?"

"Tell me something in this world that isn't strange."

Davies smiled pleasantly. "Philosophy, yes, quite. A little

existentialism to raise the tone. Excellent. But what we're wondering, Colonel, is why a manuscript belonging to Stalin would be in West Germany in the first place? And why would he launch a major operation to get it back?"

"I don't know. As I said..."

"You know as much as we do. Yes, right, I heard you. But let's put our thinking caps on for a moment, shall we, Colonel? I'm perfectly willing to take it on face value that you don't know too much but what I'd like you to do is make a few suppositions. Can you do that?"

"Suppositions?"

"Yes, you know, 'best guess' kind of thing. If I were to ask you what you *think* it might be all about, what would you say? You must have some ideas."

Mikhailov considered the request but couldn't think of any reason to turn it down. "It's just my opinion, you understand..."

"Absolutely. That's all I'm looking for."

"My initial assumption was that the manuscript might have been something that Stalin sent to Hitler."

"To Hitler?"

"Before the war. When they were still friends."

"I see, yes. An intriguing notion. Why would you think that?"

"It's a theory that fits. There were many exchanges between them. Correspondence, memos... I'm sure there would have been gifts, too."

"So you think Stalin sent Hitler a manuscript as a gift. But now he wants it back... why?"

"Again, my opinion..."

"Fine."

"Stalin's getting old. He's thinking about his legacy, his place in history. He's not proud of his early friendship with Hitler. He got taken for a ride, played as a sucker, so to speak. So anything that's still around from that time is nothing but an embarrassment."

"Yes, I suppose that makes a certain amount of sense. Posterity and all that. But a major covert mission into West German territory? A joint operation between the navy and the MGB? Beria himself involved? That must be some manuscript, Colonel."

"You asked for my opinion, I told you."

"And you think we'd be interested in this, why?"

"If you get your hands on it before he does, you can do exactly what he doesn't want."

"Which is?"

"Which is to embarrass him, to let the world know what he did, cuddling up to Hitler like that."

"You think the world doesn't know?"

"I think the world forgets. You made such a big deal of him as an ally during the war, you and the Americans, that people have pushed aside what he did. All those pictures of Stalin sitting there with Churchill and Roosevelt... in Yalta, in Quebec... Like the three musketeers. All for one and one for all."

Davies looked at him across the table. "I'm getting the impression, Colonel, that you don't like Comrade Stalin very much."

"Like him? Who likes him?"

"What I mean is... admire him, respect him."

"Let's not be simplistic, Mr. Davies. I would have thought we were past all that."

"Fair enough," said Davies airily. It was an expression that seemed to come easily to his lips. Then, for a while, he scanned the file in front of him, flipping the pages, checking his notes against the directive that Mikhailov had brought. Finally, after again rubbing his eyes, he said: "Let's talk about the woman, Colonel, the target of the operation... this Lina von Osten... formerly Lina Heydrich, as I understand. What do you know about her?"

"What do I know? I know what everybody knows."

"Which is?"

"Which is that she was married to the worst criminal in history."

Davies raised his eyebrows. "Strong stuff, Colonel."

"We're talking about Reinhard Heydrich."

"Well, yes, I understand..."

"Genocide, Mr. Davies. Does that mean nothing to you? He instigated it. He was in charge of it."

"Yes but, with all due respect, Colonel, if we're talking criminals, Stalin's already killed thirty million of your own people and he's still going."

"So what are we doing here? Counting bodies? How many did the British kill in the Opium Wars, the Boer Wars, the Indian Wars, the Irish Wars?"

"I don't see your point."

"My point is that Heydrich wasn't building an empire or even purging his enemies. That's been happening since we all lived in caves. What Heydrich did was pure genocide for its own sake. The extermination of an entire people, cold and calculated. Deliberate. A thousand an hour, twenty-four hours a day, like a human production line. Gassed to death, then burned in the ovens. If you can't see the moral difference, Mr. Davies, then I'm sorry for you."

"You seem passionate, Colonel. Is it something personal? You wouldn't be Jewish by any chance, would you? Or perhaps someone very close to you?"

The last part was spoken as if Davies already knew the truth and Mikhailov wasn't sure how to react.

"That's all right," said Davies. "We all have our little secrets. We know about your wife."

"She gave up the Jewish religion a long time ago. Anyway, what does this have to do with anything?"

"You're right, it doesn't. Nothing at all. Didn't mean to be insensitive."

"Just doing your job, right?"

"Let's get back on track, shall we? Lina von Osten, formerly Lina Heydrich. Tell me more about her."

Mikhailov ran a hand through his hair and took a deep breath. Just like earlier, he knew he had to swallow his emotions and remain in control but it wasn't easy. He was more used to asking questions than answering them. "Like I told you, I don't know much. When her husband was killed by the Czechs..."

"Wait, let me stop you there, if you don't mind. Point of order. Actually, *we* were the ones who killed Heydrich."

Mikhailov stared at him. "What are you talking about? The

Czechs threw a bomb in his car."

"Well, I'm sure that's the Soviet version of history but there's a little more to it than that. Who do you think planned the mission? Who trained and equipped the Czech agents? Who dropped them behind enemy lines? Who provided the bomb?"

"That was you?"

"Yes, Colonel, that was us."

"Then you have my respects, Mr. Davies."

"Thank you, that's very gracious of you. Now, about the woman..."

"I'm sure you know more a lot more about her than I do."

"Very well, let's compare notes, shall we?"

"Compare notes? Sure, okay, why not? We've got all day, right? All tomorrow, too."

"I can assure you, I'm as anxious to be done with this as you are, Colonel. Now if you don't mind..."

"Okay, okay, the woman, fine. So, her husband is killed, they hold a big state funeral, they order reprisals against the Czechs. Now what's she going to do after that? There's nothing left for her in Berlin, so she moves back to the island of Fehmarn where she came from. Then, in 1945, a big problem. Her SS pension dries up, so she converts the family home into a guesthouse."

"All right, good. That basically corresponds to what we know ourselves."

"I'm glad to hear it."

"And this manuscript which Stalin's after. Presumably, she got it from her dead husband?"

"Presumably."

"Which he obtained how?"

"Are you kidding me? He was the head of Reich security. He could get his hands on anything."

"Even if it belonged to Hitler himself?"

"Maybe it was given to Heydrich, some sort of reward. Or maybe he stole it. Who knows? Who cares? The result is that she has it. What more do you need?"

"I need to know what it is."

"I can't tell you what I don't know."

"I understand," said Davies. "I just need to find out what you *do* know." He calmly turned a page in his file like he was turning over a new leaf. "So, this operation," he said, beginning afresh. "You were expected to do what, exactly?"

"Nothing. Like I said to the Major, the directive is only an advisory. It's just procedure."

"Procedure, yes. And who else knows about it? I mean, at your end."

"In Berlin? Nobody. I decrypted it alone. I've been through all this."

"Bear with me, Colonel. Did you decrypt it yourself because you knew you were going to bring it to us?"

"No, it was only afterwards."

"Only afterwards that you made your decision to defect?"

"Yes."

"And why was that? Why did you come to that decision?"

"Why?"

"Yes, what were the factors?"

For Mikhailov, this was difficult to explain. "The factors... I don't know. I guess you could say it's something I've been thinking about for a while."

"You miss the lifestyle?"

To Mikhailov, that sounded weak, decadent, but what could he say? In a way, it was true. "There's more to it than that."

"Like what, for example?"

"If you must know, I'm tired, okay?"

"Tired of what? Stalin? The MGB?"

"The game. I'm tired of the game. I just want..."

"Yes? You just want what? Money?"

"No, not money."

"Come on, Colonel, nothing to be ashamed of. That's the usual motive."

"Have I asked for money?"

"No," said Davies, honestly. Then he added: "Not yet."

"Look, I'm not a mercenary, never have been. And I'm not a

traitor either. I just want something else... a different life. An ordinary life. Is that so hard to understand?"

"No, not at all. I feel like that myself sometimes. Perfectly reasonable. But isn't it also true, Colonel, that you're afraid for your wife? Stalin's talking about purging Jewish intellectuals, isn't he? Doctors and such? Isn't that the real reason you're here?"

"My wife's not a doctor."

"No, but her father is. Or should I say *was*. Friend of Trotsky, wasn't he? At least, until Stalin had Trotsky assassinated. Then her father was stripped of his credentials and left penniless. That's why the family moved to Yaroslavsky, why she had to become a seamstress, isn't it? And now you're afraid that it'll all come back again, that they'll dig it all up. Isn't that right?" There was no response but Davies didn't need one. "Really, Colonel, do you think we don't know what's going on? What do you think we do all day long?"

Mikhailov had no answer to offer. Eventually, he said: "You're not from the Foreign Office at all, are you?"

At that moment, there was a rap on the door and Davies called out: "Enter!"

The young WRAC appeared and they both fell silent. She was carrying a full tray, which she set down on the table between them and then carefully unloaded: a steaming teapot, a classic "Brown Bess" as it's known, with two cups and saucers, several half-slices of lemon, a sugar bowl, plus a small plate of ginger snaps; all as neat and tidy as a church garden party.

"How's my wife?" Mikhailov asked her. "Has she had anything?"

"We've been looking after her, don't you worry about that," replied the woman. She had a pleasant smile and spoke like she was chatting to a neighbour across the fence.

"Thank you, Freda," said Davies, once she was done. Then, when the door shut behind her, he said: "Bit of a waste, I always think. We train them in military administration and then ask them to serve tea."

"In Russia, our women fire howitzers," said Mikhailov, before offering an empty smile. "Little joke."

Davies recognized the attempt to lighten the atmosphere. Then he said: "Tell me about the submarine they're using."

The change in direction caught Mikhailov off-guard for a moment and he had to refocus. "I know nothing about it," he said truthfully. "Those things are all the same. Death traps, if you ask me."

"Yes, I'm inclined to agree," replied Davies, as he set about pouring the tea. "One lump or two?"

"Just lemon, thank you."

"Happen to know the course they're following, by any chance? The precise landing site? Anything like that?"

"No, I don't."

"Right, right. You only know what's in the directive."

Mikhailov crushed the lemon into his tea and dismissively tossed the peel back on to the tray; an act of pent-up frustration. "Look, once and for all," he said, "let me make it very clear. I received the document yesterday from Moscow. As far as I know, it came directly from Minister Beria who, for some reason, chose not to include me in his planning sessions."

"Yes, but that's interesting, don't you think? That it came from Beria and not Ignatyev. Why do you think that is, Colonel?"

Mikhailov shrugged, as he had so many times before. "Who can say? I don't work at the Kremlin. I've got no idea what goes on inside those walls."

"Has there been some kind of change we don't know about? Some secret purge?"

"Not as far as I know."

"So you still report to Ignatyev at the Lubyanka?"

"I did, until this morning."

"He was the one who assigned you this position in Berlin, am I right?"

"That's right."

"And you have no problem betraying him like this?"

It was a tough question for Alexei Mikhailov. Even now, he wasn't totally sure who or what he was betraying: his boss, his department, his country, or merely his own principles? He'd tried to convince himself that it was none of them, that his actions should be framed in more positive terms. He was doing it for his wife, he told himself, as well as for his own sanity; a chance to find some much needed peace of mind. But how could he explain all this in a way the man would believe?

Eventually, he replied in the simplest of terms: "I'm here, aren't I?"

Davies looked at Mikhailov for some time, as if wondering whether to pursue the question, then appeared to let it rest. "All right, let's go on, shall we? You received the directive... and then?"

"And then? And then, nothing. Like I told you, I worked alone all night to decrypt it, then I took it home. That's where we made the final decision, my wife and I. Then she sewed the damn thing up in the lining of our suitcase and we drove it over here. What more can I tell you?"

"A few details would be nice."

Mikhailov sipped his tea. "Why?" he said simply. "You've got more than enough."

"Really? How so?"

"I should have thought it was obvious. All you have to do stake out the von Osten place on Fehmarn and wait for the raid. When it happens, you catch them in the act. What more can you ask? You'll be able to grab whatever it is they're looking for... plus, of course, you'll capture the team they're sending in, which you can later exchange for your own people caught over there. Sounds like a pretty good deal to me."

"Well, yes..." said Davies, " I must admit, when you put it that way, it does sound appealing. But you see, the problem is that you're no mere file clerk, are you? I mean, if you were, it would be so much easier. You lift a document, you hide it in your suitcase, you bring it to us. Bravo! Well done! But you're not a file clerk are you? You're a colonel in the MGB and you've got a head full of names we'd love to know."

"Those names are not for sale."

"There you go, you see? My point exactly. The fact is, Colonel, you've crossed over. You're sitting in our office and now we've got you. Not very nice, I know, not very welcoming, but I'm afraid that's how my bosses will see it and there's nothing to be gained by hiding that from you. I'm afraid we're stuck with each other, so we should probably make the best of it, don't you think?"

"What I think..." Mikhailov put his cup back down on the tray before completing his reply. "What I think is that I've done all I'm prepared to do, so we should probably make the best of that."

"Yes, well, I'm afraid if that's your attitude, then we may just have a problem. And before you say anything, let me ask you this. What's the worst thing that could happen to you right now? You don't get the standard of living you want in London?" It was a rhetorical question. "No, that's not the worst, believe me. The worst is that we decide we don't need you and simply drive you back to your own side with a note pinned to your chest saying 'Thanks, here's your traitor back.' What do you think they'd do to you? You and your wife?"

"Why don't we just leave my wife out of this?"

"Getting upset, are we, Colonel?"

Mikhailov gazed across at Davies. "What's your code name, Mr. Davies?" There was no answer. "You're not Foreign Office, so my guess would be MI5, probably G Section... which means you have a code name. I could look it up if I had my files, just like you looked me up, but as it is..."

"Sycamore," said Davies.

"Sycamore... Ah yes, a tree, I believe. That's very sweet. Mine's Axel."

"Yes, I know."

"Yes... yes, I'm sure you do," said Mikhailov. "Well, all I want to say is that you're a smart fellow, Sycamore. You know about me, you know about my wife. So what I'm proposing is very simple. You settle us comfortably in London. Okay, not luxurious, but comfortable. A decent place, some transport, a way to earn an income. Any kind of job, I don't care. You know my father was a fishmonger? I can do that if I have to. It's okay, I don't mind. I know a cod from a herring. At any rate, if you do all that, I'll think about cooperating."

"You'll *think* about it?"

"Let's call it an incentive. A juicy carrot dangled in front of your nose."

"Yes, thank you, I get the idea, but you'll have to do better than that."

"No, I don't think so. *Quid pro quo*, Mr. Davies. Let's think of the operation on Fehmarn as just a deposit. A show of good faith. Give me a new life, make it secure and I'll pay you the balance. It'll be worth it, I promise you."

"Ah, a promise. In that case..."

"Let's not get into that mode, shall we? I've had enough sarcasm for one day."

"You know," said Davies, "we can always accept your deal, milk you dry and send you back anyway. There's nothing to stop us from doing that."

"You're right," replied Mikhailov, "but there's also nothing to stop me from going straight to your famous Sunday papers. Perhaps *The Sunday Times*. Or how about *The Observer*? I've always liked *The Observer*. What do you think they'll pay? Ten thousand? Fifteen? And in exchange, I'll tell them the full story, all about how I was prepared to give you everything, but you loused up the agreement. And if we're talking about names, Mr. Davies, the first name I'll give them is yours."

"Is that a threat I'm hearing, Colonel?"

"You threaten me, I threaten you. Isn't that what the Cold War is all about?"

Davies sat back, deep in thought. "I hate to pour cold water on your fancy scheme, Colonel, but we can clamp down on the Sunday papers, you know. Little thing called the Official Secrets Act."

"Not a problem. I'll just go to the American press."

"And the FBI will do the same thing."

"Fine, so I'll use the Swiss, or the Swedes... or the Irish, come to that. The Irish do love to embarrass you Brits, don't they? The point is, Mr. Davies, it doesn't matter to me. As long as one newspaper somewhere in the world accepts it, then it becomes reported news and your own press can print it, irrespective of your precious Act. You see, I do know something of your laws too, so let's not try to bullshit each other, all right, Sycamore? We're both too old and too tired."

Mikhailov paused at this juncture. He'd made his point, he'd exposed the bluff and there was nothing further to be gained from rubbing the man's nose in it.

"Look," he said, trying to sound more amenable, "what you have to appreciate is that I risked everything to bring this stuff over to you. Everything. You know what that means? It means not just my life, or my wife's, but also my only daughter and perhaps even our entire family. It's not just the MGB I've crossed but Stalin himself... and, as you may be aware, he's not always so rational. Or so gentle. So please, don't treat me like I'm just another agent off the street trying to sell you a low-grade memo. What I've given you is valuable enough for us to make a deal... especially since you'll have hard proof of its authenticity in about... let's see..." Mikhailov looked at his watch, the Timex he received as a leaving gift from his consulate colleagues in New York. "I'd say in about thirty-one hours from now."

Davies didn't respond at all. He just closed the file in front of him, scraped back his chair and got to his feet. "They'll be sending in some lunch soon, I expect. Shouldn't be too long." Then he put on a jaunty smile, the same one he'd worn when he came in. "Nice chatting with you," he said, resuming that perfidious British brightness. Then he simply strolled out, closing the door gently behind him.

With all his experience, Mikhailov still didn't know whether he had a deal or not and he gazed out forlornly through the dusty window, with nothing to contemplate but the wisdom of his approach and the uncertainty of his fate. Outside, the walls of the stadium and the bland skies above were almost the same colour and it didn't do much to create a sense of optimism. On the other hand, they hadn't yet thrown him into a jail cell, which was something to be thankful for. Perhaps, after lunch, they'd even let him see his wife.

In the end, he decided, it had probably gone as well as he could have expected under the circumstances. And anyway, since he'd staked his credibility on the value of the information he'd brought, then obviously it all depended on the outcome of the operation. If it failed to take place or, worse, if Western agents somehow died in the process, then it would be difficult to convince anyone about anything.

Alexei Mikhailov sat back with the dawning realization that events were now completely out of his hands. By refusing to give up any further information, he'd sacrificed his leverage and lost control of the process. Whatever happened up there in the Baltic would now determine his entire future existence.

Based on the season and latitude, "H-Hour" for the Fehmarn assault must have been no later than 22:30 on Sunday, April 20. This would have provided the MGB *spetznaz* with sufficient hours of darkness to complete the mission in one night.

The designated landing site was an isolated rocky beach, approximately half-way between the south-eastern lighthouse, known as the Staberhuk, and the Sud-Badestrand promontory. The plan entailed the submarine surfacing two hundred metres offshore for several minutes in order to release a small dinghy, its motor specially baffled to reduce noise to a whisper. The forecast was for calm, clear weather, with good visibility provided by a three-quarter moon; and while they were ashore, the tides would turn in their favour, so the current would offer generous assistance for both entry and departure.

All-in-all, they couldn't have hoped for better conditions.

Once their preparations were complete, the four members of the unit descended a rope ladder and lowered themselves carefully into the small craft, with Petrov taking the rear position at the helm. They were efficiently outfitted against the cool spring temperature in full black: waterproof anoraks and pants, well-oiled boots, supple gloves and fleece-lined caps. As camouflage, they'd also daubed blackening on their exposed facial skin like ancient marauders. Since they didn't plan to stay on the island more than a few hours, each carried no more than a small backpack containing minimal supplies; a definite advantage when speed and stealth were primary requirements. The only weight would be armaments and ammunition. The weapon they'd selected was especially well-suited for the mission parameters: the recently developed Stetchkin 9.2 automatic pistol with an accuracy range of fifty metres and an effective firing rate of ninety shots a minute, including clip changes. But the firepower was only a contingency. As the unit commander, Petrov, had stated in his briefing, there should be no need to use it.

For the first hour or so, everything went smoothly. The crew of the S-80 was able to complete the launch process and the four-man team made the approach within the time allotted. The section of beach was a little rockier than expected but the small rubber craft was well-constructed and survived the haul ashore. They pulled it up into the shadows but made little attempt to hide it. They figured that a more thorough job would waste too much time and, anyway, the plan called for them to be back here before dawn. Unless somebody actually stumbled over it, there'd be little chance of discovery.

The target location was situated eight kilometres from the landing site, which meant they'd have to travel cross-country to reach it. The assigned field navigator was the youngest member of the unit, Filshin, who'd earned a citation in the subject at the academy. His talents were augmented by a clever map light that he'd invented himself, which allowed him to see the chart without using an exposed bulb. It was like a photographer's loop but totally enclosed in black metal. To find directions, he just had to place the small instrument flat against the map, click the eyepiece release and peer through, which he did at every opportunity. After forty minutes, he ascertained they were due south of Meeschendorf. From here, they had two roads to cross before reaching their ultimate target: the guesthouse owned by Lina von Osten. It was said to have a fine view of the Burgstaaken harbour.

By the time they reached the first road, it was already 23:45. The four-man group traversed it one at a time, with Petrov waving them over like a school crossing guard. As they reached the fence on the other side, a dog began to bark. It sounded like a large breed, perhaps a kilometre away, the noise magnified by the night air and carried over on the light breeze. In reaction, they froze, crouching low and gripping their weapons just in case of a problem; but then the silence returned and Petrov motioned for them to be on their way.

The next section was more difficult, a plowed field having replaced the previous meadowland, and it made the going more treacherous. It would be all too easy to twist an ankle in the deep furrows. Filshin stopped midway across to take a reading and then, when he was certain, he readjusted their track to a more westerly direction, holding his arm straight out ahead of him in the dim light. Just like a Nazi salute, thought Petrov, but he didn't say anything. He, himself, had given the order for zero verbal contact. The cloud cover was also a little heavier than they expected, making visibility more difficult and more rapid progress impossible. By the time they reached the second road, it was well past midnight and they'd fallen a few minutes behind schedule. All was still quiet but, in the distance, they could see a couple of lights from the small hamlet of Neue Tiefe. Filshin indicated they needed to be just to the south to reach their target.

When they finally arrived at the guesthouse, there was nothing to see. The place was in darkness, conveniently closed until June to allow renovations to the roof, just as they'd been told by their West German contact who'd visited two weeks previously, posing as a tourist.

They knew that the living quarters were in a small wing of the building, accessed by a separate back entrance, but they didn't approach. Not yet. Even though they were behind schedule, they followed Petrov's plan to the letter and squatted down in silence to keep the building under observation for a full ten minutes.

What they didn't know was how many were inside or how prepared they might be. The briefing had indicated that the von Osten woman would be there alone but, as Petrov could testify from long experience, combat briefings were far from infallible. Maybe some of the staff had returned unexpectedly. Or maybe she had house guests. If so, they might be armed. If they put up resistance, even minimal, it would change the whole equation.

In the meantime, as the MGB *spetznaz* hunkers down to assess the situation, it's perhaps worth pausing to offer my own, personal impressions of their mission target, Lina von Osten, since she plays such a critical role in this account.

I first met her in my capacity as a freelance journalist, right here on her home island of Fehmarn. It was very soon after the war, in September, 1946, to be exact. The Berlin I'd known had been buried under mounds of rubble and I only discovered where she was living by searching through endless Reich files at the Allied Documentation Centre at Clay Allee. At the time, I was trying to re-establish my credentials and I had it in mind that an interview with the widow of the worst war criminal in history might make for a fascinating article, perhaps even of Pulitzer calibre - or so my vanity hoped. Unfortunately, it didn't quite turn out that way.

She agreed to meet me readily enough and, during the few hours I spent with her, I have to say she was nothing but gracious. She even offered me lunch. Physically, she was typically Nordic, a lean woman, a little taller than average, with straw-blond hair and alabaster-hued skin. Her one bad habit seemed to be that she smoked too much, revealing a nervous and suspicious disposition; but, by the end of my allotted time, I'd also learned that she could be vain, pretentious and extremely devious - a manipulator of the highest order.

Like any reporter, I was searching for insight but she had her own agenda and it was soon evident that she was still dedicated to the memory of her assassinated husband: SS Obergruppenführer Reinhard Heydrich, wunderkind of Third Reich security, instigator of the Holocaust, and potential successor to Adolf Hitler. The way she spoke about him, it was as if some god of fate had commanded her to carry his flame in perpetuity and she spent a good deal of energy both defending his beliefs and rationalizing her own motives for supporting him. She even told me that, in his own way, he was simply "advancing the cause of higher civilization." Those were her exact words and I recall wondering how anyone, after all that had happened, could still utter such nonsense and expect anyone to believe it. She also outlined in considerable detail how her marriage to Reinhard Heydrich had been less a traditional marriage than an "alliance" - that was how she put it - a mutual ambition that would have propelled them to the very apex of Nazi domination. She saw her husband as the new master of the "master race" and herself as the mistress.

When I asked her why the supposed master race had ultimately been defeated, she blamed any number of reasons: the British for not seeing sense in 1940; the Japanese for goading the Americans at Pearl Harbor; the Italians for not fighting with sufficient aggression alongside Germany. In other words, she managed to point the finger at everyone except the Führer and his delusional regime.

I wrote up the article accordingly but it wasn't exactly what my client, the editor at *Der Spiegel,* was expecting to see, nor what his subscribers wanted to read about. During that immediate post-war period, it seemed they were looking for more in the way of regret and remorse from such people, possibly even some kind of tearful apology. I could hardly write what hadn't happened. As a result, the piece was never published and I didn't bother returning to Fehmarn, having decided to cut my losses and give up the idea of the article. I knew there'd be nothing more forthcoming from a woman like that.

By the time the MGB came calling in April, 1952, the world had pretty much lost interest in Lina von Osten and she'd descended into a kind of bitter resentment, brooding alone for the most part, but fully capable of resorting to either furious tantrum or icy ruthlessness, depending on the circumstances - as the *spetznaz* was about to discover.

The ten minutes were up.

The unit commander, Vladimir Petrov, glanced at his big Soviet chronometer under the moonlight, then cast his eye one last time over the entire guesthouse. All seemed as it should be. Nothing had stirred and no light had come on, either in the section being renovated, or in the owners' private apartment.

At his silent command, his team edged closer and worked their way around to the side of the building. Beyond, hardly visible, lay the distant crescent of Burgstaaken harbour.

It was the sergeant, Mischa Borovik, who applied the suction cup and glasscutter to one of the ground floor windows. That's when he discovered, to his own surprise, that the guillotine mechanism wasn't even locked. He offered a smirk to Petrov before lifting it open to its maximum extent. They were big men but the space was sufficient for each of the four, in turn, to crawl through into the hotel's conservatory.

The next step was to wake someone. They needed a hostage. Petrov found an ashtray and threw it to the floor with some force, a shattering sound that reverberated around the house. Then, they all faded into the darkest shadows of the corners to wait for whoever came down to investigate. It was the cold Likhachev who stood beside the door, his knife unsheathed.

The moment the door opened, he wasted no time. He grabbed the bare wrist, pulled it in and saw that it belonged to the owner herself, Lina von Osten, wearing just a loose robe over a flimsy nightdress. He seized her from the back and placed his heavy hand over her mouth before she could cry out - but she didn't give up, as he might have expected. Like an animal caught in a trap, she began to struggle violently, biting his forefinger with such savagery that she nearly took it clean off at the joint. By the time she let go, his blood was smeared over her face and dribbling from her mouth like a vampire. In reaction to the shock, Likhachev gave out with a vindictive curse, then curled his muscular arm tight around her neck, choking off most of her air. The knife was still in his other hand and, in a flash, he brought the steel blade to within a millimetre of her throat. He was ready to slice it open, a quick, deep gash from the windpipe to the jugular, but a sharp order from Petrov restrained him. They needed her alive in order to find the manuscript.

For a few moments, they waited, just in case the sounds had alerted others in the house. A long minute passed but they detected no movement, no creaking of floorboards or stairs. There was nobody at all.

The woman was still gasping for air as Petrov leaned in close to her; close enough to sense whatever light fragrance she was using. "Anybody upstairs?" he whispered in his rough German, a residue from his wartime training. His grammar and accent were poor but he could make himself understood.

She gave a single shake of her head, about all she could manage.

Then Petrov said: "We're going to let you go but, if you try to run or scream, we'll kill you instantly. Do you understand?"

A very slight nod.

"You're sure?"

Another nod, this time a little more definite.

At Petrov's gesture, Likhachev loosened his grip so she was free to stand on her own but he continued to hold the knife very close. She watched it nervously, her line of sight never venturing far from its menace.

"What do you want?" she said, attempting to keep her voice steady.

"You know what we want," replied Petrov coldly. "The manuscript. We want the manuscript."

"I don't know what you're talking about."

"Is it worth your life?"

"I'm telling you, I don't..."

Before she could finish, Petrov stepped forward and brought the back of his hand harshly across her face, which caused her to cry out involuntarily and slump to the floor at Likhachev's feet.

It was that sound, passing through the open window, that raised the alarm and, at that exact moment, an outside searchlight was switched on, flooding the room in its macabre white glare. Almost immediately, the firing began.

First to be hit was Likhachev, followed by the youngest, Filshin. It was the two veterans, Petrov and Borovik, who made a fight of it, wheeling, ducking and returning fire. The intense sound of their machine guns echoed around the walls and reverberated inside their ear drums.

Petrov's first burst extinguished the floodlight and the room returned to black; but this seemed an even deeper black thanks to the trick the light had played on their pupils. It was the alert Borovik who knew instinctively that he was closest to the woman and he edged towards her position. Too late. She'd vanished and he knew that she was either dead, lying somewhere beyond in her own pool of blood, or, more likely, she'd seized the chance in the confusion to scramble to her feet and escape through the door.

Petrov kept firing until he'd emptied his first clip. There was no way of telling who was out there or how many. He couldn't even identify them from their weapons, because the sound was like nothing he'd ever heard before, somehow lighter in tone. But it was effective, nonetheless, and its rapidity was keeping the two of them pinned down.

There was obviously no exit through the windows, so Petrov reached out to tap Borovik on the arm, indicating that they should follow the woman through the only door. He was assuming his other two men were dead but, even if they weren't, their rescue would depend on him and his sergeant staying alive, so that was the priority. He'd have to risk leaving them here.

Petrov told Borovik to go first. Then, a few seconds later, he too made the dash into the passageway. One direction led to what appeared to be a kitchen store-room but a quick glance, even in the dark, suggested there was no way out from there. The only other option was a flight of stairs and he took them two at a time, emerging onto some kind of wide landing with several rooms leading off. Which one? Which door to take? His eyes were gradually becoming used to the darkness and there was something, or someone, lying there on the far side. Three long strides and he saw it was his sergeant, unmoving with a large knife in his chest. It was not a professional's weapon, just a kitchen tool for carving. Was it the woman who'd done it or had somebody entered to help her?

Petrov stood up and waited a moment to get his bearings. That's when he felt a slight breeze coming from one of the rooms. The door was slightly ajar. He moved closer, then kicked at it with his foot, pushing it wide open. The room beyond was a bedroom but it seemed empty. Over on the far side was another open door that led outside to an iron fire escape. He could see it clearly outlined against the night sky.

He glanced around, his Stetchkin at the ready, but there was nothing: nobody behind, nobody in front. He was alone. His *spetznaz* team was down, either dead or seriously wounded. The mission was a complete shambles and, to survive, he'd have to try to make it back to the landing beach in the dark without a field navigator. Even then, even if he made it that far, he'd have to launch the dinghy on his own and rendezvous with the S-80 at exactly the right time. The plan was for the vessel to surface at 04:00 while there was still total darkness and show just a solitary light, the same kind used on local fishing boats. It would remain stationary until dawn but, after that, it would have to submerge and the rendezvous window would be gone.

All this went through Petrov's mind in a matter of moments. Was he up to it? He wasn't sure but he had no alternative. He thought of his sergeant, Mischa Borovik, who'd survived an entire four-year war only to end up dead on a fool's errand like this. Petrov was damned if he was going to let that happen to him. He was anxious to return downstairs to see if the younger men were still alive but, even if they were, what chance would he have? How could he carry even one of them? With Mischa, they might have been able to share the load but on his own? The idea was doomed from the start and, reluctantly, he let it go. There was only one way out and that was by himself, via the fire escape. It might be a trap but there was no alternative.

Cautiously, he emerged on to the metal platform and eased his way down, one step at a time, trying to minimize the noise of his boots. Eventually, he felt his feet on the gravel path at the base and he paused. Everything was still and he spent a second or two peering into the darkness to try to decide the best direction, a little disoriented to be on this side of the house.

Just as he was about to move off, there was a sudden light: not a floodlight like before, but a flashlight shining in his face. He could hear soft footsteps and, instinctively, he raised his weapon. But before he could fire, a heavy blow from behind knocked him to the ground and, in an instant, they were all over him. Three, four... he wasn't even sure how many. His arms were pinned, his wrists were handcuffed and somebody was addressing him in German. It was an easy voice, very smooth, with a gently mocking inflexion.

"Greetings, comrade. On behalf of Herr Gehlen, may I be the first to say 'Welcome to the West.'"

Petrov didn't reply. He knew all about Gehlen and his organization. They'd begun during the war as members of German military intelligence operating on the Eastern front but, by the end of hostilities, they'd learned so much about the Soviet forces that they were hauled out of their various POW camps and re-united by the Americans in order to be their clandestine intelligence capability in the new Cold War, based in Munich but with tentacles reaching right across to East Berlin and the rest of Soviet-dominated Europe. To Vladimir Petrov, however, the Gehlen Organization was, and always would be, a "Nazi" outfit and some of its senior members, he'd been reliably informed, were still key figures in ODESSA, the support group for escaping SS. He was also aware that, in a bizarre case of historical irony, Gehlen himself bore the given name of Reinhard. So now, here they were on the island of Fehmarn, the men of Reinhard Gehlen guarding the widow of their old SS leader, Reinhard Heydrich. They must be very proud, thought Petrov bitterly, to be called upon for such duty.

As they hauled him to his feet, they informed him that the rest of his team was all dead and that he was now alone: an official prisoner, required by international convention to give only his name, rank and serial number. He was then led away, with his hands shackled behind him, around to the other side of the house where a canvas-covered truck was parked. One of the men helped him to clamber up and they settled opposite each other on the truck's slatted benches.

That's when Petrov became interested in the weapon the man was holding. It was a short, automatic firearm of unusual design and Petrov guessed it was one of the weapons which had pinned his unit, causing so much damage. It seemed to fit comfortably into just one hand, yet it wasn't a pistol like the Stetchkin: it was a full, automatic rifle with the breech almost fully recessed, allowing the barrel to be encased within the housing. For a moment, the animosity he felt for his captors gave way to a professional soldier's curiosity.

"What *is* that?" he said to the man, in his rough German.

The man lifted the weapon to show it off. "New design," he

replied. "They call it an 'Uzi.'"

"Never heard of it," said Petrov. "Who makes it?"

"The Israelis."

Petrov nodded. An interesting development, he thought. The Nazis were now carrying Jewish guns. But he didn't say anything and nor did he have time to dwell on it because, a moment later, the driver of the vehicle ground noisily into gear and they lurched unevenly away into the night.

Vladimir Petrov was now a prisoner of the people he despised the most. They'd obviously been lying in wait at the von Osten house and, as far as he could work out, there were only two possible ways they could have known about the operation. The first was that the Danish frigate had indeed detected the submarine and had called ahead to warn the West German authorities. For Petrov, this was an extremely unlikely scenario. Even if they'd somehow managed to track the vessel to its destination, how would Gehlen's people have known exactly which building to stake out? The only other explanation was that the entire mission had been compromised from the very start. This was far more serious, because it meant that somebody from his own side had deliberately offered up the information; but who that might have been, or how it might have happened, Petrov couldn't even begin to guess.

As Petrov was being driven away into captivity, Lina von Osten was escaping in another direction, sitting in the passenger seat of an Opel sedan with the prized manuscript in her lap, her heart still pumping and her lips still stained with Russian blood.

Driving the vehicle was her ODESSA bodyguard, Karlheinz Oehring: a big, competent man who'd once been her late husband's adjutant. He'd been out for the evening and had heard the gunfire on the way back. He was the one who'd entered the house through the rear and killed the MGB sergeant, Borovik, stabbing him through the heart, Roman style, just as he came up the stairs. Even then, he'd never have managed to spirit the woman away without the passive complicity of the Gehlen sympathizers, who couldn't bring themselves to forget their prior devotion to her dead husband, even as they were being paid by their former enemies, the Americans.

In their minds, this was no paradox. As far as they were concerned, loyalty to the Nazi cause was still paramount and it only proved that, seven years after the Third Reich's unconditional surrender, the war still wasn't completely over - not for ODESSA and not for Lina von Osten.

I've heard it said that Moscow's massive central security building, the Lubyanka, holds such dread for ordinary citizens that they surreptitiously cross themselves whenever they pass by.

Personally, I've always tried to avoid going anywhere near the place during my own visits to the city but I can well understand their terror and trepidation. The mere sight of its yellow, baroque facade is enough to elicit nightmares about all that's happened behind those walls.

The structure was originally built under Tsar Nicholas in 1897 to house the All Russia Insurance Company but, after the Bolsheviks seized power in 1917, it was commandeered by Felix Dzerzhinsky and became the national headquarters of his Cheka secret police. It was on these premises that interrogation by torture became standard procedure during the Lenin era and it's been reported that the screams of the victims once echoed around the hallways at all hours of the day and night.

Since that time, a whole series of directors have been installed on the Lubyanka's elite third floor, the most recent being MGB chief, Semyon Denisovich Ignatyev. A stolid, stalwart *apparatchik*, Ignatyev proudly wore his proletarian blue suit with a lapel full of Party pins and, under it, a stiff white shirt of poor quality that always seemed a couple of neck sizes too small. As a result, his collar was invariably open and his tie permanently loose, which made him appear both scruffy and threatening at the same time, especially compared to Lavrenti Beria, who was physically softer but infinitely more devious. Due to their different personal styles, the two ministers clashed often, both inside the Politburo and out. Yet, since their duties overlapped - with Ignatyev's MGB in charge of covert intelligence and Beria's MVD controlling internal security - they were often required to work together, even when it was against their own better judgment.

The Fehmarn mission was one such joint assignment. Although Beria had been given final responsibility by Stalin himself, he couldn't handle it without the special expertise of Ignatyev's *spetznaz* units. That's why, during the early morning hours of Monday, April 22nd, they were together in Ignatyev's large corner office, anxiously awaiting news from the third member of their operational triad, the Soviet Navy, which was supplying transport, communications and other resources.

As the time passed, Beria and Ignatyev became involved in yet another of their frequently heated discussions, this time about a seemingly unrelated issue: the sudden disappearance and possible defection of the MGB's most senior Berlin operative, Alexei Mikhailov. They were sitting on opposite sides of the enormous desk. Ignatyev was in his swivel chair, as usual, with Mikhailov's file open in front of him and he was flipping the pages back and forth, looking for something, anything, that might offer a clue to the man's behaviour. Eventually he leaned back, exasperated. There seemed to be no reason, nothing that could shed any light on why such a faithful, experienced servant of the Soviet Union would do such a thing.

Adjacent on the desk were numerous photos of Ignatyev's own family, plus several black telephones which he glanced at occasionally, as if willing them to ring. Elsewhere in the spacious office, there were easy chairs and side tables, plus a tall glass cabinet containing a fine collection of service memorabilia dating back all the way to Dzerzhinsky. However, the grand historical trappings were of little comfort on this day, because the loss of an asset like Alexei Mikhailov was a telling blow. It was Ignatyev who had appointed him to the position in East Berlin, a matter of great personal trust. But now that the trust had been shattered, he just couldn't seem to figure out why; and, since Beria had also worked with the man, Ignatyev took the unusual step of voicing his thoughts.

"Did you know his wife is Jewish?" he said.

"No," came Beria's reply. "What of it?"

Ignatyev shrugged. "They hear the rumours, even in Berlin." Ignatyev was referring to the recent speculation that Stalin was considering a purge of Jewish intellectuals. "Maybe he's worried about her. Maybe that's his motive."

"Maybe," said Beria, "but if you ask me, it's more likely a problem with a mistress."

Ignatyev shook his head. "I doubt it. According to reports, he's devoted to his wife."

"Devoted!" Beria laughed out loud. "Well, there's a lesson, right there. Never trust a man who doesn't have a mistress."

"Yes, well, you of all people should know about that," replied Ignatyev, in allusion to Beria's own penchant for sordid sexual activity. The man's preference for pedophilia - primarily virgin, pubescent country girls - had both appalled and fascinated his hypocritical colleagues. In this case, it may have been a mistake on Ignatyev's part to mention it, since he was the one looking for help, but he had such a dislike for Beria that, sooner or later, most of their conversations descended into insult, no matter how polite they began.

Beria removed the rimless spectacles he wore and polished them carefully on a pristine white handkerchief. It was an attempt to remain in command of the situation, a way to avoid losing his temper. He genuinely believed that, at fifty-three, a man of his age should be proud, not ashamed, of his masculine accomplishments, but he didn't say those words out loud. He didn't need to invite further ridicule. Instead, he added some quiet threat to his voice, as much as he could muster without going too far.

"My personal business is my own and nobody else's," he said, "and I would advise, Comrade... I would *strongly* advise... caution on your behalf."

Ignatyev was very tempted to toss the words right back into Beria's round face, along with his own sizeable fist, but in the end, he decided it wasn't worth it. He'd made his point and, besides, he still had the Mikhailov problem to solve.

"I'm always cautious, Comrade Minister," he answered slowly. "That's why I'm still here. Now, should we get back to business, or should we continue with our pissing contest? What do you think?"

Beria responded by folding up his handkerchief into a perfect square and returning it to his jacket pocket. It was a sign that he, too, was willing to discontinue the antagonism, at least for the time being. "What's the name of his Jewish wife?" he asked, his voice back to an even tone.

"Irina."

"All right, so Alexei is devoted to Irina, is that what you're telling me? Well, I suppose it can happen, even in the Soviet Union. So maybe she just doesn't like Berlin, as simple as that. Maybe she misses New York. Do they have children?"

"A daughter," replied Ignatyev, hunting for the relevant page in the file. "Olga, twenty-eight years old, unmarried. A nurse... currently working in China."

"China? Well, that's a whole other story. What if it's a little influence from our new comrades in Beijing?"

"That doesn't seem likely."

Beria thought about it but was forced to conclude that, for once, Ignatyev might be right. Why would the Chinese need to compromise the head of MGB intelligence in Germany? There was no possible benefit and, anyway, the newly installed Chairman Mao had enough problems of his own without making an enemy of Stalin.

"Of course," said Beria, "we may be overlooking the obvious."

"Which is?"

"He may have already been turned by the West. Maybe he left because he felt he was about to be discovered."

"Impossible," replied Ignatyev, perhaps a little too defensively. "If that were the case, I'd have known about it."

"Would you?" asked Beria. It wasn't a question so much as an implicit accusation.

Ignatyev responded by getting to his feet and pacing his way slowly around the room. His polished black shoes squeaked a little and his weighty footsteps were loud on the parquet floor. Eventually, he stopped by one of the tall windows and gazed out. It was still dark and all he could see were a few street lights, plus his own reflection. He was recalling an old joke about the number of times the MGB changed directors: *"The Lubyanka has a great view... from the third floor, you can see Siberia!"* But he didn't say it out loud, because Beria already knew it. Besides, at the present time, it just wasn't that funny.

"Let me remind you," added Beria, still seated. "We do need to find a reason for his absence. If he has indeed gone across, then we need to take action now, today, to protect our assets."

"You think I'm an amateur, Comrade?"

"Amateur or professional, I'll tell you one thing for sure. If I were you, I wouldn't go in to see The Boss without having some answers." Along the high level corridors of the ministries, the expression "Boss" was the ubiquitous slang for Stalin.

Before Ignatyev could respond, one of the desk phones finally rang, interrupting his thoughts and reminding him of their first priority that Monday morning: the joint operation on Fehmarn. He quickly stepped over to grab the receiver, then sat down in his large swivel chair and deliberately turned away from Beria in order to gain some privacy. Whatever the news, he wanted to digest it first.

There was nothing Beria could do, so he just sat there on the other side of the desk, straining to hear the barely audible conversation. Eventually, Ignatyev turned back around to face him and that's when Beria knew there was a problem. He could see it on Ignatyev's face.

"What's happened?" he said.

"That was Kuznetsov," said Ignatyev, his expression sombre. He was referring to Admiral Nikolai Kuznetsov, recently brought back from Pacific exile to spearhead Soviet naval development and the man in charge of military support for the Fehmarn operation. "The captain of the S-80 is reporting that he failed to pick up the *spetznaz* at the coordinates."

"What? Shit!"

"He remained on the surface as long as he could until daylight required him to submerge. They're waiting for further orders. What they're saying is that they can't stay around much longer."

"No, no, they have to stay," said Beria. "They must pick up the unit. The directive said 'at all costs.' The orders were specific."

"I understand. But Kuznetsov's not willing to risk his best sub. Not without a direct order from The Boss."

"Dammit, is he out of his mind? We can't go back to Stalin with this. Call him back, tell him to follow orders or he'll be back out in Vladivostok."

"He says we put him in charge of naval development and the S-80 is his newest boat. He's not going to risk five years of design and an experienced crew for a mission that had less than a fifty percent chance of success anyway."

"What? That was *his* assessment, not mine."

Ignatyev was about to reply when he received another call, this one on an internal line. As he listened, his eyes registered a sense of urgency, then slowly changed to something more like resignation. As he took down notes, he held his head in his hands.

"All right, got it," he grunted eventually, then hung up and looked at Beria. "We just received a call from a source in Munich, relayed through the Control Commission. He claims to speak for Gehlen. He says the organization intercepted a four-man MGB unit on Fehmarn today at 01:40. He said there was brief resistance and three of the four are dead. The man they've got in custody is the unit commander, Petrov. The service number provided is correct."

At that point, Lavrenti Beria got up from his chair. "Shit," he said again, this time in his native Georgian, then repeated it several more times, adding ever-more-vulgar variations to the theme.

For his part, Ignatyev spoke only Russian. "If that means what I think it does, I tend to agree. The source also said that Gehlen won't go public in anticipation of a future exchange."

"An exchange? For a lousy unit commander? Forget it. He's not worth it."

Ignatyev was about to protest, to say that Petrov was too a good man to lose, but he held back. It would be better, he decided, to find a quiet way to make the exchange when all the dust had settled. "Just one damn thing after another," he was saying, almost to himself. "First Mikhailov and now this. Is there anything else that can go wrong today?"

Meanwhile, Beria was still muttering and shaking his head in frustration. But that was precisely when his brain made the connection for the first time and there was a long moment of shock. His face seemed to turn as pale as an Arctic winter and he just buried his face in those fleshy palms.

"What?" said Ignatyev, but there was no response. He pounded his fist on the desk. "*What?*" he yelled.

That's when Beria looked up very slowly. There was no way to hide it or to avoid it. "The operational directive," he said very quietly. "It was sent to Mikhailov."

That's when Ignatyev caught on and he, too, looked stunned as the realization set in that their two problems were linked. "You mean the Fehmarn directive? You sent it to Mikhailov? Why, in the name of all that's..."

"It was procedure."

"Procedure! Who the hell cares about procedure?"

"It's required to send a copy to the local head of station via the Control Commission in the receiving territory. You should know that."

"So what are you saying?" said Ignatyev. "You mean the Commission might have seen it too? Who's down there?"

"Chuikov."

"Ah yes, the hero of Stalingrad. That's all we need."

"No, no, he never reads that stuff. He would've just sent it through unopened."

"You mean it just landed on the desk of Mikhailov, like a gift from heaven? That means he must have known everything, even about the manuscript. And now... now he's defected. My God!"

Beria wasn't really listening. He, too, was visibly shaken and he just rubbed his eyes, which seemed to have become bloodshot under the strain. "That's why Mikhailov left. We gave him the opportunity. We handed him a free ticket back to the West."

"Not we... *you!*" said Ignatyev, emphatically. "You, Comrade, and nobody else. And now he's spilling his guts out to a gang of Americans, who can't believe their own dumb luck."

There wasn't much Beria could say in his own defense and nor was there any need, so he chose to focus on the issue at hand. "Not the Americans," he replied eventually.

"What?"

"I don't think he'd take it to the Americans. Hoover already has a file on him and now, with that guy, McCarthy, running wild... No, Mikhailov's too smart. I don't think he'd have risked that."

"So, who then? The British?"

"That would be my guess. He went to the British and they were the ones who alerted Gehlen."

"Without telling the Americans?"

"The Anglo-Saxons may seem like a family, but even the best families guard their little secrets from each other."

"So where's the damn manuscript?" Ignatyev asked. "You think Gehlen's got that, too?"

"Not necessarily," replied Beria. "Lina von Osten's not going to give it up unless she's forced."

"And we don't know where she is now?"

Beria just shook his head in frustration. Already, he could begin to see all the consequences lining up in front of him. Denunciation, exile... perhaps even a bullet. He tried to wipe the negativity from his mind and think his way through. Suddenly, it occurred to him. There was a way out, he could see it clearly, but it meant he'd have to move against Ignatyev - and move fast. Without any warning, he reached across and picked up the external phone to access the switchboard operator. "I need a secure line to the MVD," he said rapidly.

That's when Ignatyev's large thumb came crashing down on the receiver cradle to cut off the call before it could be made. "No," he said flatly, "I don't think so."

Beria screamed at him: "Take your hand off the phone!" He attempted to grab the man's wrist and prize it away but Ignatyev was stronger and fitter than the out-of-shape Beria. The hand was immovable.

"If you think you can just order my arrest and put all the blame on me, you're dreaming," said Ignatyev, his hot, smelly breath close to Beria's face.

Beria was fuming. "This is outrageous," he said. "I demand..."

"Demand nothing! Say nothing! Just listen... This was your operation. You were in charge. If you'd wanted it kept quiet, you shouldn't have issued the directive."

"But without a directive..."

"It was your choice to make," said Ignatyev. "I'll tell you this right now, I'm not going to take the fall and, believe me, our naval friend, Kuznetsov, won't take it either. I know, because he already told me. That leaves you, Comrade. So if I were you, I wouldn't be too quick to call out your dogs. They won't get through *these* doors, I guarantee it, and they certainly won't get far at navy headquarters either. Not without explicit orders from The Boss. And you're not really going to divulge this mess to him right now, are you?" There was no immediate answer forthcoming, so Ignatyev said with greater force: "Are you, Comrade?"

Beria didn't answer. But he hadn't survived all these years by allowing himself to be intimidated by a crude *apparatchik* like Ignatyev and his mind was already a step ahead.

As I understand it, the Russian word "*dacha*" means country home and, in common slang, the privileged few who can escape the city at weekends are called "*dachniks.*"

It was a tradition that began during the time of Peter the Great but, after the revolution, all such places were initially denounced as bourgeois and seized in the name of the state. Then, just like a page from Orwell's *Animal Farm*, they were gradually reassigned to Party leaders. As with the use of official vehicles, the weekend *dacha* became a major perk, which could be awarded or denied depending on the individual's standing.

During his thirty years in power, Stalin had enjoyed several such retreats in various parts of the USSR. In the later stages of life, however, the *dacha* he preferred was Blizhnyaya, within easy driving distance of Moscow. It was not palatial compared to some but it was large enough to invite his ministers to dinner and even to hold Politburo meetings if necessary, when he didn't feel like returning to the city.

As a member of Stalin's close-knit fraternity, and a fellow Georgian, Beria was a frequent guest and found that his leader's attitude often changed towards him while they were there. Conversations became more intimate and confidences were exchanged more freely than within the intense pressure cooker of the Kremlin. On certain occasions, he was even made to feel like part of the family, although that was strictly dependent on the temperament of The Boss, which could change with frightening speed. No matter how convivial the moment, there was inevitably a degree of trepidation as Beria and other guests watched for the telltale signs of a shift. It could be anything from a subtle scratching of his chin to a more obvious clenching of his fist. Trying to read Stalin's moods was like predicting the weather by just watching the sky and it had become an ongoing obsession.

The best times were definitely the evenings, when the food was plentiful, the vodka flowed freely and laughter was easy. There were card games, film shows and music; always music, either in song around the piano, or from a professional performer who would be invited out to give a recital. There were even times when Stalin insisted that everyone should get up and dance, including his daughter, Svetlana, who had reached the age of twenty-six by 1952 and had already been twice married. At such times, she was often obliged to suffer the humiliation of sweaty hands and clumsy feet but she endured it because, like the men around her, she also knew that her father was more mellow when drunk. She, too, had reason to fear his disposition.

Nevertheless, despite all of that, Lavrenti Beria decided to drive out here after his discouraging morning at the Lubyanka. He knew that Stalin had decided to make it a long weekend and that it would be better to give him the bad news here than wait for him to return. Beria was both unexpected and unannounced - but when Stalin spotted him removing his coat in the doorway, the greeting was effusive and he was immediately clutched in that familiar bear hug.

"Lavrenti Pavlovich, where've you been? We started the party without you." Stalin neither knew nor cared that Beria wasn't on the evening's official guest list.

"Sorry, Boss, I was busy."

"Busy..." repeated Stalin. "You're always busy. What happened to that sense of fun you used to have, my friend? I miss that side of you. You should lighten up, relax a little. Come, have a drink with us." Then Stalin leaned in and whispered: "Lavrenti, do you have enough women in your life? Is that it?"

Beria laughed, but much of it was simply in relief, glad to see Stalin so jovial. Hopefully, this mood would help when the time came to take him aside and confess the failure.

In the large salon, there were over a dozen people, sitting or standing around, talking or telling jokes, to the background accompaniment of a violinist from the Moscow Radio Orchestra playing sugary-sweet selections from Tchaikovsky. They'd already eaten dinner and were sampling a case of foreign liqueurs that had been specially brought in. The Grand Marnier was proving to be especially popular with the ladies and they, too, were a little flushed. Among the notables present this evening were Nikita Khrushchev and his wife, Nina, as well as Georgi Malenkov, who had come alone. Both men were key members of the Politburo, as well as the Party secretariat, but there were major differences in their personalities. Khrushchev was verbose and bombastic, with a bald head and a squat, wrestler's physique. Malenkov, by contrast, was taller and more conservative, a traditionalist who rarely put a foot wrong and remained in place by the great trick of managing to please everybody, especially The Boss.

As Beria entered this elite gathering, the first person he happened to come across was Nikita Khrushchev's wife, Nina. He greeted her by gallantly kissing her hand but, at that exact moment, her husband happened to notice the two of them together and stormed over. Khrushchev sometimes liked to act in an oafish, bullying manner just for comic effect and predictably, he grabbed Beria by the lapels, threatening in a loud voice to beat him to a pulp for daring to romance his wife, then placed his large fist in front of Beria's nose. For Beria, it was an ugly recall of Ignatyev's manners that morning but, of course, on this occasion it was all merely in jest and the rest of the gathering was highly entertained.

Even Stalin laughed heartily. "When I said women, I didn't mean that one," he called over, and everyone laughed again, even though they weren't sure what the joke was about.

Beria continued around the room, attempting small talk. Meanwhile, his mind was working, trying to figure out how he was going to approach the subject of the disastrous operation. Eventually, he sank down into a sumptuous sofa with a glass in his hand. He didn't even know what was in it; he was just glad for the moment to relax.

"You look preoccupied, Comrade Minister."

Beria looked up from his thoughts to see Stalin's daughter sitting in a winged armchair, very close by. He hadn't even noticed her there. "Svetlana Josephovna... You startled me."

"Some bad news for my father?" she said, perceptively. She had a wary personality, with a slightly ravaged look to what should have been a pleasant young face, the years of obedience and fear, as well as the two failed marriages, having taken their toll.

Beria attempted a pleasant smile. "You know," he replied, "every time I see you, you're more like your mother, may she rest in peace."

Of all her father's associates, Svetlana perhaps loathed Beria the most, mainly because of his reputation as a pedophile. She could recall being seated on his lap during evenings like this when she was a young child, being cuddled and tickled by him, but today just the thought of such behaviour made her want to vomit. Even now, she still couldn't understand why her father ever allowed it.

"You're lucky he's in a good mood tonight," she said to him. "I hope for your sake that it lasts."

With that, she got up and Beria was left alone to sip his drink and continue his anxiety.

Of course, this wasn't the first time he'd ever brought Stalin bad news. There'd been many such times over the years. The problem was that, as The Boss aged, he seemed to be even less predictable, even more eccentric in his whims - and this business with the manuscript was a very personal matter. There was no way of telling how he'd react to such a disappointment and the only idea Beria could think of was to fall back on an old strategy: to wait until Stalin had drunk enough and then address him in their native Georgian for the sake of nostalgia. Sometimes the trick worked and sometimes it didn't but Beria felt he needed every possible advantage.

The evening didn't go exactly as planned. While the violinist played endless Bolshoi favourites from *Swan Lake* and the *Nutcracker*, Khrushchev was leading the conversation, speaking stridently and extravagantly about the perils of the new United Nations organization: about how it would inevitably be engulfed by the NATO agenda and how it was therefore Soviet duty to destabilize the existing international order as much as possible. Stalin himself took no part in the discussion but it was sufficiently lively that he controlled his alcohol intake and remained relatively sober. For Beria, this was not a good sign, exactly the opposite of what he desired, yet he knew he had to divulge the information tonight if he had any hope at all of deflecting the blame.

It was close to midnight when the guests finally began to leave but Beria deliberately stayed behind, waiting to the last. He could already feel the constrictions in his chest.

"So, Lavrenti..." said Stalin, finally walking over to where Beria was sitting. "You want a bed for the night?"

"No, no, thank you, I'll be leaving soon. But... there's something I need to talk to you about."

"It sounds serious. Is that why you're speaking Georgian? Speak Russian, Lavrenti. Be proud of your Russian."

Beria had no choice but to oblige, although the change of language also changed the tone. For him, Russian was a lot less collegial. "There's been a defection," he said quietly.

"What's that? Speak up, speak up."

"A defection," Beria repeated, a little louder.

Stalin grunted. "Another bastard who doesn't know when he's well-off? Well, let him rot in hell, whoever he is. If he wants to go, we don't need him. Shame it wasn't Khrushchev. I could've done without his loudmouth talk tonight." A big laugh. "Who was it, by the way?"

"MGB... Head of the First Directorate in Berlin."

"MGB? Then why isn't Semyon Ignatyev here telling me this? Why do you take it upon yourself?"

"Because the defection compromised..." Beria felt the man's gaze and could hardly bring himself to say it. This wasn't the scenario he'd planned.

"Compromised what? Speak up."

"The operation."

"What operation? Don't talk in riddles. We have many operations."

"The operation to retrieve the manuscript."

It was at that moment that Stalin's expression retreated from joviality to a blank mask and Beria instantly knew the line had been crossed. A tremor ran through him and all he could do now was wait to see on which side the man's wrath would fall.

"It failed?" said Stalin. "The operation failed?"

"We had everything planned correctly. The navy did their job well enough but I'm afraid the MGB..." Beria shook his head in an attempt to signify gross incompetence.

"Who has the manuscript now?"

"What happened was that the defector went to the British, who told the Germans..."

"Who has it?"

"The woman. We think the woman still has it. She escaped before..."

"Lavrenti Pavlovich, listen to me carefully." The words were spoken very, very slowly. "Are you listening?"

"Yes, I'm listening." Beria could feel the sweat trickling inside his shirt. This wasn't the violent temper that Stalin usually employed to invoke fear at the Kremlin. This was more like a cold fury that, in some ways, was even more frightening.

"Good," said Stalin. "It's very good you're listening, because this is important, do you understand me, Lavrenti? Do you?"

"Yes, yes, I understand. Believe me, I understand."

"I want that manuscript."

"Yes, I know... and I'll get it for you, I promise." By this time, Beria's voice was almost hoarse and it was all he could do to answer coherently. "You can rely on me. This is just a temporary setback, something I couldn't have predicted."

Stalin wasn't interested in excuses. "How, Lavrenti?"

"How?"

"How will you get it back? Do you have a plan?"

Beria was reluctant to answer but he had no choice. The man's eyes were on him, waiting, waiting. "I'm working on it."

"I see," said Stalin. The calm in his voice was ominous. "So now it's a race to see who can get to it first, am I right?" Once again, Stalin put his arm around Beria's shoulder, this time squeezing it tight. "You against them, Lavrenti, you against them."

"I'll find it first, Joseph Vissarionovich. I swear to you on my father's grave. I'll find it first."

"Yes," said Stalin, "you will."

It was a clear threat, which Beria understood only too well. He chose to remain silent, hardly daring to breathe as the seconds ticked by until Stalin offered the slightest of nods, almost imperceptible. Was it a nod of understanding? A nod of acceptance? Beria found it difficult to tell.

Eventually, Stalin lifted the glass that had been in his hand all this time and threw back the remains of the liqueur. "Don't let this ruin our friendship, Lavrenti," he said and turned away, finished with the conversation.

For Beria, it was a delicate moment and he crept away as softly as he could. The ordeal was over and he'd survived. The palpitations inside his temples began to subside. But that's when Stalin turned back and Beria was again frozen into inaction.

"By the way," said Stalin, scratching his chin thoughtfully. "About this MGB business, this defection in Berlin... Tell Ignatyev to make an appointment."

As Beria knew well enough, the phrase "to make an appointment" was a well-known euphemism for a tirade. "Yes... yes, of course."

He quietly left the room, then said a polite goodbye to Svetlana in the hallway as he pulled on his coat, but it was only when he was safely in the back of his own car that he could begin to regain some composure. He wound down the window to let in some of the cool night air and breathed deeply as he watched the dark countryside flash past. He was still under the heaviest pressure to find the missing manuscript before the British could lay their greedy hands on it but, on the whole, he felt he'd managed to emerge relatively unscathed from such a calamitous day and that his luck hadn't totally deserted him.

It was time to celebrate and he decided to do it in his own special way. He would call up Giselle.

★ ★ ★

Madame Giselle was a Latvian who'd spent some time as an exotic dancer in Montmartre before the war and now liked to pretend she was descended from French nobility. Her professional name was inspired by the famous imperial ballet and she even spoke her Russian with a fake Parisian accent, addressing her clients as *"comrade cheri."* But Lavrenti Beria didn't mind her pretensions because she knew his tastes and requirements. Indeed, that was the main reason she was in business.

With Beria's help, she'd taken over a large old house not far from the main Sadovaya Boulevard and it was there that she kept an exclusive supply of girls just for him: all of them virgins who were barely past puberty. Every couple of weeks she'd have a fresh supply transported in on a special bus from the small villages and collectives in the Moscow hinterlands. When they arrived, they were bathed, fed and dressed by a couple of assistants. After that, they were thoroughly inspected by Giselle herself. Those who passed were placed in a special dormitory and trained to satisfy her unique client's demands. If they were compliant, they were well-treated; if not, they were chained up for the night as punishment because Beria didn't want to see the marks from any beating. The girls, when delivered to his private apartment, had to look wholesome and pristine: in other words, virginal. Once he'd finished with them, however, he never wanted to see them again, so they were usually sold off to one of the neighbourhood pimps. For the shrewd Madame Giselle, it had turned into a flourishing business with a quick turnaround and handsome profits. Not only that but, as a bonus, she could count on the full protection of the MVD, the Ministry for Internal Affairs, should the need ever arise. And it was all due to her most exclusive benefactor, the chubby, bespectacled gentleman from the Kremlin, the one whose name she never dared mention.

In return, Beria was able to indulge his whims at very short notice. This evening, just a few hours after leaving the *dacha*, he was playing a favourite game he called "the flower arrangement." It was usually played in the late hours here in his private apartment and involved a group of nubile young girls, personally selected by Giselle and transported over in a covered van.

Tonight there were eight of them. They were completely naked and kneeling on all fours in the centre of the room with their heads together, thus forming the shape of a flower. Slowly, he paced around the ring, inspecting each girl closely before deciding which one he wanted. It was a fine crop tonight, Giselle had done well. But there was one who immediately caught his eye. She had long legs, white-blond hair and a real country look to her, as if she'd just come in from milking the cows.

"You," he said, pointing, and saw her glance up at him with her pale blue eyes. "What's your name?"

"Anna-Marie," said the girl shyly.

Beria smiled. A fine Russian-French combination. "Is that what Giselle told you to say?"

"Yes."

"Good, good. It's a pretty name. It suits you. Stand up, please."

Obediently, she got to her feet and he gazed at her slim body and limbs; at her long neck; at her small, upturned breasts with their delicate pink tips; and finally down to the main focus of his attention, her groin, its pale hair delicate and almost invisible.

"Come with me, Anna-Marie, I have a surprise for you."

"What kind of surprise?"

"Ah, you're confident. I like that. You answer me when I talk to you. Are you afraid of me?"

"No…" she said, but she was a little more hesitant with this reply.

"No, of course not. Nor should you be. I'm just a big teddy bear and tonight… well, I have to say that tonight is very special for me. It's kind of a celebration, like a party, and that's why I'm going to give you a big surprise. You want to see what it is, my big surprise?" He saw her nod. "Good, so please, Anna-Marie, come with me and I'll show you."

He took her by her slim fingers and led her into the next room, his own master bedroom suite, furnished with an antique Persian carpet, heavy velvet curtains and a broad, sumptuous bed covered in brown silk. He saw her look around questioningly, so he said: "No, no, the big surprise is over here." That's when he slowly reached down to the front of his gray wool pants and began to undo the buttons of his fly, one by one, enjoying the sight of her blue eyes transfixed on the thick, growing bulge. "Don't be nervous," he said in his most soothing voice. "You're going to have a good time."

He was just about to take a step towards the young girl when an abrupt thought entered his head and he couldn't seem to extricate it. *"Lavrenti, do you have enough women in your life?"* Those were the words The Boss had used. Was he being funny? Did he know about this little arrangement with Madame Giselle? Why would he have used those words, if he didn't know about it? And if, in fact, he did know about it, who could have told him? Not Giselle certainly. Why would she do that? Then it must have been Semyon Ignatyev. Did he call Stalin the moment Beria left the Lubyanka? Or was it all just paranoia? As cunning as Beria was, he just couldn't seem to work it out.

The girl, Anna-Marie, was watching him intently, wondering what was happening. She was still fearful, waiting for that monstrous thing to emerge, to invade her, to thrust its way inside her, but the thing had vanished. All she could see was a man paralyzed where he stood, a blank expression on his face and an erection that had completely subsided.

The turmoil was crowding Beria's brain and he tried to shake himself free. It wasn't fair, he thought. Even at this moment, when he was merely trying to relieve the pressure, the sudden thought of Stalin was able to spoil it. Was there no escape from the man's terrifying shadow?

I personally read about the failed Fehmarn operation in a week-old issue of the *International Herald Tribune*. I was still in Barcelona, where I'd been residing for several years, and that worthy paper was just about my only source of world news.

The story was no more than a few lines, tucked away on an inside page, but my eye caught the small headline and recognized the name of the island. The brief text that followed reported that a guesthouse near Burgstaaken harbour had been invaded and the perpetrators apprehended. No clue was offered as to means or motive - but, to me, it seemed suspiciously like the place in which I'd conducted my ill-fated interview with Lina von Osten. This was then confirmed when the piece finally mentioned, almost as an afterthought, that the property was owned by the widow of the late Reinhard Heydrich, head of the Reich Central Security Office.

In fact, the only reason I even cite the article at this point is to demonstrate that, although both London and Moscow were taking the matter seriously, the world at large knew next to nothing about it. There was no major announcement, no great propaganda coup, simply because neither side had yet gained the advantage. At this stage, the only notable beneficiary in the entire mess was the defector, Alexei Mikhailov, and the British were still keeping him under tight wraps. Even the Americans didn't know about him.

So far, the information he'd brought across had completely checked out and the MGB *spetznaz* had been duly apprehended. Of course, the manuscript was still missing but that was hardly Mikhailov's fault. As a result, he and his wife were granted provisional asylum by Her Majesty's Government and personally escorted by the MI5 officer in charge, Malcolm Davies, from Charlottenburg to

Tempelhof and then, by BEA Viscount turboprop, to Heathrow.

Their arrival didn't go unnoticed, however. Moscow wasn't ready to give up this undercover war so easily.

The man assigned to shadow the Mikhailovs when they landed was a veteran operative, based at the Soviet Embassy on Kensington Gardens. He'd been doing the same kind of observation job for years, as revealed by an almost permanent expression of resignation. His thin hair was combed over in a vain attempt to cover a spreading bald patch and his sunken brown eyes were surrounded by shadow-filled lines and creases. Sometimes, he sighed for absolutely no reason at all. I never discovered his real identity but his code name was Tobias and, on this day, he'd been sent to follow the Mikhailovs from the moment they cleared airport customs.

Tobias knew exactly which flight they'd be taking, thanks to the secretary responsible for travel arrangements at the British military administration in West Berlin. Like so many involved with minor espionage activities, her recruitment had nothing at all to do with either politics or ideology. She just needed the cash to get married and had been led to believe that the morsels of information she supplied were so minuscule that they couldn't possibly harm anyone.

What the MGB didn't know, however, was exactly where MI5 would station the defector and his wife. A safe house in the city? Some secluded farm in the middle of nowhere? In theory, it could have been anywhere in England. The operative, Tobias, was therefore assigned to monitor the large blue Vanguard until it deposited both the Mikhailovs and their luggage, wherever that happened to be.

From the airport in West London, he kept them well within sight all the way into town, staying as close behind as he dared. It would have been all too easy to lose them in the traffic through Hammersmith. Then, at Earl's Court, he saw the Vanguard cut north through a bewildering maze of side streets, weaving nimbly past construction barriers and parked delivery vans. The maneuver was evidently designed to show up any possible tail but Tobias, in his black Morris Minor, refused to take the bait. Instead, he attempted to outflank the Vanguard by taking parallel streets, the idea being to meet up with it at a later intersection. It was a clever ploy, one he'd used successfully before, but it didn't work this time and he cursed quietly to himself in Russian. He'd lost them and all he could do after that was devise a makeshift search pattern and hope he'd see the vehicle parked somewhere. It was a forlorn hope and, after about fifteen minutes, he'd just about given up when he spotted the distinctively curved profile of the car on the other side of Bayswater Road. It was just pulling up outside a pub called the Paddington Arms, situated not too far from the rail terminus of the same name. He could hardly believe his luck.

Slowly, Tobias cruised the area until he found a parking spot, then stepped out onto the pavement. He'd come prepared and his outfit included a briefcase, an umbrella, a black bowler hat and a folded copy of the *Daily Express* under his arm. His English still had an accent but, as long as he kept his mouth shut, he could easily be taken for a typical City bank clerk running some private errand on his lunch break.

Playing his role to the full, Tobias strolled right past the pub, then stopped, looked at his watch and seemed to decide that he had the time to "nip in for a quick one," as the English like to say. Leaning up against the bar, he pointed casually to the beer pump and opened his paper to the sports section. It was full of the upcoming Cup Final at Wembley stadium between Newcastle and Arsenal. The experts were divided as to who they thought might win but his own deep interest in football was just a well-rehearsed distraction so he wouldn't have to speak to the barmaid and reveal himself as Russian. She was a mature woman with rounded shoulders and big, curly hair, dyed ginger. Her clothes were modest, a plain knit sweater over a dark tartan skirt but she augmented it with brash costume jewellery in fake mother-of-pearl: a matching necklace and bracelet, with large, circular earrings. To any amateur observer, she'd be the least likely person to be on the MI5 payroll. However, for an experienced agent like Tobias, her appearance only served to bolster his suspicions.

As the brimming pint glass was placed in front of him, Tobias nodded his thanks, then glanced around. Over to one side, a small, wood-panelled entrance led into a hallway where a metal sign on the wall announced the "Paddington Arms Inn," the letters forming a red circle around the blue trademark of the Royal Automobile Club. Underneath were the two stars that the inn had been awarded. The name of the establishment was all Tobias needed to know and there was no need to stay any longer.

Continuing his role, he suddenly looked at his watch again, as if remembering some prior appointment; but since no ordinary Englishman would ever leave a glass of ale totally untouched, he quickly drank a few gulps before leaving. Then, he folded his paper with expert ease, threw some loose change on the wooden counter to pay for the drink and left as silently as he'd arrived.

Once he'd eased himself back into the confines of the Morris Minor, Tobias allowed himself another of his long sighs. He knew he'd been extremely fortunate to spot the car again outside the pub and he was all too aware that, in his business, it was often such random luck that determined success or failure and, sometimes, even life or death.

To prove this point, we now shift from London to the other side of the world - all the way to Beijing, capital of the new People's Republic of China, the revolutionary regime led by the rosy-cheeked dictator with the Marxist ideals, Mao Zedong.

It was there, in that ancient, poverty-filled land that Olga, only child of Alexei and Irina Mikhailov, had been based for several months, engaged in a program of smallpox vaccination for the Bethune Institute of Public Health. The project, which included nursing staff, medical supplies and support vehicles, had been offered as a gesture of friendship and solidarity from Stalin to his new fellow Communists.

Olga had inherited the sandy hair and delicate facial features of her mother but was solidly built like her father. She'd even become a little paunchy since she'd arrived here in China, the result of the poor quality diet. There was little protein available, even for foreign aid workers, and her daily subsistence was nothing more than glutinous rice, stale cabbage and watery, fish-head soup. It was fortunate that she'd also inherited her mother's attitude, with the same deep reserves of patience and tolerance. They served her well in her current assignment.

On the day the two Soviet agents arrived, she was working in the hard-pressed Wukesong district of the capital, located an hour's bicycle ride west of the Forbidden City and consisting primarily of ramshackle housing, smoke-belching mills and spartan military barracks. Her clinic had set up tents just outside one of the traditional community enclaves known as a *hutong*, which was nothing more than a warren of hovels, each pieced together with planks of old wood overlaid by sheets of rusty, corrugated metal, and intersected by unpaved alleys, ripe with open sewers. Here, a thousand or more malnourished humans eked out an existence, surviving as best they could on the scrawny, disease-infested chickens and goats that they raised in their tiny backyards, as well as the occasional cart-load of mouldy, pest-ridden vegetables that the new government dropped off as part of its own socialist mandate. It was the perfect recipe for an epidemic and the sheer fear of its potential was the only reason the Chinese authorities had put aside their pride in order to accept Soviet help.

By eleven in the morning, there were several hundred parents and children lining up as ordered, each waiting for the dreaded needle prick in the arm. They weren't sure what it was all about or how such a thing could work but they'd been told that, without it, they and their offspring would surely die a terrible death. One by one, they entered the canvas tent, only to be shocked by the sight of a blond woman, the first that most of them had ever seen. Worse, she was wearing her Soviet supplied uniform of stark white, which Chinese superstition holds as the colour of death. To their eyes, she was a living ghost but she was used to the reaction and she tried to calm each new patient with a warm smile and a cheery "*Ni hao,*" the everyday greeting.

It was after a young mother with her screaming, wriggling baby had finally left that the three men entered through the flap. The two in plain clothes were Russian, their bulky stature making them seem like giants compared to the diminutive Chinese military officer who accompanied them. The Russians smiled at her but their icy presence dominated the tent.

Olga's immediate anxiety was that she was being drafted. The Korean War was in its third year and had reached something of a stalemate, a long standoff in which neither side could gain a true advantage. But the guns were still firing and the casualties were still mounting, and all sides had need of as many medical personnel as they could ship in. That's why she feared that her transfer to the war zone might happen at any time, despite the fact that both she and the Institute were doing everything possible to resist such a move. In her view, her work here was equally essential and far from complete.

"Olga Mikhailov?" said the Russian who entered first.

He was about thirty and wearing a wartime aviator's jacket that he might have picked up in some Moscow flea market. One of the sleeves was ripped, she noticed, and she couldn't help thinking of her mother, the seamstress.

"Yes," she replied firmly. "Who are you?"

"It doesn't matter who we are. All you have to do is focus on this."

From a holster inside his jacket, the man pulled a small calibre pistol, then spread his body into the classic, two-fisted marksman's position and levelled the weapon directly at her. As his finger found its way to the trigger, a look of stunned realization set into Olga Mikhailov's face and her mouth opened as if to cry out. At that same moment, just as the gun's hammer clicked against the empty chamber, the other man stepped forward to take a close-up photo of her expression. The sudden blue-white light of the flashbulb blinded her, freezing her movement and silencing her scream. Once the picture had been taken, the first man put his gun away.

"*Xie xie*," he said, speaking his own version of badly-accented Chinese and bowing to her with mock gallantry. The phrase means "thank you."

With that, all three men left, the two Russians plus their Chinese escort.

An empty silence seemed to permeate the tent and all the young woman could do was stare blankly after them until the tears began to flood her eyes. She couldn't help it. She was confused and shaken. In the normal course of events, Olga Mikhailov didn't cry easily but the sudden shock had completely unnerved her.

Olga's parents, Alexei and Irina Mikhailov, weren't displeased with their London accommodation at the Paddington Arms, except for the fact that they had little privacy. For their own protection, Malcolm Davies had assigned one of his MI5 juniors, code name Lupin, who spent his time either reading the papers or dozing in an armchair.

The apartment they'd been given was in a separate annex from the rest of the establishment and furnished by the counter-intelligence agency as a safe house. It had a living room, a bedroom, a kitchenette and a bathroom, all reasonably spacious, and a good light entered through the lace curtains. The only problem was that, because it was situated in the front of the building, it was subject to considerable street noise, especially when the big, red double-deckers rumbled past right under the windows. Still, it was far better than the Mikhailovs' dump of a place back in East Berlin and they were thankful just to be here. The water was hard but drinkable, the gas stove lit with an even flame and the electricity worked from every socket. Irina had also been delighted to find that, in addition to the crockery, cutlery and fresh linen, some thoughtful person had even stocked the place with several of the latest appliances: in the living room, a quality radio and record player; in the kitchen, a pressure cooker, a toaster, an iron and a good set of pans; plus, in the bedroom, twin reading lamps and a hair dryer. It was very cozy and she took a small delight in each new discovery.

When she asked about shopping for groceries, young Lupin

informed her in his nasal Midlands monotone that, for the time being, they couldn't leave. His manner was polite enough but he had an impassive air about him, with a humourless demeanour and no ability for small talk. In the same boring voice, he went on to tell them that their meals, like their laundry, would continue to be serviced by the inn for the time being. Meanwhile, he'd taken the liberty of ordering them soup and sandwiches for lunch.

Faced with such bland officialdom, Irina had little choice but to shrug and comply. She didn't wish to upset her husband's chances of negotiation, so she sank back into her familiar mode of perseverance and tried to accept the situation for what it was. Her way was just to get on with things, so she began setting the table. However, before she could even arrange the place mats, there was a polite knock on the front door.

Lupin was instantly on his feet at full alert. "What?" he said through the door.

"It's just me," replied a female voice from the other side. "Come on, luv, I haven't got all day."

It was the barmaid from downstairs, Barbara, and he opened the door a crack. That's when she passed the sealed envelope through to him. On the front, there was handwriting, scrawled in thick pencil: "For the Russians."

"Who gave you this?" he said softly. Until he knew more about it, he didn't want the Mikhailovs to hear.

"Some bloke who came in."

"What sort of bloke?"

"Dunno. Seen 'im before though, same day your Russians arrived. Never says nothing."

"And you didn't think to mention it?"

"He was just an ordinary customer. How was I supposed to know?"

"So he just gave you this in your hand?"

"Nah, left it on the bar when my back was turned. Before I knew it, he was gone."

"Can you describe him?"

"Not really. Was just average, like." Then she thought about it some more. "Bit of a City gent, if you ask me, but not quite... like he was one of the lower downs. Aren't you going to open it?"

"Yes, in private," Lupin replied rudely. Then, he thought better of it and added: "Thanks." But she was already disgruntled, so he just shrugged and shut the door after her.

"What's in there?" asked Alexei Mikhailov from the other side of the room.

Lupin realized it was too late to conceal it. "Looks like it's for you," he said, before brazenly opening it himself. It was part of his job. But all he found inside was a grainy snapshot, taken with the glare of a flashbulb. It showed a blond female in her twenties, in a white nurse's uniform, with a frightened expression on her face. There was no note. "Do you know this girl?" he said, passing the photograph over to Mikhailov.

By this time, Irina had come over to join her husband and it was her muffled gasp that partially answered Lupin's question. She seemed as if she were about to faint and had to be helped into a chair.

Lupin looked at her, waiting for an explanation, but it was her husband, now kneeling next to her, who spoke the words.

"Our daughter, Olga," he said in a low voice. "It's a warning."

"What kind of warning?"

"From our friends in the Kremlin."

"And it means?"

"Isn't it obvious?"

"You tell me."

Alexei Mikhailov was tempted to mouth off at Lupin, to vent his frustration in a torrent of abuse, but decades of discipline took over and he was able to control his anger. No point taking it out on the young man who was supposed to protect them. Instead, Mikhailov answered as calmly and patiently as he could manage: "In simple words, it means 'shut up or else.'"

★

As it turned out, Alexei Mikhailov's fate was finally sealed, not in London or Beijing, but in Moscow, when an infuriated Joseph Stalin ordered his MGB director, Semyon Ignatyev, to dispose of the traitor once and for all.

They were in Stalin's grand office in the Pantheon, the triangular building with the green cupola, just a few hundred metres from the Spasskaya Tower on the northeastern side of the Kremlin. His rage was audible even in the anteroom but it was nothing the aides hadn't heard before. Sometimes, they imagined, the sound of his tantrums could carry beyond the high red walls, all the way out to Red Square, where the proletariat mingled on the cobblestones: minor officials hurrying across town; provincial families come to see the sights; war veterans, some on crutches or in wheelchairs, paying their respects at either Lenin's tomb or St. Basil's Cathedral, depending on their convictions.

Although Stalin had originally shrugged off Mikhailov's defection when talking to Beria at the *dacha*, he'd since changed his mind; or, to be more accurate, he'd forgotten his earlier reaction. Such random mood changes were by no means uncommon and, on this particular day, it was Ignatyev bearing the brunt. The defector had been MGB? According to Stalin, no matter what the circumstances, the responsibility lay with the service director.

When Ignatyev tried to suggest several courses of action, Stalin just screamed "*Nyet!*" at each one of them. He didn't want Mikhailov's daughter threatened, nor his wife, nor anybody else. He didn't want to issue warnings. He just wanted the man eradicated and he wanted it done as soon as possible.

The order was therefore wired through to the *rezidentura* at the

Soviet Embassy in London, demanding immediate action.

When the opportunity duly presented itself, it was less a product of MGB planning than an unfortunate tactical error on the part of Malcolm Davies.

The catalyst was the photo of the Mikhailovs' daughter, which was making the couple apprehensive, especially Irina. Due to increased Chinese involvement in the Korean War, it was proving impossible to get a line through to Beijing, even for MI5. As a result, the couple's nerves were fraying and Davies was very much afraid that the pressured atmosphere just wasn't conducive to the kind of voluntary cooperation from Alexei that he required.

The best solution was to get them away somewhere, perhaps to transfer them to the agency's rural safe house in Hertfordshire, but Irina point-blank refused to go. She wanted to remain, to keep trying to get through to Olga, and she knew there was a much better chance of accomplishing that from the centre of London than from the depths of the countryside.

The alternative option was simply to get them out of the apartment for a while, just to get their minds off the problem. It was Alexei Mikhailov himself who came up with the idea of a sightseeing tour and Davies reluctantly agreed. Looking back, it was a tragic mistake but it was his best judgment at the time and he even insisted on precautionary measures. They would have to be driven door-to-door and accompanied at all times by two of the department's handlers: the cautious Lupin, who would do the driving, plus a beefy young man to supply the muscle, code name Nasturtium. He'd once been a useful middleweight boxer and had the broken nose to prove it.

After some negotiation, there were only two places on the itinerary, both very public. For Alexei, the history buff, they would visit Westminster Abbey along with all the other tourists. For Irina, it would be Fortnum & Mason, the exclusive food emporium on Piccadilly, famous for having served seven British monarchs. It was at the latter location that the lethal incident took place, right in the centre of the main food hall on the ground floor.

While Irina was marvelling at the spectacular selection of cheeses, everything from Wensleydale to Mozzarella, her husband was over by the fish counter, renewing his acquaintance with the varieties he'd seen his father handle. He was enjoying the familiarity of the raw smell, the silvery sheen of the scales and the chill of the crushed ice on which they were stacked. Both Lupin and Nasturtium were in close attendance but, afterwards, neither of them knew for certain exactly what had taken place. There had been no gunshot, no stabbing, nothing at all to disturb the normalcy of the day and all Lupin could recall was that the assailant was probably the middle-aged man in the suit who seemed to bump into Alexei Mikhailov accidentally: just the kind of meaningless incident that can occur in a busy store at any time. Nobody thought anything of it but later, back at the Paddington safe house, Mikhailov began to feel drowsy while listening to a BBC concert on the radio: Mahler's Symphony No.1 in D Major. He'd always enjoyed Mahler. It was during the second movement that he completely collapsed, slumping sideways into the arms of his panicked wife as his heart finally surrendered.

It was only after the Crown coroner had finished his autopsy several days later that MI5 knew the cause of death: a chemical of unknown origin that activated on contact with the victim's skin. In terms of delivery, the assumption was that the assassin had applied the fatal dose merely by brushing against Mikhailov's bare hand, possibly by means of a sponge or a vial hidden in the palm of a protective leather glove. For the Special Branch officers conducting the investigation, these findings were difficult to believe, like something out of science fiction, until a technical team based in Crawley confirmed that the Soviet Union was indeed believed to be developing such methods at an installation called Laboratory 12, a covert section of TsNIIST, the Central Research Institute of Technology.

To anyone's knowledge, this was the first time the substance had ever been used operationally and an ominous development in the ongoing East-West intelligence wars.

To fully appreciate how the story unfolds from here, it's necessary to understand that the loss of the defector, Alexei Mikhailov, was of enormous consequence to Malcolm Davies. It was more than just his reputation or his ego, as might be expected; more than just a professional loss. The episode profoundly affected his entire psyche.

He'd had a major Soviet asset in his hands, one of the most important defections in a long time. Yet, somehow, he'd managed to foul it up by trying to be too nice. He could have moved the couple out to the country, by force if necessary, but he didn't because they were still trying to contact their daughter in China. He could have also refused the sightseeing expedition but, no, he felt sorry that they were so cooped up in that little apartment. Even then, he could have insisted on beefing up the assigned escort but he didn't do that, either, because he wanted to make them feel welcome, not like prisoners. As a result, Alexei Mikhailov, ex-colonel of the MGB First Directorate and British intelligence prize of the highest order, was assassinated in broad daylight, in the very centre of crowded London. It was a foul-up of vast proportions and Malcolm Davies couldn't help the feeling that he was personally responsible.

It was illogical, he knew that. In his line of government work, the accepted method of dealing with such circumstances was to pass the blame on down the line: in this case to the minders, Lupin and Nasturtium. Yet, despite his better judgment, he couldn't do it and a large part of the reason was the guilt factor triggered by the funeral service. Several years previously, Davies had lost his own wife, Emily, to a metastatic brain tumor. She'd died while pregnant, losing their child in the process, and all the memories of that painful, wrenching period came flooding back when he saw Irina's unrestrained show of grief.

Perhaps it was his self-identification with Alexei: two operatives working different sides but at the same level, with the same motivations. Or, perhaps it was simply the final product of so many years of tension and stress. Whatever the reason, he felt a massive weight on his narrow shoulders and he just couldn't seem to shake it loose. He'd now lost his wife, his unborn child and his career, so what was left? He had no real hobbies, except for a minor collection of first edition stamps; he didn't much care for sports; and the only exercise he'd ever taken was the occasional Sunday stroll with Emily on Hampstead Heath. These days, he didn't even do that any more. He lived only for his work: a conscientious functionary who toiled long hours and sometimes took his duties too seriously.

The evening after the funeral, he found himself sitting in his untidy Bayswater flat, just staring out at the darkening sky, alone and depressed. The cheery disposition he'd always tried so hard to maintain had collapsed like a house of cards. He couldn't read his newspaper, do the crossword puzzle, or even listen to the radio. He had no appetite for supper and no taste for scotch. Instead, he just sat there like a zombie until, at some time close to midnight, he decided there was nothing left. That's when he actually began to contemplate suicide.

The more he thought about it, the more convinced he became that it was a viable solution to everything. Now, the only question in his mind was how to go about it.

He didn't keep a gun at home and a leap from his third floor window would probably just break a few bones. So how, then? By putting his head in the gas oven? By slitting his wrists with a penknife? Or simply by swallowing down a bottle of Aspirin tablets in a comfortable armchair? Obviously, the last option was the preferable way to go but there was another problem: he didn't have any Aspirin. He looked at his watch. By this time of night, the neighbourhood shops would all be closed and he could hardly wake up the people next door. What would he say? "Excuse me, could I borrow the means to kill myself?" It was laughable but he couldn't see any humour in the situation. For Malcolm Davies, it was merely frustrating and, lacking any definitive course of action, he just drifted off into a fitful, unsatisfying sleep.

It was close to dawn when he awoke, aching as if he'd just fought a major battle and survived. He vaguely recalled some distant dream in which he was with Henry V at Agincourt. Or was it Wellington at Waterloo? He couldn't really figure it out. All he knew was that his entire attitude had changed overnight. He was done struggling with fate, and tired, too, of wrestling with his own conscience. His real war, he suddenly realized, was elsewhere - and the first thing one needs in a war is an ally.

The Gryffon was one of those secluded little pubs which locals know intimately but strangers take an age to find. It was tucked away in a narrow Mayfair mews, conveniently close to the American Embassy on Grosvenor Square and therefore ideal for the kind of quiet, unofficial meeting that Malcolm Davies had in mind.

From outside, the place was not much to look at but, inside, it was a intriguing warren of interlocking rooms, all grouped around a central bar area. The low ceilings were supported by exposed beams and the irregular walls were crammed with all manner of framed artwork: hand-drawn maps of London boroughs, soft watercolours of the Thames, and the kind of erudite, pen-and-ink cartoons that were once published in magazines like *Punch* and *Tatler*.

When Davies arrived, his lunch guest, a long-time acquaintance, was already there. This was the immensely tall Phil Rankin, almost doubled over just so he could lean on the bar.

The man's full name was Philip Stewart Rankin III, a native of Pennsylvania and a senior grade officer of the Central Intelligence Agency, stationed here in London. Although he was wearing a well-cut suit, it was difficult to hide the fact that he still retained the physique of the junior league pitcher that he once was. By all accounts, he might even have made it to the majors if it hadn't been for the war. He came from a good family and his father happened to be an old school buddy of "Wild Bill" Donovan, the man who turned the OSS from a bunch of enthusiastic amateurs into the professional and respected outfit it finally became. That's how the young Phil Rankin got involved with the fledgling service: a personal introduction from his father. But the big college jock was happy enough to start at the bottom, just like everybody else, and eventually progressed up the ladder through dint of his own honest toil, a worthy career if somewhat unspectacular. These days, one of his principal assignments was as liaison to the Gehlen Organization, over in West Germany.

After the initial greetings were over, Davies took it upon himself to order beer for the two of them, since he was the one who'd issued the invitation. This was no ordinary "pint," however, but a special brew and, despite his bleak mood, he forced himself to show some enthusiasm.

"Now, what you've got to do," he told Rankin, "is to watch very carefully as the barman pours it."

"Yeah? Why would I wanna do that?"

"Just watch." Sure enough, the beer was tipped in extremely carefully, with about a third left still in the bottle. "See the stuff that's left?" said Davies. "That's sediment."

"In a bottled beer?"

"Ah, but this is no ordinary bottled beer. This is India Ale... the original. Very rare, these days. This is one of the few places you can still find it."

"Sorry, Malcolm, but warm beer is warm beer."

Davies made a show of being shocked, then just shook his head sadly. "Phil the Philistine," he muttered, as the big glasses arrived in front of them, white foam dribbling down the sides. "Wash your mouth out with that, will you?"

Rankin sipped at it, before pronouncing his verdict: "Okay, not bad."

"Not bad? *Not bad*? What you're holding there, my son, is a classic. You see, when we still had an empire, we'd try to send beer out to the troops in India but it took weeks to get there and the beer used to go flat in the ship's hold. So some Victorian genius invented a beer that was still actively brewing as it travelled and when it arrived... *voilà*... perfection."

"So this is it? The same stuff?"

"India Pale Ale. The very same. Except that, instead of maturing on the boat, it now does so on the shelf. When they get a fresh batch, they're not even supposed to serve it until the sediment settles. And then, when somebody orders it..."

"They have to pour it carefully or that somebody's going to get a mouthful of sludge. Okay, I get the picture. Very impressive, Malcolm. Another anecdote for the folks back home. Now, why don't you tell me what all this is about?"

Davies realized he was maybe over-playing his role of genial host and allowed his smile to wither away. "To be honest, Phil, I'm looking for a favour."

Rankin gazed down at him from his greater height. "Something of a personal nature?"

"No, no... nothing like that. No lusting after secretaries, no missing expenses, I can assure you."

"I'm glad to hear it."

"Shall we order some food, by the way? I recommend the steak and kidney pie."

They found a table in a hidden back corner, out of earshot from the bar, but it was a cramped affair and it was all Rankin could do to tuck his stilt-like legs underneath. Such places weren't built for American athletes.

"So, what's the favour?" asked Rankin.

Davies drank some more of his ale while he considered how to talk about it. What he was about to divulge was technically illegal. "This conversation is completely off-the-record, all right?"

"Never happened."

Davies nodded but, for a brief moment, he wondered whether to back out. It was still possible, even now. He could just make his apologies and talk about something else. Then he remembered the farce of the missing Aspirin and his courage returned. In his own mind, he had nothing left to lose. And, from that moment until the food arrived, he spoke in hushed tones, relating the strange tale of the Mikhailov defection: the bungled raid on Fehmarn; the interception by Gehlen's men; the disappearance of Lina von Osten with the manuscript; the ODESSA faction within the Gehlen organization who'd helped her escape; and, finally, to his own everlasting shame, the blatant hit on Mikhailov in central London.

Rankin waited until after the barman had brought over the plates of food. "Some story," he said finally, as he began forking into his lunch. It was steaming hot and he had to drink some of his beer to quell the burning. If he was surprised by the revelations, he was professional enough not to show it. The unauthorized British contact with the CIA-sponsored Gehlen Organization was especially galling but he knew it had taken a lot for Davies to open up like this and he was curious to see how it might play out. "But I still don't know the favour," he added.

"Yes... the favour," said Davies, blowing carefully on his own food in a practiced manner. "I want to find that manuscript, Phil. I want to embarrass the hell out of Stalin and I want you to help me do it."

"Me? Why come to me? Why not your own people?"

"Because we don't control Gehlen," replied Davies. "You do. And Gehlen's the key to all this."

"What gives you that idea? You think he knows where Lina von Osten is hiding herself?"

"I'd say it's a pretty safe bet."

"Yeah, well, I don't know so much."

"Really? I should have thought it was obvious."

"Maybe to you on your side."

"I'm not following."

Rankin looked at him and then, in the frank spirit of the exchange, decided on a little of his own candour. "I'm going to be honest with you here, Malcolm. We really don't know what Gehlen's doing half the time because, well, he doesn't want us to. Which is fair enough, I guess. But a few of us suspect he hides a lot because he doesn't always know what's going on himself. Oh, he plays a pretty game and he sure acts the part, all that dash and charisma, but when it comes down to it..."

"You think ODESSA operates without his knowledge? Is that what you're saying?"

"No... no, that's not what I'm saying at all. Look, Malcolm, it's a freelance organization, which means they're all just a bunch of damn mercenaries, even the best of them. And the worst? They're into all kinds of garbage, from smuggling war criminals to local racketeering. Christ, they may even be robbing banks for all we know. The point is, we turn a blind eye because..."

"Because they're useful. I understand. But you still haven't answered my question. Can you do it, yes or no?"

"Can I do what?"

"Control Gehlen."

"Malcolm, I just finished telling you..."

"You just finished telling me that he's a mercenary."

"It's not like that. How many more times? Sure, we pay Gehlen and he serves us well enough, which is all very nice, but that's as far as it goes. It's a buyer-seller relationship, not one of your British master-servant deals, you get what I'm saying?"

"Yes, thank you," replied Davies, feeling a little patronized. "I get it."

"Look," said Rankin. "In the end, he's a West German national. He'd like nothing better than to get rid of us and report directly in to the Chancellery, so if you must have a name, the only person who can really control him is Adenauer." He was talking about 76-year-old Konrad Adenauer, first post-war Chancellor of the new West Germany.

"Good, excellent," replied Davies. "Now we're getting somewhere. All you have to do is put pressure on Adenauer."

Rankin gave out with a laugh, until he looked across at Davies and saw that the man's face was perfectly serious. "What? Are you kidding me? Dream on, buddy boy."

"I need your help to do this, Phil."

Rankin brushed a hand through his thinning brown hair. "All right, all right, you got my attention." He was prepared to admit that much, at least. "So just lay it out straight for me, would you? Starting right now at this pub, what would you like me to do? Me, personally." He watched for a moment as Davies unscrewed the top of what looked like a bottle of thick, brown ketchup, then couldn't help asking: "What the devil is that?" He didn't even try to hide his expression of disgust.

"What *is* it? How long have you lived here? You don't know about India Ale, you don't know about HP sauce... You've really never tried it?"

"No... but then I've never tried jellied eels or mushy peas, either. These days, I value my health."

"You don't know what you're missing." Davies spent another minute fooling around with a knife to get some of the thick substance out onto his plate. "It's very simple," he said, switching back to their conversation without any warning. "All you need to do is get a personal word to Gifford."

"I see. A personal word to Gifford, just like that. Hell, Malcolm, what do you think we're running here? I don't get to speak with him that often, especially not on a personal basis. I can't just drift into his office and say 'Hi there, Wally, what's going on? Mind if I just bend your ear for a few minutes?' Believe it or not, we've got a reporting structure to follow."

Walter Sherman Gifford was American ambassador to the UK and nominally in charge of all matters inside the Embassy. His full title was "Ambassador Extraordinary and Plenipotentiary to the Court of St. James" but, as grandiose as that sounded, it wasn't important. What was important, at least as far as Malcolm Davies was concerned, was that Wally Gifford had once been a close adviser to Roosevelt and, more recently, had become a stalwart friend of his presidential successor, Harry S. Truman. However, unlike Roosevelt, who had a special wartime relationship with Stalin, it was well known that Truman held the Soviet dictator in total contempt. Indeed, some even went so far as to claim that he dropped the two atomic bombs on Japan just to show Stalin what he could do.

"Think of the potential," said Davies, trying to summon up some encouragement. "If Gifford likes it, he'll take it upstairs and you know his old pal Harry's just going to love it."

"Well, that's as may be. But I can't do it, Malcolm."

"Of course, you can."

"No, I really can't. I don't report to State. I'd have to cross departmental lines and go around a dozen different people. Maybe even as far as DC. It's impossible."

"Nothing's impossible if you want it badly enough."

"I don't want it at all."

"Really? You'd pass up the chance to embarrass Stalin? The thanks of a grateful President? The thrill of whispering afterwards that you were the one who did it? You'd become a legend in no time, then wouldn't your dad be proud?"

"Yeah, you think so? My dad doesn't even like the CIA. Thinks we never should've disbanded the OSS and you know what? Sometimes, I think... Well, never mind what I think. Look, even if it were possible and we could somehow put the squeeze on Gehlen, what makes you think he could flush Lina out from wherever she is? Like I said..."

"He may not even know. Yes, I heard you, Phil. But, like it or not, he's the best chance we've got."

"We?"

"Absolutely. You and me. I get redemption, you get the glory."

"Yeah, well, glory or not, it can't be done."

Davies couldn't help reacting to the outright rejection. Before coming here, he'd told himself to stay calm no matter what happened, to remain professional, but now the pressure inside his head felt like it was going to explode. His face took on a mask of aggrieved fury and, suddenly, all the depression and the frustration reappeared, spouting up like a geyser.

"Jesus Christ, Phil! I ask for you for one lousy favour..."

"I think you'd better keep your voice down."

"One little favour, that's all I need."

"It's not that little."

"Isn't it? *Isn't it*? Just a quick word in the man's ear... along the corridor, on the back stairs, in the damn toilet for all I care... what's so hard about that?"

"Hell, Malcolm..."

"Don't give me that 'hell Malcolm' rubbish. What's that supposed to mean? I'm being unfair? I'm being unreasonable?"

"Yes, in a word. I think you are."

"Dammit, you think this is easy for me? All right, look... you say you'd have to cross departmental lines? Well, what do you think I've done, just by coming here? We've known each other a long time, Phil. You think I make a habit of doing this? You think I enjoy cutting my own people out of the loop? Do you?"

"No, I get it, I really do. I'm honoured you called me."

"Honoured?" scoffed Davies "*Honoured*? Fine, thanks a lot, Phil. Sorry to have disturbed you. Sorry to have wasted your precious time. Oh, and thanks for not telling me what a cretin I am to have the nerve, the temerity, to ask the saviours of our poor, besieged little island for a favour."

At this, Rankin sat back and just shook his head. From his perspective, this was not only unseemly, it was also embarrassing. If it hadn't been for the sake of friendship, he'd have gotten up and simply walked out.

Davies, meanwhile, was breathing hard from his outburst. He was still upset, still in an emotional state from the other night, when he'd actually thought about ending it all. Yet the deeper, more rational side of him knew only too well that such demonstrative behaviour was not only unprofessional, but also counter-productive. The more upset he became, the less likely it was that Rankin would buy in.

For several minutes, they both sat finishing their food in a kind of aggrieved silence, until Davies chose to break the stalemate with a different approach.

"Come on, Phil..." he said, sounding a bit like a boy scout leader. "Where's your sense of adventure? Where's that ol' OSS spirit? What would Wild Bill have done?"

Rankin glanced at him. "Cheap shot, Malcolm."

Davies gave a wry smile. He could see that Rankin's hard line might just be softening. "Is that a 'yes' I'm hearing?"

"It most definitely is not."

"How about a maybe?"

"I told you, no."

"A *possible* maybe, then?"

Rankin offered a shrug of those lanky shoulders. In truth, he wanted to be accommodating. He really did. As his father used to say, never refuse a man asking a favour, because you never know when you'll need one in return. "Let's just say, a very tentative 'maybe'... at the outside."

"Splendid!" Davies exclaimed, instantly changing the mood. As far as he was concerned, victory was nigh. The cavalry was on its way. "Then let's drink to 'maybe,' tentative or otherwise. Cheers!"

Less than two weeks later, that private little lunch between two old friends at the Gryffon pub took on the makings of a full-scale, geopolitical issue.

It happened when Phil Rankin of the CIA finally found a way to circumvent embassy protocols. Instead of following the prescribed line of authority through his CIA superiors, he managed to broach the matter directly with Ambassador Gifford under the guise of casual gossip during an otherwise boring cocktail reception. As predicted, Gifford immediately sensed it might be just the kind of Cold War mischief which would appeal to the President and, the following day, he sent off a coded personal cable to his good friend in the Oval Office.

As a consequence, we now shift our focus to Chancellor Adenaur's austere office in the West German capital of Bonn, so we can listen in to the call which came through his switchboard from the White House on June 23 at 14:00, local time. At the other end of the line was Harry S. Truman himself.

A highly conservative man of staunch opinions and old-world manners, Konrad Adenauer sometimes found the populist Truman a little too folksy for his personal taste. On a political level, however, the two needed each other and they'd managed to develop a sound, if somewhat formal, working relationship.

"Good afternoon, Mr. President," said Adenauer, in his very correct but strongly accented English. There was no need for an interpreter and he sat alone in his simply furnished office. A depressing drizzle splattered the windows.

"And a very good morning to *you*, Herr Chancellor." Due to the time difference, Truman was still eating breakfast in the Oval Office. "How're you doing today?"

"I'm very well, thank you," replied Adenaur. "And yourself?"

"Just dandy."

"And your good wife, Bess?"

"She's very well too, thanks for asking. Herr Chancellor, I've got a couple of my ol' pals here with me, Dean and Beetle. There's a small matter we'd like to discuss."

Truman glanced at the other two who were with him on this occasion. Facing him was one of the most able of US diplomats, Secretary of State Dean Acheson, his white eyebrows and mustache contrasting sharply with a conservative dark suit and the spotted bow-tie that he invariably wore. Near him sat CIA Director Bedell Smith, a taciturn ex-military man, who had once served as US Ambassador in Moscow. He was called "Beetle" for no reason other than his name but the Chancellor evidently had trouble recognizing it.

"Beetle?"

"Bedell Smith," replied Truman. "Central Intelligence Agency."

"Ah, yes, of course... Beetle... I must remember that."

"Now, this thing we're talking about here. I want you to know it's not critical but, well, it may be kind of interesting. I'll let you be the judge."

"Mr. President, it's a rare pleasure to receive a call that's not critical."

Truman laughed heartily. He was in fine form. "In that case, I think you might enjoy this one. It's about a way we might be able to embarrass the Soviet Chairman while he's alive and perhaps even affect his legacy once he's gone. Does that sound interesting to you?"

"I'm listening."

"Fine. In that case, if you don't mind, I'll put Beetle on the line. He can explain it all far better than I can. Hold on, Herr Chancellor, he's right here. I'll just step aside, let you fellers get at it..."

All-in-all, the Transatlantic call lasted less than twenty minutes.

The tone continued in the same easy, almost jovial manner, but no contact at that level is ever innocuous, especially when the richest nation on Earth contacts a war-torn dependant, struggling to rebuild. As casual as this matter sounded, it didn't take long for the serious ramifications to trickle down.

It began as early as the following morning, when Konrad Adenauer welcomed Reinhard Gehlen to his office for a private, one-on-one meeting. It wasn't on the official Chancellery agenda and no aides were present.

"Ah yes, Reinhard, come in, come in. I don't have long I'm afraid. I'm just on my way to Brussels, so I'll come straight to the point if I may."

Gehlen was his usual gallant self. "Of course, Herr Chancellor."

"I want you to cooperate with the Americans on this stupid affair, this manuscript business. Can you do that?"

"Well, yes, normally I'd be glad to do anything…"

Adenauer cut him short. "You have a reason not to do so?"

For a very brief moment, Gehlen thought about telling the truth - that if he tried to chase down Lina von Osten, the ODESSA faction in his organization might not appreciate it and they had a lot of influence on his people, more than he liked to admit. But then he caught himself in time. He knew that the old man had always been staunchly anti-Nazi and had no sympathy for a mercenary gang of ex-SS, none at all. To bring it up might therefore be the very worst thing that Gehlen could do at this moment. He had his own ambitions - a grand plan to graduate from his US dependency to become the official intelligence agency of the newly sovereign West German state - but he wouldn't be able to achieve anything without Adenauer's full support.

In the end, Gehlen's answer was succinct. "It's a delicate matter, Herr Chancellor."

Adenauer stopped packing his briefcase for a moment and looked across at him, trying to gauge the level of opposition. Then he gave a half-smile, an unusual occurrence. He hardly ever smiled. "But you're so good at delicate matters, Reinhard. That's why we like you."

"Thank you, Herr Chancellor. I appreciate your confidence, as always."

Adenauer closed his bag, his face thoughtful. "My advice? If it's too difficult for you to handle, get somebody else to do it."

"Somebody else?"

"I can see why you don't want to go meddling in your own filth, so plant a spy. You can do that, surely? You know about spies."

"Excuse me, Herr Chancellor? You're suggesting I plant a spy in my own organization?" For Gehlen, it wasn't the concept that was so strange, it was the fact that it was coming from Adenauer, a dignified man in a starched collar whose usual way was to avoid such grubby issues.

"Reinhard, please. I don't have time for this. I survived two world wars and all the madness in between. You think I don't know how things work? Now listen. It's very simple. Go find someone acceptable to both you and the Americans, someone very low profile, and put him in with your people. You let him roll around in the dirt for a while and then, after a suitable time, you pull him out."

Gehlen nodded his understanding. "It might be risky."

Adenauer was about to march over to the door but paused. He had a car waiting downstairs and a plane standing by at the airport. "Let me be perfectly clear," he said. "I don't care if your man succeeds or fails. Truman obviously wants the manuscript but, to me, it's an irrelevance. Worse, it's an annoyance. So all I want is to show him we're making an effort, you hear me, Reinhard? Do this for me."

Without waiting for any further reply, he left the office, leaving Gehlen with no room for maneuver. The so-called advice had turned into a direct order and, although neither Gehlen nor his organization officially reported to the Chancellery, he knew that, if he ever wanted to fulfill his own ambitions, he had no choice but to obey.

The only issue now was finding someone foolhardy enough to take on such an assignment.

★

"Forget it, Siegfried," I said for the umpteenth time, as we sat there in the shaded heat of late afternoon. "I told you 'no' and I meant it."

We were sitting at an outdoor café on the Ramblas in the centre of Barcelona, where I'd been rooted for the past couple of years, and opposite me was my sometime friend from pre-war Berlin, Siegfried Wachter. He was a large man in every direction and he liked to live large, too; the only one of the old crowd who ever had any cash to throw around. On this day, he was dressed in his colonial outfit: a handsomely-tailored tropical suit of beige linen, complete with navy handkerchief in his top pocket; a sky-blue shirt of the finest Egyptian cotton, with silk cravat to match; plus a rakish Panama hat to protect his massive bald head from the Mediterranean sun.

"All right, dear boy, keep your hair on." It was his version of a self-deprecating joke. In addition to his native German, he also spoke fluent Russian as well as an impeccable English, complete with upper-crust accent. "But, if nothing else," he added, "you have to admire my persistence."

"What I admire," I replied, "is your talent for making money."

He knew I was being facetious but that didn't deter him. It never did. He'd survived the war handsomely by trading commodities and now, here he was in Barcelona, lording it over my poverty and grandly interrupting my wine-induced trance.

"You know, Ed, it strikes me you could use a few lessons in the art of making money yourself." He sipped some of the expensive cognac he'd ordered for the two of us. "Of course, you know what *your* problem is. You don't see the big picture, you never have. You can't make money if you don't see the big picture."

"I'm not sure what that means."

"Ed, please..." he said. "Just think about it for one minute, will you?"

I was thinking but I still couldn't see what he was talking about. He'd told me the sordid tale of Stalin's missing manuscript and it didn't take me long to recognize that the raid on Fehmarn was the same affair that I'd briefly read about in the *Herald Tribune*. He'd also told me that Reinhard Gehlen himself had initiated the search for "a unique individual" to track it down - that's precisely how he put it - but, for the life of me, I had no idea what such a role might entail. I couldn't figure out how I qualified, or why I should even consider it.

"Okay, I give up," I told him. "What's the answer?"

"My poor boy, you do have a hard time seeing the obvious, don't you? The answer is that this manuscript is an item that everyone wants."

"You don't even know what's in it."

"Who cares what's in it? First lesson, Ed... An item that everyone wants is valuable by definition."

"Everyone? Who's everyone?"

He gave a long sigh. "Well, Stalin's the one pushing, so *he* wants it. Then there's his lackey, Beria, who's taking all the heat, so there's no question he wants it, too, if only to please Stalin. Then, on the other side, we've got Herr Gehlen and his most generous sponsors, the Americans, God bless their little greenbacks, who each want it for their own selfish reasons. And I'm sure there are others involved too."

"So what do you intend to do once you find it? Sell it?"

"Sell it, trade it, maybe even auction it. I don't know yet."

"Auction it? You mean play one off against the other? Isn't that...?"

"Isn't that what? Dangerous? My dear boy, I've done this before, you know."

That was true enough and I couldn't deny it. Trading commodities between nation states, friendly or otherwise, was not exactly without risk.

"You know, Sieg," I told him, "it's people like you who cause revolutions."

He grinned broadly. "On the contrary, dear boy. It's people like me who *lead* revolutions."

"You think so?"

"Of course. Think about it... Cromwell, Robespierre, Lenin, Mao... The only thing they've all got in common is that they were willing to adapt in order to win the game. So in that sense, yes, they're just like me."

"So what you're really telling me is that there's no morality in this world. It's just winner-takes-all, right?"

"Don't be silly. Of course there's morality. That's what keeps it all from falling apart. Ninety-five percent of the planet is basically moral, which is a blessing. Thank heaven and praise the Lord! But I'm not talking about those people. I'm talking about the other five percent."

"The people like you."

He stared at me for a long moment. "Now look, Ed, I'll say this once." He was back into serious mode. "I'm as moral as I have to be, as moral as my own conscience requires me to be. I've never shot anyone, never even yelled at anyone as far as I can recall, so I really don't need your insults to mess up my day, all right? I'm offering you a chance to pull yourself out of this... this fug you're in... yes, 'fug'... and I'm doing it for old times' sake. We were good friends once, Ed, back when Berlin was still a fun place to be. We had a good crowd and we shared some good times... and, personally speaking, that's what I choose to remember. So it's up to you, yes or no. Sit here and drown your sorrows, or get up from that damn chair and return to the land of the living."

That was the annoying thing about Siegfried. He could flutter around a subject like a damn butterfly. Then, in one instant, he'd metamorphose into some kind of stinging hornet and zoom in to pierce his target with uncanny accuracy.

For a few seconds, I said nothing. I just watched the faces passing by on the Ramblas and it occurred to me that I'd been sitting here for so long, they'd become nothing more than a peripheral blur. In my own mind, I'd become a tragic figure, injured by life and love in equal measure. It was something of a romantic delusion, I admit, but it suited me to play the role as I wasted away, yearning after Katharina, the woman I left behind in Berlin.

How I actually wound up here in Spain is an unlikely tale but, then again, the immediate post-war period was an unlikely time. The people of Europe were all trying to pick themselves up off the floor as best they could and some found themselves in very strange circumstances. In my own case, I'd decided to return to my old stomping ground of Berlin in order to try earning a living, once again, as a freelance journalist. The newly independent press had need of people like me: an experienced professional who knew the landscape, spoke German like a native and who, as a North American, could parlay his way into the various echelons of the occupied power structure. One of the first assignments I gave myself was to scour the records for Lina von Osten and then travel north to Fehmarn for that useless interview - but, try as I might, I couldn't find any trace of the one person I was really seeking, the woman I'd fallen for all those years previously: the stunningly elegant Katharina Vollbrecht, woman-about-town and heir to the Vollbrecht estate. I searched every archive, every file, but she seemed to have vanished without trace.

Eventually, in frustration, I accepted a position in the Middle East with an international wire service. The region was just heating up prior to Israeli independence and, potentially, it was a great opportunity to be in the right place at the right time: a foreign correspondent's dream. Sadly, it didn't turn out as I envisaged. Not long after I arrived, a bomb went off in a Jaffa souk and I was on the receiving end of a piece of shrapnel which lodged itself deep into my hip, putting me out of action for several months. In the meantime, the wire service replaced me, so when I could finally walk again, I was out of a job. That's when I came up with a very creative idea. I made use of some Israeli government contacts to meet with the fledgling Mossad intelligence agency and came up with an offer.

At that time, in addition to serving the needs of state security, one of Mossad's side functions was to track down Nazi war criminals, a mandate for which they had little appetite, as well as a chronic shortage of resources. I therefore told them that, for a small stipend, I would become their resident agent in Barcelona, the Mediterranean port which had become the central staging post for such escapees on their route to South America. After some hesitation, the Israelis finally saw the logic and agreed. Thus, without putting too fine a point on it, I became an officially credited bounty hunter. In other words, I was paid a commission to identify members of the SS who were still on the run. Yes, I know it sounds like a daredevil job but, truth be told, it was all fairly mundane. After my decade in pre-war Berlin, I had both the dialect and the slang, so the SS who passed through tended to trust me - or, to be more accurate, they *wanted* to trust me. I was like a welcome friend in an insecure world. But no sooner had we shared a litre of wine than I was on the phone to my Mossad case officer with names and details. And that's all I had to do, because that's where my responsibility ended. The surprising thing was that we were reasonably effective. In the end, we managed to nail quite a few that way and my Israeli cohorts were satisfied enough.

By the time Siegfried Wachter arrived in the summer of '52, however, such work had all but dried up. Most of my potential targets had already been caught or else flown the coop. So there I was, a more or less permanent fixture at Jose's café, drinking myself into a pathetic stupor while wondering what the hell I was going to do with the rest of my life. My hip had pretty much healed but my mental state hadn't, and it was easier to sink into a depression than to get myself together in order to actually do something.

"You haven't even told me what the job is, exactly," I said in a quieter voice. To Siegfried, it must have seemed like the first dent in my armour.

"I've told you all I can for now."

"Right, to help search for some manuscript, or whatever it is. But what have I done to deserve this privilege?"

"All will be revealed. You just have to come to one meeting. If you like what you hear, we can move on from there. If you don't... well, that's a pity... but it'll be your choice. Now who can say fairer than that?"

"Where will the meeting be?"

"Somewhere civilized, I promise you."

"I don't know, Siegfried."

"How about if I told you there might be an incentive?"

"What kind of incentive?"

"Let's say a percentage on the sale."

"How big a percentage?"

"Oh, my dear boy, far too early to be discussing that."

"So how do I know..."

He didn't even let me complete the sentence.

"When have I ever lied to you? When have I ever cheated you out of anything?"

I thought about it but he had a point. He'd never done either of those things. I was running out of excuses. "All right, all right," I finally told him. "I'll come to this precious meeting, if that's what you want." He'd finally managed to wear me down and I could see that annoyingly self-satisfied grin on his face. "Two conditions though. You fly me first class, okay? And you give me a nice hotel, five-star, with all expenses."

"Done."

"Even with all that, I want it absolutely clear, I'm not making any promises."

I thought it was a good piece of negotiating, a last ditch effort to put me back in the driver's seat, but tactics like that didn't work with Siegfried. He just drained his cognac and gave a single, imperious nod of that huge head.

"I'll be in touch," he said.

Then he stood up and walked away, like a champion leaving the field, and all I could manage was to stare after him, wondering if I'd made the right decision. I'd made no commitment, none whatsoever, but I was already beginning to regret it.

While I was meeting up with Siegfried Wachter in Barcelona, another reunion between two old friends was taking place in the centre of London.

It was July 10th and the man who'd facilitated the Mikhailov assassination strolled out of the staff door of the Soviet Embassy on Kensington Gardens. He was in his fifties, with an "everyman" appearance augmented by deliberately dull clothes: the kind of gray worsted suit and boring blue tie that any office manager might wear. Over the years, his waist had thickened and his wavy, mid-tone hair had receded a little but his features remained undistinguished and he was still the kind of person nobody would ever look at twice: a prized quality in his own field of endeavour. His name was Yuri Modin and he'd been in the covert intelligence business a long time.

Originally, Modin had been a protégé of Lavrenti Beria, when the latter was director of the NKVD. It was an association that had paid many dividends over the years and, later in Modin's career, when he was posted to London, he was given full responsibility as case officer for the treasonous British spy ring that had been recruited from Cambridge University in the 1930's. These were the notorious sleeper-agents, or "moles" as they're often called: upper class, left-wing sympathizers who successfully burrowed their way deep into the very heart of the British establishment and passed so many vital secrets along to the Soviets. This included the notorious pair, Guy Burgess and Donald Maclean, who'd recently made headlines by fleeing to Moscow in order to evade capture; also John Cairncross, another member of the academic elite, who gave away the celebrated ULTRA cipher codes and then, after the war, offered up even more critical information about the British nuclear program.

Now, Modin was on his way to see yet another of his former star assets: someone who hadn't yet been fully exposed but was under heavy suspicion at MI5 and had been for several months.

From Kensington High Street, he travelled by Underground - or the "Tube" in daily parlance - because traversing crowded stations and changing trains frequently is just about the best way of losing any potential tail. In this case, he could have gone directly to his destination by way of the Circle line but, after changing five times, he wound up on the Bakerloo line and surfaced at Charing Cross on The Strand. From here, he strolled across the stately Trafalgar Square at its southwest corner and passed under Admiralty Arch, gateway to a more imperial London. Through this high portal is a gracefully landscaped oasis of mature greenery and white columned facades. Personally speaking, it's one of my favourite areas of the city, a living history that harkens back to the days of Empire, when British industry and naval prowess held dominance over a quarter of the world. Carving its way through this well-preserved refuge is the ramrod-straight, mile-long avenue known as The Mall, which leads directly to the ornate stone structure of Buckingham Palace, central seat of the monarchy since the reign of William IV.

Yuri Modin, however, wasn't here for the sightseeing, glorious though it may be. On this occasion, he was all business.

After crossing Horse Guards Road, he sidetracked left into St. James's Park, a pleasant diversion where the thrushes sang, the squirrels scratched leisurely and the aromatic smell of damp grass was a welcome change from exhaust fumes. Being a weekday, there weren't too many around and the only people to pass him were a retired couple, quietly discussing the jonquil beds as they slowly walked their Labrador, and a uniformed nanny pushing a large, ornate baby carriage: a fast-disappearing sight in this modern era. But this lack of pedestrian traffic was exactly why Modin came here. There was no risk of eavesdropping and there'd be absolutely no record of anything having taken place.

The man he was due to meet was waiting at their pre-arranged rendezvous point: a certain lakeside bench that was isolated from any shrubbery by a radius of thirty yards.

"Hello, Kim," Modin said softly, in his well-practiced English.

The real name of Modin's contact was Harold Philby but he'd been known since his earliest schooldays in colonial India as "Kim," a nickname derived from the famous Kipling volume about a fictional child spy.

Like Modin, Kim Philby was middle-aged and just about average height, with black hair swept back and ice-blue eyes; but, while Modin was steady and methodical, Philby was more complex, relying on both the power of his intellect and the chameleon-like quality of his personality to regulate his life. He could be either dashing or slovenly, detailed or casual, highly motivated or maddeningly off-hand, all depending on the circumstance and who he was trying to impress at the time. On this occasion, he'd chosen a Savile Row suit in classic pinstripe, a crisply laundered Turnbull & Asser shirt and his Westminster school tie, as if to prove that he was still a man of substance and that none of the accusations bothered him in the least.

"Ah, there you are, Yuri," he replied. "I'd just about given you up."

The bench was just across from the promontory known as Duck Island and several of the waddling inhabitants had ventured over to snatch at the tiny morsels of sandwich that Philby was throwing them. Next to him was the tightly furled umbrella that he invariably carried.

As Modin sat down on the same bench, he glanced around one more time, a matter of habit. From half a mile away, the chimes of Big Ben rang out their three-quarter pattern and he checked his watch. It was already 3:45.

"Sorry," he said, "the trains weren't cooperating today."

Philby nodded his appreciation. He'd had to go through a similar rigmarole on the Underground to get here himself. Although their meeting could be categorized as something of a risk under the circumstances, they'd calculated that St. James's Park was an ideal place to do it because it was so obvious. Even if they were, indeed, spotted together, it could be easily rationalized. What more natural explanation could there be than two old diplomatic acquaintances meeting by accident in a public space that was central to everywhere? Why wouldn't they stop and pass the time of day? If pressed, they'd say they were just reminiscing, asking after each other's families. What was wrong with that? Who could prove otherwise?

"So, how're things?" said Modin.

Philby smiled wryly at the profound nature of the question. "Remember during the war, how people said everything would be so much simpler once it was all over? The funny thing is, I never felt like that at all. At one point, I recall thinking that all we have to do is defeat the fascists. One target, one goal, with everybody working towards it, all together. Simplicity itself. Only when it's done will things get more complicated."

Modin nodded in that gently reassuring way of his. "Always the visionary," he replied. In fact, he was glad to see that Philby was back to a more relaxed mood than of late. The strain of so much suspicion had been starting to show. "I have some news," he said cheerfully.

"News?"

"One of your problems has been solved."

Philby immediately caught the gist. Without any further explanation, he knew that the problem to which Modin was referring was Alexei Mikhailov. "Is the solution permanent?" he asked.

"Very."

"Good," he replied. "Thank you, that's a weight off my mind."

From a personal point-of-view, Kim Philby had been extremely concerned about Mikhailov's defection and the evidence which might emanate as a result. They'd known each other in the US, each having been stationed there for a couple of years during the war, and had met on several occasions to exchange information. Specifically, Philby had been the SIS liaison in Washington during the time that Mikhailov was with the Soviet Consulate in New York and much of their communication concerned who knew what about Project Manhattan, the covert development of the atomic bomb at Los Alamos, Nevada. While Philby didn't pass on the secrets of nuclear fission himself, he played a vital role in covering the tracks of those who did.

Modin looked at his old friend and breathed a long sigh. "So now, Kim, I need something from *you*, if you don't mind."

Philby glanced at him for a moment, then continued his gaze out towards the lake. "Tit for tat," he said. "I suppose it was ever thus."

"It's nothing much, I can assure you. Just a little information."

"Information... A rare commodity these days, Yuri, at least from my end."

"Well, fortunately, this one dates back a bit. What do you know about a man called Wachter?

"Wachter, Wachter... now why does that name ring a bell?"

"Full name, Siegfried Hendrik Wachter. Trades commodities for a living."

"Oh, yes, right. Big, round type. Rich as Croesus, or so I was told. German national... also spoke perfect Russian and English. Worked all sides, if I recall. Quite adroit at it, too."

"That's him."

"Yes... I wouldn't say I actually knew him well but I did run into him a couple of times before the war. Here in London, as a matter of fact... formal functions, that kind of thing. Actually, I heard the suggestion that he might be some sort of courier for Ribbentrop and Molotov... you know, when they were negotiating the pact." He was referring to the alliance that the two foreign ministers signed in 1939, the ultimate conclusion of the early friendship between Hitler and Stalin. It shocked the world and, for a while, realigned the entire balance of power, until Hitler shattered the pact in 1941 with his surprise decision to invade Russia. "Of course," added Philby, "the whole affair was very hush-hush at the time... especially the part about Wachter acting as go-between. I must admit, I wasn't even sure whether to believe it."

"And now?"

"You mean with the benefit of hindsight? Certainly, I believe it. Is he still around?"

"Large as life and twice as wealthy."

"Well, good for him. What's your interest, if I might be so

bold?"

"Just wanted your impression."

"Don't be coy, Yuri, it's not your style. Play all the games you want, I really don't mind, but please don't be coy."

Modin thought for a while before answering. "All right," he said, finally. "I suppose we've known each other long enough. You know all that business with the manuscript?"

"Beria's little caper in Fehmarn, yes, I heard something about it. Total fiasco, as I understand. Wasn't it Mikhailov who put the kibosh on it?"

"Yes, as a matter of fact, it was. If you must know, that's how he defected. He alerted the British and they sent Gehlen running off to intercept... except that, somehow, in all the chaos, the manuscript went missing and so did Lina von Osten."

"Gehlen let her go?"

"That's right. And now he's coming under pressure to do something about it."

"Pressure from whom?"

"Mostly MI5, since Mikhailov was their defector... but now they've got the Americans involved too."

"Ah, the big boys."

"I believe there was even a call from Truman to Adenauer on the subject."

"My, my, heavy stuff. So now Gehlen's got everyone breathing down his neck. But what does all this have to do with Wachter?"

"I'm not exactly sure... but, if I were to hazard a guess, I'd say Gehlen wants to defuse the situation by distancing himself from it. So what does he do? He hires someone to infiltrate his own organization."

"Really? How intriguing. And may I ask how you come to this conclusion?"

"It's a theory, nothing more."

"Must be based on something though."

Modin gave a shrug. "You know how it is, Kim... Gehlen watches us, we watch him. Always far more bits of gossip than we ever need. But, occasionally, a tiny morsel comes through that justifies all that time we waste."

"A morsel?"

"If I knew more, I wouldn't need to be here, would I?"

"No, right, I suppose not."

"So what do you think?"

"Of what?"

"Of my little theory."

"You mean about Wachter infiltrating Gehlen's outfit? Well, to be honest with you, I wouldn't have thought he'd really be suited to that line of work."

"No? So what if he's simply been charged with finding someone. He knows a lot of people."

Philby considered this new thought. "I'd say, of the two options, that would be the more likely. Any guess as to who it might be?"

"That's what we need to find out."

"And how do you intend to do that?"

"Well, that's where it gets interesting. Wachter has a history of playing it both ways and I was wondering, if I were to approach him, whether he'd be willing to do it again."

"Interesting notion," said Philby thoughtfully.

"You think it's possible?"

Philby laughed a little. "You forget, I only met him twice, Yuri. And that was a long time ago."

"That's twice more than I did."

Philby sat back on the bench and spent a few seconds thinking about it. "My experience? If a man's done it before, he's usually got no inherent scruples about repeating the act, so I'd have to say yes, it's possible."

"Possible? No more than that?"

"Yuri, please."

Modin shook his head, as if he realized how stupid all this must sound. "You know, Kim, the real problem here is that I've been asked to do this, so I have no choice in the matter, whether I agree with it or not. I think what I'm really trying to ask is that if you were me...?"

"How would I go about it?"

"Yes."

Again, Philby took the time to think. At last, he said: "From what I recall, I'm fairly sure the rattle of money would work with a man like Wachter... but I'm afraid it would have to be a rather substantial amount. He's already got more than your entire country." A pause. "That's a joke, by the way."

"Yes, thank you. I love your British humour. Unfortunately, my budget is far from substantial."

"Yes, I can certainly vouch for that. So if it were up to me, I'd try blackmail."

"With what?"

"My dear Yuri, you only have to meet him." Philby leaned over to whisper but it was merely a theatrical gesture. There was clearly nobody around but the ducks. "Homosexual," he said with his finger to his lips.

That's when the dawn of possibility struck Modin's face and he fell into a contemplative silence. Homosexuals were no longer openly persecuted as they were under the Nazis but such behaviour remained a criminal offense in most European countries, including the UK.

Meanwhile, Philby used the opportunity to look at his watch. He was obviously getting a little nervous about the length of the conversation and decided to make a unilateral move to conclude the meeting. "Anything else I can do for you today, Yuri?"

Modin brought himself back from his thoughts. "No... No, I think that about covers it, thank you."

"In that case, I think I'll be getting along," said Philby, as he stood up. "A pleasure, as always. Give my regards to your good lady."

With that, he simply strolled away towards Birdcage Walk, tip-tapping his brolly on the pavement as if he hadn't a care in the world. It was an amazingly smooth show he put on and he'd been doing it for so long that it had pretty much taken over his entire persona.

As for Modin, he chose to remain seated on the park bench for a while. It was far more pleasant here than his stuffy embassy office and even the most experienced operatives occasionally need the time just to sit and think.

In deference to the increasing pressures, he knew that this whole business with the manuscript would have to be handled with exceptional delicacy, since it was now being watched from on high by both sides: not only Stalin and Beria, but also Truman, Adenauer and heaven-only-knows who else. Even worse was the fact that, as of now, he, Yuri Modin, was slap in the centre and, reputation notwithstanding, it could easily rise up and destroy him. As he told Philby, he didn't have a choice about whether to approach Wachter. That decision had already been made back in Moscow. The real issue was how best to do it. The homosexuality angle was as good as any but should it be directly with blackmail, or indirectly with something else - like a good, old-fashioned honey trap for example? This insight from Kim Philby had certainly brought forth a whole range of options.

The predicted rain clouds were beginning to roll in as Yuri Modin heard Big Ben strike five, so that's when he, too, got up from the bench. He was a little stiff from sitting so long and couldn't decide whether his body needed a pot of tea or a shot of scotch. Either one, he felt, would be very welcome.

Siegfried Wachter was as good as his word. The meeting to which I'd been invited was due to take place on Thursday, August 5. The London location was unexpected - I thought it might be Berlin - but I had no idea what to expect or who I was actually going to meet. This was Siegfried being his usual enigmatic self, annoyingly smug and self-important about the secrets he guarded. But I will say this about him. He did live up to our agreement, flying me in first-class elegance from Barcelona and then providing me with exceptional accommodation, all expenses paid, at the refined Lanesborough at Hyde Park Corner. Okay, it wasn't the Savoy or the Dorchester but it was one of Siegfried's favourites nonetheless and he's a man of impeccable taste.

The first evening, I indulged in a fine solo dinner of roasted lamb accompanied by a good burgundy, which was followed by a sound night's sleep on crisp white linen. By the time the car arrived for me at nine the following morning, I'd enjoyed an excellent pot of coffee and was beginning to feel distinctly mellow.

I should have known it wouldn't last.

For a start, the car happened to be an ordinary police vehicle, with an un-talkative officer at the wheel who wouldn't tell me our destination and even declined to say good morning. From the way Siegfried spoke, I thought I'd be taken to some chic rendezvous point, perhaps a Chelsea penthouse with a private elevator, or some Tudor mansion with butlers and stables. I thought we'd munch on *petit-fours* while we discussed the state of the world. Fat chance. As it turned out, the drive took less than ten minutes and, once we got to the Victoria Embankment, we turned into the gates of the large, red brick building familiar to every Londoner. This was Scotland

Yard, the busy, workaday headquarters of the Metropolitan Police and about as non-chic as it was possible to get.

"Here?" I said to the officer but, again, he didn't say a word. Instead, he politely held the car door for me, then escorted me in through an entrance in the rear. The structure was bigger than it appeared from the street and something of a maze. At the back, on one of the upper floors, was a large conference room and it was here that they were all waiting for me - all ten of them. It was more like the editorial board of a major daily newspaper than a clandestine intelligence session and the people around the table were already looking like they had better things to do. So far, I wasn't too impressed.

"Please take a seat, Mr. Schaeffer." The voice came from the far end of the long table: a hollow-cheeked man with a horseshoe bald patch and a civil servant's attitude. On the wall above him was a framed portrait of the new heir apparent, Elizabeth II, just eighteen years old and already looking regal. Her father, George VI, died in February but her official coronation wouldn't be for another year.

After a brief round of introductions, I learned that the man speaking was Sir Humphrey Pender of Special Branch who was chairing the meeting at the personal insistence of the Home Secretary. Although Special Branch was devoted to issues of national security, they were officially a police division, which was why we were at Scotland Yard and not some place more private. Also present was Malcolm Davies of MI5, the lanky Phil Rankin of the CIA, plus a man with film star looks who turned out to be none other than Reinhard Gehlen, living up to his billing. There were others around the table, too, presumably aides and assistants, but these four were obviously the principals. The one person I expected to see, Siegfried Wachter, was conspicuous by his absence. Since he seemed to be such a key person, I found that a little strange.

Pender began with a few brief comments, mostly to remind everybody that it was against the Official Secrets Act to repeat anything outside this room. Obviously, the people gathered had no need for such a warning and his tone was a little patronizing. Then, once he was done, he passed the meeting directly over to Gehlen, who took the time to light up one of his American cigarettes before speaking. I have to say that, for a man who had the pressure of the world on his shoulders, he seemed remarkably relaxed. He was in good physical shape, with a firm jaw, cool blue eyes and a full head of hair that was graying handsomely at the temples. He also had an elegant charm just oozing out of every pore but that, too, was part of the legend. It was said that, after his surrender, he managed to talk his way out of the POW camp and on to the US Army's payroll within mere days.

"So..." he said, leaning back in his chair to gaze at me, "you're the Mr. Schaeffer I've been hearing about." His English was almost as good as Siegfried's. "May I call you Ed?"

"Sure... as long as you don't expect me to call you Reinhard."

He gave a gentle smile, well aware of the effect that his first name had on some people. The only other Reinhard that most people had ever heard of was Reinhard Heydrich and, although I didn't know what this guy had done in the war, or what kind of atrocities he might have committed, I can still say with some certainty that the name association with the prime architect of the Holocaust was a little unnerving.

"I gather," he went on, "that Mr. Wachter has already explained to you what the job entails."

"To some extent. You want me to infiltrate your organization and find out which of your goons can lead me to the manuscript."

"Good," he replied with great nonchalance. "Very succinct, Herr Schaeffer. That's it exactly. You and my goons. One big happy family."

"I hope they see it that way."

I saw a slight smirk play around his lips but that's all it was. I had the impression that the only time this guy would smile would be at some glamorous hostess in a nightclub. But maybe I was just being unfair. He took a long drag on his cigarette but nobody around the room took up the dialogue so I guessed this was just going to be him and me. Then he stubbed it out in the ashtray as if he'd changed his mind about smoking and sat forward in his chair. Time to get serious.

"You'll get a complete briefing in due course," he said, "but first, I'd like to ask you a few questions, if I may."

I gave a slight shrug of my shoulders to signal I didn't much care for questions but that I'd tolerate him for now. Charm or not, I was more than aware of what he once represented and I couldn't get it out of my head.

"Let's start with your language credentials, shall we? Mr. Wachter says they're excellent."

"They are."

"Good, very good, but you won't mind if I hear for myself. Speak to me in German, if you will." He turned to the rest of the room. "Excuse us for a few moments."

"What do you want me to say?" I said in German.

"A little more than that, please."

I thought about it, then I told him a joke I'd heard in 1938 using as much of the old Berlin slang and syntax as I could muster. The humour came from a time when all spare factory capacity was being rapidly converted to armament production and the story concerned a man who worked at the Volkswagen automobile plant in Lower Saxony. One day he had an idea. He thought that if he could just smuggle out one part every day, eventually he'd have enough to put together a family car. So every day, he took out a part and finally began assembling them in his back yard - only to discover that, once he'd finished, he'd built a tank.

Gehlen must have heard the joke before but he was polite enough to applaud the way I told it. Nobody else in the room had understood a word, so he switched back to English for their benefit. "All right, Ed, very good. You pass the language test, so let's move on, shall we? What do you know about the SS?"

"In English or German?"

"Oh, English, I think. Let's share it with everyone, shall we? Now, please... what can you tell us?"

It took a while but, piece by piece, I put it all together, everything I knew from Berlin, plus all the rest I'd learned from my post-war years in Barcelona. Some of it wasn't pretty but I made no attempt to go easy on him, even if he was supposed to be on our side now.

"Sounds to me like there's some personal animosity in there," he said when I'd finished. "Is that how you'd describe it, Ed? Personal?"

He waited but I didn't feel like answering. As far as I was concerned, dislike of the SS was a personal matter for every civilized human on the planet. I looked around the room for a little support but all I saw were faces of stone. Up to now, nobody else had said a word and it seemed like they had no intention of doing so. Davies, for his part, had a disgruntled look on his face because he wasn't chairing the meeting, even after everything he'd done to initiate all this. Rankin, too, could have been aggrieved but he didn't seem upset, just terminally bored with the proceedings. As for Pender at the far end of the table, he was the most sphinx-like of all.

"All right," said Gehlen, unperturbed with my non-response. "Let's move on to exam question number three... a little personal history. You were deported from Germany, were you not?"

"That's right."

"And why was that?"

"I had a minor disagreement with your leaders." He didn't even flinch at the intended insult of lumping him in with Hitler, Göring, Himmler, Goebbels and company - to say nothing of his namesake, Reinhard Heydrich.

"Could you perhaps elaborate?"

I was growing a little tired of all this. He must have seen my file, otherwise I wouldn't have even been there. My history would have been analyzed and vetted every-which-way-to-Sunday, including my stint working with Mossad, so why I had to sit and respond to such idiocy, I had no idea. "All right, once and for all... Before the war, I was a journalist in Berlin. For more than a decade, I kept my nose clean... well, fairly clean. But then, in the autumn of '38, I got into something I shouldn't have and caught some serious flak which, if you recall, was not that difficult for anyone who disagreed with the Nazi regime. Now, what I suggest, Herr Gehlen, is that you either throw me out or we get on with it, okay? I don't care which, as long as you make up your mind."

"That's quite an attitude you have there, Ed."

"Thanks, I'll take that as a compliment. Now, is that it? Are we done?"

"No, not yet, if you don't mind. One last thing. You already met the woman, Lina von Osten, I believe."

"Sure, after the war."

"In what capacity?"

"Excuse me?"

"In what capacity did you meet her? What were the circumstances?"

"The circumstances? I was a journalist. I was conducting an interview. What else would I be doing?"

"What I'm trying to ascertain is your standing with her. Do you think she'd remember you?"

"She might. Why? Will I be running into her?"

"In all likelihood, yes. We believe she still has the manuscript."

Maybe my mouth was open, I don't recall. Siegfried had somehow forgotten to apprise me of that little detail. "Let me get this straight... We're talking about Lina von Osten, formerly Lina Heydrich. She's guarded on all sides by ODESSA, who hero-worshipped her husband. And you want *me* to go chasing after her? Is that about right, or have I missed something?"

"No," replied Gehlen, "that's about right."

I looked across at him, at the handsome face, so confident and twinkle-eyed. Then I simply stood up. "You're out of your mind," I told him.

"Sit down, Mr. Schaeffer."

"Is that an order I hear?"

"It's a request."

"In that case, request denied. This meeting's over."

"Wouldn't you like to know who you'd be working with?"

"I don't give a damn who I'd be working with."

I turned to go - and suddenly there she was. How long she'd been standing there, I don't know, but I couldn't move.

"Hello, Ed," she said, very softly, in English.

She'd said hello to me. I'd heard her, but I was incapable of responding. I hadn't seen her since that last night before I left Europe and, in all those years, I'd thought about no one else. But it was as if she'd disappeared from the face of the earth. Sometimes, God help me, I even thought it would be better to know that she was dead, just so I could move on.

"I see you know each other," he was saying, but he was just being a smart-ass, playing to his audience. "Katharina will be your liaison," he added. "I take it you have no objection?"

The people around the table responded with a few shy smiles but other than that, they remained in the background, no more than a blur, because I was fixated. *It was her!* Katharina Vollbrecht... the same as I'd always remembered, elegant without even trying. She was just as slim, just as polished, with that familiar willowy stance that always appeared so casual, and hazel eyes that gazed at me with that same penetrating intensity. It seemed like she'd hardly aged at all, except for her hair. The chestnut I so vividly recalled had turned mostly silver. It still flowed soft and lustrous to her collar but the change took me by surprise and I had the vague impression that my impolite stare was making her a little self-conscious.

"Gentlemen," Gehlen said to the assembled gathering, "have you any further questions for Mr. Schaeffer?" His eyes searched back and forth but they all demurred: Davies of MI5, Rankin of the CIA and even the chairman, Pender, of Special Branch. Nobody had anything to say. "In that case," Gehlen went on, "I suggest we adjourn, what do you think, Sir Humphrey?"

"As you say," said Pender, before adding "meeting adjourned," as if it were necessary. A born bureaucrat if ever there was one.

Chairs were pushed back as they got up to leave and I was left standing near Katharina. It was weird but, after fourteen years, all I could think of to say was: "You work for Gehlen?"

She nodded her assent. Was there a touch of sadness creeping in to those intense eyes? I couldn't tell. I was too busy trying to manage my own emotions.

It was all just too hard to believe. When I last knew her, she'd been an art dealer, the rich heiress to the Vollbrecht family fortune, but now here she was, an operative for the Gehlen Organization, the CIA's central Europe surrogates. No wonder I couldn't locate her after the war. She'd gone undercover.

It was a neat trick that Gehlen had pulled but, in a way, the joke was on him because, for the moment, I'd forgotten all about the task they'd laid out and forgotten, too, about the manuscript. I'd even forgotten about Siegfried Wachter who'd sent me there. It had all been chased from my mind. All I could focus on was the woman standing in front of me. I desperately wanted to reach out to hold her, to feel her next to me, but I couldn't move. I was frozen to the spot, so I just stood there like an idiot.

As it happened, my good friend Siegfried Wachter didn't attend the meeting because he was attending to more important matters: at least, they were more important to him. That's because he, too, had met someone. In his case, however, it wasn't an old flame. It was someone new, something totally spontaneous and it was all very unlike him. Sure, he enjoyed what he called a "fling" every so often, but to fall so completely, so instantly, was contrary to everything I knew about him.

The young man in question turned out to be a Welshman, name of Owen Timothy Rhys. He had a wiry physique with unruly brown hair and possessed all the Celtic passions for which that small nation is famous. Plus, he worked in the same field as Siegfried. That is to say, Siegfried was a commodities trader and Owen, having escaped his working class origins through a combination of natural intellect and raw ambition, was a bright prospect at the London Metal Exchange, or LME as it was known, on Leadenhall Street.

Before it was closed for the duration of the war, the LME traded only in copper, lead and zinc but now that it had reopened, there were moves afoot to expand its range and Siegfried was one of those leading the charge. Specifically, his interest was nickel, just as it had always been, an element essential in the manufacture of a wide range of armaments. Originally, Siegfried had built the bulk of his fortune by helping to pioneer the Norilsk deposits of Siberia during the 1920's. Although a native Berliner, he spoke Russian fluently, thanks to his mother who taught the subject at Humboldt University, and his luck was in opening up this immense deposit for the German market just in time for Hitler to take advantage. In fact, the nickel trade was one of the economic foundations of the Nazi-Soviet pact and it became Siegfried's entry card into the world of high-powered diplomacy between the Chancellery and the Kremlin.

After the war, he was right back at the same game, except this time he was attempting to prise open the London markets with Canadian nickel extracted from my own home province of Ontario. There's an area to the north of Georgian Bay around the city of Sudbury where several major nickel corporations conduct their mining operations and it was through the UK office of one of these companies that Siegfried was introduced to the dashing young Owen Rhys.

It didn't seem to matter to either of them that there was such a wide difference in their ages, because they had so much in common. Not only did they have mutual professional interests but they also shared a taste for good wine, an appreciation of opera, plus a great enthusiasm for classic vintage automobiles, of which Siegfried himself possessed several. Yet beyond the shared pastimes, there was also a strong chemistry based on the kind of intangibles that define any human relationship, homosexual or otherwise. In this case, it consisted of a ready wit, a hedonistic philosophy and, perhaps more than all of that, a nice sense of appreciation for the narrow parameters in which their minority survived. They lived on society's cusp and they each instinctively understood what it took for the other to maintain that existence. For Owen Rhys, it was a revelation to find someone so experienced in sheer survival, while for Siegfried Wachter, it was good to be able to confide in a partner again after all those years of caution and secrecy under the Nazi regime.

At any rate, Owen Rhys was the reason Siegfried didn't attend the meeting at Scotland Yard.

Specifically, he'd promised to take the young man to a performance at the Royal Opera House at Covent Garden: Maria Callas performing her signature role in *Cavalliera Rusticana*. They were prime tickets and, for almost anyone else, impossible to obtain but, after several telephone calls, Siegfried finally managed to pry loose a couple of front row seats from one of his many connections.

The invitation was a purely romantic gesture, a total surprise, and it forced Rhys to give up a prior appointment. As it happened, that same evening, he'd been scheduled to check in with his Soviet case officer, Yuri Modin, the same man who'd met Kim Philby in St. James's Park.

In fact, Rhys hadn't even been that difficult to recruit. With all his climbing of the English social ladder, the one thing he'd never forgotten was that his late father had been a committed member of the Communist Party, a man who worked tirelessly between shifts at the coal face as a union organizer for the hard-pressed miners of the Rhondda Valley. So while the young Owen Rhys genuinely enjoyed the finest things that capitalism could provide, he was also dedicated in his own strange way to keeping faith with his father, something that remained carefully hidden within the depths of his Welsh soul.

It was an aspect of Rhys' personality that dear Siegfried, with all his worldliness, knew absolutely nothing about; and nor would he until it was far too late.

After the meeting at Scotland Yard, Katharina and I took a taxi to lunch at a small French bistro on Wardour Street, the kind of place populated with producers and designers: a chic, stylish crowd who inhabited worlds I didn't know about, like fashion and drama and advertising. With her family pedigree and impeccable dress sense, she seemed to fit in perfectly here but I remember feeling uncomfortable; although whether it was the surroundings or the circumstances, I'm not totally sure.

So far, our conversation had been of the small talk variety, some polite but meaningless chitchat about the city and the weather and the sights we each wanted to see while we were here. We were like strangers, which was indeed strange since we'd once been as intimate as it's possible for two people to be. Eventually, I'd had enough. It was time for some truth between us.

Once the white wine and crusty baguette had been duly delivered to our table, I just looked at her straight. "I thought you were dead," I told her.

The blunt force of my admission had its effect, stunning her first into silence and then, a few moments later, into an equally honest response.

"I thought you were dead, too," she replied quietly. "When you were deported... I just assumed... I'm sorry, Ed, I didn't know."

There was a great deal of hesitancy on her part, as if she wasn't sure how things were between us, or even how she wanted them to be.

As for me, I'd spent the last fourteen years dreaming of this day, of meeting her again and, as with all such dreams, we tend to create a mental picture of what it would be like, almost a fantasy. I thought that, if it ever happened, we'd be in raptures. I thought we'd fall into each other's arms, thanking whatever fates were responsible that we were together again and that nothing else mattered. I know, I know... impossible notions. My only excuse is that hope can be a powerful driving force and it was basically all I'd lived on since 1938. If I hadn't maintained that sense of hope, I'm not sure how I'd have survived at all.

I gazed at her across the table, completely immune to the noisy hubbub around us. Yet, still, I couldn't speak the words. I couldn't tell her how much I'd longed for her and I don't know why. It's possible that, with her hesitancy, I didn't want to push too hard but, truth be told, I think I had a very real fear of rejection. I just couldn't allow the dream to wither so I chose to tread carefully, attempting to gauge the progress of our reunion by picking up the signals. It was not how I imagined it was going to be but this was how it was and I was determined to find my way through it.

"Tell me about Gehlen," I said, for want of a better subject.

Instinctively, she looked around but nobody had the slightest interest in what we were talking about. They were all far too busy with their own affairs: their gossip and their jokes and their deal-making. Nevertheless, she switched to a semi-whispered German just to be on the safe side and I followed suit.

"What do you want to know about him?" she said.

"I don't know. Tell me how you met him, how it all happened. I mean, the last I knew, you were staying in Germany to be with your father."

"He was very sick."

"Yes, I know."

"Yes, yes, of course you do. I'm sorry, it's been so long." Her father had once been among the leading horse-breeders for the Kaiser's army but, while the family name was still highly respected, his age, his heart condition and his old-world Prussian attitudes had made him irrelevant within the newly burgeoning power structure of the Third Reich. "After you left," she said, "I took care of him at the estate for over three years. Yes, for a while we tried to follow what was happening in Berlin with phone calls and newspapers but he just wasn't interested in it any more. You know, he despised the Nazis."

"Yes, I know that too."

"It depressed him that Hitler was having so much success... Poland, Belgium, Holland, Norway, Denmark, France..." She was reeling off the countries like fallen dominoes which, in essence, they were. "Then came Russia and I think that's when he began to believe there'd be no end. The thousand-year Reich. It seemed to be more of a reality every day... and you know the sad thing? He died before the tide turned. He never even lived to see the possibility that there might be some other outcome."

"Maybe, wherever he went, he had a hand in it." I don't really know what made me say that. I'm not especially spiritual and she immediately rounded in on it.

"You still believe in that kind of thing? Even after everything that happened, everything we went through?"

"I was just trying to make you feel better."

She didn't reply and, for a while, we sat in silence. The Chardonnay we were sipping was excellent but it wasn't enough to make us feel relaxed and the tension between us only grew.

"Go on," I encouraged her. "What happened after your father died?"

She looked at me as if deciding whether she wanted to continue. There was a look of weariness on her face. Then a minor shrug. "I didn't want to stay at the estate alone. I mean, what was the point? So I just closed it all down and went to France."

"Where, Paris?" Like most of northern France, Paris had been occupied by the invading German Wehrmacht and was being run by the Vichy French collaborators.

"Yes, I stayed in Paris for a while. I had the idea... stupid, I know... I had the idea I could work with the galleries to help safe-guard the artworks."

"Not so stupid."

"But then I met someone."

"You... you met someone?" It's astonishing, astounding, but that thought really hadn't occurred to me and it hit me like an errant bolt from what had otherwise been drifting clouds. "What kind of someone?"

"He was French. Rich, mature, well-connected. It was, I don't know… I guess it was like a dream. He had a chateau in the Loire valley, with vineyards and horses… but he was also involved in the Resistance. He knew de Gaulle personally. It was very tempting."

I could feel myself going into cardiac arrest. I didn't care about de Gaulle. All I wanted to know about was this man, this damned aristocrat she found so tempting. "Did you…" I wasn't sure how to ask the question. Or even what question I wanted to ask.

"Did I what?"

"What I'm trying to say is… did you love him?"

"I don't think that's what you're trying to say. But the answer's no, Ed, I didn't love him. We didn't have any romantic involvement at all. Not that he didn't try, of course, but…"

"But?"

That's when she changed the mood, turning it from vacillation into a kind of accusation. "Dammit, Ed, what do you want me to tell you?" She'd raised her voice a notch or two and, even though it had been seven years since the war ended, the loud use of German in public places was not really recommended.

"Maybe we'd better switch back to English," I said quietly.

She obliged without even thinking about it and her voice became soft again. "I was fine until I met you," she said, shaking her head slightly at her own folly. "I was part of society, I had an art business. I had a life."

That's when I saw a tear appear in the corner of her eye and it made me realize what was going on. This was a confession and I'd just been too dumb to see it. Now I had to try to make amends in some way.

"My God, Katharina, I begged you to come with me."

"I couldn't."

"I know, I know, your father was sick. But that wasn't my fault. You can't blame me for that."

She didn't reply. Instead, she dried her eye on the corner of her napkin and we descended into a kind of neutral silence. Then, of her own accord, she said: "That's where I met Gehlen."

For the moment, I was nonplussed. It seemed we were back to the Gehlen story, which I'd almost forgotten. "At the chateau?" I asked, trying to recover.

"Yes, at the chateau. It was in the spring of 1944. I remember the blossoms, white and pink… so beautiful that year. He came for dinner. He was a Lieutenant Colonel, working with Hube on the Eastern front. He was young, in his forties, and already a senior intelligence officer with the General Staff."

"Impressive."

"Yes... but he'd been approached by von Stauffenberg."

"The bomb plot?" I said, incredulously. Von Stauffenberg, together with von Tresckow, Stülpnagel and others, was responsible for placing a bomb under the table at a meeting that Hitler was attending. The blast injured him but failed to kill him and the proposed coup was aborted. "I didn't know Gehlen was a part of that."

"One of the few who didn't get caught. That's how smart he is. Anyway, he'd heard of my father's efforts against Hitler and he'd been told that I shared the same sympathies. That's why he came to the Loire. He wanted to meet me. He said he'd be returning to the Eastern front soon but he needed someone to keep him in touch with what was going on."

"You mean in Berlin?"

"Yes, in Berlin."

"Just like you used to do for your father."

"That's right."

"So you went back?"

"Yes, I went back to my old life in Berlin. Lunches, theatre, social events..."

"And espionage."

"I wouldn't call it that."

"No?"

"It was just bits here, bits there, nothing more than gossip really."

"Very useful gossip."

"Perhaps. Sometimes. Except I wasn't doing it for my father

any more. I was doing it for Gehlen and he knew how to use it. That was the difference."

"Must have been tough being back in Berlin. You could have just stayed at the chateau for the rest of the war."

"No, Ed, I couldn't. Don't you understand? How could I stay there and keep refusing the man's advances? If you must know, Gehlen arriving like that... It was the best thing that could have happened. It was... It was a way out."

"Out of the frying pan, into the fire."

"Sorry?"

"An English expression. What happened after the bomb plot failed?"

"Well, what do you think? We had to be very careful. We knew there wouldn't be another chance, so we changed strategy. Instead of trying to kill Hitler, we made plans to contact the Americans as soon as we could. By that time, Gehlen had been in the East for over two years. He knew a lot about the Russians and he thought it would be valuable when the time came."

"He was right."

"Right? He was more than just right. It was a masterstroke, Ed. The man's a genius."

"You sound like you're quite taken with him."

As soon as I said it, I regretted it. The look she gave me was more piercing than a knife in the ribs. "Are we going through all that again?" she said.

"No," I replied sheepishly. "It's just that I need to know, Katharina."

"What, Ed? What do you need to know?"

"I need to know about us." That's when it came pouring out before I had a chance to prevent it. "You have no idea what I've been through, just thinking about you, waiting for you..."

"But you thought I was dead. You said so."

"I know I said so. But I didn't mean it. Inside, I always felt... It was the thought of you that kept me going, kept me alive." I wasn't good at this. I'd kept it all bottled up for so long that I was babbling. I sounded like a fool, even to myself. Fortunately, the waiter arrived to save me from any more embarrassment and I was able to stop talking while he took our order. She chose the quiche lorraine and I simply asked for the same. I hadn't even looked at the menu.

"Will you take the job?" she asked me, once he'd gone.

And just like that, the mood changed. It was mercurial. She was back to business and I had to shift my brain into another gear in order to readjust.

"Gehlen said I'd be working with you," I replied.

"I'd be your liaison, yes."

"Then of course I'll take it."

"Ed, please."

"What?"

"Don't do it for me."

"Are you kidding? Why else would I do it?"

"There *are* other reasons, you know."

I sat back, trying to figure it out, trying to make some sense of why I'd just agreed to volunteer for an undefined assignment, perhaps even a suicide mission.

The truth was that we were different, Katharina and me. She lived for a purpose, a greater meaning, first against the Nazis, then against the Soviets. As for me, I just tried to survive as best as I could. Sure, I recognized the importance of her ideals and, to a great extent, I shared her loathing of Hitler, Stalin and every other tyranny but I simply wasn't the crusader that she was and it was no use pretending otherwise. Her motives were political; mine were personal. It was as simple as that. The only reason I was willing to go above and beyond in this instance was Katharina herself. I'd have done anything for her, just to be with her, just to live up to her expectations.

Siegfried once told me that love is a form of insanity and it was true, both for him and for me. He had Owen Rhys and I had Katharina Vollbrecht and, at that same moment in time, we were both power-less to alter our respective fates. Is that an over-dramatization? No, on balance, I don't think so. As a portend of what was to happen, I'd say it's a fairly accurate summary.

As it turned out, my job initiation period wasn't much fun and I didn't even get to see Katharina very often. I received some basic training in this and that, which didn't really teach me a great deal but did at least serve to shake me out of my self-obsession for a few hours each day. In that sense, if nothing else, I suppose it was time well-spent.

For my first serious excursion, a doughy-faced constable of the Special Branch accompanied me to the King's Cross rail terminus, bought me a first-class ticket and put me on a train called the "Flying Scotsman." But it didn't "fly" at all; it chugged along as if taking its own good time. And my destination wasn't Scotland, it was somewhere far less picturesque: the dour city of Leeds, known since the Industrial Revolution for its wool trade and now the centre of the ready-to-wear clothing industry that turned out de-mob suits by the thousand for legions of returning servicemen.

Nevertheless, despite the grim, rainy landscape passing by the window, I tried hard to make the most of my trip. The dining car served me a fine breakfast of buttered kippers followed by toast and marmalade and, while I ate, I scanned the morning's papers. The big story of the day was an announcement by General Clark, recently named commander of the UN forces in Korea, who wanted to break open the stalemate along the 38th Parallel by bombing bases across the Yalu River within Red China. It was a discouraging escalation but I refused to be depressed about anything.

I was well aware how difficult my own task might be but I also knew that Katharina would be there to support me. If I needed to speak to her, I just had to call the operational number that Special Branch had given me. I learned it by heart.

★ ★ ★

The train deposited me fifty-six minutes late at Leeds Central, a sombre, Victorian-era station that seemed to be permanently covered with layers of smoke and soot. The putrid fumes from the locomotive hung in the air. I handed my ticket to the guard at the barrier and looked around but there was nobody waiting for me. The man I was supposed to meet was said to have had a seven year history inside the Gehlen Organization and would perhaps be able to give me some clue as to how I might proceed.

Just as I was about to go find a pay phone, I felt a tap on the shoulder and heard a male voice. The tone was slightly amused.

"Mr. Maple?"

It was the code name they'd assigned me and here was somebody making fun of it. In fact, I suspected that all the flower and vegetable identities the British handed out were nothing more than self-parody, a little light trivia to brighten up their agents' sad lives.

I turned at the greeting. The Gehlen people had shown me a photo but I'd never have recognized him from it. He'd dyed his hair black and, instead of the SS swagger, he'd developed a slight stoop and walked with a cane. To complete the disguise, he'd grown a thin beard and wore half-moon glasses. When I nodded my reply, he put a single finger to his mouth, silencing any further conversation as he led me out to the car park, where he unlocked a tiny, pale green Austin. It was only once we were squeezed inside and he'd started the engine that he permitted any conversation.

"Surprised at my appearance?" he said in German, as he backed the car out.

"You could say that."

"Good, good. Here I'm no longer Ludwig Maurer of the SS Totenkopfverbände. I'm Laszlo Mayer from Austria, modest watchmaker from the Jüdenplatz and survivor of Buchenwald."

The SS unit he'd named had been the special guard division for the "Kz" system of concentration camps, while the Jüdenplatz was a district in central Vienna from which thousands of Jews were sent to those camps.

"From guard to victim," I answered, trying hard to keep the loathing out of my voice. "That's one hell of a transformation."

"Thank you."

"And they say Germans don't understand irony."

I saw him offer a brief smile in response as he manhandled the shift and bounced us out of the station car park onto the city street.

"Just out of interest," I said, "do you actually know anything about watch making, or is that made up too?"

"My grandfather," he said. "I trained with him when I was a boy. Now I've got a little repair shop of my own right here, in this God-forsaken place. It's not much of a business but it gives me something to do. Want to see it?"

I shook my head. "Not especially."

We were threading our way around a public square with a large equestrian statue of a medieval knight. There were pigeons perched on his metallic head and their continual droppings had already desecrated his neck and shoulders.

"From the fourteenth century," he said, when he noticed my glance. "He was known as the Black Prince, which is a joke in this town, because everything's black from the dirt." He laughed but, when I didn't respond, he glanced at me. "Lighten up, Herr Maple. You need a sense of humour around here."

I did my best with a smile. "You're not happy?" I asked him.

"Happy?" he seemed to consider the word for a few moments. "Sure, why not? I do all right. Each morning I leave to do an honest day's work and each night I go back to a fine, big woman. She makes me a nice dinner and then, for dessert, I screw her brains out. What more does anyone need in life?"

There was a strong undercurrent but it wasn't lewdness as much as melancholy. The man was far from happy. "Does she know who you really are?"

"No. And, if you tell her, I'll kill you."

I looked at him and saw that, this time, he was serious. Meanwhile, we were stuck behind a double-decker streetcar, known in the local dialect as a "tram." The tracks ran down the middle of the street and, if other drivers weren't careful about overtaking on the inside, they could easily mow down the disembarking passengers.

According to the briefing I'd received, Maurer began working for the Allies soon after his capture in 1945. He was interred in the same US Army POW camp as Reinhard Gehlen but apparently the two didn't know each other. So, while the youthful-looking Gehlen was busy buying his salvation with a combination of sweet-spoken charm and hard-nosed information, the sly Americans were offering this older weasel, Maurer, what they called a "shadow" deal. They'd already figured out that, if they were going to set up Gehlen as their European master-spy against the Soviets, they'd also need somebody on the ground to keep a close watch on Gehlen, so they foisted Maurer on him. It worked, too, or so the Americans thought. What they didn't know, however, was that Maurer was playing by his own rules. As soon as he received his offer, he immediately completed the triangle by making an even more profitable deal with Gehlen to look the other way as more and more ODESSA members were recruited.

It was clever but it all came to an end in the spring of 1951, when Maurer became either over-confident or greedy, depending on your point-of-view, and demanded even more from Gehlen. The latter not only refused but felt he'd established enough credentials that he could cut out Maurer completely without harming his relations with the Americans too much. Of course, the Americans still had no idea that Maurer had played a double game and still considered him a major asset who they might be able to use in some future capacity. So in the spirit of the newly formed NATO alliance, they asked the Brits to furnish him with a temporary visa and a false identity - and this was the situation in which I found him when I arrived from London. He was in a kind of resentful no-man's-land, neither employed nor retired, neither a citizen nor a refugee, and every day he half-expected the decision to come through that he was of no further value, in which case he'd no doubt have his UK visa revoked and be cut off from CIA largesse without a dime.

The drive from the station wasn't far, taking us just across town to where Maurer lived: a massive oval structure, twelve stories high and a mile in circumference, known locally as Quarry Hill. Architecturally, it had a certain Bauhaus functionality but the result was gray and forbidding, in some ways more like a penitentiary than the largest apartment complex in Europe. At compass points around its outer walls were giant, echoing arches that allowed access for vehicular traffic.

"Looks like it should be in Berlin," I told him.

"Funny you should say that," he replied. "Ever hear of Operation Sea Lion?"

"Sure, the German plan to invade England back in 1940."

"That's right," he said. "And, under those plans, you know what this place would have become? I'll tell you... The northern headquarters of the SS. I'm one of the few who knows about that and you know why? Because I was the one who studied the options and made the original recommendation."

"Is that why you live here?"

"No, I live here because it's cheap and convenient. But that's not to say a few swastika banners wouldn't improve the place."

He offered me an empty smile as we passed under one of the arches and entered the interior of the complex. Here there were yet more buildings of the same bland design, interlaced with cracked roads, pedestrian pathways and bits of lawn that were once green but were now mostly threadbare. Not far from where we parked, two older women carrying a basket of laundered clothes took a wide berth around a few grime-stained men who were unloading hefty sacks of coal from a horse-drawn cart. The animal was an enormous dray, or "shire" as they're known in England, the same kind that armoured warriors like the Black Prince once rode into battle. But this was no proud war-horse; this was a mundane worker, old and well-used, and it just stood there placidly with its eyes blinkered, immune to both the activity and the ugliness around it.

"Nice," I said to Maurer, as we climbed out of the car.

He must have seen the look on my face. "I'm planning to move," he said flatly, "as soon as I can squeeze the Americans for more money."

"I'll put in a good word."

He laughed. "No, you won't."

Inside, the building smelled of cats. Then, when we stepped into the tiny elevator, the stench changed to stale fish 'n' chips and we rode the slow, cranking contraption up to the fourth floor in silence.

"She's not home yet," he said to me as we entered his apartment.

My watch said a little past five. "What does she do?"

"She's a stripper."

I looked at him but saw he was just teasing and I smiled dutifully. I later found out she worked as a shorthand typist in a municipal office.

We passed along a narrow hallway, decorated with beige, flowered wallpaper. An opening on one side led to a minuscule kitchen with a blackened range and a coal-fired oven. Beyond was a small balcony where they kept the coal. At the end of the hallway was the main living space: a square-shaped room with a small fireplace that appeared to back on to the oven and share the same chimney.

"Tea?" he asked me.

"No, I'm fine, thanks."

"Don't blame you, I'm beginning to hate the stuff myself. Grab a seat... if you can find one somewhere." He gathered up some newspapers that had been lying around and put them in a neat pile by the grate. Then, once we were both settled, he said: "So, what's *your* story? Why'd they give *you* the job?"

"I'm not sure," I replied.

"Oh, come on. You're not German yet you speak a perfect Berlin dialect."

"It's not really important who I am."

"No, you're right, it's not. I was just trying to get the conversation started."

"You think we need to break the ice?"

He gave a gentle smile and crossed his legs. "You don't trust me very much, do you, Herr Maple? I'm still a German to you, still just another damn Nazi, despite everything I've done for the Americans. Well, not to worry. We both have our own reasons for cooperating, so we'd better get on with it, don't you think? Now, what is it you want to know?"

"I want to know about the Gehlen Organization."

"So I understand. But what exactly?"

"If I knew, I wouldn't be asking." It was an instinctive reply and not very helpful. I decided honesty might be a better approach. "I guess I want to know what Gehlen won't tell me. Does that narrow the parameters?"

"It might," he replied, "but I'll still need some kind of clue."

Was he being open or cagey? I didn't know. On a couple of occasions, I asked Katharina whether I should reveal our objective but, other than repeated warnings about the man's duplicity, she failed to give me a definitive answer. Obviously, she told me, it was better to give away as little as possible but each case must be judged on its own merits. A good operative knows how to strike the balance: how much he must give away in order to get what he needs. She said there's no way to train for that.

I made a decision. "I need to make contact with Lina von Osten."

"Heydrich's wife?"

"Yes."

"Gehlen can do that for you."

"I was told he couldn't."

"Couldn't or wouldn't?"

"Does it matter?"

"I see. All right, so let me ask you something else. Who's driving this thing? The Americans or the British? Who really sent you up here, Herr Maple?"

"I'm only an operative, Herr Maurer, just a messenger."

"Oh, I think you're a little more than that."

I smiled at him. "All I can say is that there are several interested parties. Now, can we get back to the topic? Lina von Osten?"

"It all depends on what you want to know."

"Let's start with her standing, shall we? What exactly does she do for ODESSA?"

"For ODESSA? Nothing, as far as I know."

"Nothing? I find that hard to believe."

"Why? She never actually did anything for anybody, even when she was married to Heydrich. She was just a provincial girl who had visions of being the wife of the next Führer. The only difference now is that her husband is dead and so is his cause, so she's become a kind of... I don't know, some sort of a symbol. She's only revered by ODESSA because of what she stands for, nothing else. Plus, maybe a wagonload of nostalgia. What else can I tell you?"

"How would I reach her?"

"She lives on Fehmarn."

"No, she doesn't. Not any more." I saw him smile, as if he knew all about that little escapade with the MGB. I wasn't pleased. "All right, we've had our fun," I told him. "Now, can we stop fooling around?"

He sat back and I could almost hear his brain calculating the odds. If he didn't give me something, he figured he could probably say goodbye to his CIA income and maybe even his UK visa too.

After a few long seconds of deliberation, he said: "I think the best thing I can do is give you a name and you can take it from there."

"Okay, I'm listening."

"The name is Oehring."

I recognized it immediately. "You mean Karlheinz Oehring?"

"You know him?"

"I've met him."

"Is that right?" he said slowly, as if carefully digesting each new morsel of information he could pick up.

As it happened, I met Karlheinz Oehring twice. The first time was in Munich in 1938, back when he was still working for Heydrich: an adjutant of some sort. The second was in Barcelona about three years ago. He was on the run, wondering whether to board a ship for South America or stick around and help ODESSA. I bought him a couple of beers, then gave his name to the Israelis. I guess he managed to elude them. But I wasn't about to tell any of this to Maurer. I was far more interested in what he could tell me.

"Why Oehring?" I asked him. "What's so special about him?"

"Special? Nothing at all. He's a soldier... brave, loyal and stupid.

One of those clowns who kept saying 'I was only following orders.' I could name you a dozen just like him."

"Meaning?"

"Meaning he was faithful to Heydrich and now he's faithful to Heydrich's wife."

"He's her bodyguard?"

"He was the one got her away from the Russians at Fehmarn."

"Was he indeed? And how exactly would you know that?"

The slightest of shrugs. "Word gets around."

"Even here?"

"I'm not completely out of touch."

"No, I'll bet." Obviously, the amount he was prepared to divulge was strictly limited. But he'd told me the one thing I needed to know, so I didn't much care about the rest. "So, if I find Oehring, I find von Osten, is that what you're saying?"

"I'd say there's a good chance."

"And how do you suggest I go about it?"

"The hard way. You'll have to get inside the organization."

"That tells me nothing."

"What do you want? A secret password? Try saying '*Heil Hitler*' a couple of times. You'll get the hang of it."

It was a poor attempt at humour and I deliberately ignored it. I was trying to stay focused. "Do the Americans know about Oehring?" I asked.

He scoffed at the idea. "The Americans! What do they know about anything?"

"You don't like the Americans?"

"On the contrary, I love the Americans."

"You just don't respect their abilities."

"Let's just say they're well-meaning."

"How about Gehlen?" I asked, changing the subject. "What's *his* relationship with Oehring?"

Again, a long moment's thought before he spoke. "Here's some free advice," he said. "Be careful of Gehlen. Listen to him but don't believe him. Observe him but don't follow him."

"Does that come from experience?"

Before he could answer, we both heard the key in the door and a female voice calling out from the hallway.

"Laszlo? You home?"

"I'm in here," he called back. "We've got a guest."

She came in and immediately added a lot of energy to the room. As Maurer said, she was a big woman: blond and handsome in that straightforward, northern English way. When she leaned over to kiss his cheek, her mighty breasts tilted and pressed into his shoulder, the cleavage straining under her thin sweater. Instinctively, he placed his arm around her hips and I could easily see how much he both liked and enjoyed her. But at the same time, I had a strong feeling that it was more than just physical. He seemed to come alive when she came in. His eyes shone and the smile came far more readily to his face. It was as if Laszlo Mayer, the watchmaker, now had a far better existence than Ludwig Maurer, the SS camp guard, could have ever imagined or deserved. For him, the gloomy city was merely an inconvenience. It was the relationship that mattered - and that was something I could well understand, considering what I, myself, was going through.

He switched immediately to English. "Sandra, this is... what was your first name again?"

I guess I could have made something up but I didn't. "Ed," I replied.

"Sandra, this is my good friend, Ed... Ed, this is my better half, Sandra."

She gave me a wide, toothy grin as she stood upright and smoothed out her clothes. "Pleased to meet you, Ed. Don't mind us. We're a bit too lovey-dovey for some people."

"I don't mind at all."

"You're not from Vienna though."

Obviously, she could tell from my accent, which I didn't try to disguise when speaking English. "No, originally from Canada."

"Oh, right. We had a lot of you lads over here during the war."

"I'm surprised you remember the war," I said with fake gallantry.

"Uh-oh," she said. "We'd better watch out for this one, Laszlo. A proper charmer, if ever I saw one."

"Yes, he's a slippery customer, our Ed," added Maurer. Then he looked up at her. "We were just on our way to the pub. Feel like joining us?"

"No, you boys go along. I'll have some dinner ready when you get back."

I had the impression I was being invited to share their meal. "No, not for me, thanks."

"You're not staying over?" said Maurer. "We've got the spare room."

It was nice of them, I suppose, but the truth was I didn't feel like it. Sandra seemed very agreeable but with Maurer, it was different. Maybe it was the hypocrisy of the story he'd concocted for himself, or maybe it was something else, I don't know, but I really didn't feel like staying. Nor did I feel like listening to him "screw her brains out" in the next room, thank you very much. Not when I couldn't get Katharina out of my mind.

Ludwig Maurer and I spent a couple more hours together, sipping Tetley's bitter at a market pub just behind the central bus depot. We didn't talk about anything special: a little sport, a little politics; also about some of the places we both knew back in pre-war Berlin.

It was all very chummy, yet I couldn't shake the feeling that he'd double-cross me without thinking twice about it, same as he had with the Americans. He'd given me the name of Oehring, to be sure, but I had no guarantee he wouldn't send a warning the moment I was gone, either to ODESSA or, worse yet, to Lina von Osten herself, in which case my entire infiltration would be compromised before it even began. I needed to warn him against making a mistake like that.

After we left the pub, he gave me a ride back to the Queen's Hotel on City Square, an art deco-style structure conveniently situated next to the railway station. I'd be able to take the first train out in the morning. But just before I said thanks and goodbye, I turned to look at him.

"Laszlo," I began. Then I corrected myself by switching to his real name, just for effect. "Ludwig... Listen, we've had a pleasant evening and everything, but I think it's important you know something." I saw him glance back at me, waiting for whatever might come out of my mouth. I think he sensed what I was about to say. "I don't know what you were offered for this little service you're providing here... but I have to tell you, there could be a problem if... well, let's just say if things don't proceed too well."

The anger showed immediately on his face and he didn't try to hide it. Speaking in German, he demanded: "What *is* this? I bring you to my home, I introduce you to my lady friend and you thank me with a threat?"

"It's not a threat."

"It damn well sounds like one to me."

"Earlier, you asked: who sent me? What you should know is that the meeting I attended just before coming here... It wasn't just with Gehlen. There were people from the CIA, MI5, Special Branch and God knows who else. I don't even know all their names."

"So what?"

"So what? You know as well as I do that a meeting like that doesn't occur unless it's been ordered from on high, with all parties agreeing. You understand what I'm saying? This thing goes all the way up the ladder and, if someone were to... what's the word I'm looking for... Let's say if someone were to *jeopardize* my progress, it would have implications all the way back down the line."

"Yet it's not a threat," he repeated, with some venom in his voice.

I tried to remain calm. "No, it's not. I'd say it's an honest warning based on a realistic assessment."

He nodded gently, as if to show his full understanding. "Well, it's been good to meet you, Ed," he said, before turning on me with full force. "Now, get the hell out of my car."

I was about to reply in kind, to throw it right back at him, but I told myself that a response like that would be childish. He'd given me the information I needed and I'd issued the necessary caution. What more was there? So, instead of a slanging match, I just waved my hand as I got out, friendly as you like. Maybe the sight of it infuriated him even more because, as soon as the door was closed, he put his foot down hard, causing the tiny car's tires to squeal as he accelerated away.

Once he'd gone, I checked into the hotel, dumped my bag and, even though I'd eaten nothing since the kippers on the train, promptly went back outside with a pile of coins, as per my instructions.

Across the street was one of those quaint red phone booths that they have in England: phone "boxes" they're called, an appropriate term since they have no supply of air. This one seemed impregnated with stale cigarette smoke but I put up with it because I was calling the one person I most wanted to hear.

She picked up the receiver after the second ring but didn't say anything.

"Hi, it's me."

"You're supposed to say 'Control, this is Maple.'"

I began to laugh but she interrupted me.

"File your report," she ordered sternly, like a sergeant addressing one of the ranks.

I retaliated by making light of it. "Thanks, I'm fine," I replied, "how about you?"

"No familiarity. Just file the report."

"Don't worry, nobody's listening. It's a pay phone, just like you told me."

"It doesn't matter. This is business and we should keep it that way, all right? I said, *all right?*"

"Yes, yes, all right. Jeez."

I really wanted to chat, to know what she was up to, to find out how her day went, anything just to listen to her voice, but she was determined to get on with it. She was a professional case officer and she was demanding we follow tradecraft procedure.

"Did you contact the source?" she demanded.

What could I do but reply? I figured that even discussing business was better than nothing at all. "Sure, I met him but he was nothing like I was expecting..."

She interrupted. "What did you ascertain?"

"Listen, can't we just talk for a few minutes? I mean, like normal people? This is ridiculous."

She wasn't having any of it. "What did you ascertain?"

I sighed to show my frustration. "He gave me a name."

"A name to contact? Within the organization?"

"That's right."

"All right, don't tell me on the phone. Wait until you get back."

"I'm not a complete dummy."

"Better safe than sorry."

"Yes, well, talking of safe, there's something else you should know. It's important this doesn't get back to your friend."

She knew I was talking about Gehlen.

"Can you explain?"

"No, not here. I was told not to trust him."

"And you agree with that?"

"I do."

"Well, I don't."

"Yes, but you're not the one filing this report, are you? I'm the agent in the field and I want it noted that we shouldn't trust him. Don't tell him I've found a name. Don't tell him anything."

I could be professional too and I think the shift in our roles threw her a little: enough that there was a short period of silence. I was hurt and more than a little annoyed, which I'm sure was evident from my tone. All day long I'd looked forward to talking to her and now, here we were, discussing all this as if we didn't know each other, as if we were perfect strangers, just thrown together for the sake of the job. It was a joke, the whole thing, and I wasn't sure if I shouldn't just get out while I still could. To be honest, I was starting to think I'd have a greater shot at rekindling our flame if I just hung around London and sent her flowers like any normal guy.

"Your report is duly noted," she said eventually.

Cold and abrupt but I guess I deserved it. "And you'll pass it on to OC?" The initials stood for "Operational Commander," which meant Sir Humphrey Pender of Special Branch, the civil servant who'd chaired the committee.

"You do your job," she replied, "and I'll do mine." There was another pause but she didn't hang up. Instead, she just said very quietly: "I'm sorry."

Actually, I was the one who needed to apologize. She was insisting on strict protocol for the sake of security, especially mine, and I was just being a jerk about it for my own selfish motives.

"Me too," I told her.

Then I heard her voice soften even more, as if business had been forgotten for the time being and she was willing to break her own rules.

"When this is over..." she began.

That's what people kept saying to each other during the war: "When this is over." I waited anxiously for her to complete the thought.

"I was just going to say... When this is over, maybe we'll have more of a chance."

That was the best news I'd heard so far and, even though I was in a depressing northern city two hundred miles away, I was ecstatic.

"I hope so," I said quietly. "I really hope so."

After the call, I went back to the hotel and ate an overcooked steak with an undercooked baked potato. I'd had enough beer for one night. Then I sank down on to the bed fully dressed and just closed my eyes. I'd been promised five thousand Sterling on successful completion of this assignment, a considerable amount for someone like me, and that was in addition to anything Siegfried might throw my way. As a result, I was fairly pleased with myself. All-in-all, I felt I'd made a pretty good start.

But I also had to remind myself that none of it meant anything unless Katharina was with me and, as I drifted off, I resolved to try even harder to be the good little agent she wanted me to be, if that's what it was going to take. Professionalism would be my watchword. I would eat, sleep and breathe my assignment. I would become a model intelligence operative, even if it killed me - which, in the end, it damn near did.

★

That week, fortune also chose to smile on Lavrenti Pavlovich Beria.

After all those weeks of frustration, he finally caught a lucky break: Lina von Osten had been spotted in Paris - and, yes, her escort was Karlheinz Oehring.

It had been a chance observation as they stepped out of a taxi at the exclusive Hôtel Raphaël on Avenue Kleber, just a few hundred metres from the Place de la Concorde. Von Osten was heavily disguised, her choice being a dark wig, black clothes and a widow's veil, and Oehring was masquerading as her valet, but that didn't stop them being recognized by one of the people who knew them best: Hedda Neuberg, who'd once worked for the Heydrichs as a housemaid, back in the Zehlendorf suburb of Berlin.

After the war, it seems that Hedda took up with one Louis-Philippe Beauclair, a mid-level administrative officer in the French sector of Berlin, who then brought her back to Paris. He had little money of his own, so he boosted his income by feeding bits of this and that to the Soviets. It was no real surprise. They'd infiltrated the British and the Americans, so why not the French, too?

In fact, there was no reason for either Beauclair or his Russian case officer to find the random sighting of Lina von Osten to be of any interest whatsoever. They were, neither of them, privy to what was going on and, under normal circumstances, who would care about the wife of a long-dead Nazi? But, like any informant, Beauclair had an ongoing need to prove his usefulness and good information had been scant recently, so he delivered the snippet to the Russian anyway who, in turn, passed it on up the line to Moscow, just to add a little more volume to the regular package. Neither of them thought any more about it and it was only once the item reached the Lubyanka clearing station that a senior analyst was alert enough to dig it out of the general debris and place it into some kind of context.

On receiving the news, Beria moved rapidly, galvanizing his resources with an immediate directive to the Soviet Embassy *rezidentura* on Boulevard Lannes in the 16th arrondissement. His orders were to focus all attention on the city centre with twenty-four hour surveillance of the Raphaël. The only problem was that Lina von Osten wasn't actually staying at the hotel; she'd only stopped by for coffee and, by the time the Soviet stakeout had been organized, she'd long since disappeared. Nevertheless, it was felt that a well-to-do German woman would certainly be noticeable if she ventured out into society, no matter how cleverly she was disguised, and all employees, contacts and connections of the Soviet and other Eastern Bloc missions were instructed to make this their highest priority.

Of course, if Lina von Osten had retreated to some quiet French farmhouse, it would have been almost impossible to trace her, but she didn't. She was sick of living in hiding and now that she was in Paris for the first time, she wanted to enjoy it: to go shopping, to take in a movie or cabaret, maybe even have dinner on one of the *bateaux mouches,* the floating restaurants that she'd heard so much about.

Inevitably, she and Oehring were spotted by one of the many freelance stringers that the Soviets employed for such work. They were identified at the main entrance to the Galeries Lafayette department store, opposite the Opéra on the Place Diaghilev. Once the sighting had been reported, the MGB unit moved into place, following discretely and handing off their target from one to the other as smoothly as a training mission, all the way across the river to a modest, unobtrusive apartment building on the *Rive Gauche*, the Left Bank, just off Boulevard St. Germain.

Lina von Osten called Karlheinz Oehring her "*Kampfhund*" (attack dog) and Oehring was the kind of man who took that as a compliment. In personifying similar traits to a pedigree German Shepherd, he could be described as big, handsome and fiercely loyal; but, as with any such animal, there was always a glint in the eyes that revealed the truth. No matter how domesticated or how well-trained, there remained a certain element of raw savagery, the genetic instinct of that species to return to a wild state at any random moment.

During their travels, they always kept a discrete distance from each other and there's no evidence to suggest that they were in any way intimate. Perhaps Oehring felt it might be disrespectful to her late husband, SS Obergruppenführer Reinhard Heydrich, the man he once served so faithfully. Or she, herself, might well have felt that he was beneath her status. Whatever the reason, they invariably slept in separate bedrooms, which turned out to be the deciding factor in countering the MGB's next violent assault.

For himself, Karlheinz Oehring would never have come to a place like Paris. It was just too much of a metropolis for his liking: too much security and too much risk of being recognized. But Lina von Osten was desperate, or so she claimed. She'd spent so many years on that rural Baltic island, she told him, that she just had to come to a place like this, or she'd go insane. In the end, she gave him an ultimatum: Paris or London. Don't argue, she instructed him, just arrange it.

Given the choice, Oehring chose Paris for one reason only. He knew of an arms cache that was still buried here and had been since the Wehrmacht evacuation in 1944. Since he couldn't take any kind of serious weaponry across the border from Germany, this would at least give him a chance of defense if the MGB came calling again.

The first day they arrived, they found the Left Bank apartment through an ODESSA source. It wasn't luxurious but it was fairly spacious, a rarity in Paris, and conveniently located. Then, on the second day, while she unpacked and made herself at home, he borrowed an old van from the same contact and drove out to the far western suburb of Châtenay-Malabry in the Hauts-de-Seine. It's a pleasant district with quiet lanes and well-preserved forest areas and it was here, to his great relief, that he found the ordnance in the exact place where it had been left: several packing cases hidden beneath the rotting floorboards of a disused barn.

The story of how it got there was simple enough, a minor footnote to the great drama of the "D-Day" invasion that the world knows so well...

When the Allies hit the Normandy beaches on that morning of June 6, 1944, the general staff of the Wehrmacht was genuinely taken by surprise. They knew there would be an invasion attempt at some point but some clever Allied subterfuge led them to believe it would take place at the Pas de Calais, the shortest crossing point of the English Channel. All available reserves had therefore been transferred to that sector, too far away from the fight to do any good. After a few days, they had no alternative but to fall back, one option being to make a stand within the tightly packed streets of Paris, where the Allied superiority in tanks and aircraft would be severely limited. In theory, the plan was sound, so they ferried in as much light weaponry as they could, since it was both easier to manufacture and more convenient to transport. As it turned out, the Allied advance was just too swift and, within a few weeks of the initial beachhead, the Paris strategy had to be abandoned. Whatever the departing troops couldn't carry away, they hid as best they could in order to prevent it falling into enemy hands - and it was a small part of this cache that Karlheinz Oehring was looking to retrieve.

Strictly speaking, the barn was on somebody's private property but it was hidden behind an empty farmhouse and he didn't care about such legal niceties. He pulled open the big doors and allowed the bright sunlight to stream in for the first time in years. Inside, it was dry and dusty and still smelled vaguely of the animal dung that seemed to permeate the very pores of the structure. Carefully and methodically, he began to examine every square metre of the floor area, kicking aside thick webs and old straw bales. There were pigeons nesting in the rafters and, at one point, he disturbed a large family of rats. They didn't faze him. In his life, he'd seen far worse.

Eventually, after a couple of hours, he found what he was looking for buried in the dark earth under the flooring: a half-dozen sealed crates with German markings. Using the van's tire iron, he pried them open to find even more than he'd dared to hope. The weapons were still wrapped carefully in oilcloth, still in factory condition and seemingly ready to use. Three of the crates contained the standard Type-24 stick grenades that the Wehrmacht infantry carried for most of the war. The other three were of greater interest and, to his immense satisfaction, held sub-machine guns plus a substantial number of ammunition clips. He unwrapped one and hoisted it in his hands, feeling the weight and the balance. It was a model he recognized immediately: the Sturmgewehr StG44, one of the most advanced German hand weapons of the war, with a deliberately slow rate of discharge to allow for superior control and accuracy. Had more arms like that been delivered, the Wehrmacht might just have made their stand in Paris - but their loss was Oehring's gain and he gladly drove his prize back into the city, unloading the heavy crates into the apartment by the rear janitor's entrance under cover of darkness.

When the MGB finally showed up, as he suspected they might, he not only had a plan, he also possessed the necessary firepower to carry it out. He was ready for them.

Despite the failure on Fehmarn, Lavrenti Beria authorized a six-man combat team: another MGB *spetznaz* commanded by another war veteran, a Ukrainian from Kiev by the name of Ilko Sawczyn.

This time, it could hardly be a joint military operation, not in the centre of the French capital. It would have to be covert, a night mission with a careful plan of attack. According to the details Sawczyn had worked out, it was divided into five distinct phases... One: secure the exits at both front and rear. Two: launch a brief incursion into the building to eliminate the janitor and his family. Three: set the building ablaze. Four: eliminate the bodyguard as he emerges from the smoke. Five: seize and remove the von Osten woman in order to extract information concerning the whereabouts of the manuscript.

What the Soviet team didn't know, however, was that Karlheinz Oehring had his own strategy figured out, and that he wasn't alone.

With him were two hardened ODESSA colleagues who'd been sent in specially. Part of their mandate was, indeed, to help defend the widow of Reinhard Heydrich but the other part was to ship all the spare armament crates to their émigré factions in South America, where such weapons could be used against local gangs who tried to threaten them with blackmail or extortion. While the two men were here in Paris, however, they were under the orders of Karlheinz Oehring and, every night before turning in, they prepared themselves according to his precise specifications. After sending the janitor and his family off to sleep with relatives, they occupied the ground floor apartment and set up a web of trip wires: long strands of strong black sewing cotton, invisible at night to the naked eye, which were attached to the men's wrists while they slept. It was an elaborate system which took time to prepare but it meant that any movement in the building would trigger the silent alarm and instantly wake them.

Thus, both sides had their plans, the Soviet attack and the ODESSA defense, but both were conceived under difficult circumstances. As it turned out, when it came to execution, each of the plans failed and both opponents had to improvise.

The catalyst was Sawczyn himself, the veteran *spetznaz* leader, whose sharp eyesight picked out the fact the curtains weren't drawn in the janitor's apartment and sensed there was a problem. He didn't know for certain, however; so, rather than abort such a highly classified mission, he withdrew his team to the street in order to consider his options, taking temporary cover inside his operational transport, a commercial moving van painted over in unobtrusive gray.

At about 2:30 in the morning, Karlheinz Oehring was woken up, not by his guards but by the smell of smoke. It was seeping in through the space under his door from the second floor landing. That's when he heard the sound of a female coughing and he was immediately on his feet. He was dressed only in his undershirt and shorts but he didn't care about that as he grabbed up the StG next to his bed, plus the leather workman's belt he'd adapted to take eight extra ammunition clips, as well as four grenades. He strapped it on as he crossed the room, then swung open the door.

A quick peek on to the landing brought a round of automatic fire from a figure in a gas mask crouched by the stairs and Oehring stepped back inside, feeling his heart pounding and the rush of adrenaline coursing through his body. In his mind, he was ten years younger and back on the Eastern front, once again in a damaged building surrounded by Russians. He unhooked one of the stick grenades from his belt, hoping age hadn't diminished either his reaction speed or his instincts. With his forefinger, he yanked the pin and tossed the grenade towards the figure outside before retreating inside the room and slamming the door closed.

The blast took an eternal two seconds, then shook the walls.

When he finally, tentatively, emerged on to the landing, he found charred wood, broken glass and holes ripped through the plaster, exposing timber and brick. Through the swirling dust, he could see that the masked figure had been thrown backwards and lay at a strange angle with muffled sounds emanating from his throat. Oehring could smell the burned flesh and the hot, spilled blood, yet another nauseating reminder of the wartime experience which had become so much a part of him. He paced across the landing and ripped off the gas mask that the assailant had been wearing. Was it still serviceable? He'd know soon enough. He edged back carefully through the wreckage towards the room opposite his own where Lina von Osten slept. Why had she not emerged? His mind was now working with a cool rapidity, almost an exhilaration. The action was starting to transform him back into the fighting machine he once was. It occurred to him that, if the man out here on the landing had a gas mask, then there might well be people in the smoke-filled room with Lina. How had they entered? By the landing? It was difficult to understand how they'd managed to evade every single one of his trip cords. The only possibility was that they'd somehow managed to scale the exterior of the building up to the narrow iron balcony. They might have used ropes or, perhaps, extension ladders, and he cursed himself for not having prepared for such an eventuality. Obviously, he was not as battle-ready as he thought. He'd never have made a mistake like that back in the old days.

From downstairs, he heard a male voice calling out his name: "Karlheinz!"

It was one of his own men, reacting to the sound of the grenade blast, but Oehring couldn't reply. If, as he guessed, there were people in the room opposite, he'd be giving away the element of surprise. Instead, he just moved. With his foot, he kicked open the door and stepped out of the way. There was the blinding flash from a muzzle and a shattering, reverberating noise as the ammunition rounds flew past and crashed deep into the landing wall behind him.

This time he couldn't throw a grenade because Lina might be still in there with them. Using the billowing smoke as his own cover, he dove down onto his belly, fastened the stolen mask to his face and crawled into the room, hauling the StG behind him. Despite the mask, he was finding it difficult to breathe and he tried to resist the cough that would give away his position by holding each intake of air as long as possible. Slowly, he crawled forward, eventually finding a position of relative cover at the side of the bed. By raising his head, he could just about make out a tangle of three figures out on the balcony. One of the two men was holding the woman over his shoulder in a fireman's lift and appeared to be maneuvering her over the balustrade, while the other was standing guard with a machine pistol.

Oehring deliberately waited a few seconds until the man carrying Lina was over the ledge, which would leave only one threat. Oehring's eyes were burning and streaming from the smoke but he had no choice. He had to move to the window or be asphyxiated right there on the floor.

Gathering himself for the effort, he took a deep breath, then threw down the mask and sprang to his feet. One long burst from his weapon and the man with the machine pistol was thrown backwards by the force. The major threat was gone and Oehring used the opportunity to spring forward to the balcony and gulp in some of the outside air. Sure enough, there was a ladder resting against the forged ironwork of the ledge and he peered over to find the figures already half-way down. He couldn't fire because all he could see from that angle was Lina's limp body over the man's shoulder. Nor could he climb down after them, because he'd be facing backwards and vulnerable to any sniper waiting on the ground.

He paused, uncertain what to do. He could hear the distant sounds of police klaxons in the night air, still a few kilometres away. Although lights were now on in several of the surrounding buildings, none of the neighbours had yet been brave enough to venture into the street.

That's when he came to a decision. He knew it was a risk and that he might injure Lina in the process but he had no alternative. He had to separate the two of them. Grabbing the top of the ladder, he heaved it forward, away from the ledge. It was heavy and took all his considerable strength to raise enough momentum but the ladder continued on its way, arching slowly at first, then accelerating rapidly as gravity took hold and pulled it towards the ground. Sure enough, the two figures were thrown off, landing awkwardly but separately. It was the break that Oehring needed. He rapidly swung his own weapon downwards and fired towards the spot where the man lay. This was the value of the StG, its control and accuracy major advantages in this kind of situation. The man twitched violently as the bullets ripped through his body and, for the moment, it was over.

A few metres to his right, Lina von Osten was lying on the ground, unmoving, and Oehring couldn't be sure whether she was alive or whether the fall, together with the smoke inhalation, had finished her off.

"Franz!" he yelled down to his colleague. "You there?"

"Karlheinz? Is that you?"

"Get the woman inside!"

Oehring stayed on the balcony to provide Franz with covering fire but it seemed that Franz's partner, Ernst, was already thinking the same way, spraying several bursts out into the shrubbery. There was nothing more that Oehring could do from up here, so he turned and made his way down the partly-destroyed staircase, hoping it wouldn't give way under him.

When he reached the ground floor, he ran straight towards the front door where he found Ernst still crouched behind his weapon, while Franz had just about dragged the prone woman inside. By this time, there was almost continuous machine pistol fire from the opposite side. They'd held off while their own man was in trouble but, as soon as they'd realized he was already dead, there was nothing to stop them.

Oehring instantly took charge. "Ernst, hold your position here. Franz, how is she?"

"I don't know," Franz replied, hoarse from the exertion. "She's still alive but..." He just shrugged.

"Take her to the back door and wait there for me."

"Where are you going?"

"I forgot something."

With that, he dashed all the way back upstairs, bounding up two at a time. Near the top, his left foot crashed through a broken plank and a large splinter of wood tore into his shin, causing him to wince as blood seeped from the gash. It wasn't bad enough to stop him but was sufficient to slow him down and he limped back into what had been Lina von Osten's smoke-filled room, cursing and coughing with every painful step. From under the bed, he pulled the locked leather case that contained the manuscript and allowed himself the briefest smile at such Russian stupidity. It had been there all along. There was no need to have abducted her. They could have just shot her where she lay and reached down for it, easy as anything. They hadn't been too smart on the Eastern front either, Oehring recalled. It was his opinion that attrition and manpower had won them the war, not intellect.

He hobbled back downstairs, taking greater care this time, carrying the case in one hand and cradling his StG in the other. Once he was on the ground floor, he negotiated his way through the passageway to the back door where he found Franz and, next to him on the floor, Lina von Osten, with her eyes half open. It was good to see that she was conscious.

"*Mein Kampfhund*," she whispered when she saw him.

Oehring touched her hand, then peered out at the darkness of the rear courtyard. "Anyone out there?" he said to Franz.

"I don't know. Probably."

"All right, here's what we do. We're going to get over to the van." He indicated the vehicle parked in the yard about four metres away, the same as he'd used to find the weapons. The van had been reversed in to the courtyard and its back end was facing them. "I hurt my leg, so you'll have to carry her. I'll cover you."

"You're going to leave in that thing? It's madness."

"Maybe, but it's our only way out. If I switch on the lights and make enough noise, they'll realize I'm leaving with her and they'll have to scramble to follow. That should give you and Ernst time to get out of here before the police arrive. You with me?"

"Can you drive?"

"I'll manage."

They made it to the back of the van, opened up the doors and bundled Lina into the back, followed by the locked case. Then Oehring quickly shook his colleague's hand, handed over the weapon plus the ammunition belt, then climbed inside, too. He closed the back doors behind him and found his way past the woman to the driver's seat. His leg was hurting all the way down to his foot and, despite his bravado, he really wasn't sure if he'd have the strength to work the clutch. This ancient van wasn't the easiest thing to drive, even in the best of circumstances.

The moment that Oehring started up the engine and switched on the beams, the firing began. He tried to ignore the flashes in front of him as he released the brake and jammed his good foot down on the gas pedal. But the other limb was far less flexible and he released the clutch too quickly, causing the van to lurch forward. With a piercing screech of metal, the front fender smashed into the concrete of the gatepost. Fortunately, the wheel housings escaped damage and the vehicle was able to swerve out onto the street.

It was not yet three in the morning and traffic was sparse. Up ahead, he could make out the lights of Boulevard St. Michel and he tried to keep his speed in check as he headed towards the thoroughfare. He knew that a damaged van travelling too fast would only cause attention. In the mirror, he could make out the flashing blue police lights homing in on the building he'd just abandoned and he hoped that the two men, Franz and Ernst, had managed to break out of the trap in time. But he couldn't worry about that now. First, he had to get away, out of Paris, and find some medical help, both for Lina and for himself. He was still a little dizzy from the smoke inhalation, as well as the searing pain of his gashed leg, but he was afraid to stop in case his leg seized up and his nervous system gave way to the trauma he knew might set in. He'd seen it happen with men at the front. They'd go into shock and start shaking uncontrollably. As long as the adrenaline was flowing, he knew his body could keep going but, once it had a chance to relax, there was always the danger of collapse. To try to cope, he made a point of concentrating on his driving, using the darkness of the road and the need for navigation as a way to focus his remaining energies.

It was not until he'd cleared the city limits that he actually realized they were both still undressed. He was still in his shorts and undershirt and his lady passenger was wearing nothing but a black lace negligee.

While all this was going on, I was back in London with Katharina. It was August and we were taking a sightseeing boat trip along the Thames, just like any normal couple. It was cool for the time of year, with a fresh breeze off the river that made our hair blow, but that just made it all the more pleasant.

My invitation for such an activity had been nothing more than a whim, a hope, but to my infinite surprise, she'd said yes, she'd be delighted. So now, here we were, along with a couple of dozen other tourists, listening to a loudspeaker commentary as the vessel chugged its slow way downriver towards its destination, the borough of Greenwich, where the famed observatory had become the historic reference mark for the meridian of zero longitude. For some reason, I'd always wanted to see it, to straddle the line with my left foot in the Eastern hemisphere and my right in the West, and this somehow seemed like an appropriately symbolic time.

Our journey began at the Embankment, not far from Scotland Yard. Once we reached the iconic Tower Bridge, we were advised to look left, towards the formidable structure of the Tower of London itself. Within its stout walls, we were duly informed, various Stewarts, Tudors and other unfortunate members of royalty were either imprisoned or beheaded, including Charles I, Mary Queen of Scots and two of Henry VIII's six wives. We were also told that, among the Tower's inhabitants was a flock of coal black ravens, which were fed and coddled by the traditional Beefeater guards because of an ancient legend that said that if the birds ever left, England would fall.

"Perhaps somebody should have told Hitler," Katharina whispered to me. "Instead of the Luftwaffe, he could have just sent over a flock of hawks. It would have all been over before lunch."

I laughed out loud, much to the surprise of the nice family from Shropshire next to us, who found nothing at all funny in the notion of England falling.

After that, we passed the financial district, then the great dome of St. Paul's Cathedral and, farther on, the East End docklands; but, after that, there was less to see and the commentary continued with anecdotes of life during the Blitz. This was of special significance to the Americans on board, who'd listened avidly to the famous wartime broadcasts of Ed Murrow, but of less interest to Katharina, especially when the guide threw in his own selection of German epithets.

To avoid it, I led her back towards the stern, where the loud-speaker was less grating and the stiff breeze much reduced. She smiled gratefully and passed a hand through that flowing hair, replaying the fantasy vision that had been with me for so long. She was fourteen years older than my memories but still as naturally elegant as ever and her long fingers still combined into beautiful angles, just the way I remembered.

"Perhaps I forgot to mention," she said, "how much we all admired the job you did with Maurer. The committee was quite impressed."

I looked at her, not really knowing what to say. She was trying to give me a compliment, so I guess I could have been a little more gracious but this was not exactly the conversation I wanted to have. She was still trying to be the consummate professional, whereas I was far more eager to be close-up and personal.

"I didn't do much," I replied.

"You extracted the information we needed."

Extracted? That was a strange word to use, in any language. Made me sound like a masked torturer in one of King Henry's medieval dungeons. "You know," I said, "getting people to give up information is what journalists do all the time... especially freelance journalists who need to pay the rent. It's not that hard."

"Then perhaps we should recruit more journalists."

"How about your friend, Gehlen?" I asked, recalling our last conversation. "Was *he* impressed?"

"In his own way."

"Which means he wasn't."

"I'm afraid Reinhard is a little... upset... at the present time."

Reinhard... I noticed the use of the first name. "Yeah, well, what the hell does he have to be upset about?" It came out a little more harshly than I intended but I didn't care. "The whole world revolves around him."

"Not lately."

"I don't follow."

"He thinks he's being left out."

"Left out of what?"

"The information you gave me."

"About Oehring?"

Instinctively, she looked around when I mentioned his name but there was nobody close enough to hear. "Of course. What else are we talking about?"

"Why? I mean, why would you leave him out?"

"Not me, the committee."

"All right, why would the committee leave him out?"

"For heaven's sake, Ed, you were the one who recommended we don't tell him. You said Gehlen's not to be trusted."

"I know. But I didn't think anyone would listen."

"Well, they did."

"So now he's upset?"

"Yes."

"How did he find out?"

"The business in Paris."

I nodded. By that time, just about everyone involved in the manuscript affair had figured out who was responsible, even if the pair hadn't yet been apprehended.

Meanwhile, Katharina had returned to a more distant mode, staring out at the river as a floating train of barges edged slowly past us, its cargo wrapped under heavy tarpaulins. Did she ever have some kind of a relationship with Gehlen? She'd denied any kind of romance with the count at the Loire chateau but she'd said nothing about Gehlen. I made a conscious effort to dismiss the notion but it was difficult and it was bugging me. She always spoke about him with such admiration in her voice that I couldn't help resenting him.

The boat was still making its leisurely way down towards Greenwich and I suddenly decided I didn't want to talk about Gehlen any more - or anything else, for that matter. For some reason, my mind had returned to our first dinner date, at Horcher's, one of Berlin's most exclusive restaurants. We were dancing, swaying to a small combo playing Piaf melodies and I felt as if all of society was watching us, wondering how the heiress to Germany's largest horse breeding estate could be in such close proximity to a low-grade hack wearing his one good suit. But their gaping looks didn't matter a damn to me. We were in a bubble, just floating our way across the floor.

"You know what?" I said. "I just had an idea."

"Tell me."

"You talked about when all this is over. That's what you said on the phone, right? Okay, so here's my idea. I was in *your* country, let me invite you to *mine*. Just you and me and... and none of this. We'll ride, we'll skate, we'll do whatever you want." I was talking about Canada, of course, the land I left behind, but I was making it sound less like an actual place on a map than some distant fantasy where politics and suspicion have no place. "It's a long way from anywhere," I added, and that's when I saw her piercing eyes soften and the gentle smile returning.

"Sounds nice," she replied quietly.

I knew that I hadn't fooled her at all, that she was responding to the dream more than the reality, but it was of no consequence. She reached for my hand and I felt that, finally, we were starting to connect. I'd been worried that it would never happen but the moment had arrived and my relief was profound. Suddenly, there was no boat, no tourists. After all this time, we were back in the bubble, once again swaying to the music.

From the Embankment, we took a black cab back to the hotel at Hyde Park Corner, where we enjoyed an excellent dinner: roasted lamb with mint sauce, very English, accompanied by a fine Bordeaux, all courtesy of my friend, Siegfried Wachter, who had reserved these exquisite accommodations. Okay, the food was a little overcooked to my taste but the wine was excellent, the mood was mellow and the candle on the table was reflecting in the depths of her hazel eyes.

We were talking about art, of which I knew little, and horses, too, of which I knew nothing at all; but both were subjects very close to her heart, so I asked questions and tried to understand. Meanwhile, I was simply marvelling at just being there with her.

And later, after I signed the cheque, we strolled towards the elevator, still chatting casually as if it were the most natural thing in the world. It was as though it was taken for granted that she would spend the night with me and neither of us had to mention it or be embarrassed about it. That was the beauty of what we had, perhaps the beauty of any powerful relationship: the unspoken communication that provides the true connection.

In the room, we undressed each other slowly in the darkness, taking all the time in the world because time had come to a standstill. Everything was forgotten: missions and assignments; agencies and procedure; Gehlen and Rankin and Davies and Pender and von Osten and Oehring; all of it. There was nothing but us. I touched her naked skin and a charge went through me, just as it had all those years before.

We fell onto the bed and intertwined our limbs until every part of us was joined. I could feel the warmth of her body and inhale the delicate strains of her perfume. The small, pert breasts rose and fell a little more with each breath and I could see the pink nipples gently darkening as they began to extend. I was fully taut and she fingered me gently towards her, guiding me inside, deeper and deeper until she was full. I was on the brink, hardly moving, but I could begin to feel her back arching and her breath quickening as her fingers dug into my shoulders. Yet still we delayed, trying to maintain the moment, to preserve what we had, because neither of us wanted it to end. Once it did, we would be back to reality and we had to avoid that for as long as possible, to hold the universe at bay, to keep the precious bubble intact. Still, there were no words as she encouraged an increase in rhythm, a slow acceleration that gained in momentum and intensity. And when it was impossible to hold any longer, we shared the mutual release, exploding and crushing, until we collapsed in the afterglow, almost numb, content just to be there with each other, as close as any two beings can be.

Later, as we lay there, I thought I detected the beginnings of remorse but she just shook her head and looked the other away. I touched her bare shoulder but she didn't respond.

"Katharina?"

That's when she turned back and gazed at me, her eyes hard as diamonds.

"What?" I said, quietly. "What is it?"

Once again, she didn't answer. She just closed her eyes tightly as if she didn't want to look at me any more. Was there a tear there, too? I couldn't tell and I was afraid to find out, so I said nothing and just retreated into my own space.

What was I supposed to do? Get up and leave? Now that I'd found her after fourteen years, did she expect me to just walk out? Is that what she wanted? For the life of me, I didn't know. I really didn't know.

While we were at the Lanesborough, Reinhard Gehlen was staying in one of the small guest rooms on the top floor of the US Embassy on Grosvenor Square, which he invariably preferred to a hotel for reasons of both convenience and security.

At some time after midnight, he was woken by the harsh ringing of his bedside phone. "*Ja?*" he said into the receiver, before he remembered where he was and switched to English. "Yes?"

The switchboard voice was pure American Midwest: "Sorry to wake you sir, but there's a woman demands to speak with you, name of Helga Kreiss, says it's very urgent. She says you would know."

In fact, Gehlen didn't know, not for sure, but he had a strong suspicion. "Okay, put her through."

There were the sounds of a long-distance connection and then a soft, almost plaintive voice through the hiss.

"Reinhard? Is that you?"

This time the language was German and he knew exactly who it was: Lina von Osten, calling from God-knows-where. "Hello, Helga," he replied, continuing the masquerade. "Where are you?"

"Can they hear me? The Americans?"

"Yes, probably."

"Then I won't tell you where I am."

"Is your 'friend' with you?" He was talking about Oehring.

"Yes, he's here. Sleeping on the floor. We're in a small place, a hotel. Reinhard, listen... What happened in Paris..."

"Not on the phone."

"You knew?"

"I guessed."

"I thought you would."

"What will you do?" he asked.

"I don't know. Keep going, I suppose. What choice do I have?"

"You know, they'll keep coming after you."

"Probably."

"So will we."

"You too?"

"What you've got, both sides want."

"What should I do?"

"You've got to get rid of it."

"It's worth a fortune."

"Not if you're dead. Look, why not just give it to me? You want money, I'll get you money."

"You'll just give it to them, to the Americans."

"I might."

"No... the answer's no, Reinhard. Not to the Russians, not to the Americans. Not after what they did to us. Never."

"Listen to me, all right? The war's over. It's finished. We've all changed sides now."

"Not me. And not Karlheinz."

"I told you, it's an open line."

A pause. "Yes, yes, you're right. I should be careful."

"Yes, you should."

"Reinhard?"

"Yes?"

"You know, I always liked that name."

Reinhard Gehlen, Reinhard Heydrich... He could see that, for her, there were many similarities but he felt no compliment. "Don't compare me to *him*. That's not right. He's dead and his world is dead and the sooner you realize that, the better."

There was a long silence before she spoke again, with no sound other than the crackle of the long distance line. "Can you help us?" she said, eventually.

"I'm sorry, not if you won't give it to me."

"Damn you! You're just like them. I should have known."

He heard a click, then nothing. She'd hung up and Gehlen lay his head back down on the pillow. After a few seconds' thought, he sat up again and got the switchboard. "Find me Phil Rankin, will you?"

"Sir, he's left for the night."

"I know, that's why I said 'find him.'"

"Yes, sir."

Gehlen got out of bed and transferred over to a small armchair. Next to it was a small round table and he turned on the lamp. The room wasn't large but it was comfortable enough and even contained a small bar. He thought about pouring himself a scotch but decided against it. Instead, he lit the unfinished cigar stub he'd been smoking earlier that evening. Cigars always helped him to think and, right now, that was what he needed to do.

The phone rang again.

"I have Mr. Rankin, sir."

"Thanks, put him through."

"Reinhard?" said a sleepy voice. "What time is it? What the hell do you want?"

Gehlen could easily imagine the big American in his striped pajamas, bleary eyed and scratching his head. "Wake up, Phil. I just heard from Lina."

It took a few moments before Rankin could get his head together. "Lina von Osten?"

"Yes. She called me here."

"What? At the embassy? Hell, some nerve."

"She's using the name Helga Kreiss."

"What did she want?"

"She wanted me to help her."

"And what did you say?"

"What do you think I said? I told her to give me the manuscript."

"And she said?"

"She said 'no.'"

"Why, in God's name? What good is it to her?"

"She thinks it's worth money."

"Okay, so let's buy it from her."

"Forget it. She won't sell to either you or the Russians." Then, by way of explanation, he added: "She's still fighting the war."

"Yeah? Well, she'll lose again."

"I know, I told her."

"So what do you want to do?" asked Rankin.

"Me? I want to go back to bed."

"You and me both, buddy boy. But first tell me what you want to do."

"I don't know yet. Let's sleep on it and talk tomorrow."

"Yeah... yeah, okay."

"Good night, Phil."

"What's left of it."

Reinhard Gehlen hung up and stamped the remainder of the cigar into the adjacent ashtray.

He couldn't help smiling a little at Rankin's first instinct: "Okay, so let's buy it." Such a typically American response. But as Gehlen sat there thinking about it, he realized it wasn't such a bad idea. If Lina wouldn't sell it to either side, then maybe they needed a third party to make the approach. It was worth some consideration.

For Gehlen, this whole thing was becoming a major pain in the rear end, an extra problem he just didn't need, but, in the end, he was hoping it might be worth all the trouble. Although the Chancellor had clearly said when giving the order that he didn't care about success or failure, Gehlen knew that if he could actually produce the manuscript, against all the odds, it would make the old man look good in front of Truman - which, in turn, would shine a highly favourable light on his own ambition.

★

It was just after seven, with the morning light hurting my eyes, when I called down for coffee. I didn't know what to say to Katharina: whether to pick up where we left off last night, or to try to make a new start. Did she have feelings of remorse about what happened? I still couldn't tell - and I still didn't want to ask.

In the end, she made the decision for both of us by returning to business. In no time at all, she was showered, dressed and full of questions: wanting to know my next steps, how I would proceed and the obstacles I envisaged. Ever the professional.

I made like it was too early to discuss such things; but the real truth was that, even if I'd wanted to answer her, I didn't have a clue how to go about it. I'd chased down difficult facts as a freelance journalist and I'd lain in wait to catch Nazis on the run but, in this kind of agency role, I was strictly an amateur. I simply didn't have enough experience to know what was possible and what wasn't, so my only recourse was to make it up as I went along, reinventing everything based on my own version of common sense. It wasn't the most efficient way of doing things and I could feel she was becoming a little impatient with my lack of enthusiasm.

"Ed…" she said eventually. "Do you want to back out?"

"I didn't say that."

"No, not out loud."

I didn't respond.

"You know what I think?" she went on. "I don't think it's the risk at all. I did at first but not now."

"So what do you think it is?"

"I think it's the idea of impersonating an SS officer that's getting to you."

I looked over at her for a moment. She had the knack of surprising me in many ways. "I knew what I was getting into," I replied, which was not really true.

"Nevertheless..."

"Why, you don't think I can do it? '*Jawohl! Sieg heil!*'" I raised my right arm and repeated the stock phrases in cartoon Nazi fashion, but I could see she wasn't amused.

"That's the problem," she said quietly. "I'm afraid you won't take it seriously enough."

I gazed at her, more infatuated than ever. "Are you worried about me?"

"I'm worried about the operation." That's when her face opened up into a broad smile and, once again, she was the same Katharina, the woman I'd fallen for all those years ago in Berlin. "Idiot," she said, "of course I'm worried about you."

We were downstairs finishing breakfast when Siegfried Wachter arrived, his massive shape forming a dark shadow over our table.

"What's this?" he asked. "Business and pleasure together? My dear boy, I do believe you're finally learning."

"Hello, Siegfried," I replied, ignoring his obvious insinuations. He'd warned me he might show up. "Grab a chair, join us."

He did as he was told but, instead of hauling the furniture around himself, he just waved a hand in the air and the waiter came running. When he was settled, he placed his order, taking enough time to make sure the man understood: smoked salmon but it had to be Norwegian, not Scottish; plus a mushroom omelet, which had to be made with brown-shell eggs, not white; and mushrooms, Portobello, not the garden variety. He also demanded rolls, not toast, as long as they'd been baked this morning; and a pot of coffee, Jamaican, not African. The waiter didn't even flinch at all this. He just stood there nodding because Siegfried just had that way about him.

He was dressed this morning in business attire. That meant an impeccably tailored three-piece suit the colour of charcoal, a fine shirt with a thin gray stripe and a hand-sewn tie of royal blue. As he made himself comfortable, his sleeve shifted sufficiently to reveal the heirloom Breguet wristwatch he always wore.

"So, my friends, here we are," he said, beaming at the two of us like a rich relative who's come gate-crashing. "How clever of us all to be sitting here like this."

"Sitting here like what?" I asked.

"Why, like souls that got sent to hell and, somehow, through their own instinctive guile, found their way back up to heaven."

"Oh, you mean self-satisfied."

"Now don't ruin it with your cynicism, Ed, there's a good fellow. Katharina and I are appreciative enough, aren't we, my dear?"

He reached over and put his fleshy, manicured hand around Katharina's, the essence of European gallantry. If he hadn't been who he was, I might have fallen prey to a whole new bout of jealousy. As it happens, they'd known each other back in Berlin long before I ever came along, having once moved in the same grand circles: diplomatic receptions on Wilhelmstrasse; opera at the Kroll; art auctions on the Linden. To anyone unaware of the circumstances, it was hardly a picture of hell. But it has to be recalled that Katharina was working with her father to try to control the rise of Hitler - totally in vain, of course - and Siegfried was desperately maintaining his balancing act with contacts and influence in order to avoid the homosexual pink triangle of Dachau.

"I'm not sure I'd label this as heaven," she answered him.

"No?" said Siegfried. "So what would you call it?"

"I'd call it scheming and operating, which is all I seem to have been doing ever since I can remember. To me, it's just more of the same."

Siegfried was magnanimous enough to concede the point. "Yes, I can appreciate that. But there *is* a difference, you know, and, personally, I believe it's one worth celebrating."

"And what would that be?"

A big grin spread across his face, like nothing I'd ever seen before. "The SS are no longer the predators, they're now the prey. And that alone, my friends, fills me with unbounded joy."

I nodded my agreement and even Katharina was obliged to acknowledge the point. It was the most basic fact of our entire post-war existence.

With that, the mood changed and we chatted about other things as we drank our coffee and waited for his breakfast to arrive. The news headlines were still full of the Korean impasse, as well as developments in what was known as the Malayan Emergency: a full-fledged jungle insurrection by ethnic Chinese Marxists, which was being put down by various British and Commonwealth forces. Both conflicts were related to the same Cold War frontier we were facing here in Europe but they still seemed very remote to us and we were able to converse somewhat dispassionately about the issues involved.

Only after Siegfried's food was placed in front of him and he pronounced it satisfactory could we start into our real topic concerning the affair at hand.

"Despite appearances to the contrary," he informed us, "I've actually been doing something worthwhile with my time."

"Business and pleasure together?" I offered, just throwing his own words back at him, but he chose to ignore my remark.

"I may have found another access point."

Katharina was immediately back on track. Since Karlheinz Oehring was now a fugitive, he was basically useless in that respect and both she and the rest of the team had been busy trying to find a new way in. "Who?" she said.

"His name is Klaus Hoeffler."

Katharina knew the name right away. "Klaus Hoeffler from Zurich?"

"The very same."

"Who is he?" I asked.

"Someone you should know about," Siegfried replied.

"Why?"

"Because he's the man who funds ODESSA."

"And he's Swiss?"

"German-Swiss, actually, with the emphasis on German. Jumped on the Hitler bandwagon in 1933. Saw it as an opportunity at first, then fell in love with the ideology. During the war, he was quite influential, moving money around for several of the leading lights. A good friend of Heinrich Müller, or so I'm told."

Heinrich Müller, also known as "Gestapo" Müller, was someone I did happen to know about. A thug of a man, he was head of that particular security agency under Lina von Osten's husband, Reinhard Heydrich, but he fled Berlin in the chaos of '45 and was never captured. "Was Hoeffler the one who helped Müller escape?"

"I wouldn't know, dear boy. Perhaps your lady here can answer that."

"She doesn't belong to ODESSA," I told him, leaping to her defense with perhaps a little too much vigour.

"I never said she did. I just said..."

"I know what you said."

Katharina put her hand on my arm. "It's okay, Ed."

I did my best to calm down. "So what's this Hoeffler doing now?" I asked, trying to continue the conversation with Siegfried as if nothing had happened. "Why would he be our 'access point,' as you call it?"

"Why? Because he's involved in a relationship with Lina von Osten, that's why. According to the gossip, he's proposed to her on several occasions."

That was a stunner. Even Katharina looked surprised.

"How do you know all this?" I asked him.

"Actually, dear boy, I found out by complete accident."

"Nothing happens to you by accident."

"Well, this did. I happen to be acquainted with the manager of the Majestic, where the two of them were having a drink together. That's a hotel in Cannes, by the way." This last part was for my benefit. He could be a patronizing bastard when he wanted to be. "They were chatting in the bar, carefree as you like, when I walked in and the manager introduced me, simple as that. We even shook hands."

"I can't believe she'd show her face in public."

"Well, as a matter of fact, she didn't. She was wearing a dark wig with a pair of large sunglasses. I was told her name was Helga Kreiss, also from Zurich, but she didn't fool me, not for a second."

It was almost the same disguise she wore in Paris and it hadn't worked there, either. That time, it was her ex-maid, Hedda Neuberg, who'd spotted her. On this occasion, it was Siegfried Wachter. It made me wonder if she had some kind of psychological need for celebrity status, like a Hollywood star who secretly hopes to be recognized, even when she's trying to hide.

"When *was* this?" I asked.

"You mean when did I see her? What difference does it make?"

"I'm just wondering why we find out about this now."

"Is that some kind of a critique, dear boy? I do hope not."

"Don't be sensitive, I was just asking."

"Well, if you must know, it happened the day before yesterday."

"And you couldn't call?"

"You sound like somebody's mother."

It was Katharina, once again, who had to step in and separate the squabbling children. "You think she's still there? In Cannes?"

Siegfried sipped at his special blend of coffee, holding the Wedgwood porcelain with his pinkie finger slightly raised. "I doubt she's staying at the hotel… but I do believe Hoeffler's got a villa somewhere in the vicinity. That would make sense."

He was right. Lina von Osten still had half the police in Europe chasing her. Where else was she going to go? Who else would hide her? "Does she still have Oehring with her?" I asked him.

"No way of knowing."

Meanwhile, Katharina's mind was already racing ahead. "How about we arrange for Ed to meet him?" she suggested.

"Meet who?" said Siegfried. "Oehring or Hoeffler?"

"Hoeffler… We're talking about Hoeffler."

That's when I interjected: "You mean change the plan?"

"What plan?" she replied. "Since Paris, there's been no plan."

That's when Siegfried came up with the idea. "All right, listen, dear friends. Three weeks from now, I'm due to host a small function on my boat… a few traders, a few finance people and so forth. I don't know Hoeffler personally but I venture to say he'd probably fit right in."

"So that's perfect," she said enthusiastically. "You invite Ed at the same time."

"He'd need an alias. And a good excuse for being there."

"No problem. We'll find something suitable."

They were discussing this whole scheme as if I weren't even there. "Don't I get a say in this?" I sounded ridiculous, even to myself.

Siegfried just laughed. "Does the meat get a say when it's put in the sandwich?" This was his own version of humour and he evidently found it highly amusing. He could be charming when he wanted, a chivalrous companion and a witty raconteur, but it was almost as if he couldn't maintain that persona for more than a few minutes before revealing a snide aspect to his character that could be almost malevolent. It reminded me yet again why I both enjoyed and despised him in equal measure.

Did he really meet Lina von Osten just by chance at the Majestic? I must admit, I had my doubts but I didn't say anything, primarily because there were only vague suspicions at best. I was such a new-comer to the game that I hadn't yet learned to trust my instincts.

After he left, Katharina also went on her way, still wearing the clothes she'd worn for our boat trip to Greenwich. With this new plan in the offing, she had work to do.

We kissed in the lobby but it was merely a farewell kiss. There was no talk of her staying longer and I didn't bring it up. Perhaps, with hindsight, I should have expressed exactly how I felt and offered declarations of my undying devotion but, once again, I recall think-ing there was no point trying to speed things along any faster than they wanted to go.

The fact remained that I still had no idea where our relationship stood. Had it all just been a passing flirtation for her, just another chapter in her life? Would we ever make love again, or were we just going to revert to our alter egos of case officer and field agent? All good questions, with no answers in sight.

★

For the time being, Lina von Osten had exchanged the company of her *Kampfhund,* Karlheinz Oehring, to that of her sometime lover, Klaus Uwe Hoeffler, the rich Swiss banker with his thinning white-hair, a lazy right eye and a taste for Italian haute couture.

While Oehring was satisfying his own lusts in the maid's quarters, Lina and Klaus were watching from the plush comfort of a love seat, as a handsome teenage couple writhed around naked on the fur rug in front of them. The slim limbs and lithe torsos inter-twined with each other, their hands searching and stroking every erogenous zone: from breasts to buttocks, from mouth to crotch. Although the young couple was as blond and Nordic in appearance as Lina herself, the theme of the performance was the Kama Sutra and the quiet music accompanying the well-practiced movement was vaguely Indian in origin.

"He's more beautiful than she is," Lina whispered.

"I'm glad you think so," came the reply. "It means we'll have no arguments later."

They were in Klaus Hoeffler's private villa, perched high in the hills overlooking Cannes. The basic concept of this evening's spec-tacle was that the performing couple would continue for as long as it took to arouse each other as well as their two spectators. Then, at a suitable point, the young male and female would split and lead their new partners, Lina and Klaus respectively, into separate bedrooms for a more private, more intimate experience. On a side table was exotic tropical fruit: lush and ripe, in keeping with the activities. As yet, it hadn't been touched. Only the wine was flowing, a fine vintage, drawn from the depths of the cellars just for the occasion.

Lina hadn't been too eager at first and she'd felt a little silly when they sat down to watch but, now, with the glass in her hand and the couple in front making a good job of feigning their thrill, she was warming up to it. She and Klaus were wearing nothing but white silk bathrobes, Japanese style, and she was starting to feel the kind of flush that she hadn't felt in some time. She was conscious of her arousal and, from the corner of her eye, she could see the beginnings of an erection from Klaus - something else that hadn't happened in a while. Artificial as it was, the performance seemed to be having its effect, so she decided to give up her innate resistance and just go along for the ride.

For the first time in ages, she could relax and she breathed out a long sigh, the way people do when they first arrive on vacation: a combination of release and freedom, which stems from the simple removal of stress. All thoughts of ODESSA and the MGB and the manuscript had faded and she sat back, her eyes half-closed and her robe half-open, content to let the orgiastic mood envelop her.

As the world knows, the Swiss remained officially neutral throughout the war. However, that word "neutral" can have wide parameters and it's not every citizen who automatically follows national policy. Many Swiss followed news of the conflict in their own language - German, French or Italian – and, as long as it lasted, they maintained their own private opinions and prejudices, much the same as anybody else.

In German-speaking Zurich, for example, there were many who had some affinity with the Nazi cause and Klaus Hoeffler was one of them. Whether his sympathies came from personal conviction, or whether he just thought it was better business, hardly mattered. Either way, as chairman and principal of his family's private investment bank, Argon Hoeffler AG, there's no doubt that he profited on an immense scale, both during and after the war. Since 1945, his company had become the depository of millions, perhaps even billions, in unaccountable wartime funds, all protected by the strict privacy laws for which the Swiss financial industry is famous. From the richer victims came artwork, jewelry, bullion and bonds, either laundered into cash on the black market or stashed in the huge vaults exactly as found. From the poor came millions of tiny amounts, either seized from the emptied homes or collected in the warehouses of the death camps: everything from the tiny diamonds hidden in the lining of ragged clothes to the gold teeth prized out of dead mouths before the bloated, soiled corpses were transferred to the ovens. Not surprisingly, many of Hoeffler's old contacts were the senior SS officers who ran those camp operations and it was through friendship, as much as anything else, that he authorized the release of such anonymous funds to the ODESSA organization.

As far as Lina von Osten was concerned, Klaus Hoeffler had money, he had influence and he supported the cause. In a way, it was natural that they would also become lovers. In truth, however, the relationship between them had never been easy. She was only too aware of his reputation as an opportunist, only interested in what he could obtain, and she was never totally sure whether he wanted her for herself or for the connections that her widowhood opened up. After all, the name "Heydrich" was a legend in the SS. In the end, she kept her emotional distance and never allowed him to get too close. Although she was the first to admit that she enjoyed both his company and his lifestyle, she still didn't trust his motives.

As a result, the manuscript was not in his bank's central vault as might have been expected. It was still in her possession, locked away in her briefcase, just as it had been in Paris. In her mind, the manuscript was the only insurance that could guarantee her independence and she wasn't about to give it up easily to anyone.

"You're leaving already?" Lina's eyes were half-open and the Mediterranean sunlight was already penetrating the louvred windows of the master bedroom.

Over by the dresser, Klaus Hoeffler was fastening his peacock tie under his crisp white collar. His skillful fingers adjusted the knot to perfection. "Eight o'clock," he said, glancing at his Patek Philippe wristwatch, just one of a prized collection. "I told you I was going."

"Did you tell me where?"

"Just up the road."

"Where 'up the road?'"

"Monte Carlo."

"You didn't tell me that."

"Yes, I believe I did."

"Well, I forgot. Can I come with you?"

"You can, if you want to be arrested."

"Monaco won't arrest me. They don't even like the French."

"Possibly, but I'd prefer not to take the risk if you don't mind. I've got some interests there I'd like to maintain."

"Interests here, interests there..." She made a silly, childish face. "It's not fair."

"Nothing's fair."

"Will you be playing the casino? Visiting the palace?"

"As it happens, I'll be meeting some very dull commodity traders on a boat."

"A luxury yacht, no doubt."

"Well... yes, I suppose so. In a minor way."

"I knew it. Damn it, why can't I ever have any fun without..."

He glanced at her. "Without what?"

"Nothing."

"You know, you still haven't told me what that whole affair was about."

"What affair?"

"Lina, come on. What were the Russians after in Paris? Why can't you tell me?"

A coy smile. "Because if I told you, my *Kampfhund* would have to kill you."

He gave her a cynical glance, then finished his tie-knot. "I should be back within a couple of days," he told her, as he adjusted his hand-stitched Milanese jacket and took a final look in the mirror. "In the meantime, I suggest you and your canine friend remain on the property."

★

That same week, Joseph Stalin was attending a Party conference in Leningrad. As he often did when travelling, he decided to hold his regular cabinet meetings right on schedule, which meant that every member of the Politburo had to make the journey out there, whether they were involved in the conference or not - and that included Lavrenti Beria.

It was therefore early on the morning of August 20th that Beria received a personal call at the Grand Hotel Europe, in the historic Nevsky Prospect. He was still half asleep when he picked up the receiver and was stunned to hear the sound of The Boss himself on the other end. To his recollection, that had never happened before, not once in twenty-five years.

"Lavrenti Pavlovich..." said Stalin. Somehow the tone was ominous. "Meet me downstairs in ten minutes. Don't be late."

Although he'd been half-asleep, Beria was immediately on full alert. "Yes, yes, of course, I'll be there."

The young, local girl was still there from the night before and he gave her naked rear a hard slap to chase her out of his bed. It left a pink hand-print across the small round globes of her buttocks and she yelped in response; but she obeyed without further objection, no doubt a wise decision on her part, given the circumstances.

It was just a little over nine minutes later that Beria came puffing through the main doors of the hotel. Directly in front of the building was a convoy of five black limousines, all with chauffeurs standing smartly to attention, each holding the nearside rear door open at the ready. Beria knew the sequence and crossed the sidewalk directly to the central car, the big ZIS-110. It was a Soviet-built model, copied directly from a pre-war American Packard, and Stalin possessed eight of them which he kept in different parts of the country for his exclusive use. Under the hood was a massive eight-cylinder engine that could propel him at speeds of up to 175 kph where the roads permitted and, sometimes, when he was in the mood, he liked to feel the full power unleashed.

Today was not one of those days, however, and, as Beria slid into the back seat, he sensed the chill of the man next to him. Stalin was facing straight ahead and didn't even glance sideways to acknowledge Beria's entry.

"Lavrenti..." said Stalin. "You know about American culture, I believe."

"A little."

"What's that game they play?"

"Game?"

"One man throws a ball, the other hits it with a big bat."

"You mean *baseball*?" Beria used the English word.

"Yes, that's right... *baseball*. Now, as I understand, the man with the bat has three chances, am I right?'"

"That's right," replied Beria, and, all at once, he had an inclination of where this was going. A drop of moisture managed to find its way from his temple down to his cheek but he didn't dare wipe it away. It would show fear and, worse, weakness.

"He tries to hit, he misses," Stalin was saying in the same even tone. "He tries to hit again and he misses again. Are you with me, Lavrenti? Then he has one hit left, am I right? Now tell me... what happens if he misses a third time?"

Beria had no choice but to answer. "He's out."

"Yes, well done. You really do know the Americans. He's out. Thank you. Now, leave."

Beria looked at him for a moment. The analogy was clear and all the more threatening by the way it was delivered. First strike, Fehmarn. Second strike, Paris. And the third? Beria was fast running out of chances. But he couldn't say a word. All he could do was exit the vehicle, as ordered.

Breakfast was a worrying time for Lavrenti Beria. Spread before him was yogurt, black bread with cream cheese, plus a large dollop of the hotel's homemade plum jam, but he'd lost his appetite and threw the food back down on the plate, spilling his coffee in the process.

The only thing the Paris team had managed to accomplish was to light up the city and set up a nationwide competition with the French police to find the fugitives, who presumably still had Stalin's precious manuscript in their possession. It was a race Beria couldn't hope to win and, once again, he was left cursing the stupidity of that damned fool, Ignatyev, and the incompetence of the MGB.

By the time the sealed and classified note was delivered to his room, he was desperate enough to seize at anything, no matter how small the chance.

It turned out to be a wired communication from Yuri Modin at the Soviet Embassy in London, sent to Leningrad via Beria's own MVD headquarters in Moscow. The report was based on a contact with Owen Rhys, the young man they'd planted to become the lover of Siegfried Wachter. According to Rhys, a man to watch might be Karl Uwe Hoeffler, a Swiss banker with ODESSA connections, who was believed to have an amorous relationship with Lina von Osten. The report also mentioned that both Rhys and Hoeffler had been personally invited to an upcoming event on Wachter's boat in Monte Carlo. The final words said "stand by for further developments," but Beria had no intention of just standing by.

Faced with The Boss's cold wrath, he was just too anxious. He couldn't leave it to Ignatyev and the MGB again. He had to act and, this time, he was determined to get involved personally. This time, he needed a home run.

The next time I saw Siegfried Wachter was on his boat, "Guinevere."

At a hundred and twelve feet, it was really more of a large motor launch than a true luxury yacht, but he was immensely proud of it nonetheless and he strutted about the main deck as if to say to the rest of us: "I own this floating whimsy and you don't." Today, he was wearing the appropriate blue blazer with gleaming gold buttons and, on his top pocket, the emblem of the Monaco Regatta Society: a gift, he claimed, from Prince Rainier himself. Completing the nautical theme were white slacks with a knife-edge crease, deck shoes of English leather and, on his bald head, a Greek captain's hat to protect him from the sun.

By the time I arrived, there was already a crowd of about thirty carefully selected guests, plus a crew of ten, including no less than five black-jacketed waiters serving champagne, caviar, oysters, truffles and other showy treats. "Hideously expensive," Siegfried confided, as he welcomed me aboard. "But what else is money for, dear boy?"

I was about to reply "paying the rent" but, just in time, I remembered who I was meant to be. Here in Monte Carlo's picturesque harbour, I was no longer the hard-up, time-ravaged Ed Schaeffer, freelance hack and Nazi hunter, but exactly the opposite. For this role, my alias was to be the successful and well-preserved Erich Schultz, celebrity journalist and secret Nazi sympathizer. The story we'd prepared was that I was covering the affair for *Vogue*, the New York fashion magazine; a personal arrangement between the CIA's Phil Rankin and the venerable editor, Edna Woolman Chase, who was prepared to back me up should the need arise. In case anyone asked why I should be working this event for an American female readership, my angle would be that I was tracking down Europe's richest and most eligible bachelors: a handy camouflage, invented by Katharina, which fitted Klaus Hoeffler perfectly and would allow me a plausible approach.

Even more interesting, however, was my supposedly hidden "biography," as discretely leaked by Siegfried. Word had it, he whispered in Hoeffler's ear, that I'd learned my trade in pre-war Berlin under Joseph Goebbels, writing and editing international editions of his slick propaganda organ, *Signal*. It was produced in multiple languages and, by the height of Nazi power in 1942, was being distributed to all the conquered territories. This included a version in English, my own specialty, which was produced solely for the Channel Islands, the only part of Britain ever occupied during the war. As a juicy footnote, it was also hinted that I was now, like Hoeffler, a silent contributor to certain ODESSA factions, with contacts and sources that even he didn't know about.

Meanwhile, as Siegfried and I sipped our Dom Pérignon from Waterford's finest fluted crystal, I was being regaled with the history of the boat, which was Siegfried's own version of deck-side small talk.

"Why is it called 'Guinevere?'" I asked him.

"Not 'it,' dear boy. A boat is always called 'she.' And she's called 'Guinevere' after the wife of King Arthur. You know, Camelot and so on."

"I thought she was German."

"Who, Guinevere?"

"No," I sighed, "the boat."

"Oh, my word, no. Couldn't be more English. Built for the Royal Navy at the Solent yards in Hampshire. First used as an ambulance out of Portsmouth and then, after the war, she was auctioned off and became a smuggler."

"A smuggler?"

"I know, terribly romantic. Classic Bogart. Ran all kinds of despicable merchandise between Gibraltar and Tangiers, until the Admiralty arrested her in 1949."

"And then?"

"And then she was sold off again… this time, to me. Amazing bargain, actually. They almost gave her away. Of course, I had to refurbish her completely but, on the other hand…"

"What else is money for?" I said, repeating his well-worn phrase.

It was at that moment that his young friend arrived: half his age and half his weight, too. He had cool green eyes, dimples on his smooth cheeks and a mousy tangle of hair.

"Ah, let me introduce you," said Siegfried, touching his arm. "Owen Rhys… this is our special guest, Ed…"

"Erich," I corrected him. Fortunately, no one around us seemed to have heard. The slip could have been a genuine error on Siegfried's part, or it could have been because his boy-pal was already in on the game. I wasn't sure which but, either way, I was immediately on alert.

"Yes, of course," said Siegfried. "How silly of me. I do apologize. Owen, this is Erich Schultz."

"Pleased to meet you," said Rhys, reaching out to shake my hand. His voice had a pleasant lilt to it.

"Welsh, I take it."

"Which gave me away, the name or the accent?" The question was rhetorical and he laughed good-naturedly at what must have been his own long-standing joke. "What do you do, Mr. Schultz, if you don't mind my asking? Finance or commodities?"

"Neither, I'm afraid. Just a lowly scribe, here to write about wealthy bachelors for my lonely heart readers."

"Ah, a journalist. Interesting. And would those lonely hearts happen to be male or female?"

"All female."

"In that case, I doubt you'd want to mention the likes of me."

Another big grin, this time accompanied by a quick wink. He really seemed to enjoy his own humour. I noticed it was all directed against himself, usually a mark of total self-confidence, or high insecurity. In his case, I wasn't sure which.

"And you, Mr. Rhys? What's your profession?"

"Oh, nothing as exciting as yours. Metals mostly, just like Siegfried here. Boring stuff, really."

I would have asked him about nickel, except I was meant to be a society reporter, so I said: "Do you happen to own a boat, too?"

He laughed. "No boat, no chateau, not even a measly Jag, I'm afraid. But I'm starting to think I could get very used to all this, if you know what I'm saying."

"I do indeed."

On the whole, he seemed pleasant enough. He was young and attractive, with a lively intellect, and I could easily see why Siegfried was gazing at him, smitten as a lovesick schoolboy. Of course, at that moment, both Siegfried and I were completely unaware that Owen Rhys, too, had a secret life - as a long time member of the British Communist Party.

In the meantime, I had my own covert activity to take care of and I was reminded of it when Klaus Hoeffler was introduced to our small group. The language switched to German.

"Herr Hoeffler, please join us," said Siegfried. " Is there anything I can get you?"

"No, no, everything is excellent, thank you. This is a fine vessel, Herr Wachter. My compliments."

"Thank you, you're very kind." Siegfried turned to us and changed back to English for the benefit of his young friend. "May I present Herr Klaus Hoeffler of Argon Hoeffler. This is Owen Rhys, with the London Metal Exchange. We've been working nickel together..."

"Yes, the Canadian project," said Hoeffler. "Most interesting. I look forward to talking to you about that, Mr. Rhys."

"I'd be delighted," replied the young man.

"So you should be," added Siegfried. "Herr Hoeffler owns his own bank."

There were guffaws all round until, finally, Siegfried gestured in my direction. "And this fine gentleman here... this is the journalist I was telling you about earlier. May I present Erich Schultz, currently working with *Vogue* magazine... something of a traveller and, may I say, perfectly at home in both languages."

"A man of the world," said Hoeffler, shaking my hand firmly.

"Just a man with a job to do," I replied, attempting the kind of accomplished modesty that might appeal to the Swiss upper class.

"He's interviewing wealthy bachelors," said Siegfried, mocking me a little. "Come to think of it, Herr Hoeffler, you'd make the ideal subject."

"Me?" said Hoeffler.

"Why don't we leave the two of you alone for a while? Come, Owen, let's mingle a little. You can talk nickel later."

With that, Siegfried shamelessly took his young friend by the hand and led him off towards the stern, where another small group of well-dressed financiers had gathered. That left me alone with Klaus Hoeffler, exactly as planned.

For a few minutes, I peppered him in German with questions about his lifestyle: his hobbies, his club memberships, his taste in women and so on; precisely the kind of thing my supposed female readership would want to know about. This would have given me a convenient segue into the subject I really wanted to talk about - his current lady companion - but, as it happened, I didn't need it because he found a very good segue of his own.

I was asking him which fashion colours he preferred, one of my prepared questions, when he came right out and said: "Personally, I have a preference for black, Herr Schultz. I'm told it's the same for you, would that be right?"

It was the opening I'd been waiting for. I knew he was referring to the SS, commonly known as the "*Schwarzkorps*" (black unit), due to their uniforms. "I've been known to appreciate that particular colour on occasion, Herr Hoeffler."

"Yes, so I've been told. You know, there's a club for people like us."

"Really?"

"I've also been told that you may already be a member."

He was hinting at ODESSA but, to me, it was a silly conversation, all this dancing around. Nevertheless, I decided to play along. "Well, I don't exactly have a membership card," I replied, "but that doesn't mean I'm not sympathetic."

He nodded. "Good… sympathy is good. As a matter of fact…"

He stopped to glance around.

"Yes, Herr Hoeffler?"

"I was about to say, I know some people who could use a little sympathy at the present time."

"Sympathy you can't provide yourself?"

"Let's just say, the kind of sympathy they need is quite sensitive... or perhaps I should say unobtrusive... and I might be a little too high-profile to provide it. Do you understand what I'm saying?"

"I believe I do. But I'm not entirely sure what you're asking me, Herr Hoeffler."

"Just to leave here now and take a drive with me."

"A drive? A drive to where, may I ask?"

"Not far. Will you come?"

"Well, I do have a job to finish here."

"In that case, let me suggest two hours from now. Will that give you enough time?"

"Perhaps if I could know what it's about?"

"Yes, but not here. We'll talk on the way. Herr Schultz, I can assure you I wouldn't ask if I didn't consider it important. Now I really must go and talk a little business. I'll see you a little later."

I watched him go and thought about what I'd just agreed to do. But I couldn't think for too long. In order to keep my cover intact, I still had to waste time on meaningless interviews for an article which would never be written. Since I'd already made contact with my target, it was probably unnecessary to continue the subterfuge but I didn't want to run the risk of him checking up on me later.

As I walked past the galley, I glanced in on a couple of white-coated chefs preparing large quantities of shrimp and asparagus on the range. Beyond, I could just make out the small communications cabin and tucked inside was Owen Rhys, talking into the mouthpiece of a radio-telephone.

At the time, I didn't think too much about it, because I didn't know he was calling his case officer, Modin, at the Soviet Embassy in London, or that he was telling him the gist of the quiet conversation he'd just overheard between myself and Klaus Hoeffler, playboy banker and intimate friend of Lina von Osten.

What I also didn't know was that this call from Rhys would be followed up immediately on the Soviet side by two further transmissions. The first was from Modin's office to the Lubyanka in Moscow. This was then relayed directly to a non-scheduled Aeroflot flight, which had already received permission to fly over French airspace. The aircraft, a Tupolev TU-104, had just travelled from Moscow via Berlin and was due to land at Paris but, after the message was received, the captain requested a last minute diversion to Marseille. The section message was a directive to the Soviet consulate in that southern port city, demanding the immediate dispatch of an undercover team to meet up with the aircraft's sole passenger on landing. This was the Minister for Internal Affairs, Lavrenti Pavlovich Beria, arriving to take personal charge of the hunt for the manuscript. For the purposes of travel, his cover was that of a manufacturing trade representative, a subject in which he could claim some experience, having supervised various aspects of Soviet wartime production.

If nothing else, the flurry of activity proved one thing: although the vast Kremlin bureaucracy usually moved as slow as a Tolstoy novel, the security apparatus could be surprisingly agile when it needed to be.

"Where are we going?" I said to Hoeffler, as we negotiated our way out of Monte Carlo through the city's maze of tunnels.

We were in his Mercedes-Benz 300S, a burgundy-coloured cabriolet with deerskin upholstery. Back in Zurich, he engaged a chauffeur but this machine was so sleek and flattering that he invariably drove it himself when he was down here.

"I have a small villa just north of Cannes," he replied. "I think you'll like it."

"We're going on vacation?"

He glanced at me from behind the wheel, made of polished wood. "No," he said, "not exactly a vacation."

After leaving the Principality of Monaco, we paused so he could take the top down before settling in for a smooth and stately trip westbound along the French Riviera coast, following the A50 through Nice, Antibes and Juan-les-Pins. The afternoon sun was on my face, the breeze flapped at my hair and I could easily agree with Owen Rhys when he said that he could get used to this lifestyle. To my mind, the Siegfried Wachters and the Klaus Hoefflers of this world had it made, while the rest of us merely tagged along, struggling in our pathetic way to make ends meet. Even more annoying, not only did they have the wherewithal to do exactly as they pleased, they also had enough *savoir-faire*, as the French say, to know how to enjoy it.

As he drove, Hoeffler became lost in his own thoughts, tapping his finger gently on the wheel, as if in accompaniment to some melody playing in his head. Then he seemed to realize my presence and said: "Let me tell you a little story, if I may, Herr Schultz. Would you do me the honour of listening?"

"Of course."

"Very good. So, once upon a time there was a certain lady, a beautiful lady, who was the widow of a mighty warrior, slain in a great war. And, when this warrior died, he left her something, perhaps some artefact, which was very valuable. Are you with me, so far?"

"Sounds like a good story," I replied, but in fact I was more than with him. I was way ahead. While he thought he was talking to a dilettante fashion writer, my brain was working like a clandestine operative, one who knew all about the lovely Lina von Osten and her deceased husband.

"Anyway, this artefact also happened to be highly prized by a powerful neighbouring state, the same state that her husband had fought against. And, even though the war had been over for several years, the neighbouring state's leader still coveted the artefact and kept trying to take it from her."

"Gets better and better," I said.

"Yes, but the problem is that we don't yet have a happy ending. That, Herr Schultz, is where you come in."

"Me?"

"If you're willing."

"Okay, let me guess. You want me to slay the fire-breathing dragon and rescue the damsel in distress?"

A minimal smile. "Nothing so daredevil, you'll be glad to hear. No, I'm not asking you to slay the dragon, just to transport the lady out of harm's way… if you can."

I nodded, as if carefully considering the request. The artefact to which he was referring was obviously the manuscript but, from his tone and his vocabulary, I guessed that he didn't yet know what it was. Lina von Osten must have kept it secret, even from him. But he did seem to know where she was, so I said: "Would it be possible to meet this mysterious damsel?"

"Certainly."

"Is that where we're going now, Herr Hoeffler? Is she at your villa?"

"Please, call me Klaus. If we're going to be on the same side, we should be friends, don't you think?"

"And my name's Erich. But you didn't answer my question."

"That's because I have one of my own. What I'd like to know is, given such a situation, how would you go about the task?"

"Of transporting the lady?"

"Yes."

"I don't know. I'd have to give it some thought, make some inquiries."

"You do understand that I have many contacts myself."

"I understand that very well. But obviously you can't use them in this instance, which is why you're asking me."

"Correct."

"But what I'd like to know is *why* you can't use them."

"Because… well, let's just say that, as a result of defending herself against her foreign enemies, the lady happened to get into a little trouble with the local authorities."

"I see. And you're telling me the situation is too sensitive for you to get personally involved."

"I'm glad you appreciate the problem, Herr Schultz. Apologies, I should call you Erich."

"And why do you think that I, of all people, might have the solution?"

"Truth be told, I'm not sure you do. I'm simply exploring the possibility, based on the amount of information I have at the present time."

"Passed along by our mutual friend, the boat owner."

He chose not to respond. Instead, he said: "How would you start? Can you at least tell me that?"

I pretended to think about it for several seconds before launching into the story that Katharina and I had already developed. "As I said, I'm not sure how much I can tell you at this stage, Herr Hoeffler… Klaus… except that my way of accomplishing such a task would probably be a little different from yours."

"Different in what way?"

"In every way. The method of transportation… the route… the destination."

"Those differences are fairly fundamental. Can you elaborate?"

"Well, I don't know…"

"Just your first thoughts."

"My first thoughts? Fine, all right. So first off, I'd have to say I'd go by air, not by sea. I'd travel through England, not Spain. And my destination would be North America, not South." I turned my head slightly to gauge his reaction and was rewarded with a definite raise of the eyebrows. "But, as I said, I can't possibly specify any further until…"

"Until you've made some inquiries, yes, I understand."

"However…"

"However?"

"I would still like to meet the lady in question… if that's possible."

My new friend, Klaus, gave a cautious nod. "We're still driving, aren't we?"

We turned north and passed through the village of Le Cannet, then threaded our way along twisty rural lanes until I lost all sense of direction. Finally, we arrived at a turn-off not much wider than the car itself, which led up a thickly treed hillside to a wrought iron gate, supported by a pair of imposing stone pillars. Two hundred metres beyond was the villa - a low-slung, modern structure of light stone - and beyond that, the hazy horizon of the Mediterranean.

"You call this small?" I asked him.

A brief smile. "Compared to some, yes."

She was waiting for us on the broad terrace when we arrived, a wraith-like figure dressed in the sunny colours of Provence: lemons, auburns and ochres that suited her complexion well and stood out against the ocean view. Her hair was the same colour of straw that I recalled from my interview and her skin still had the delicate hue of alabaster: Lina Mathilde von Osten, once known as Lina Heydrich.

"*Guten Tag, meine Frau,*" I said formally, after being introduced. She had almost no grip at all, just the limp fingers normally associated with aristocracy. "It's an honour to meet you." I genuinely didn't think she'd remember me but I was mistaken and I saw her eyes search me suspiciously.

Even before returning the greeting, her first words were: "I know you, don't I?"

Fortunately, Katharina and I had foreseen this possibility. "You have a good memory, *meine Frau*. I'm a journalist. I interviewed you at your home on the island of Fehmarn for *Der Spiegel* in 1946."

"Did you, indeed? But your name wasn't Schultz, was it?"

"Back then, many of us were living under assumed names," I replied. "An unfortunate necessity."

"I understand. And was your article flattering, I wonder? I don't think I ever saw it."

"Actually, I was freelance at the time and, well, I must admit that it was never published." That part was true and I tried to look suitably embarrassed.

A gentle smile. "In that case, I'm sure it was *far* too flattering. Most of them only wanted to crucify me."

"Today too," added Klaus.

"Yes, today too," she agreed, her tone philosophical. Then she turned back to me. "And who was the editor, did you say?"

"Of *Der Speigel*?" It was a test but, once again, I'd been expecting it. "If I'm not mistaken, that would have been Rudy Augstein. A fine editor but, with all due respect, I don't think I was one of his favourites. Why do you ask? Did you know him?"

"No, not really, Herr... I'm sorry... Schultz, is it?"

"Erich," I replied.

"Erich," she repeated, as if getting used to it. "Klaus tells me you trained with Doktor Goebbels."

I glanced from one to the other. I realized that he must have called her from the boat before we left but I was trying to figure out exactly what might have been said: whether I was to be trusted or doubted. Either way, I had no choice at this stage but to continue the act and follow the party line, much as it stuck in my throat. "Klaus is quite correct. I did indeed have the privilege of working for the good Doktor. For over two years, as a matter of fact. It was just in a junior capacity but, still, I learned a tremendous amount."

"I'm sure it must have been very exciting for you."

"I think the word I'd use would be 'inspirational,' *meine Frau*. The man was a genius, nothing less."

"A time when genius was allowed to prosper," added Klaus, ruefully.

He obviously enjoyed wallowing in his Nazi nostalgia and I took it as a sign that, so far, I was making the grade. An elderly valet arrived with a bottle of white wine, some kind of local specialty, and Klaus thanked him in accented French.

"You have a large staff here?" I asked him as the glasses were poured.

"No... but then, unfortunately, I'm not here as often as I'd like to be."

"A shame. It's incredibly beautiful. You're a lucky man, Klaus."

"Thank you. So... shall we drink to the cause?"

We all sipped our wine but I have to say it kind of stuck in my throat.

The end of the afternoon passed pleasantly enough, full of polite conversation on appropriately refined topics: wine vintages, a little art, international real estate; all subjects that Katharina had force-fed me during my training sessions. I was glad now that she'd been so thorough. Occasionally, they also threw some intriguing political references into the mix, as if they were still sizing me up: questions about German reunification, the upcoming American election, the revolution in China and, yes, about the Soviet leadership, too - in particular, who I thought might succeed Stalin. I tried to be cagey with my answers, phrasing every issue as a choice of options: if *this* happens, then *that* follows; if *that* takes place, then *this* might occur. I was cautious to a fault. I couldn't help feeling that if I were to fail in some way, things might become a little less friendly.

This villa may have been Klaus Hoeffler's vacation retreat but it was also his lair and I knew it couldn't all be as casual as it seemed. Even though I'd only met the two of them, plus one aging retainer, I thought that, with a guest like Lina von Osten, there had to be an armed guard or two somewhere on the premises. In particular, I was very conscious of the fact that her friend, Karlheinz Oehring, alias the *Kampfhund*, had yet to put in an appearance.

At around seven, I was shown to my room so I could freshen up before we all met again for dinner. Apparently, I was expected to stay and I was glad I'd taken the extra minute to grab my overnight bag from Siegfried's boat before leaving. At least I had some toiletries and a change of shirt.

As I shaved in front of the bathroom mirror, I couldn't help asking the reflection a whole series of silent questions: "What in God's name am I doing here? Why am I involved in this? Why am I putting my life at risk, a rank amateur trying to convince himself he's some kind of professional operative, able to pry dark secrets from liars and killers? Am I insane? Am I so much in love with a woman from my own past that I'm ready to risk my life like this?" But the harder I thought, the more I realized I just didn't have any answers to give myself.

The real problem was that I simply hadn't learned any lessons in life. I'd been through all this fourteen years previously. I'd been just as smitten the first time around, back in pre-war Berlin, and yet here I was again, cast in the same movie, going through the same motions, like a sucker for punishment. Back then, it ended when the SS deported me as a threat to Third Reich security, but I could have easily suffered a more drastic fate. They could have done much worse than just sent me packing. Had I gained nothing from the experience? Where was the so-called wisdom that's supposed to come with the passing years? Had it all just left me untouched, as if I wasn't even worth the effort?

As I finished getting ready, I watched the evening sun turn to burnished gold and settle over an indigo sea. I knew they weren't done probing yet, that there'd be more questions over dinner and, if I slipped, or if I drank too much and let down my guard, then I might not make it through to morning. So far there'd been no intimidation of any kind, yet the implication was there. I could feel it all around me, hanging in the sweet-scented air. This villa in the sleepy south of France was perhaps the closest thing I'd ever seen to a paradise, yet to me it was more like a holding cell.

Through the open window, I could hear various species of birds and I envied not only their freedom but the utter predictability of their lives. Eat, shit, mate, sleep, then wake up and do it all over again… what more is there to existence? Maybe that's what gives them the ability to sing.

Dinner turned out to be a grand affair, even though there was still only the three of us present. Both Klaus and Lina had changed for the occasion: he into a lightweight Italian suit in pale cinnamon, with an open white shirt and an ostentatious gold medallion around his neck; and she into a slim black dress with thin straps and deep cleavage, which teasingly revealed her delicate pink nipples as she moved. Adornment was hardly necessary but she'd chosen turquoise jewelry - matching necklace, bracelet and earrings - plus an overly generous daubing of Chanel.

We sat around a large circular dining table in a room that looked like it had been professionally designed to match the local style. The theme seemed to be "farmhouse simplicity" but the furniture was too well-polished, the decor too perfectly matched, to be authentic. We were treated royally by a staff of five to whom I was formally introduced: the same aging valet who, this evening, was acting as sommelier; a fussy, rotund woman who served as waitress; an eccentrically mustachio'd chef and his assistant, who were probably only engaged when guests were present; plus a middle-aged, no-nonsense woman acting as a kind of overseer, who I suspected was also the manager of the property when Klaus Hoeffler wasn't here. I nodded polite greetings to each of them as they were paraded in front of me. Yet still no guards or security of any kind. It was strange and I began to wonder if maybe the old retainer had some kind of weapon sheathed in his cummerbund.

The soup, when it arrived, was a clear beef consommé with goose liver. It was excellent but we hardly had time to enjoy it before Klaus opened up the conversation.

"So, Erich, perhaps you could explain to us a little more about your plan."

"My plan?"

"The escape plan we were discussing in the car."

Obviously, he'd already mentioned something to Lina about our brief discussion but I hesitated in my response, because the waitress was still in the room, busy grinding pepper and handing out bread rolls, still warm from the oven. I broke one open and chewed at the crust.

"Don't worry," he told me, "none of the staff speaks German, I assure you."

Nevertheless, I still waited until she'd gone. "Well, as I mentioned, I can't be certain of the details until I make some inquiries…"

It was Lina who replied. "Yes, yes, I understand all that." She was as impatient as he'd been. "But it would be helpful to know some of the details at least, even a little of what you're thinking."

I looked at her and, for the first time, I saw a woman with a hint of anxiety in her eyes; this in sharp contrast to her attitude of superiority on the terrace that afternoon, where she'd been more like royalty granting an audience. Now that we'd actually arrived at the key topic, however, I could see the aloof, icy manner melting in front of me. In this guise, she seemed like just another Nazi fugitive from justice, the kind I'd seen so many times before, and her evident weakness gave me the confidence to pull myself together. Sure, I was as scared as any beginner thrown in the deep end. I had a right to be. At the same time, I had to remind myself that the person I was meant to be playing, Erich Schultz, man of the world and ODESSA sympathizer, couldn't appear to be like that at all. He was supposed to be confident and influential. Even being here should be considered a favour. Such a man wouldn't be nervous; he would be on top of things, demanding what his own recompense might be.

"Forgive me, *meine Frau*," I said as politely as possible, "but I'm really not sure what I'm being asked to provide. Or, I might add, even why I should provide it."

At this, Klaus glared at me. "*Why* you should provide it?" he repeated. "Is that what you said?"

"Is it such a ridiculous question?" I asked him.

"It's not ridiculous; it's an insult!"

Up to this point, he'd been the master of ceremonies. He'd been the one in control. Suddenly, with one statement, I was challenging all that and he just had to respond, like some chivalrous knight from the fantasy story he'd told me in the car, here to defend both his honour and his lady. I decided that a measured response would be appropriate, a gesture of goodwill without actually conceding anything.

"If you think it's an insult," I began, "then I apologize for that perception. I would never insult a man in his own house. But the fact remains, I know nothing of the current circumstances or why you, Klaus, cannot get involved. All you say is that it's 'delicate' and it's 'sensitive'… but I'm afraid that's not good enough. I have as much to protect as you do, perhaps even more, considering I'm a journalist with a public reputation, so I think that before I offer up any further details, I have a right to expect answers to both my questions. I therefore repeat… What exactly am I being asked to provide? And why should I provide it?"

"I thought I'd made it clear," he replied. He wasn't going to give up his position easily.

"If you'd made it clear," I said a little more firmly, "I wouldn't be asking."

"All right, if that's what you want, I'll repeat what I said. I would like you to provide a means for Frau von Osten to exit the country. And the reason you should do it is loyalty to the cause, as simple as that. What else do you need to know?"

I deliberately put down my soup spoon, sat back in my chair and smiled, as if this were all just a minor affair to be easily dismissed. "Klaus, my friend, I really don't think I'm making myself understood. First, tell me why Frau von Osten has to get out of the country so urgently. Second, I need to know why *you* can't do it. And third…" At this point, I sat forward meaningfully and raised the timbre of my voice, adding what I hoped was a layer of the old SS arrogance. "And third, Klaus, I strongly resent the implication that I'm not loyal. If you say it, or even imply it, one more time, I walk out and you'll be very lucky if I don't break your smooth banker's face on the way."

He was already half-way to his feet with outrage but Lina reached out to his arm and held him back.

"Boys, boys..." she said. "Please."

"Did you hear what he said?" Klaus asked her, his face flushed. "Did you hear?"

"Yes, I heard. But to be honest, my dear Klaus, you deserved it."

"*What!*"

"And I believe our friend's questions do have some validity."

"Lina..."

"Now, now, Klaus, let me handle it, all right? Please calm down and finish your soup while I try to explain."

I still maintained the glower I'd assumed but, inside, all I could feel was relief that I'd read her mood correctly. She badly wanted passage away from here and she wasn't going to let Klaus Hoeffler's pompous ego stand in the way of that.

"I'm listening," I said to her quietly.

"Do you recall an incident in Paris a few weeks ago? It made some news. There was some shooting..."

"Of course, on the *Rive Gauche*. All France knows about that."

"That was me. Or should I say, that was the Russians trying to get me."

I managed to feign astonishment. "The Russians? Why?"

I could see that Klaus was becoming increasingly agitated at her giving out all this information but she didn't care about his objections. She was the one in charge now.

"They think I have something they want," she replied.

"The artefact?" I asked her. When she looked bemused, I added: "Klaus mentioned something about it on the way here."

"Ah, I see," she replied hesitantly. "Yes... an artefact. You could call it that. The Russians came after it and my friends... *our* friends... protected me."

"Did they get it? This artefact, whatever it is?"

"No, they didn't."

"So they didn't get it and you obviously escaped. Congratulations on your victory."

She smiled at the compliment. "Don't you want to know what it is, this thing that I'm guarding so carefully?"

"Only if you care to tell me."

Another smile, this time far more enigmatic. "No, I don't. But thank you for not asking."

"You're welcome."

"So you understand now why I want to leave?"

"Yes, very clearly."

"And do you also understand why Klaus here can't help me?"

I glanced at him. "I imagine because he has considerable assets in France and would feel exposed."

"Something like that. And does money interest you, too, Erich? Must I bribe you to help me?"

She was baiting me but I just couldn't resist another dig at Klaus.

"I'm no banker but money always interests me, *meine Frau*." I saw her give the slightest of smiles. "But let me reassure you that's not the only reason... and certainly not the most important one."

"And what *is* the most important one, would you say?"

"I'll use exactly the same word as Klaus," I replied. "Loyalty."

She nodded proudly, like a schoolteacher when a prize student has given the correct answer. "You see, Klaus? Loyalty. Isn't that what you wanted to hear?"

By this time, Klaus Hoeffler had just about resigned himself to his secondary status. He wasn't happy about it but nor did he want to go against her wishes. "Yes, loyalty," he agreed begrudgingly. But he couldn't help a final dig of his own: "Plus the money, of course."

We were going round in circles, like amateur boxers in a make-shift ring: each taunting and threatening the other but neither willing to land a true blow. It was ludicrous.

"Yes, well, I'm sure you gentlemen can work out all those little details later. Good, so now we've got all that settled... We do, don't we, Erich?"

"For the moment."

"Good, so let's return to the main issue. How can you help?"

It was at that point that the serving staff re-emerged with the main course, *cochon-de-lait rôti*: roast suckling pig, glazed in caramelized apple sauce, stuffed and garnished with local herbs and surrounded by fresh seasonal vegetables. It was all served on one giant platter that took both the chef and his assistant to carry in.

"*Magnifique!*" I applauded. "*Un vrai chef d'oeuvre!*" (A true masterpiece.)

"*Merci bien, m'sieur,*" replied the chef, beaming. "*Bon appetit!*"

Once we'd been served and the staff had disappeared, Klaus looked at me. "I didn't know you spoke French."

"Just a little," I replied. "I spent some time in Canada growing up."

It was all part of my "Erich Schultz" background cover, all carefully worked out by Katharina. "Don't blurt out your life story," she kept telling me, "but have it ready just in case, just enough to answer a probe. And even then, not too much. It should sound easy and natural, like second nature." She really was very good at her job. And, like a good student, I decided to change the subject.

"So, where were we?" I asked them.

It was Lina who answered. "You were about to offer some practical details..."

"Ah, yes, details, right. I presume that funds are no problem?" I looked at Klaus.

"No," he said, still not too happy. "No problem."

"Good, so, what I'd suggest is that we rent an aircraft and fly it out of some small, local airfield. Perhaps Nice, I don't know yet. We board and fly out at night, all very quiet."

"What kind of aircraft?" asked Klaus.

I shrugged. "Large enough to be impressive, small enough to be flexible. I'm no expert but I'd have to say something like a DC3 might be suitable. There are hundreds still around. Finding one should present no great problem."

Lina again: "And once we're airborne in our rented DC3? What then?"

"We head north. I'd prefer England but Ireland might be another option."

"Why England?"

"Very simple. Because I've got connections there."

"What kind of connections?" demanded Klaus.

"Good ones," I replied. It was my way of throwing his attitude right back at him.

"How about customs and immigration?" This was Lina again.

I looked over at her. "Do you have documentation?"

"That's being arranged."

"I see." I knew she meant forgery, no doubt under "Helga Kreiss" or some other name. "German or Swiss?"

"Swiss."

"How good will it be?"

"Enough to get us through."

"Us? You mean the two of you?"

"No... not Klaus. There'll be..." A hesitation. "There'll be someone else with me."

I understood she was talking about Karlheinz Oehring but I wasn't supposed to know, so I didn't push any further. "Fine," I replied airily. "If your documentation checks out, no problem. But we don't want to take unnecessary risks, so I suggest we land at Croydon, not Heathrow."

"Croydon?"

"A small airdrome in south London. I happen to know people there." This sounded impressive but, of course, it was an outright lie. I figured that, if it ever came to it, Katharina could access Pender's crew at Special Branch and they could arrange pretty much anything.

"And after that?"

"After that, you'll lie low for a while. Some nice, exclusive hotel with a discrete staff. You won't stay long, just a few days, just enough to make arrangements for the next leg of the journey."

"Which is what?"

"A flight to New York."

"Will we rent a plane for that too?"

"No, I don't think so. For that leg, you should travel commercial, from Heathrow to Idlewild via Shannon and Gander, as usual. You'll travel first class on a major airline, say Pan-Am or BOAC, because that raises less suspicion."

"And how will we get into the US without a visa? You have connections there too?"

"No, but we won't need any. We'll change your passports in England, turn you into British citizens. The US won't give you any trouble."

She gazed at me thoughtfully. "I don't know how I'd feel about being British."

"Don't worry, I'll teach you how to sing 'God Save The Queen,'" I told her, to which she smiled. I was starting to think she'd taken something of a shine to me - and maybe that was the real reason that my new pal, Klaus, was looking so downcast.

"One last question," she said, "and it's not insignificant."

"Please…"

"Why would you possibly think I'd want to live in New York?"

"Why wouldn't you? It's full of people of all nationalities… Italian, Greek, Irish… Many Germans, too. I venture to say you'd blend right in."

"And how about the Jews and the Coloureds?" said Klaus. "Would she blend right in with them, too?"

He really was a miserable son-of-a-bitch but I managed to restrain myself. "I didn't say she'd have to stay there forever. The beauty of it is that, with British citizenship and an American visa, Frau von Osten would have the credentials to go just about anywhere her heart desires… any state in the US, any country in the Commonwealth… especially if she also has a few dollars to spread around, which I'm sure you'll be able to arrange, Klaus." I turned to Lina. "Actually, I live in New York myself right now," I lied, "and, well, if you want the truth, I think you'd enjoy it, at least for a while. Theatre, shopping, restaurants…"

"You make it sound wonderful," she said, a little more motivated. "Would you show me around?"

"I'd be honoured," I replied. Over on the other side, I could almost hear Klaus Hoeffler grinding his perfect white teeth but I had no idea why that should please me so much. I disliked them both in equal measure. "However, *meine Frau*, I must caution you against too much optimism. First I must make…"

"Some inquiries," said Klaus, completing the phrase. "Caution, caution, caution... that's all you know. You sound like a broken record. For once, be bold, for God's sake. Frau von Osten needs answers, not more questions."

I pushed back my chair. "I'm sorry to cause you so much suffering, Klaus. If you like, I'll call a taxi and…"

"No!" said Lina sharply. "No need to rush away."

"I don't want to stay where I'm not welcome."

"You're perfectly welcome. Isn't he, Klaus? Tell him."

I think Klaus Hoeffler was really beginning to despise me but too bad for him. I wasn't there to win any popularity contests: not with him, anyway. I was just trying to be the kind of "alpha male" that was once so admired in Nazi society. The more I challenged him, the more I was succeeding.

"A guest is a guest," he muttered, backing down. Then he forced a laugh, as if attempting to play the big man and shrug off the whole thing. "I suppose I should try to remember, we're both on the same side."

"There's a lot of pressure on all of us," I told him. It was my own way of making peace.

Nevertheless, I have to say that remaining there for the *crème brulée* was a strain and I was more than glad to be rid of them when we finally turned in for the night. At least I'd be able to have a few hours to myself - or so I thought.

The attack began in the early hours of the morning.

They weren't trying to be quiet and the sound of guttural voices, followed by heavy boots on the stairs, woke me from a deep sleep. I found it difficult to orient myself: not just what was happening but also where I was and who the hell I was meant to be.

No sooner had I sat up than the figure burst into my room. It was too dark to see his face but the weapon in his hands sure looked like a Kalashnikov AK-47 to me: the standard Soviet automatic with that distinctive curved magazine. What was confusing was the fact that he was not yelling at me in Russian, as I might have expected, but in German: "*Raus! Raus!*" he was screaming. (Out! Out!) And, once more, ugly memories of the Third Reich came flooding back. That was how the brown-shirted thugs with the swastika armbands used to roust a building.

I felt the butt of his gun hard on my shoulder and figured I'd better do as I was told. He half-pushed, half-herded me out onto the second floor landing where the lights were already on. The sudden illumination hurt my eyes.

"What is this?" I demanded as I was marched downstairs. I received another blow across the back for my trouble.

He indicated the dining room, where I'd just spent the entire evening. Klaus Hoeffler and Lina von Osten were already there, sitting in their nightwear: Klaus in his slightly silly pajamas of purple silk, with a large discolouration on his left cheekbone; and Lina wearing a flimsier version of the lace negligee she'd worn in Paris, this time in flamingo pink. One of those small, pale breasts was now totally exposed but there was nothing she could do about it. Like Klaus, she had her arms tied behind her with electrical wire and her mouth tightly gagged with a strip of towelling. I, too, was forced down on to a chair and likewise restrained. Around us were three men, dressed in gray fatigues with no markings and all well-armed with the same Soviet-made weapons.

Then came firing from somewhere else in the house: several rapid bursts into the night. There were muffled cries of pain but, after that, there was silence again and I knew, without being told, that the household staff had been the targets. Were they all dead? I didn't know but when a fourth man entered the dining room and gave a nod to his colleagues, I had a pretty good idea. He stood at ease, like the others, with no expression. The weapon was slung loosely over his shoulders and there was a spray of blood across his chest. For him, the murder of total innocents was all just part of the job.

The seconds ticked by as if we were waiting for something - or someone. Meanwhile, the wire bit into my wrists and the rag they'd tied around my mouth smelled of kerosene. I could hardly breathe. Across the table, the other two seemed very afraid. Although Klaus was trying to hide it, he wasn't very convincing.

Finally, a short, chubby man entered, older and slower than the others. He was wearing a baggy, double-breasted suit with a brimmed hat pulled low over his forehead and he stood looking at us, from one to the other, through a pair of steel-rimmed glasses. I recognized his round face immediately.

This was Lavrenti Beria himself.

Needless to say, I was astonished to see the Soviet Minister for Internal Affairs here in France, personally supervising a project like this, and I knew it represented an ominous development. If the three of us had seen him, how could we be allowed to survive? It also seemed strange that he'd be leading a platoon of German-speakers and my brain couldn't seem to work it out. Then, in a flash, something clicked and it all became abundantly obvious. These men were "Stasi" - agents of the MfS, the East German security service. I had no idea why Beria couldn't find a Soviet team to do his dirty work but here they were and they'd already accomplished more than the MGB *spetznaz* in either Fehmarn or Paris. They'd managed to capture the SS queen-consort herself, Lina von Osten.

Beria spoke to the most senior of the armed Germans, an unshaven heavyweight he called Dieter, and gave him a quiet order in Russian which the man evidently understood. In response, Dieter then walked around and unfastened the gag from Lina von Osten's mouth.

She said nothing, even when it was removed.

Next came Klaus Hoeffler, who made the mistake of immediately spewing out a stream of blasphemy, calling the invaders Stalinist pigs, traitors to Germany and any other abuse he could come up with. It was very un-banker-like but I think his sense of panic just got the better of him, as well as the ongoing need to prove himself to his lady.

Dieter was not a man with a high degree of tolerance and he was becoming especially irate at the taunts of "traitor." At one point, he took a side arm out of his holster and waved it at Klaus in order to shut him up but that only made it worse.

Klaus spat at him and just continued his tirade, finishing up with his own version of "Long live the Führer!"

That's when Dieter's face turned crimson. Without bothering to ask Beria for permission, he forced the gun muzzle into his prisoner's mouth and fired. The back of Klaus Hoeffler's head blew out like an exploding melon, with pieces of brain and bone scattered all over the wall behind him. It was disgusting, sickening, nauseating, and I almost choked on my gag.

I thought Lina might have also reacted in some way but, surprisingly, she didn't. She just sat there, staring like a zombie, tense but still silent.

I could see that the other Stasi in the room were also shocked by the unexpected carnage but it was Beria who was the most upset. He'd had his authority challenged and he spent some time arguing loudly with Dieter in Russian, before he finally calmed himself down and made an uneasy peace. They still had a job to do, despite the mess.

However, it was at that stage that Beria began paying more attention to me. "Who's that one?" he said in Russian, pointing at me. His question was aimed at Lina von Osten but it was Dieter who translated back and forth.

"Nobody," she replied. "Just a dinner guest. An American journalist."

"A journalist?"

"He was here for an interview with Klaus."

"What's his name?"

She glanced at me but it was only a minor hesitation. She had no scruples about giving me up. "Schultz... Erich Schultz. He's from New York."

This information was duly relayed back to Beria, who looked at me for what seemed like a long time. I couldn't tell what he was thinking, or what he intended to do. I don't think he'd expected me to be there and he now had to decide whether to kill me or not. On the one hand, I'd seen him and could identify him. On the other, I was a journalist, which meant that, sooner or later, people would miss me and come looking for me and he didn't need that kind of attention, especially from the American press. For the moment, he chose to do nothing and I was able to breathe a sigh. Whether it was a full reprieve or whether my death sentence was just being held in abeyance, I had no way of knowing. At any rate, he left me bound and gagged, ignoring me while he turned his attention back to the woman. There was nothing I could do anyway.

Beria pulled up another chair, removed his hat, unfastened his jacket and sat himself down comfortably. Then he hauled out a big cigar with some matches, bit off the tip and took his own time lighting up while everyone else waited. Once he was ready, the interrogation began. As before, Beria would first ask each question in Russian, then Dieter would translate into his crude East Berlin dialect of German.

"Where is it?"

Lina gave no response.

"I'll say it again. Where is it?"

"I don't know what you mean."

A gentle smile from Beria. "You know, you're a nice-looking woman for a Nazi. Now, I'll ask you one last time. Where is it?"

"I told you already. I don't know what you mean."

Beria looked at his cigar as if considering what to do next. Then, without warning, and still with that damn half-smile on his face, he leaned forward and pushed the glowing tip into Lina's exposed breast, holding it there for a full second before removing it.

The shriek from her throat pierced the atmosphere with its intensity.

She made a conscious effort to stop but she was shaking and I could see tears of pain flooding her eyes. In my time, I've been around both injury and death but I'll never forget the pitch of that scream. On her white skin, there was now a scorched circle, blackened and inflamed. She tried to show courage but couldn't help shaking from the sheer shock.

Beria just sat back, once again puffing on the cigar. "There are more sensitive areas," he said, and this too was translated. Then he whispered something to Dieter, taking the time to explain what he wanted.

Dieter gave him a questioning look but chose to follow orders. First he untied Lina, then he forced her face down over the table, his palm firmly in her back. When she tried to struggle, he pushed her down even harder, causing her to cry out yet again. Then he lifted her pretty pink negligee, so it was up around her waist and the soft white skin of her buttocks was completely revealed. Finally, he kicked her legs apart.

Beria remained seated, still taking his time. "This is called the flower arrangement," he explained but, even after it was translated, nobody knew what he was talking about. Nobody knew of his little pedophilia game back in Moscow. It was his own private joke. Then he took another puff of his cigar, causing the ash to glow red hot. "Now, shall we start again?" he said.

It was at that exact moment that the quiet tension exploded, as a large figure came crashing through the dining room window like an avenging anti-Christ, machine gun blazing as he leapt through the air and landed squarely on the dining room table. The noise was shattering. Swinging his weapon around in a full three-sixty, he opened up on anyone standing, a deadly spray of lead that hit plaster, glass and human flesh alike; the blood across the walls adding to the previous Hoeffler carnage.

The men of the Stasi team had been standing at ease during Beria's questioning, so they were ill-prepared to cope with such an indiscriminate assault and three of them fell quickly. The fourth, Dieter, let go of Lina and managed to raise his handgun but his aim was too fast and all he managed to do was slash the muscular part of this new intruder's thigh. However, it was enough for his leg to buckle under him and he fell to the floor with a heavy thud.

Dieter used the opportunity to tend to his charge, Lavrenti Beria, who'd taken cover by crouching on all fours while the fight raged on above his head. Dieter hauled Beria up by the arm and urged him towards the doorway as best he could in an effort to get him out of there as quickly as possible.

But the intruder wasn't done yet. He couldn't get up but he could still fire and he let go another wild round towards the door. He was too late. Within seconds came the sound of an engine starting up, followed by the squeal of tires. The Stasi agent and his Soviet master were gone.

It was hard for me to believe I'd emerged unscathed. Despite all the random firing, I hadn't been hit, not even once. I looked over at our rescuer lying on the ground. His thigh was oozing blood and he couldn't move easily but he didn't seem too badly hurt because he was grinning back at me, almost panting with his own sense of satisfaction: Karlheinz Oehring, the attack dog.

Lina von Osten also managed to escape the fusillade. In her case, it was by ducking under the table. Nevertheless, she was in bad shape, both from the pain and the trauma of what had happened a minute earlier. Eventually, she managed to stagger her way over, remove that disgusting gag from my mouth and undo the wire that was binding my wrists. I began to reassure her, telling her I'd call for help, but I must confess that I thought seriously about deserting the scene. It would have been easy. Neither she nor Karlheinz were in a position to stop me.

But in the end, I didn't do that. I stayed, continuing the Erich

Schultz masquerade. I'm not exactly sure why. No doubt it was due to some subconscious sense of duty: not to the job or to the mission, but to Katharina. It was what she would have expected of me. So, while Lina von Osten got busy fashioning the white linen tablecloth into a makeshift tourniquet for Oehring's thigh wound, I went off to find the phone in Hoeffler's private study.

I asked the operator to put me through to an unlisted number in Cannes. It was Katharina herself who answered the phone. She'd set up a safe house in the town so she could remain close.

"What happened?" she asked me in German, no doubt mindful of any French telephone operators who might have chosen to listen in.

"We had a visit," I replied. "You won't believe it. This was Beria himself."

"No names."

"So how am I supposed to tell you?"

"Are you sure it was him?"

"Of course, I'm sure. With a gang of Stasi."

"It's an open line."

"Nobody can understand us."

"Nevertheless, you must follow…"

"Protocol, yeah I know. Would you prefer I send you a letter? It was a bloodbath. Three of the bastards are dead. So is our fine host. All his staff, too, I think."

"Are you all right?"

"It was touch and go for a while but the *Kampfhund* arrived late and saved us. He's wounded and so is the woman. What do I do?"

"Can they move?"

"Just about. They both need medical attention."

"Okay, I'll arrange it. But you must get out of there. You have transport?"

"Yeah."

"In that case, best thing is to bring them here. Drive around the back. There's a small alley, turn off your lights. Make sure nobody sees you. How about the objective?"

"No idea," I replied. "They tortured her but she wouldn't give it up. Crazy, if you ask me."

"Okay, enough talk. You should leave now. I'm... I'm glad you're all right."

She hung up but I was already feeling a whole lot better: not just because she was close by, but also because she was glad I was all right. She'd taken the time to say so.

I struggled to get them both into Hoeffler's big Mercedes. It wasn't easy. Oehring must have weighed two-thirty, maybe more. Then, at his insistence, I went back to gather up as many of Lina's things as I could carry. He didn't want to leave any evidence. That gave me the opportunity to flip through the various items to see if I could find anything that looked remotely like a manuscript but there was nothing at all. Had she hidden it on the premises? Inside a wall, perhaps, or under a floorboard? Or maybe buried somewhere in the grounds? There was no way to tell and I couldn't stick around to find out.

Once I was done packing everything into the car, I had to go back into the house yet again and search around for the damn ignition keys, which I'd forgotten. I cursed myself for being such an amateur. Eventually, I found them on a hook in the hallway and found my way back, just about exhausted from the effort. I wasn't really wounded but my wrists were chafed raw from the wire and I was reeling from everything I'd witnessed: a man with his brains blown out; a woman savagely tortured; several others cut down in a hail of fire, with enough blood and guts around the room to fill a sink. Not exactly my usual night out.

"Where are we going?" Oehring demanded.

I was still catching my breath in the driver's seat and they were both behind me in the back. When I turned, I saw that his grin had disappeared. The attack dog was now barking at me.

"Cannes," I replied.

"Where in Cannes?"

"To a friend of mine."

"What kind of a friend? What's his name?"

"Not male, female. And you don't need to know her name."

"How do I know we can trust her?"

I had no time for his suspicions, so I swivelled around and said: "If you like, you can stay here and wait for the police to show up. That's if you don't bleed to death first. Up to you."

He didn't seem too convinced but then Lina touched his arm, just like she'd done with Klaus Hoeffler earlier in the evening.

"It's all right, Karlheinz," she said gently, and it seemed to quell his anxiety.

I turned the key and the big engine came obediently to life, a comforting sound. I was hoping I'd be able to find my way to Cannes. It wasn't far but the narrow lanes were dark and confusing. After a few minutes, we came to a T-junction and I was thankful to see a signpost pointing the way: Le Cannet one direction, Cannes the other. Now all I had to do was stay alert long enough to get us there.

"What were they looking for?" I asked Lina, over my shoulder. "I mean, what exactly?" I was still Erich Schultz, still playing my role, so it was a natural question.

It was Oehring who took it upon himself to answer. "None of your business," he said gruffly.

"I need to know," I insisted.

That's when Lina cut in. "It's a... document."

I glanced at her in the mirror. "Valuable?"

"In a way."

"But they didn't find it."

"No, they didn't. That's because I don't have it."

"So where is it?" I hated sounding like the Stasi but it couldn't be helped. "I need to know where they'll strike next," I lied. "I need to be prepared. Is it in Hoeffler's house?"

"No."

"His bank?"

"No."

"Did you destroy it?"

She managed a smile, despite everything. "If you must know, you're too late," she said. "You and the Russians and the Americans...

you're all too late."

"What's that supposed to mean?"

"It's up for auction, highest bidder wins. You want it, Erich? How badly? Just name your price."

I looked in the mirror again and saw her laughing openly: no doubt a hysterical reaction to what she'd suffered, more than any genuine humour. She must have still been in severe pain from the untreated burn.

"Look," I said, "all I'm asking…"

"Don't ask anything," said Oehring, with more menace in his voice. "Just drive."

I did as I was told. A dog is even more dangerous when wounded. The conversation seemed to be over anyway and I thought it better not to force it for the time being.

I managed to find the way to Cannes all right but it took me several circuits of the deserted streets before I found the small apartment building and then another few minutes to negotiate the big car around the back without lights. The alley was both dark and narrow, and I really couldn't see much at all. I was afraid of crashing a fence, or worse, the garbage cans, which would probably wake the entire neighbourhood. By the time I switched off the engine, Oehring was unconscious. Despite the tourniquet, he'd lost a lot of blood and, when I opened the rear door to try and help him out, I could feel a sticky pool on the leather seat. There was no way I could manage alone in that state, so I made a quick decision.

"Come on," I said to Lina.

"We can't just leave him."

"He'll survive here until help arrives. Let's just get you inside, okay?"

She was reluctant but she had no choice, leaning on me as I helped her out. We entered through a rear door and found our way slowly up two flights of stone stairs, guided by a single, dim light bulb. This was not exactly Hoeffler style. I didn't know who was living in the building but no doors opened and nobody peered out; obviously, the kind of place where people kept to themselves, which was just as well for us.

Katharina was waiting on the top floor landing, a Uzi subma-chine pistol cradled in her arms, same kind the Gehlen squad used at Fehmarn. It was a precaution on her part but when she saw who was with me, just a pale woman, injured and traumatized, she placed it down inside the door and reached to give me a hand. I was glad to see her, more than glad, but we kept it very straight, merely a nod of greeting. She was dressed in old clothes: a faded khaki shirt and a pair of cotton work pants, suitable for both the climate and the neighbourhood - no makeup, no jewelry and with her hair tied up at the back. I'd never seen her like that but it suited her. Actually, anything suited her.

"You?" said Lina von Osten, the moment she set eyes on Katharina.

"Yes, me," replied Katharina bluntly. "You have a problem with that?"

Lina paused for a second, then a faint shake of the head.

I knew they'd met before, through Gehlen, but I didn't know if there'd be any recognition. It seemed as if Lina von Osten had a good memory for faces: first me, then Katharina. It was a valuable asset for someone on the run. She was still leaning on me as I helped her into the spartan apartment and sat her down in an old armchair.

"A doctor will be here soon," said Katharina, gently easing Lina's nightwear aside to inspect the damage to her breast. "Don't worry, he's one of us. How did they do this?"

"Beria's cigar," I replied.

"My God."

There were now concentric shades of yellow, red and purple spreading across much of Lina's chest. She'd be lucky if it wasn't infected. While Katharina went to the kitchen to find some first aid, I used the opportunity to press my case for the manuscript. Not nice, I guess, to do that to someone in her condition but I wasn't required to be nice: not to her and not to her attack dog. In the end, they were nothing more than unrepentant Nazis, still at war with the Soviets and still at war with the West too.

Was she beginning to suspect that I wasn't who I made myself out to be? I neither knew nor cared.

I knelt down next to her, so I could talk quietly. "I really do need to know about the document," I said but she just shook her head, an outright refusal. "All right," I continued, "let me spell it out, shall I? Klaus is dead and Karlheinz is half-dead, so I'm all you've got left."

"Reinhard," she whispered.

To her, "Reinhard" was a familiar name which sprang easily to her lips; but whether she was talking about Reinhard Gehlen or just indulging in nostalgia for her dead husband, Reinhard Heydrich, I wasn't entirely certain.

"Nobody's coming," I told her. "Not Reinhard, nor anybody else, which makes it very simple. You either trust me or you don't. If you do, I can get medical help for Karlheinz and I can get you out of here. If you don't, then Karlheinz dies down there on the street and you're in a French jail for the rest of your life."

Needless to say, it was no more than an empty threat. I didn't really think Oehring was in mortal danger from his wound - the man was indestructible - and nor did I know anything about how the French justice system might treat her. It didn't matter. My words had the desired effect and, for an instant, she looked at me as if I'd disappointed her. It was a brief flash of the previous Lina, the arrogant Lina, the SS queen-consort. But then, nothing happened. Instead of speaking, she just leaned her head back and closed her eyes. I touched her arm slightly but it was no use. She was still alive but the trauma had finally set in and her nervous system had simply shut down. I was none the wiser about anything.

I climbed wearily to my feet just as Katharina was returning with her hands full: a bowl of hot water and a small medical kit. And that's when it hit me from out of nowhere. I realized exactly who had the manuscript. Why it had taken so long to register, I don't know. Maybe I was too tired, or maybe the night's drama had frozen my brain, but I was being played for a fool and I wasn't happy about it.

"I need your car," I said to Katharina. I couldn't use the big Merc with Oehring still in it and I knew she'd rented a vehicle when she arrived. "Where are the keys?"

"Why?"

"Katharina, please… Where are the keys?"

"In that drawer."

She indicated an old, scratched cupboard unit near the door. Next to it, still standing upright in the corner, was the Uzi she'd brandished when we arrived and I briefly considered grabbing it along with the keys. For a moment I hesitated, but I felt bad depriving her of her only means of protection, so I left it there. With hindsight, it was a serious error.

"Where are you going?" she called after me.

"To an auction," I replied.

It was just as I emerged from the building that medical help arrived: a young doctor of North African descent with a very earnest demeanour. I quickly explained the situation, speaking my basic French. I hoped he'd understand: "Man in the car around the back, gunshot wound. Woman upstairs, second floor apartment, bad burn."

He mumbled his acknowledgment and carried his bag immediately towards the alley where I'd indicated. To be honest, I was starting to feel a smidgen of guilt about having just left Oehring there alone. After all, the man had saved my life. Without his crazy intervention, I'm sure I'd have suffered the same fate as Klaus Hoeffler, with the Stasi splattering my brains across the dining room wall.

I couldn't afford the time to think about it. I was still searching for the black Renault that Katharina had rented. Eventually, I found it parked out front but it was hardly in the same class as the Mercedes. It started all right but the engine sounded rough, the shift was stubborn and the shocks felt like they were worn. At least the route was easy to find. All I had to do was hit the shore road and turn left towards the faint hint of dawn in the eastern sky.

For once, I was in luck. The yacht "Guinevere" was still at her moorings in Monte Carlo harbour, just as she'd been twelve hours previously. I'd half-expected her to be underway by now, carrying my friend Siegfried to whatever port-of-call he planned to visit next: Naples, Athens, Cairo... the entire Mediterranean was his playground.

This morning, however, I was in no mood for play. I left the car on the quay and went storming up the gangplank, only to be met at the top by a burly Greek deck hand.

"I need to speak to Mr. Wachter," I told him.

"He asleep," said the man in broken English.

"It's urgent."

"You come back later."

I tried to go past him but he stood his ground, effectively barring my way. He had forty pounds and several inches on me and I had neither the strength nor the energy to barge my way through. "Now look…"

"No trouble, okay?"

"You don't understand. I was a guest here yesterday and I need to speak to him again."

He poked his finger in my chest. "No, is you no understand. I say come back later, you come back later."

I'd had enough of this. "Siegfried!" I called out at the top of my lungs. One way or another, I was going to get through. "Hey, Siegfried! Get your ass out here!" To hell with being fancy Erich Schultz from *Vogue* magazine, I was now back to being good ol' Ed Schaeffer from the Ontario sticks.

"You shut up!" said the deck hand, pushing me so hard in the stomach that I nearly lost my footing.

I backed off a few paces down the walkway so the man couldn't reach me as easily. "Siegfried!" I yelled again.

I saw a light flick on inside the boat. Then a door opened. His bald head emerged first, reflecting the shipboard lights, then came the rest of him, dressed in pajamas and bathrobe with his hands in his pockets. "All right, dear boy. No need for all this fuss. I'm awake now."

He said something to his man, who moved away sullenly. Then, to me, he said: "Well, you may as well come aboard. Anything to stop that infernal racket. What's wrong with you, anyway? You're normally more civilized than this."

"I don't feel very civilized tonight, Siegfried."

"It's morning, dear boy, nearly five o-clock. Want some coffee, since I'm already up?"

In fact, coffee sounded like an excellent idea, so I put my anger on hold for the time being and accepted his offer. We went inside and planted ourselves in his handsome stateroom, while he called to someone beyond named Dimitri to organize some breakfast. Plush carpet, mahogany, leather chairs: we were surrounded by Siegfried's impeccable taste in luxury.

"Now," he said, "why don't you tell me what on earth you're so upset about."

By that time, some of the fury had gone out of me, which was probably just as well. I needed to think logically. "When did she sell it to you?" I asked him.

"When did who sell what to whom?" He was being annoyingly nonchalant.

"Come on, this is me, okay? I just want to know when you got your hands on that manuscript. Recently... or before all this began?"

"Ed, I really don't know why you might think..."

"Siegfried," I interjected, "I saw a lot of bad things tonight and I only just escaped myself. Now, are you going to answer me or do I have to call out the guard... and, in case you're wondering, I'm talking about the CIA, MI5 and maybe even Gehlen himself. I haven't decided yet."

He just smiled and got to his feet. "Just going to see about breakfast."

He could have been buying himself some time or even going to talk to someone, I didn't know which. At any rate, I didn't say anything, I just waited. A couple of minutes later, he returned, leading a thin crewman with a large tray, as promised.

"Thank you, Dimitri," he said, "just leave it here if you will." Then he sat down and began to organize the food like a mother taking care of her family: coffee, croissants, yogurt and fruit.

Eventually, I couldn't wait any longer: "Are you going to answer me?"

"First things first," he replied softly. "Do you know why we maintain civilization? I'll tell you. Because it's our prime duty to do so. If not us, who? If not now, when?"

I knew Siegfried of old. When he was in this mood, he could be very deceptive and I was determined not to be side-tracked. Maybe direct accusations would be better, after all. "I know you've got the manuscript, Sieg, so either you tell me now…"

"Or what? You'll carry out your threat? You know, I think you've forgotten who got you into this in the first place."

"You. And you've been lying to me from the get-go."

"Not true. In Barcelona, I told you I'm just in it for the profit and nothing's changed as far as that's concerned."

"All right, granted." I was prepared to be magnanimous up to a point. "But you've lied about everything else."

"Only by omission."

"Lies are lies. And tonight they nearly killed me."

There was a long pause until he sat forward in his chair. "How do you like your coffee? Black or with milk?"

The word "black" reminded me of Hoeffler's verbal segue into the subject of the SS. It was just the previous day but it seemed like an age ago. Now, just the thought of his head being blown apart in front of me made me feel sick to my stomach. I swallowed some of the hot liquid just to keep down the vomit.

"All right," I said, "let's try something else. What *is* the manuscript?

"What *is* it?"

"Yes, what kind of a manuscript is it? What's it all about?"

"Nobody told you? Not the CIA or MI5? Not Gehlen? Not even your lovely Katharina?"

I was offended that he'd bring her into this, although I don't know why. She was my case officer. "No," I replied emphatically but, even as I said it, I was beginning to wonder. Why *hadn't* they told me? Was I so far down the line that I didn't need to know?

"Eddie, Eddie, Eddie… What are we going to do with you? You really should stick to journalism, you know. You're just not a very good secret agent."

I'd had enough. "Is that right?" I replied. "Well, look around,

Siegfried. Who else do you see here? I'm the only one who's managed to put two and two together. That's not bad for a beginner. And, since we're talking of lies, I also recall you saying you'd cut me in on the deal. What happened to that?"

A gentle smile of admission. "Yes…" he said slowly, letting the word play itself out. "I did say that, didn't I?"

"As a matter of fact, that's what led me back to you… when our mutual friend Lina started mumbling something about an auction. It took me a while, what with one thing and another, but eventually I worked it out."

"Clever you."

"Yes, well, maybe not so clever, because I still don't know what's in the damn thing. But you're about to fill me in, aren't you?" I decided to repeat it, just to make my point. "Aren't you, Siegfried?"

There was a silence as he finished the last remnants of a croissant and sat back thoughtfully with his cup in his hand. Then he said: "Oh, very well." It was like he was indulging a curious child. "Tell me, have you ever heard of something called *The Protocols of the Elders of Zion?*"

"Sure. Is that what the manuscript is?"

"Actually, it's the original. The hand-written first draft."

I knew the tract to which he was referring. It was supposedly a Jewish plot to take over the world, as written by a secret cadre of rabbis. Time and again, experts with impressive credentials had furnished convincing proof that it was a forgery, yet all manner of tyrants continued to use it as anti-Semitic propaganda to further their own ends.

I asked him: "Why are the Russians after it?"

"Because they're the ones who created it in the first place."

"They did?"

"A brief history lesson," he said in that smug way of his. "During the latter half of the nineteenth century, the Tsarist regime became more and more worried about revolutionary stirrings… and, since many Jewish intellectuals were involved with that kind of progressive socialism, a few of the Tsar's advisers came up with the idea of blaming the whole thing on the Jews. That's why the pogroms began at that time, sending so many Jewish refugees to the West. That was the start of it. The violence was often made to look like outpourings from local populations but they were encouraged, organized and often paid for by the Okhranka."

"Okhranka?"

"The Tsar's secret police. Not very nice people, as you can imagine. At the time, the head of the Okhranka was a man called Rachkovsky and he was the one who decided to take it all one stage further. Seems he'd heard of some earlier nonsense by a French citizen called Maurice Joly entitled *The Dialogues in Hell*, so he sent his own man down to Paris to meet with Joly's son, Charles, who happened to be a writer with *Le Figaro*. Anyway, to cut a long story short, the two of them sat down together, extracted many aspects of *The Dialogues*, some of it almost verbatim by the way, and the result was the first handwritten draft of the *Protocols* manuscript. It even has some of Rachkovsky's notations in the margins."

"It was the Okhranka who first published it?"

"That's right. First in a St. Petersburg newspaper in 1902, then on a wider scale in 1905. But it was only around the time of the 1917 revolution that factions still loyal to the Tsar began to promote it worldwide. They said the prophecy it contained was coming true and that the Bolshevik revolution was the work of what they called the 'international Jewish conspiracy.'"

"That's exactly what Hitler was saying in 1924."

"Correct, but not just Hitler."

"Sure, Mussolini too, I know."

"Not just him either. *The Protocols* also became a bestseller in dear little England, can you believe that? And in the States, Henry Ford himself sponsored half a million copies... he was a well-known anti-Semite, you know. The Vatican also knew about it, as did the Arabs, who latched on to it as a way to counter the spread of Zionism."

"Fine, fine, I get the idea. Everybody's got an agenda. But why does Stalin want it back? I mean, why now especially?"

"Isn't it obvious? Stalin sent it to Hitler. Now that he's getting old, he's embarrassed by it. He wants to preserve his legacy as the

'Great Patriotic Hero,' the man who defended Mother Russia against the vile Teutonic invader."

It made a certain amount of sense. And it even explained how the manuscript came to be in Lina von Osten's possession. Stalin gave it to Hitler, who in turn must have given it to Lina's husband, Reinhard Heydrich, perhaps as some kind of reward from an admiring Führer to the man who planned the Holocaust. But it still didn't completely add up. Not to me.

"Let me get this straight," I said. "Moscow sends an MGB team to Fehmarn in their best new submarine, risking capture and detention. Then, when that doesn't work, they go to Paris and start a minor war on the Left Bank. Finally, Beria himself comes down to Cannes to supervise round three. And all for what? An old manuscript?"

"Beria's here?"

"Yes, with the Stasi. Didn't I mention that?"

"No, you didn't."

"They're the ones who made my evening with Lina and Klaus so entertaining."

"Are they dead?"

"Klaus, yes... Lina and Karlheinz, no."

"How about Beria?"

"No, he escaped. But we're straying a little from the point."

"Which is?"

"All that effort? All that firepower? Just for an old Tsarist manuscript, full of obsolete propaganda? Who cares? I mean, I know some people love to collect originals but this is absurd. What's the real story, Siegfried? No more games. If I'm being bribed with this thing, I should at least know what it's worth."

He gave me that enigmatic half-smile of his. "I must say, Ed, you sometimes have a pithy way about you."

"I know, I'm a barbarian. Now, are you going to tell me or do I have to summon the dragoons?"

"My Greeks won't even let you off the boat."

"What are you going to do? Kill me? Kidnap me? You think Katharina doesn't know where I am?" As a matter of fact, she didn't, but that didn't change the effect.

He opened up into an even broader smile. He seemed to be really enjoying himself with all this and it occurred to me that, beyond all the show and the fine living, he really did see his own role in life as the master of intrigue. Nevertheless, he was boxed in and he knew it. I'm pretty sure he hadn't expected me to figure it out and come back here this morning, much less to call his bluff with my open threats.

"Let me show you something," he said at last.

He got to his feet and padded his way over to where an oil painting of an ocean regatta hung on the dark wood panelling, perhaps another gift from Prince Rainier. I had no doubt that Katharina would recognize it immediately as a fine example of some master French Impressionist but, to me, it was just another symbol of Siegfried's extravagance. He touched a hidden button and both the picture and its frame swung out on hinges to reveal his shipboard safe. Then it took just a few practiced turns of the brass combination before the heavy door clicked open. From deep within, he lifted out an old-fashioned container: rectangular, about twelve inches by eight, with a red velvet covering and a gold tassel to fasten it. Very carefully, he brought it over to the low table where we were seated.

I moved some of the food plates so he could place it down. "That's the manuscript?" I said. "Looks like a chocolate box."

"Not just the manuscript…" he replied teasingly and stopped there, as if still reluctant.

"Siegfried, once and for all, let's stop fooling around, okay?"

"Relax, I'm getting to it. You know, you're far too intense for this career. You'll have a heart attack."

"Just open the damn thing already."

Another fleeting smile. Then, gingerly, he opened up the ornate box and leafed through its contents until he produced a single sheet of paper that didn't have the same appearance as the rest. Even from where I was sitting, I could see it was more official, with a Soviet hammer and sickle at the masthead.

"You want to know what it's all about, this whole affair? Well, this, my dear Eddie, is it. This single piece of paper, hidden in the manuscript. A signed letter from Joseph Stalin, addressed to his good friend, Adolf Hitler."

"Dated when?" I asked him.

"When do you think?"

"I don't know, I'd say end of '38, maybe early '39." There had been a great deal of personal correspondence before the war, when they were still allies.

"What would you say if I told you that this letter is dated December 21st, 1942?"

"But that would have been..."

"At the time of Stalingrad, yes."

The Battle of Stalingrad was the ultimate turning point on the Eastern front. After Hitler broke the Nazi-Soviet pact with his surprise invasion in June 1941, his Wehrmacht rolled a thousand miles across Western Russia as Stalin's Red Army fell back before them. But the city of Stalingrad was symbolic. Not only was it named after Stalin himself but it was also the key obstacle in the German drive towards the oil-rich Caucasus, so if the Soviets were going to make a stand, it would have to be there. The only advantage they had was their old friend, winter. It had defeated Napoleon a century before and it would do the same to Hitler. All they had to do was hold out long enough and wait for it to arrive. Sure enough, the German supply lines became overstretched and got stuck in the early snows. The ill-equipped men suffered severe frostbite. The mechanized units simply froze in their tracks. By the end, over two million died in the carnage and the city itself was reduced to rubble. But the Soviet lines held and the Germans advanced no further.

All in all, the struggle for Stalingrad lasted from the end of August 1942 to the beginning of February 1943 - so the date Siegfried mentioned would have represented the mid-point of the siege, long before the Soviets could see any kind of positive outcome. On the contrary, this would have been the bleakest time, when all hope seemed lost. And, from that, I began to realize what the letter might be.

"Wait a minute," I said. "The only reason Stalin would have sent Hitler a gift with a letter attached during Stalingrad..."

"Was to sue for peace, that's right. Well done, Ed. I knew you'd get there eventually. Would you like me to read you the letter? It's in Russian…"

"By all means."

Thanks to his mother, Siegfried was as fluent in Russian as he was in English. Having travelled there often to open up the nickel deposits, he knew both the language and the culture - and that's why he'd once been so effective as a personal courier between the Nazi Foreign Minister, Joachim von Ribbentrop, and his Soviet counterpart, Vyacheslav Molotov, when the two were still friends.

"My dearest friend Adolf," Siegfried began, translating directly into English for me.

"At this time in the history of our great nations, I must pause and ask myself how it has come to this. We were friends and our people were friends. Our Foreign Ministers signed an agreement. Why are we now at war? Is the world not big enough for us to live in peace?

"You have achieved a magnificent triumph in the west. You have defeated your old enemy France. You have taken Belgium, Holland, Denmark and Norway. England is on her knees. You have a friend to the south in Italy and you have an ally in the Orient with Japan. Why not now reach out your hand to your old comrades in the north? It is the perfect time. We can save our armies from annihilating each other if we act now.

"Join me, dear friend, in achieving this noble ambition. This manuscript I offer is meant as a token, a Christmas gift, sent to you on the day of the Equinox when everything changes. Yet it is merely a promise of more to come. As you know, I too have the misfortune of several million Jews in my own land and I ask you to think what we could accomplish in removing this plague if we act together, in harmony. I have read with interest of your new facilities at Auschwitz-Birkenau and other places. God willing, we can build more such camps in Poland and possibly Ukraine. You will transport these vermin from the west and I will transport them from the east and, in half the time, our dreams will be realized - a Jew-free world.

"Think of it, my good friend Adolf, and let me know your response

at the earliest convenience. Our great destiny awaits your reply.

"With my warmest personal regards, I sign this letter of peaceful intent by my own hand:

Joseph Vissarionovich Stalin."

When Siegfried finished the letter, he placed it carefully back in the box with the manuscript, then sat back, very pleased with himself at having astonished me.

The idea of Stalin suing for peace during the epic Stalingrad battle, and offering the genocide of Russian Jews as a bargaining chip, was a major historical rewrite and my first words to him were: "Is it genuine? Has it been authenticated?"

"Authenticated?" he laughed. "My dear Ed, I was the one who originally delivered it."

"You?"

"Yes, me."

"You went to Moscow to get it?"

"No, of course not. It was total war. Nobody could get through the lines. If you must know, I received it personally from Molotov in Stockholm and then hand-carried it to Ribbentrop in Berlin. Took it right to his office on the Wilhelmstrasse."

"And then what? He just walked it over to the Chancellery?"

"I presume so."

"Why do you think Hitler rejected the offer?"

"Why? Because he thought he was winning, that's why. And anyway, he only put up with the alliance in the first place as a way to buy time. Underneath it all, he despised Stalin. To him, the Slavs were all sub-humans, not much better than Jews... or homosexuals for that matter. How can you be friends with a sub-human?"

"So what are you telling me? You've been sitting on this whole secret for ten years?"

"In a manner of speaking. But a secret's no good unless you've got proof, so I've also been trying to get hold of this letter for ten years."

"And you couldn't have told me all this in Barcelona?"

"You wouldn't have believed me if I had."

It wasn't a real answer but I left it alone. "And how about Gehlen and the rest of them? The British and the Americans... Do they know about the letter, too, or do they still think we're chasing some stupid manuscript?"

"The ones at the top know about it, I'm sure. The ones lower down just do as they're told, as with everything. But if you're asking me about your lovely lady, I'd say no, she probably doesn't know... if that makes you feel any better."

It did but not by much and I just shook my head. I was way past being annoyed. "One thing I still don't understand," I said.

"Just one?"

I ignored his sarcasm. "How did Lina von Osten get hold of it? I assumed that Hitler gave the manuscript to Heydrich and that Heydrich left it to his wife when he was killed. But that's impossible because Heydrich died in the spring of 1942, several months before Stalingrad."

"Which only proves that your assumption was wrong."

"So what happened? How'd she get her grubby little hands on it?"

He sighed, as if telling me all this was a lot of trouble and I should be suitably grateful. "The gift and the letter were officially part of German state records, so Ribbentrop kept them under lock and key at the Foreign Ministry. But in the spring of 1945, Ribbentrop was fired from his post and tried to escape. Like so many, he thought that, with all he knew about the Russians, he could switch sides and work for the West but, as we know, only a few like Gehlen managed that little trick. Anyway, Ribbentrop needed money, so he sold the manuscript and the letter to our friend, Lina, who was smart enough to know a good investment when she saw it and used up so much of her dead husband's savings to get it. That's why she had so little left at the end, why she had to convert her house into a hotel."

"But if *you* wanted it so much, why didn't you just buy it from Ribbentrop when he was selling?"

"Don't be silly. You think I was hanging around Berlin in the spring of '45? The Soviets were pulverizing the place. Everyone was being raped, arrested or murdered... and I wasn't too keen on any of those options, thank you very much."

"Couldn't Molotov have protected you?"

"Well, yes, he might have tried. But do you seriously think the Red Army gave a damn about politicians like Molotov? They were on a rampage. Even Stalin didn't have control."

"So where were you at that time, just out of interest?"

"Back in Stockholm."

"Busy planning your post-war career, I suppose."

"Is that a rebuke I hear in your tone? Am I to be pilloried for wanting to survive?"

"You worked for both sides, Siegfried."

"So did General Motors. So what?"

There was no way to win an argument like that with someone like him, because he thought he had all the answers. And in a way, he did. All wars produce their share of heroes and villains but far more numerous are the people like Siegfried who inhabit the gray zones, the millions who just try to get through it any way they can. Behind it all, he was a vilified homosexual, caught between the Nazis and the Bolsheviks, a potential prey who managed to outwit his predators by making himself useful to both. He wasn't looking for glory. As he said, he was just trying to survive and, if he was able to succeed through a natural flair for intrigue, who could really blame him?

"So what happens now?" I asked him. "You auction it off to both sides, see who's willing to pay the most?"

"Don't worry, Ed, you'll get your share."

That's when there was another voice from behind us, a voice with a Welsh accent. "And will I get my share too?"

I turned and saw the curly-haired Owen Rhys, standing there with a small calibre Beretta in his hand, the kind the Italian forces once used. He was aiming it at Siegfried but he was talking to both of us. He must have heard every word we'd said. We both stood up as he confronted us.

"Owen?" said Siegfried.

"Don't 'Owen' me, you bastard."

"What?"

"You heard me... you... you sad bloody excuse for a human being."

"I don't understand. What are you saying? What are you doing with that gun?"

"What does it look like I'm doing?"

"I honestly have no idea."

"No, you don't, do you? You really don't have a clue. Well, for your information, what I'm doing is returning that box to its rightful owner."

"And who might that be?" I asked him.

For the first time, he turned to look at me, the disdain evident. "Comrade Stalin," he replied.

I could see that Siegfried was taken aback. He was shrewd and calculating but he hadn't reckoned on being faced down by his own young lover.

I looked at them, from one to the other and it was immediately clear that I wasn't the only one that Siegfried had kept in the dark. "Don't tell me, let me guess," I said to Rhys. "You knew about the manuscript but not the letter, am I right? Hey, welcome to the club."

"Shut up, Ed, or whatever your name is. This has nothing to do with you. This is between me and that lying old bastard over there."

"Old?" replied Siegfried. "I resent that." The humour was his way of trying to regain his composure but it didn't work too well.

"You think you're so damn smart with your clothes and your money and your smarmy jokes," Rhys said to him. "Let's see how smart you are with a bloody hole through your heart."

"Now, now, Owen, put the gun down, there's a good boy. You're not going to shoot me."

"Be careful, Siegfried," I said. "Didn't you hear him? He said *Comrade* Stalin. Nobody says 'comrade' any more except the truly committed."

"Or the truly delusional," added Siegfried.

"Shut up," said Rhys again, "the both of you. Yes, I'm a Communist and damn proud of it. My dad worked down the pit all his life, while you people..."

"Yes, what about us people?"

"You're all born with a bloody silver spoon in your mouth. You make me sick, the lot of you."

I wasn't sure how I got lumped in with Siegfried Wachter and his well-heeled crowd, unless Rhys was getting me mixed up with my cover identity, Erich Schultz. It didn't matter though. Through the eyes of an angry young socialist, I was no doubt fair game because I hadn't worked in a Rhonnda Valley colliery, shoulder-to-shoulder with people like his father. Personally, I was prepared to let it go but, for some reason, Siegfried chose to continue the discussion.

"Owen," he said, "just who do you think you're kidding with this nonsense? You're no more a coal miner than I am. At day's end, we're exactly the same."

"No! Never! I'm nothing like you. I don't betray anyone."

"Except your country."

"My country? That's rich, coming from you. And since when was England my country anyway? I'm from Wales, or don't you know the difference? But then it's all the same to you, isn't it? Germany, Russia… England, Wales… It's all just a way to make money."

"You'll make money, too. A few more years, I dare say you'll have your own yacht. No doubt a lot bigger than this one."

"No, I don't think so. I give most of *my* money to the Party."

"Really? Well, more fool you."

"Oh, I see. I'm a fool, is that what you think? Was my father a fool?"

"For heaven's sake, Owen, that's not what I meant and you know it."

"You know your trouble, Siegfried? You believe in nothing beyond your own selfish pleasure."

"I believed in you. Was that nothing?"

Rhys didn't answer. Couldn't or wouldn't, I'm not sure. As far as he was concerned, the debate was over.

"Give me the box," he said to Siegfried.

"Do you think you can really pull that trigger?"

"You want to try me?"

"I think he means it," I said to Siegfried, but I'm not sure he was listening.

"*You!* Shut it!" said Rhys, turning on me. "I won't tell you again."

But that was when Siegfried made his mistake. I don't know if it was a lapse in judgment or whether he really was deeply hurt by this turn of events but, whatever the reason, he chose that one moment in his life to be courageous. He used the distraction to throw the box at Rhys and lunge forward. The young man was caught off guard by the movement but only for an instant. Instinctively, he lifted his arm to deflect the clumsy projectile and then fired at the oncoming Siegfried. The noise reverberated around the cabin.

I watched helplessly as the single bullet smashed into Siegfried's big ribcage. The air was forced out of him as his lungs caved in and he staggered backwards across the room.

But even if Rhys was a Stalinist sympathizer, he was no professional assassin and there was an immediate look of horror in his eyes at what he'd just done. With the gun still in his hand, he ran over to where Siegfried had fallen and knelt down, muttering apologies until there were tears in his eyes.

"God, I'm sorry, Siegfried! I'm sorry, I'm sorry!"

I didn't want any part of it. Siegfried and I had known each other for many years and I, too, was shocked at what had just happened, right in front of my eyes. But, at the same time, I knew he was gone and there was nothing I could do about it. I was very conscious of the nearby box, which had clattered to the floor, so I leaned over, quietly picked it up and then moved as slowly as I could towards the door. I almost made it but, at the last second, Rhys spotted me and, once again, his Celtic temper took over. He began to stand up and all I could see was that damn gun rounding in on me.

Before it could reach its target, I was out of there, racing upstairs and out onto the main deck with the box under my arm. Too late, I'd come up on the wrong side of the boat. Instead of the gangplank facing me, I had the rail and the open harbour. I cursed loudly. I looked around and saw a couple of the Greek crew running to see what the gunfire was all about but they weren't the problem. The real concern was Owen Rhys, who'd followed me up on deck and still had the weapon in his hand. His tear-streaked face was turning crimson and I could see he was nearly hysterical, torn between his convictions and his emotions. He'd been set up by his Soviet handler as a honey trap but he'd fallen seriously in love with Siegfried and, at that moment, I was the nearest target for his guilt and his anguish.

I had no choice. Before he could fire again, I was up and over the rail, jumping feet first into the cold, salty waters of Monte Carlo harbour, while still clutching tight on to the box, with the manuscript and the letter inside it.

I'm a good swimmer, always have been, but I couldn't do much with that damn box in my arms, so I just let it go. Slowly, it floated down towards the bottom. It was a shame after all I'd been through but I figured the water would have ruined it anyway - at least, that's what I kept telling myself, as I struggled to get myself as far from the boat as possible before hauling myself ashore.

Drenched, exhausted and chilled to the bone, I staggered to the Renault and drove it all the way back to the safe house in Cannes. By the time I'd dragged myself up two flights of stairs, I was ready to fall into Katharina's arms.

"What happened?" she asked, as she helped me in.

"I decided to take a dip."

I sank gratefully into the armchair but that's when it struck me. This was exactly the same place we'd put Lina just a few hours ago. "Where is she?" I said. "At the hospital?"

"No, in custody. They both are."

"You turned them in?"

"First things first. Get out of those wet clothes, I'll make you some tea."

"No, wait, Katharina… Before you go, I just want to tell you… I found it. What I mean is, I took it and now it's a total mess but there's more to it than that. There's a letter, or at least there was, but that's messed up too…"

"Ed!"

"What?"

"I've got no idea what you're talking about. Now, listen to me. I want you to go and get changed before *you* end up in the hospital, all right?"

"But…"

"Later."

"It's important."

"It can wait."

And that was it. She'd laid down the law and I must say I liked this mode she was in, caring for my welfare. It was a lot better than just being my case officer. Towels, blankets, tea… maybe a hot bath, if we could ever get the plumbing to work. Why couldn't it always be like this?

Within ten minutes we were back, sitting together with steaming mugs in our hands. Technically, I suppose, this was a debriefing session and we were making our respective reports but it felt more like camp story time, especially with the outlandish tales we each had to tell.

"You first," she said to me.

Slowly, and a little more logically, I took her through what happened: how I knew that Siegfried was the one with the manuscript; the 1942 letter from Stalin to Hitler and what was in it; how we were both taken by surprise by Siegfried's lover, Owen Rhys; and, finally, how both I and the manuscript box ended up in the harbour. The strange thing was that she didn't offer any reaction. She just listened, nodding and offering expressions of understanding in all the right places. Was she back to protocol or was it her own way of showing empathy for what I'd been through? It was hard to keep track of who she was or what she was really thinking at any given moment.

"You think we should go back?" I asked her.

"Go back?"

"To the boat. Siegfried's body…"

"The villa, the boat… I'll say this, Ed… you certainly know how to leave your mark on a place."

"Yeah, thanks." I drank some of my tea. "Okay, your turn."

She was still pre-occupied with her own mental gyrations but then she realized I was waiting for her to say something. "My story's not as exciting as yours," she told me. "No flying bullets. No secret correspondence."

"I'd still like to hear it."

She shrugged slightly. "Well, the doctor arrived just as you left..."

"I know, I saw him."

"We helped them as much as we could. We patched up the woman but Oehring needed a transfusion. He'd lost a lot of blood. We had no choice but the local emergency room."

"And you called the police from there?"

"Not me, the hospital. Standard procedure for a gunshot wound. I couldn't do much about it."

"So what happened?"

"I telephoned Reinhard for instructions. Within an hour, he'd made a deal with the French Ministry of Justice. I think it may have been through Adenaur's office, I'm not sure. Anyway, the deal was that if von Osten was willing to testify against Oehring for the Paris affair, charges would be dropped against her and she'd be released."

I nodded. To me it stank but it was the way of the world. To ODESSA, she was an icon. Gehlen couldn't just stand by and see her indicted, he'd have a revolt on his hands. "And she agreed to that?" I asked.

"Apparently."

"Typical," I replied. "So what happens now? Lina just takes the cash that Siegfried paid her and what? She goes back to Fehmarn as if nothing happened, while her attack dog gets euthanized? After all he did for her?"

"I imagine it'll be something like that, yes."

"Nazis and Communists... the species that eat their own."

We sat in a kind of trance for a while, sipping our tea in silence. The morning sun was already bright and lighting up the room, a burst of radiant optimism in a depressing world. Eventually, it was Katharina who broke the spell by glancing at her watch.

"We should get out of here."

"Right."

"Ed... I'm sorry about your friend, Siegfried. I kind of liked him."

"Yeah, me too. I guess we had our differences but he was a

character. One of the last true eccentrics. What the English like to call 'a gentleman player.'"

"Would you have taken the money?"

"The money?"

"From the sale of the letter. You said he was going to auction it off to the highest bidder and give you a share of the proceeds."

"Do I ever know what I'm going to do from one minute to the next?"

I was joking around but she didn't smile. She chose to take it seriously, managing to turn my silliness into some kind of psychoanalysis.

"You know," she said, "you're a lot better at all this than you think."

"No, I'm not. I might be if I had some conviction but it's just not there. It's just not me."

"Yes, it is. You just don't want to admit it." She shook her head as if I were a lost cause and some of that carefully tidied hair fell loose. She swept it back with a flick of those long, elegant hands.

"Katharina…" I saw her look up as I spoke her name, perhaps sensing what I was about to say. I'd put it off long enough and it was about time I really told her how I felt. Yet, it was difficult and awkward and I hesitated just long enough for her to reach over and take my hand in hers.

"It's all right," she said softly. "You don't have to say it. I know. I've always known. My problem is, I love you, too."

We abandoned the safe house, took the Renault and checked into a modest guesthouse in the main part of Cannes: just an average couple on a touring holiday.

That evening, we ate seafood at a small bistro, then went for a quiet walk along the Cannes beachfront. Behind us, the lights glowed from the busy hotels lining the Croisette but down here, near the lapping waves of the Mediterranean, we could be alone. It was a warm evening with just a slight breeze coming in off the sea and she kept pausing to shake the gritty sand from her shoes. As she did so, she leaned on my shoulder for support and it felt good in a symbolic sort of way. Stupid, I know, but each time it happened, I wanted the moment to last.

"Do we really need all this?" I said to her at one point.

"All what?"

"All this stuff we do. I mean, what's it all about? Who are we fighting? Stalin? He'll be dead soon."

"You think it'll all come to an end when Stalin dies?"

"We can't bring the whole empire down. That'll take years, maybe decades."

"Perhaps... but if we don't keep trying, it'll never happen."

"And you think it's our responsibility? Yours and mine?"

"Don't ask me that, Ed."

"Why not?"

"Because responsibility was the way I was brought up. My father..."

"Yes, I know about your father. I know how he struggled against Hitler but..."

"But what?"

"He died, Katharina. He died in the attempt and I'm afraid that's what might happen to you."

"You almost died yourself, last night."

"Yes, but I did that for you."

"For me? You did it for me?"

I stared at her. As intelligent and perceptive as she was, she hadn't even recognized that simple fact. "Why do you think I did it? For freedom? For democracy? For future generations?"

"What's wrong with doing it for those things?"

"Nothing... nothing's wrong... except I didn't, that's all. I did it for you. If you hadn't been there that day, in that room with Gehlen and all those people... the British, the Americans... I would have just walked out."

"Would you?"

"Yes, I would. And Gehlen knows it too. That's why he had you there. As a lure to get me involved."

"A lure? Is that what you think I am?"

She was annoyed now and I had no idea why.

"Look, Katharina, I'm sorry if..."

"Ed, you're such an idiot sometimes. Do you really want to know why I was there? Do you? Because I volunteered, that's why. I didn't know if you were alive or dead but I never stopped thinking about you. The first time I heard Reinhard mention your name, I couldn't believe it. And when it was confirmed, I insisted on being there, just so I could see you again."

This was a confession she was giving me and it stopped me cold. "Really?" I said quietly.

"Yes, really. What do you want me to say, Ed? You wrecked my life from the moment you walked into it fourteen years ago. Fourteen years."

"I wrecked your life?"

"That's what love does. It destroys things. It pushes aside anything in its path. Don't you know that by now? Don't you even know that much?"

She was annoyed and I had no idea how to respond. To me, it was simple - I loved her, she loved me - but to her, it was far larger than that. To her, it was an issue to handle, like duty or responsibility, something to be compartmentalized, and if it happened at the wrong time or with the wrong person, it became a hindrance. I was about to ask her deeper questions, the kind of questions ordinary people ask, about the chances of settling down, building a home, finding some happiness, that sort of thing. But I didn't get that far.

"Well, well, fancy meeting you here."

The voice came from behind us. Once more, I recognized the Welsh lilt and looked around so fast that Katharina, who was again leaning on my shoulder to empty her shoe, almost lost her balance. And yet again, I found myself looking down the barrel of the same gun. It was Owen Rhys, back to haunt me.

"How the hell..." I was about to ask how he found us but the only way could have been if he'd followed me from Monte Carlo. I'd parked the car near the dock. He knew I'd return for it and all he had to do was follow at a safe distance with his lights off. There was no way I could have been aware. Once in Cannes, he probably didn't want to enter the apartment building - he didn't know who else might be up there – so he just sat and watched the car until he saw the two of us leave this evening. Finally, like fools, we led him here, to this quiet spot on the beach.

But all this was just supposition and, anyway, it didn't really matter. The fact was that he was here and babbling almost incoherently, even worse than when he was back on the boat.

"My father gave his life," he was saying. "Died for what he believed in. That's why I took the job when they asked me. I'd have done anything, you know that? Anything. But then I met him... Siegfried... and..." There were tears forming in his eyes. "I thought I could do it. I thought I could do the job... I thought I could have it both ways. Maybe I would, too, but then you had to come along, poking your damn nose into everything. It's your damn fault he's gone. You ruined everything!"

I was transfixed by that stupid little gun in his hand, yet all I could think about was how much like Katharina his argument sounded. It was an almost a replica of what she'd just been telling me, the same struggle between emotion and conviction, between love and keeping faith with a cause. The only difference was that Rhys was certifiably crazy - and very dangerous. Yet again, I found myself longing for the comfort of the Uzi that was now hidden safely in the trunk of the car.

"You're the one who shot him, Owen," I replied, "not me."

"You were supposed to be his friend. Some friend you turned out to be."

"So now you're looking for someone else to blame, is that it?"

"Ed..." whispered Katharina. "Take it easy."

But I didn't feel like taking it easy. I'd seen five people killed in the past twenty-four hours. I'd also seen a woman tortured, I'd barely escaped being shot myself and, to top it all off, I'd almost drowned. I was sick of taking it easy.

Next to me, Katharina was sharp enough to sense my mood. She must have thought I was about to lose my equilibrium so, despite her warning, she decided to make a play of her own.

At first, it looked inconsequential, a natural movement to put her shoe back on but, before I knew it, she was pulling the old trick of throwing sand in his face. Although some of it missed, it was enough to distract him and I used the chance that I'd been given. I lunged forward and dove for his gun hand. I almost made it, too, but I was slower than he was and he managed to raise it, just out of my reach, a repeat of what happened with Siegfried. This time, though, it was different. My flying trajectory took me crashing into his wiry frame and he fell backwards, dropping the gun. For a second, we were both scrambling to regain our balance. It seemed like an even contest - but speed and agility will usually have an advantage over age and weight and he reached the weapon first.

I'd lost and I knew it. He was kneeling up in front of me, aiming straight at the centre of my head, his finger about to squeeze the trigger.

I really believed it was the end, not just for me but for Katharina too. Then I saw the slight smile on his face as he turned the gun ninety degrees towards his own temple and fired. From that range, the small-gauge bullet crashed through the cranial bone and bulldozed its way into the soft brain tissue, causing Rhys to fall over sideways with a crater oozing gore from the side of his head.

I put my arm around Katharina and could feel her clutching on to me, as we both stared at the mess before us. There was a dark patch spreading slowly over the sand and, once again, she was urging me to move, to get out of there. An ugly suicide on a public beach would have been impossible to explain. What could we have said? That Owen Rhys had just lost the great love of his young life? That he'd been a dedicated Soviet agent, assigned as a honey trap, but that he'd fallen for his own victim? That the conflict within him had finally torn him apart? How would anyone have understood?

In a way, it was tragic; and yet, as we made our escape, driving away into the night, I couldn't help feeling a strong sense of relief. Rhys had surely been the last, because everyone else had either been murdered or arrested. The fact that he took his own life seemed to me like some kind of closure.

I couldn't have been more wrong, though, and the next threat came at me when I was least expecting it.

★

When we got back to London, it was raining and I had no place to stay. There was no longer any reservation at the Lanesborough and, belatedly, I realized it was Siegfried himself who'd funded my first sojourn there. However, I didn't mind too much, because Katharina offered to put me up at the apartment maintained by the Gehlen Organization, situated in the desirably middle-class district of St. John's Wood, not far from Lord's cricket ground. Since Gehlen himself usually stayed at the US Embassy on Grosvenor Square when he was in town, we had the place to ourselves.

The official debriefing for the operation took place once again at Scotland Yard, but not in the same room, nor with the same crowd. Actually, there wasn't any crowd. This was just a small, bare office with four chairs, one behind the desk and three in front. Hosting the meeting was the bureaucratic Sir Humphrey Pender, here only to wrap things up. Also present was Reinhard Gehlen, looking as if this were a total waste of his time, plus Katharina and myself. That was it. There was no one else: no MI5 and no CIA.

"Where is everybody?" I said, trying to inject a convivial note into our small, sombre group.

Nobody answered and, in the end, there was no need. Word had spread along the corridors of the various agencies that the mission had failed and it was obvious that anyone who'd been involved was now trying to stay as far away as possible. This wasn't so much a debriefing as a wake.

The project had been originally set up in the somewhat optimistic hope of finding the manuscript and, presumably, the compromising letter it contained. That way, Malcolm Davies of MI5 could redeem himself after the loss of the defector, Mikhailov; and Phil Rankin of the CIA could be a hero in the last days of Truman's White House, perhaps rounding off a long and worthwhile career with a Congressional Medal of Honor, or some such bauble. But since the prize was lost when I jumped into the harbour, the only thing that remained for them was to wonder why they'd bothered to place their faith in such a fool's errand in the first place.

Only Katharina remained loyal, both to the intent and to the realistic inevitability of the outcome, and I must say she defended our actions with vigour. Naturally, both Pender and Gehlen assumed she was biased towards me, so they paid little heed, but I must say I was impressed and I couldn't help beaming proudly in the warmth of her convictions. The way she portrayed my exploits, I was a well-intentioned and industrious amateur who'd risked my life for what was, after all, nothing more than a piece of paper. Surely, she argued, I deserved some thanks and, at the very least, a modicum of respect.

"Of course, of course," replied Pender, but he didn't mean a word of it. Instead, he questioned me again about the circumstances at the Hoeffler villa and on board Siegfried's boat. "And you're positive," he said for the third time, "that it was Lavrenti Beria who questioned the woman."

"Yes, I'm positive."

"The Soviet Minister for Internal Affairs."

"How many Lavrenti Beria's can there be?"

"It's just that, you see, we have no confirming reports, either that he left Moscow or that he ever arrived in France."

"Are you calling me a liar?"

"No, no, of course not. I'm merely asking you to consider the possibility that you were under a great deal of stress and…"

"Okay, once and for all. We were together in the same room for over half an hour. I was tied up with a gag in my mouth but there was nothing wrong with my eyesight, or my brain, and I'm telling you that, without a shadow of doubt, this was Lavrenti Beria, Soviet minister and member of the Politburo. There's not a one percent chance, not even a tenth of one percent chance, that I'm mistaken. Is that clear enough?"

Pender didn't respond. He just continued in the same tone of voice. "And you say he was leading a team of Stasi?"

"That's right."

"How do you know they were Stasi?"

"Because they were speaking German, not Russian. And, before you ask, it was the leader of the team, a man called Dieter, who translated."

"Dieter what?"

"I don't know if that was his first name or his family name. They just called him Dieter."

"But he was able to translate from Russian to German?"

"Yes, and back again."

"Unusual, don't you think?"

"Not at all. He might have fought on the Eastern front. Or he might have spent some time in a Soviet POW camp. Or he might have been sent to Moscow after the war for retraining. There must be thousands of East Germans of that age who speak some Russian."

"I see, yes. All right, let's move on. You say it was Beria himself who inflicted the burn on Frau von Osten?"

"That's right."

"With his cigar."

"Yes."

"Well, at least that part's consistent with medical reports."

"At least? What do you mean, at least?"

"Ed," said Katharina, "it's not helpful if you get upset."

She used the same tone as she did on the beach at Cannes with Owen Rhys. I almost expected her to throw sand in Pender's eyes but that wasn't an option. Carpet dust, perhaps, but not sand.

The problem was that there seemed to be no independent corroboration. Lina von Osten had been released and wanted nothing more to do with anything. Well, why would she, with her pockets full of Siegfried's money? And Oehring, who was awaiting trial, had clammed shut on the advice of his ODESSA-sponsored lawyer. For all I knew, it was Gehlen here who'd arranged it. Meanwhile, Pender was still asking his ridiculous questions. It was clear that he, too, would have rather been somewhere else but, since there'd been government expenditure, he was required to file a report.

"Tell me again," he was saying, "what happened when Oehring came through the window. How come you weren't hit?"

"Not just me. Von Osten wasn't hit and nor was Beria. Come to that, nor was the Stasi commander, Dieter, as far as I could tell."

"And why was that, do you think? From what you've said, Oehring had a sub-machine gun and the firing was fairly random."

"It wasn't that random. As I already told you, he aimed high, so only those standing were hit."

"And he managed that while leaping through the window onto the dining room table? That would take considerable skill, wouldn't you say?"

"I just saw what happened."

"Right you are." Pender's tone suggested it was all highly suspicious. "And this man, Dieter... he offered no resistance?"

"Of course, he offered resistance. He shot at Oehring, wounded him in the leg."

"But you say he led Beria out."

"I presume that was his primary responsibility."

"Do you know where they went?"

"No. I heard a car engine start outside but I couldn't move. I was still tied up."

"Who untied you?"

"Lina von Osten."

"Really? While wounded and traumatized from her torture?"

"She thought I was still on her side. Once I was free, we helped Oehring out to Hoeffler's car. It was only later, at the safe house, that she collapsed."

"Strong woman."

"She had to be. She was married to Reinhard Heydrich."

A wry smile from Pender. "Now, after you arrived at the safe house in Cannes, why did you immediately go back to the boat?"

I sighed. We'd been over that, too. "Because I recalled something she said that matched something that Siegfried Wachter had originally told me."

"The idea of an auction, yes. And from that, you put it all

together?"

"It suddenly struck me."

"So without waiting for backup, without informing anybody... even your case officer... you went charging off. A bit gung-ho, don't you think? A bit cowboy. Anyone would think you're American."

"Well, I'm not. I'm just a dumb Canuck. You ask me to do a job, so I do it."

He looked at me dubiously. "All right, so you get to the boat and you face down Wachter. Go on."

"We had a conversation."

"You were angry?"

"Let's just say, I was a little upset that he'd misled me."

"Because he bought the manuscript from von Osten without telling you?"

"Yes, but more the fact that I'd almost been killed by his deception."

"Did you struggle?"

"Struggle?"

"Physically."

"You mean did I kill him? No."

"So, according to your account, he just opened up his safe and showed you both items, the manuscript and the letter."

"Yes."

"And that didn't strike you as odd behaviour?"

"Siegfried was an odd man, or hadn't you noticed?" I looked at Gehlen for confirmation but he looked half-asleep, not paying much attention to any of this.

"The letter," said Pender. "Describe the letter again, if you would."

I did the best I could from what I remembered and he listened carefully.

"What language was it in?" he asked.

"Russian, I told you."

"Do you read Russian, Mr. Schaeffer?"

"No. Siegfried translated it for me into English."

"But you're completely bilingual. Why didn't he translate it into German?"

"I don't know."

"Yet you say Rhys overheard its contents. Wouldn't it be fair to say that if Wachter had used German, Rhys wouldn't have been able to understand?"

"What kind of question is that? Who the hell knows? Neither Siegfried nor I even suspected Rhys until he pulled that damn gun."

"Were you aware that Rhys was on the boat?"

"No... but I didn't really think about it."

"Do you think Wachter knew he was a Communist?"

"Possibly, but I doubt it."

"Strange, don't you think? With them being so... what shall we say? Close?"

"No, I don't think it's strange at all. People can share a bed without sharing their politics, you know."

I resented his attitude, although why I felt the need to defend either Siegfried Wachter or Owen Rhys, I'm not sure. Maybe it's because what they'd found was real: a pair of duplicitous people who'd finally latched on to something authentic. In that context, the little scene that played out between them on the boat was genuinely heart-rending.

"And how about you?" said Pender. "You didn't suspect anything either?"

"No, I didn't. But then, nor did you," I replied. "My, my, what a surprise! British intelligence not realizing they had a Communist infiltrator in their midst."

I tried to make the insult biting but he wasn't really having any of it and simply shunted it aside without comment.

"So, let me get this straight," he went on. "You're telling me that Rhys suddenly pulled out a gun, argued with Wachter and shot him in a fit of lover's pique. And, until that happened, you didn't suspect a thing. Is that your statement?"

"No, that's not my statement. That's the truth of what happened."

"And while he was kneeling by his lover's side, feeling all kinds of remorse, you managed to pick up the documents…"

"A box. It was all in a kind of fabric-covered box."

"Oh, that's right, with a tassel."

His tone was snide but I did my best to ignore it.

"Yes, with a tassel."

"Nice touch. So you picked up the box, which was now conveniently on the floor near your feet and ran out to the deck."

"It wasn't that convenient but, basically, yes."

"And when you saw that Rhys was giving chase, you jumped over the side… which means the box and all its contents are now lying at the bottom of the harbour."

"Why don't you send in some divers?" I asked him. "You might be able to find it."

He ignored my suggestion and sat back in his chair. "Let me play devil's advocate for a moment, if I may, Mr. Schaeffer."

"Any chance I can stop you?" My outright hostility was now plain for all to see and I could tell that Katharina wasn't pleased.

"A suspicious mind," said Pender, "might just believe that your story is a concoction from beginning to end."

"A *concoction*?" I was already out of my chair.

"Please sit down, Mr. Schaeffer."

I did so but only at Katharina's silent urging. Pender waited before going on.

"And if that same suspicious mind were to go further," he said, "it might just decide that you didn't jump into the harbour at all…"

"I arrived in Cannes soaking wet."

"Yes, a good act, so you could keep whatever's inside that box and profit from it."

That was it as far as I was concerned. I was furious. I scraped my chair back and got to my feet, shrugging off Katharina's implored advice to calm down. "No wonder you people are in such a mess," I told him. Then, before I lost all control, I turned around and left, slamming the door behind me for good measure.

I vaguely heard Katharina's voice calling after me but I didn't go back. What was the point? Not only did they not believe my story, they were actually accusing me of theft and the only reason they even allowed me to leave the building was because they had no proof at all; not a single piece of evidence to back it up, other than their own arcane suspicions. Were they really that stupid, or were they just so paranoid from all the recent revelations that they now saw enemies everywhere? Or was it simply a matter of Pender casting personal aspersions in order to camouflage his own role in the fiasco? In the end, I neither knew nor cared. I didn't want any part of it.

They were waiting for me in the early evening.

After leaving Scotland Yard, I had no idea what to do, so I travelled by Tube to the zoological gardens in Regent's Park. I know it sounds strange but, back in Berlin, I'd often visited that city's famous zoo as a kind of therapy. I used to find that a mental conversation with the primates helped make things clearer and, with all their nonsensical chatter, they invariably gave me better advice than the humans I knew. In London, I'd heard about a relatively new addition to the venerable institution and, since the rain had cleared, I thought I'd go check him out, just to see what he could tell me. His name was Guy... Guy the gorilla. He was very much the strong, silent type but his all-knowing look spoke to me in volumes. And what did he say? Pretty much what I knew already: that I was a typically idiotic member of my species who'd prefer to die for the woman I pined after than live a normal life. In fact, his personal suggestion to me was to grow up. In his opinion, I was a middle-aged fool who was acting like a love-sick juvenile and his debilitating gaze told me I was an embarrassment to male primates everywhere.

Needless to say, my thirty minute confab with Guy the gorilla didn't do much to change my dark mood so, after that, I checked out the penguins, the giraffes and various other species to see if they concurred. Sadly, I never found out because they just didn't give a damn. At least, Guy had listened. These others simply went about their business without paying the slightest attention, so I left them to their own devices. At the end of the afternoon, I ate a sandwich in the cafeteria, tried on a gorilla mask in the souvenir store and left the premises even more dismayed than when I arrived.

The bus was crowded and slow heading back to St. John's

Wood, so I didn't arrive until the light was fading. As I approached the building, I couldn't see any lights on in the third floor apartment, which meant that Katharina hadn't returned yet. It was just as well, I was thinking, because I had no idea what to say to her anyway. I knew that my display in front of Pender and Gehlen had disappointed her.

However, I didn't actually get as far as the apartment, because they intercepted me in the lobby. There were two of them: both young and fit and fairly sizeable. I looked around but there was nobody to offer assistance: no other residents and certainly no friendly "bobby" who might barge in to save me because, as the cliché insists, they're never around when you need them.

One of the men had a baby face but he was the one who took the lead: "There's somebody who'd like to have a word with you."

His English was good but I could detect the Russian accent and, right away, I knew I was in trouble.

"What kind of somebody?"

"Please come with us. We have a car outside."

I looked at them, from one to the other, but neither of them showed any expression at all. Just a couple of guys doing their job. "Look…" I said, trying to sound casual, "I've had a lousy day and I'm tired. Can't it wait until tomorrow?"

The only answer he gave me was to poke something heavy and metallic into my ribs. I didn't need to look to see that it was a firearm of some sort. Yes, another one. I was getting tired of having guns pointed at me. He was hiding it under the gabardine raincoat which he carried over his arm.

"You'd kill me in the centre of London?" I asked him.

"We've done worse."

The way he said it gave me little room for doubt, so I shrugged and left the building with them. They ushered me into the back seat of a big, black Rover with diplomatic plates, where I found myself next to an older man in a slightly crumpled business suit. He looked like he may once have been an athletic type, but now had rounded shoulders and a double chin. The two who'd escorted me got into the front seats, with baby face doing the driving.

"Good evening, Herr Schultz," said the man next to me. His Russian accent was even more pronounced. "Or should I say, Mr. Schaeffer. Which one would you prefer today?"

"Who are you?"

"My name is Yuri Modin. I work at the Soviet Embassy."

"Doing what?"

A faint smile. "I'm sorry we had to bundle you in like this but I was afraid you might not have come of your own accord."

"You're damn right I wouldn't." I noticed that we'd turned north on Maida Vale where the traffic was a little heavier. "Where are we going?"

"Nowhere. Just driving around. It's so much safer when we're on the move. Oh, and please don't think of jumping out," he said. "If you try something like that, you may miss an excellent opportunity and that would be a shame."

"What kind of opportunity?"

"I believe I'm in a position to help you."

"Help me how?"

"Ah, the North American mind. Always the practicalities."

"How'd you find me, anyway?"

"Why? You think we don't know the Gehlen residence? How *is* Herr Gehlen, by the way? Not taking the loss too hard?"

"The loss?"

"Of the manuscript."

"All right, now look, you've had your fun. Tell me what you want or drop me off at the next bus stop. Either way is fine by me."

We were already in Kilburn and on our way towards Cricklewood. Were they taking me out of London? Somewhere convenient to shoot me and dump my body? After my experience in France, nothing would have surprised me. Through the windows I could see ordinary cars and pedestrians, average people going home to their sausage and mash before a quick walk with the dog and off to bed early. I envied them their normal lives and, for the moment, I was distracted by my own self-pity. But I couldn't afford to lose focus.

"Rumour has it," said Modin, "that you had the documents but you somehow managed to drop them in the water."

"Who told you that? Wait, I know, Owen Rhys. He called you before he found us in Cannes, didn't he? What are you, his case officer?"

He wasn't responding to any of my questions but I was supposed to answer his. I'd almost decided to stop playing along when he said something I wasn't expecting.

"Rumour also has it," he added, "that your own people don't believe you."

I stared at him. That meeting was just this morning. How could he have known so fast? And just who did he mean by "my own people?" Pender? Gehlen? Perhaps even Katharina? I couldn't seem to work it out and my only recourse was to bluff my way through. "Once and for all, what do you want?" I said to him. "And don't say to help me, because I don't believe a word of it."

"All right, let's be frank, Mr. Schaeffer, shall we? I'd venture to say you're in the worst possible position right now."

"I am?"

"You've been cast into no-man's-land. You've been dumped right in the middle, without a friend."

"I don't know what you're talking about."

"Of course you do. You say you lost the documents but nobody believes you. Not your own side and not my people either."

"Now just a minute. You heard it from Rhys himself."

"He's dead."

"Sure, but he was there, he saw what happened and he called you, didn't he?"

"Absolutely."

"So now you're saying you don't believe him either?"

"I wasn't talking about myself, Mr. Schaeffer. The problem is Moscow."

"Moscow?"

"A certain Minister called Lavrenti Pavlovich Beria. Naturally, I filed my report but it seems to be stuck in some kind of… what's the word? Limbo?" He smiled. "I like this word, limbo. It has a good sound to it. Limbo, limbo…"

"Christ, will you stop saying that? So what does it mean, Beria doesn't believe me? What are you trying to say?"

"What I'm saying is that he's almost convinced me he's right. After all, I only have Owen's word and he could have been playing it any number of ways... with Wachter, with von Osten... or maybe even with you."

"Terrific. That's just terrific. You said you were here to help me. Well, I gotta tell you, this isn't helping me much."

"Who said 'sarcasm is the language of the devil?' Wasn't it Thomas Carlyle?"

"Who cares?"

"I'll be candid, Mr. Schaeffer. I was prepared to ignore Comrade Beria and take young Owen Rhys at face value... but today, when I heard that even your own people don't believe you... Do you see my point?"

"No."

"No? Well, no matter. I'm just here to say that, at this stage, I could be swayed either way. I could be your enemy, or I could be your best friend."

"Which means what exactly? You want me to switch sides?"

"I think I prefer the expression 'to jump ship.' More appropriate, don't you think?"

"Very funny."

"My offer *is* genuine, you know."

"As long as I bring the documents with me."

"Well, yes, that would help."

"Too bad they're at the bottom of the sea."

"So you keep saying."

"I keep saying it, because it's the truth."

"Perhaps, but it's not me you have to convince. It's Comrade Beria. And if he ever gets hold of you..."

"Thank you, I've seen what he can do."

"That's true, so you have. Mr. Schaeffer, I think what you should remember is that, right now, I might just be your *only* friend."

"So I guess this is just some friendly advice."

"If you like. Tell you what, why don't you think about it? Sleep on it. Talk it over with that lady friend of yours, the one who works for Gehlen."

"Leave her out of this."

"Of course, of course. But if I were you…"

"If you were me, what?"

"If I were you, I wouldn't go back to that apartment. If I can find you, so can Beria."

We'd reached the Edgware Road but were crawling through traffic due to some kind of accident. The day's drizzle had more or less cleared and I could see the Hendon Underground station on the opposite side of the street.

I made a decision. "You think he can find me?" I said to Modin. "Good luck."

Before they could stop me, I had the door open and was leaping from the slowly moving car. I slipped on the damp asphalt, badly grazing my hand, but managed to roll over, get back on my feet and continue through lines of cars and buses towards the other side. I turned and saw one of the men come after me, the one from the front passenger seat who hadn't spoken a word. My only recourse was to head into the station, which was right in front of me.

To the astonishment of the ticket clerk, I clambered my way over the turnstile and made for the escalator, running down the moving stairs as fast as my feet could go. At the bottom, I looked back up but couldn't seem to see the man following me. Had he given up? I wasn't sure but, just to be on the safe side, I half-walked, half-ran to the end of the southbound platform, right next to the tunnel mouth, where I found a small alcove in the cream-tiled wall. There I waited, trying to catch my breath, until the train arrived a few minutes later. Once the doors were open and all the passengers aboard, I darted across the platform at the last minute and stepped into the car, trying to look as if I hadn't a care in the world.

Only one thing gave me away. When I looked down, I saw that my grazed hand was dribbling blood right down to my fingertips.

I found a place to stay - a small tourist hotel near Russell Square

- and checked in under the name of Erich Schultz, the *Vogue* magazine journalist from New York. I still had the passport to prove it. If they really wanted to find me, they could, but this might just throw them off for a while.

Once I was installed, I went down to a public phone and called Katharina at the St. John's Wood apartment. I was aware they might be tapping the line.

"Hi," she said, "I just got in. Where are you?"

"Can you meet me?"

"Ed... It's been a long day. Why don't you just come back here?"

"I can't. And you shouldn't be there either. It's not safe."

"Why? What's wrong? What's happened?"

"I can't explain on the phone. Just meet me, please."

I heard a hesitation, then a slight sigh. "Where?"

"Okay, you need to make sure you're not being followed. Take the Underground, a few trains back and forth at random..."

"You're telling me how to do my job?"

"Right, sorry. Anyway, finish your trip at, let's say, Holborn, any time after eight. Take the Kingsway exit and walk south towards Aldwych, understand? Stay on the same side of the street. Don't look round, I'll make contact."

"Ed..."

"Please, Katharina, just do it, okay?"

"Fine, fine."

I hung up and not for the first time did I wonder if I'd made the right decision. For all I knew, she was the one who'd called Modin but I couldn't let myself think that way. If I couldn't trust Katharina, then what was it all about anyway? I might as well just give up.

I didn't make contact with her on Kingsway like I said. Instead, I intercepted her much sooner, in Holborn station at the base of the ascending escalator, even before she had the chance to step on. I took hold of her arm and turned her around, so we could cross the platform and board the same train before it left. My reward for this initiative was a rare compliment from her.

"So…" she said quietly, once we'd settled into our seats. "I see you finally turned into a real operative."

"Thanks. I had a good teacher."

"Ed, what's going on?"

"Not here. When we get off."

"Where?"

I looked around but couldn't see anyone suspicious: a few commuters in raincoats looking bored and tired after a day's work; a couple of elderly ladies wearing hats with pins; a harried mother with two school age children who wouldn't sit still; but nobody who even remotely resembled a heavy Soviet agent with a hidden weapon. "Next stop," I replied. It happened to be Chancery Lane, situated just off Fleet Street, halfway between the West End theatre district and the financial hub known as The City. It was a pleasant area to stroll and I knew it well.

When we emerged from the station, we walked north and entered Gray's Inn Fields. With its leafy public gardens and old stone walls, this ancient institution is one of the four "inns-of-court" that form the heart of London's legal infrastructure. However, we weren't going for a consultation. It was just somewhere quiet where we could talk. Once inside the grounds, we huddled on one of the benches like a lovers' tryst. Elsewhere, the street lights were beginning to flicker on but here we were secluded. Above us, the clouds were starting to clear, the grass smelled fresh and we could even see one or two stars. In other circumstances, it might have been romantic - but this was business.

In short order, I told her about Modin and his warnings. She seemed to recognize the name.

"Do you know him?" I asked her.

"It would be more accurate to say I know *of* him."

"He didn't deny being Owen Rhys' case officer."

"No, by all accounts, that's a job he knows well."

"But what I don't understand is how he found out so quickly. I mean, he told me that my own people didn't believe me… and that just happened this morning."

"Right. And since there were only four of us present, you've been wondering which one is the traitor."

"Well…"

"I can tell you it's not me. And I don't really see what Reinhard would have to gain."

"Which leaves Pender, I know. That's where I came out. Dear Sir Humphrey. You think he called Modin right after our meeting?"

"Perhaps. But there's another possibility."

"What's that?"

"Well, he does happen to be very good friends with another man under suspicion… Kim Philby. Ever hear of him?"

"No, who's he?"

"Whitehall thinks he may be another of the Cambridge moles. They've suspended him from duty but they don't have enough to bring him to trial."

"You mean Pender would have used Philby as a go-between to Modin?"

"Not necessarily. It's also possible that Pender still believes in Philby, despite the accusations. There are many who do."

"What is it, some kind of mass denial?"

"In a way. But that's how the British establishment operates. In the end, it's just a network of friendships based on upper-class connections and old school chums. It's hard for them to admit the model's broken. Sometimes they maintain the trust, even in the face of all evidence to the contrary."

I couldn't help grinning. "Chums?" I repeated. It was an unlikely word to come from her mouth.

"Isn't that what they say?"

"Yes, it's what they say."

"So what do you want to do, Ed? Where do we go from here?"

"I'm not entirely sure," I replied. "But I think we should start with two things. The first is to find you alternative accommodation."

"Where?"

"I don't know. Gehlen's your boss; talk to him. Where does he normally stay?"

"At the US Embassy."

"Can't you move in there?"

"At my grade? I don't think so. Plus the apartment's already paid and nobody's using it."

"But it's dangerous."

"I'll talk to him."

"Katharina…"

"That's the best I can do."

"Okay, okay. But while you're talking to him, maybe you can also discuss the second thing."

"What's that?"

"I need a new identity."

"A new one? What about Schultz?"

"Compromised by Owen Rhys. Modin already knows about it."

She thought about it. "I don't know if Reinhard would be willing. The operation's over."

"Come on, it's the least he can do."

"It wasn't even his operation to begin with."

"No, but it was Gehlen who chose Siegfried, so it was his responsibility when Siegfried was targeted by Modin."

"Perhaps, but it was the British who chaired the committee, so technically…"

"Don't get all official on me. I'd go to Pender if I could trust him but obviously I can't. Hell, I don't even know if he's even going to sign the invoice I sent him."

"All right, all right… let me see what I can do."

She looked at me and I could feel her eyes piercing the dim light. She still had an immense power over me. I liked to think of myself as hard-nosed but, in truth, I was as pathetically helpless with her as I'd ever been. She said I'd ruined her life but I think the truth was more likely the other way around.

"Why don't you come stay with me?" I asked her.

"Where?"

"I don't know. We'll find somewhere."

"I left all my things at the apartment."

"So did I. So what?"

"One thing at a time, Ed, all right? First I need to call Reinhard. Let's find a pay phone somewhere."

"Then a bite to eat? How about that? I know a place that serves a pretty good Wiener schnitzel with sauerkraut."

"Here in London?"

"Yeah, can you believe it?"

She smiled as we got up but her smile had changed over the years. It was no longer warm and glowing. It was more worldly and knowing. I didn't like it as much and I wondered vaguely how I might go about bringing the other one back.

As desperate as the situation was for me, it was even worse for the man who was rapidly turning into my own personal nemesis: Soviet Minister for Internal Affairs, Lavrenti Pavlovich Beria.

There'd been a new President elected to the White House and the Moscow ministries were busy analysing what this development might mean. Dwight Eisenhower, popularly known as "Ike", ex-Supreme Commander of Allied Forces in Europe and the first Supreme Commander of NATO, had defeated Adlai Stevenson in a landslide, the first Republican victory in two decades. Any new doctrine, especially concerning the war in Korea and the struggle against Communism, was cause for concern around the Kremlin and, although they'd prepared for this eventuality, the various bureaucracies were still scrambling to finalize policy.

Thoughts of the manuscript were therefore banished from Stalin's priorities during this frenetic period but Beria knew it was less of a genuine reprieve than a temporary stay of execution. He tried to conduct his normal daily affairs as best he could but it seemed that, wherever he went, the whispers were all around him. If he walked into a room, he sensed that all conversation stopped immediately, as if they'd been talking about only him. When he met Stalin, the tone was superficially cordial but, still, Beria couldn't help feeling like the living dead, already condemned to his fate.

First Fehmarn, then Paris and, finally, Cannes. "Three strikes and you're out," that's what the man had said. But would it mean a long tribunal, or an immediate sentence? A gulag or a firing squad? He lived or died at the pleasure of The Boss and waiting for the final decision was, for him, a torture in and of itself. The constant anxiety prevented him from sleeping and even his notorious proclivity for sexual diversion began to elude him, to the extent that even Madame Giselle despaired of ever satisfying him.

Finally, he broke.

One Sunday evening, when he was alone at his private apartment with only a flagon of vodka for company, Beria began to wonder what kind of world it might be without Stalin. How many intractable problems might be solved? How many new opportunities would open up? And from there, it was just a short step to thinking about who else amongst the senior members of the Politburo might gain from Stalin's death? He began to make a list. After a long process of elimination, he came down to just three names before he collapsed on the sofa from tiredness, from tension and, above all, from alcoholic stupor. It was perhaps fortunate that no one broke his door down that night because, if they had, they would have discovered the nascent plot right there in his pudgy grasp, the pencil and paper still in his hand.

On waking from a cramped and awkward slumber, he glanced down at the list he was still clutching. But instead of tossing it away as a crazy idea, he knew with cold certainty, even through an aching head, what he had to do. His liquor-induced meanderings from the previous evening had turned into nothing less than a plan to assassinate the thirty year dictator, victor of the Great Patriotic War and General Secretary of the Central Committee of the Communist Party: Joseph Vissarionovich Dzhugashvili, as he was born, or Joseph Stalin, as he came to be known.

For Beria, all those years of friendship and loyalty now counted for nothing. Even being a fellow Georgian was of no consequence. In his mind, his only chance of survival came down to one ultimate act, a single thought that permeated his very being, sweeping all else aside. The more he considered it, the greater its momentum became until, gradually, he began to involve the others on his list. It had to be done with extreme caution, at first so nuanced that it was hardly there at all. Then, as he became more confident, he began to insinuate thoughts he could later deny as mere jokes, the kind that everybody makes about their boss, each one designed as a test to see who agreed with what.

In one respect, Beria was fortunate. He had the time. The bus-tling activity inside the Kremlin continued from the US election all the way through to the presidential inauguration, with any number of policy changes and counter-changes, each of which had to be personally presented, debated and finally approved by Stalin. Beria therefore used this period as cover, trying to analyse which of the three on his list should be his priority. Georgi Malenkov, the big, non-committal friend of everyone, was the obvious choice, if only because he was Stalin's closest acolyte and would be the biggest beneficiary as the next in line. Then there was Nikolai Bulganin, who was a Marshal of the Soviet Union and had once been Stalin's loyal agent inside the ranks of the armed forces. Bulganin was generally less favoured than Malenkov and, anyway, he was very much under the sway of the third man on his list: the squat, powerful and often headstrong Nikita Sergeyevich Khrushchev.

Against all logic, it was the notion of Khrushchev that Beria found the most intriguing. Even though he disliked the man on a personal level, there was no doubt that approaching Khrushchev would potentially reap the greatest rewards, because he carried great influence within the Politburo and could therefore carry a lot of support after the deed was done. An additional motivation came from the fact that, underneath all the ribald jokes and the boorish camaraderie, it was Khrushchev who loathed his leader the most. It was clear to a shrewd observer like Beria that Khrushchev was the one who most objected to the cult of Stalinism, seeing it as the reincarnation of the Tsar in another guise. More than that, Khrushchev's bold, outspoken aggression suggested that, of all the contenders, he was probably the man who could most successfully effect the change.

At the end of the day, thought Beria, who better than Khrushchev to have on his side? It wouldn't be easy and he knew there were major risks but, when all was said and done, what did he have to lose? If his calculations were correct, the answer was simple. Nothing at all. It was kill or be killed, betrayal or be damned: the unwritten law of the Kremlin.

★ ★ ★

On January 13, the government-controlled newspaper, *Pravda*, published an article hinting at a new, wide-scale purge, centred on the allegedly undue influence of Jewish intellectuals, starting with medical practitioners.

By that time, there was almost no rationality to Stalin's dictates but, in this instance, there were a couple of possible explanations. The first, according to conventional wisdom, was the legacy of Trotsky, Kamenev, Zinoviev and other prominent Jewish members of Lenin's original revolutionary cabal: the ideologues whom Stalin had long since purged, yet whose political philosophies lived on. Another possibility, at least for those few insiders who knew about it, was the nagging reminder of that letter he sent to Hitler at the time of the Stalingrad siege in the winter of 1942: the offer promising to persecute Soviet Jews in exchange for peace. Perhaps the notion played on his mind. Or, perhaps in some twisted way, he'd finally come to believe the genocidal nonsense he wrote at that time.

Whatever the reason, many in the Politburo were becoming increasingly apprehensive, mainly because they'd been dealing with Jews for years: not just doctors but also lawyers, physicists, engineers, teachers, musicians and so many others. When it came to Stalin's purges, even an arm's-length relationship with a victim could become the excuse for an accusation.

This must have been the turning point, too, for Khrushchev: the moment when his personal anxiety finally overtook him. His solution was to propose an informal dinner at Stalin's *dacha* to discuss the matter, suggesting they keep the numbers down in order to debate the issues more freely. Stalin readily agreed - any excuse for a good dinner - and official invitations therefore went out to Malenkov, Bulganin and Beria, the last name being at Khrushchev's specific request. The implication was that, if there were ever an ideal time to do the deed, this would be it.

The date was set for February 28th, the last day of the coldest month.

It seems that Stalin was no different from normal on that occasion: the convivial host who provided copious amounts of Balkan food, plus endless refills of Polish slivovitz and a fruity Hungarian white wine. His moods altered, depending on the direction of the conversation but that, too, was the same as usual.

There was a great deal of internal tension, however, on the part of the guests, especially Lavrenti Beria. The other three may have believed that something was afoot but still didn't know for sure; and if it were to happen, they had no clue as to either the means or the methodology. Would Beria pull out a gun? A knife? A garrotte? All they could do was sit there and wait - and try not to reveal their anxiety.

The multi-course dinner was over by about one in the morning but Stalin wasn't yet tired and insisted on leading his four guests to the cinema gallery, where a projector was set up and a movie already laced through. As he entered, he called to one of his attendants to bring him a large glass of mineral water, possibly to cope with heartburn.

That's when Beria saw his chance.

On returning from the bathroom, he waited by the gallery door, then intercepted the delivery of the water and volunteered to carry it in. He dismissed the valet and, for that key moment, he was alone in the corridor. His own stomach was churning but he knew he had to pull himself together. If he didn't do this now, his nerve would fail and he'd never get another chance. His life would be over.

With a visibly trembling hand, he reached into his inside pocket and brought out an envelope containing a fine powder: a simple rat poison by the name of warfarin, obtainable almost anywhere. This he sprinkled into the water, forming a colourless, tasteless solution. Once he was satisfied, he carried the glass into the room, handing it over to Stalin, who thanked him. Then, as the lights were dimmed and the movie was about to roll, Beria watched his fellow Georgian gulp down most of the poisoned liquid in one go.

It didn't act immediately and, even at seventy-four, Stalin had a strong constitution. By the end of the movie, he was still fine and all four guests left in their large cars a little perplexed. To Beria it was disappointing, to say the least. After all that effort, it appeared that the substance hadn't worked. To the other three, it seemed as if he'd simply surrendered to his own cowardice.

Nothing untoward occurred until late the following morning when the guards noticed that Stalin hadn't called for his habitual tea with lemon. However, even then, they dared not interfere. It often happened that, when Stalin had been up late, he didn't want to be disturbed. Sometimes he slept through the day, sometimes he got up and worked: either way, he could become irate if anyone even dared to knock on his door.

At 6:30 that evening, the duty guards were relieved to see Stalin's room light switch on and assumed that all was well inside. Yet he failed to call out or emerge, so they still didn't know what to do until about 10:00 pm when an urgent package arrived from Central Committee offices in Moscow. This gave them the excuse to enter and it was a lowly security guard called Lozgachev who was assigned the unenviable task of interrupting The Boss.

Lozgachev knocked but received no answer. He knocked again. There was just silence. When he finally found the courage to open the door, he found a mess: Stalin lay slumped on the floor, unconscious, with blood-stained vomit coming from his mouth and a bad smell from his nightclothes where he'd soiled himself.

It was at this point that irony took over. Members of the staff had heard Stalin ranting against Jewish doctors the evening before and were therefore afraid to call in medical help. All they did was lift him back on to the bed. Without expert advice and for want of a better plan, the commander of the security detachment made the decision to call Moscow, specifically Beria's old sparring partner at the Lubyanka, Semyon Ignatyev, head of the MGB. But Ignatyev wasn't sure what to do either and he certainly didn't want to handle this alone. Any misstep and he'd carry the entire blame. He therefore telephoned Georgi Malenkov at the Kremlin and it was Malenkov, in turn, who informed the other three who'd been there the previous evening: Khrushchev, Bulganin and, of course, Beria.

They still didn't know if The Boss would recover, so they deliberately waited until the following morning, hoping to give the poison more time to do its work. Only then did they travel back out to the *dacha* to check for themselves - and only then did they authorize the staff to summon medical help. By the time such help arrived, it was too late. Despite all efforts, nobody could revive him.

Yet, incredibly, Stalin still wasn't dead.

The effect on his system was slow and his passing took two more days, during which time most of the senior Politburo and military leaders came to his bedside at the Blizhnyaya *dacha* to pay tribute. Even Beria himself was seen to go down on his knees and kiss his leader's hand in front of witnesses, just in case The Boss somehow made a miraculous recovery and wanted to know who had done what. But that didn't happen.

On March 5th, Stalin suffered a major cerebral hemorrhage and, at 9:50 in the morning, his bedside medical contingent declared him officially dead.

The first I heard of Stalin's death was from Katharina.

I was at the Odeon, Leicester Square, watching a matinee performance of *High Noon*, a flick I'd been wanting to see ever since it had premiered the previous year in New York. It was all about Gary Cooper shoring up his courage to face down some bad guys in black hats who wanted to kill him. I knew the feeling.

It was right on the critical stroke of "noon" in the movie, just as the plot was reaching its climax, that Katharina arrived and sat down in the seat next to me.

"Is it good?" she asked me.

"Better, now that you're here."

In the darkness, I saw a hint of that smile again. All I wanted to do was put my arm around her and forget everything else but we had business to conduct. This was a professional rendezvous.

She reached into the purse she was carrying and took out a package of items, wrapped up in a small folder. "Birth certificate, passport and funds," she whispered.

"Great, thanks. Who am I this time?"

"Albert Koenig, a freelance journalist from Vancouver."

Albert was my middle name and the word "*Koenig*" in German means "king." It meant I was now King Albert. "Cute," I told her.

"I thought you'd like it. By the way, Stalin was pronounced dead this morning."

The entire world had been waiting for days. "It's confirmed?"

"You'll see it in this evening's papers."

"How?"

"Cerebral hemorrhage, or so they say. At his *dacha*."

"You sound like you don't believe it."

"Let's say there's other intelligence."

"Which means what exactly?"

She looked around to see if there was anyone within earshot but, with the noise of the movie as cover, we were safe enough. "We don't know yet," she replied. "We're trying to piece it together."

"You must have some theories."

"We prefer to wait for the facts."

I knew enough not to push her. She'd tell me in her own good time. Meanwhile, up on screen, Gary Cooper was preparing for the showdown. His wife had left him and most of the townsfolk had refused to join him in his lonely stand against the desperadoes. Why didn't he just cut and run? Was he brave or just foolhardy? I could have asked myself the same question. If Stalin was dead, then Beria might well assume a free hand to chase after all kinds of enemies, real or perceived, and I wondered if that would include me.

"What will you do now?" she asked me. "I mean, now that you've got your new identity."

"How much money do I have?" I indicated the package in my hand.

"Three thousand."

"Pounds?"

"Yes."

"I was promised five."

"Proceeds from Hoeffler's Mercedes. Otherwise, you wouldn't have even got that."

"How about Siegfried's boat... and all the rest of his stuff, come to that?"

"All impounded."

I must say, I felt kind of cheated after all I'd been through but, at the same time, my anger was misplaced. "Thanks," I said, a little belatedly. I knew she'd fought to get me the funds and, in the end, three grand wasn't so bad. With that kind of cash, plus my new identity, I could hide out for a while without worrying. "I was thinking about going to the Cotswolds," I told her.

"Where's that?"

"Shakespeare country."

She picked up on it immediately. "Thinking of doing some writing?" she asked me.

I knew she was trying to ascertain whether I really would try to piece the story together. "I'm not sure yet," I answered. Strictly speaking, it was no more than the truth. Much would depend on the information I could glean and what kind of sources I could unearth.

"They won't let you publish it, you know."

"I thought, maybe, with the passage of time…"

"It was a failure, Ed."

"Not to me, it wasn't." I waited until she turned to look at me. "I found *you*."

She wasn't sure whether to smile or be embarrassed until, finally, she leaned in and kissed me on the cheek. "My hero," she whispered in my ear. Then she got up and sidled her way out, just as Gary Cooper's six-guns began blazing.

I looked down at the package she'd left me and considered once again whether I should I attempt to set it all down in writing. In truth, I didn't care too much if it was published or not. I wanted to do it anyway. What's the point of being a hero, I thought, if there are no heroic tales to tell?

EPILOGUE

London: Christmas Eve, 1953

It's now been ten months since Stalin died but, in that time, the world has changed a great deal. We've seen the testing of the hydrogen bomb, the conquest of Everest and the end of the Korean War. We've also witnessed an uprising in East Germany, riots in Poland and the triumph of Nikita Khrushchev as head of the new Soviet Presidium.

Finally, we heard another announcement which, for me, was the best news of all. This was the long-awaited news from Moscow that Lavrenti Pavlovich Beria had been executed. At long last, Beria was out of my life and I could breathe easier.

Victory was mine, if only because I'd managed to outlast him.

I must say the initial rumours of his arrest had come as something of a surprise because, in the immediate aftermath of Stalin's death, Beria had actually gained in status. According to reports, he'd tried to redeem himself by starting a program of cautious liberalization, a way to distance himself from the policies and purges that he'd so often carried out under the orders of his former boss. Yet he wasn't fooling anyone, especially Nikita Khrushchev, who'd been planning all along to step in and destroy the cult of Stalinism himself. The new Chairman of the Central Committee therefore maneuvered to have Beria denounced as *"Vrag Naroda,"* an enemy of the people, and promptly had him frogmarched out to Lefortovo prison. Charges were brought and tribunals were held but, as always in the Soviet Union, the result was a foregone conclusion. Beria was found guilty and sentenced to death by firing squad.

On learning of his execution, I immediately called Katharina and asked her to join me here at Rules, one of the oldest and most prestigious restaurants in London. Being Christmas Eve, I had to bribe my way in but what does it matter? I've still got a little money left, so what better way to enjoy it? Polished wood, stained glass, deferential waiters - I'm hoping it might be a reminder of that very first evening we spent together at Horcher's, back in Berlin.

"Hello, Ed."

I'm almost surprised to hear my real name after living with an alias for so long. Yet here she is, approaching my table with that familiar, elegant sway, causing every male in the place to pause in his conversation and glance her way. Today, she's wearing a dark, tailored suit over a cream blouse and the chandeliers are causing the silver in her hair to shine like swathes of platinum.

"Great entrance, as always," I tell her.

Given the surroundings, a modest smile and a discrete peck on the cheek is all I receive before she sits down. I order a good bottle of Macon from the hovering waiter but it's only after he disappears that I reach over to touch her hand. Her long fingers stretch out towards mine.

"You must be feeling pretty good," she's saying to me.

"Best in years."

"How's the report coming?"

"Almost done. Still a few holes... you know how it is."

I see her nod but, in fact, she's been the one who helped me the most. Gehlen authorized the information because he wants the account of what happened as potential evidence, just in case he ever has to disassociate himself in a hurry from Sir Humphrey Pender.

"Ed, you do understand, it'll never be published."

It's not the first time she's told me. "I'm aware of that."

"It'll just be filed and forgotten. All that work, just to end up on a dusty shelf."

"We'll see."

She gives me a look to suggest I'm wasting my time. "Well, at least there's no need to stay in hiding any more. What will you do now? Any ideas?"

"Yeah, I've been thinking about that."

I'm instantly aware of a new crowd being seated at the next table: a group of City bankers in their sober pinstripes. I try not to let them distract me. This might well be the most important con-versation of my life.

"And?" she asks me.

"And I guess what I do now kind of depends on you... or should I say, on *us*."

She takes a moment or two, then offers an awkward smile. "I don't know what to say."

"That's easy. Say you want to be with me."

"I do but…"

"But?" The word sounds ominous.

"Ed, I've been asked... I've been asked if you'd like to join us."

"To join you? I don't follow. You mean a job? Katharina... you're offering me a job?"

"Effectively, yes. Well, not me personally..."

"Gehlen?"

"He's got big plans. As soon as Adenauer makes it official, we'll be reporting to the Chancellery instead of the CIA."

"That's been rumoured for a while."

"Yes, but now that Eisenhower's in office, the talks have already begun. Anyway, the point is that, when it happens, the ODESSA faction will be the first item on the agenda. Adenauer won't turn a blind eye, like the Americans."

"That's good to hear."

"So... what do you think?"

"Of joining you? In what capacity?"

A slight shrug. "We don't know yet."

I find myself gazing at her, peering into those hazel eyes, trying to penetrate that beautiful mask she wears so well. "Katharina, tell me the truth. Is this really coming from Gehlen, or did you arrange it yourself?"

There's a moment's hesitation. "We... had a discussion."

"That's what I thought."

"But I didn't have to persuade him. He was very receptive."

"Another bribe, just to make sure my story stays hush-hush?"

"No, you're wrong about that."

"I am?"

"Well, no, not about the story."

"Ah."

"But he wouldn't have offered you a job on that basis, believe me. Despite what you think, he was actually impressed with your performance."

"I didn't bring him the manuscript."

"No, but you got a lot further than he ever thought you would. And you managed not to die in the process."

I can't help a grin. "Not that I didn't try."

"Look, Ed, I can assure you, the offer's real... if you want it. Do you? Are you even interested?"

"Would I be working with you?"

"Yes... I mean, it's not really my decision, but I would hope so. But that's not the reason..."

I interrupted her. "Then, naturally, I'm interested."

"No, Ed, what I'm trying to say..."

"I know what you're trying to say."

"Do you?"

"Katharina..." I reach for her hand again. "Let's make a deal, shall we? Let's agree to stop playing games. Can we do that?"

"Games?"

"Between us. Hiding everything behind this... this professional wall we keep building. I just want to know. Do we have something or not?"

She looks down at the slim fingers that always seem to form such graceful angles. "I think you know the answer to that," she says very softly.

"I need to hear you say it."

"Say it? The minute you called this morning, I dropped everything... several meetings, a dozen calls, a half-day conference. I cleared everything and came here. What more do you need?"

She has a point. "How about Gehlen?" I ask her. "He doesn't mind?"

"About what?"

"About us."

"Reinhard's only interested in results. He says that if we can make it work, so can he." A pause. "But you still haven't answered me."

I manage a further delay, as the waiter arrives with the wine and we go through the rituals of tasting and pouring. The real truth is that I don't know how to answer her. I want to be with her - yes, I can even say desperately - but to make a decision like this? To work for Gehlen? To live a life of endless deception?

"Can I make you a counter-offer?" I ask her.

Immediately, she's on the defensive. "I can't quit my career, Ed. Don't ask me to do that."

"That's not what I was going to say."

"No?"

"Not at all."

"What then? What's your counter-offer?"

"I was just wondering... when was the last time you took some time off?"

"A vacation?"

"We talked about Canada, remember, on the boat ride to Greenwich."

"I'm sorry, Ed, that's impossible."

"You want to live in a democracy? That's one of your rights, to take a holiday when you need it. Better get used to it."

"I'm in the middle of something."

"Okay, so it doesn't have to be tomorrow. Whenever you're free."

"I don't know, Ed..."

"Come on, it'll do you good."

"Isn't it cold in Canada this time of year?"

"Frigid." I see her smile again. This time it's the big one, the one that can bring a whole room to life, and I decide to press home my advantage. "We can ski, drive a dogsled, build an igloo... whatever you like."

"Build an igloo?"

"Sure, they're very cozy.'

"And, I have to say, you're very crazy."

"Yeah, well, I'm feeling kind of crazy today. Stalin's dead and

Beria's dead but we're alive and I want to make the most of it. What do you say?"

"Will you think about the offer while we're there?"

I can feel myself hesitating. I just can't see it. Me, as a full time operative: a life of case officers and safe houses, encryptions and false identities; and, yes, the constant threat of exposure. On the other hand, what the hell? What am I so worried about? The MGB? The Stasi? If I really think about it, they're the ones who brought Katharina and me back together. Maybe I should write to Moscow and offer my thanks.

"Okay, I'll consider it," I tell her. "I'll do anything you want. Just say you'll come."

She shrugs. "Do I have a choice?"

"I'm trying not to give you one."

She looks at me for what seems like an age. Then, once again, she surprises me by raising her glass. "In that case... to the frozen north!"

I lift mine to match. "As long as it's not Siberia."

This time, she not only smiles, she laughs out loud. The joyous sound reverberates around the room, causing the business types around us to stop their chatter and glance in our direction. They may be making money but I'm making headway and, for me, right now, that's more than enough.

★

AUTHOR'S AFTERWORD

Weaving fictional concepts into well-established facts is the hallmark of any political thriller, so a final word of explanation might be of some interest.

On the historical context

In the three decades that Stalin was in power, his Soviet regime became the epitome of the totalitarian state. Even his closest acolytes existed in a state of constant fear. Numbers vary as to how many of his own countrymen Stalin had killed in his purges but some historians put the figure as high as thirty million, which would make him the bloodiest dictator of all time. In the worst instances, these mass murders were carried out on a quota basis: so many thousands from this town, so many hundreds from that village; in other words, based on nothing but sheer, personal whim. Fear as a means of installing obedience has been around since before the Romans but this was a more callous disregard for his own people than even the Tsars could have contemplated.

His pact with Hitler in August, 1939, shocked the world and created a whole new balance of power, until Hitler personally decided to break it by invading the Soviet Union in June, 1941. This surprise move forced Stalin to switch sides, joining Churchill and Roosevelt to become one of the principal Allied leaders in World War II. As a result, his image was moderated in the West - to the extent that the media often referred to him as "Uncle Joe."

However, despite this wartime alliance, the Soviet intelligence services continued their astounding success rate in prying crucial secrets from the US and the UK, even as they collaborated closely and accepted billions in aid.

By far the most serious result of such activity was the Soviets' rapid nuclear deployment and it was this factor, more than any other, which made the early Cold War so dangerous. The period covered by this novel, 1952/53, was especially critical because, just as the 74-year-old Stalin was gaining access to atomic warheads, he was also becoming more imperial in his leadership, more arbitrary in his decisions and less stable in his mental processes. There were even worries that he might just trigger a war through senility.

As regards the events surrounding his death, I've done no more than draw on evidence that many researchers have already uncovered: that he may not have died from natural causes, as officially reported, but may well have been fed rat poison by fellow Georgian, Lavrenti Beria. Along with Malenkov, Bulganin and Khrushchev, Beria was there at the Blizhnyaya *dacha* on that fateful night and was very much afraid of being purged. Further evidence comes from the auto-biography of long-serving Foreign Minister, Vyacheslav Molotov, who claims that Beria confessed to him that he was indeed the one who betrayed Stalin and committed the fatal act.

Following Stalin's funeral, it was Malenkov, as next in line, who assumed the Soviet leadership, with Bulganin as his Minister of Defense. However, their powers were soon superseded by the irrepressible Nikita Khrushchev, who eventually denounced what he called "the cult of Stalinism." It was primarily due to Khrushchev that the era of irrational mass purges came to an end, with Beria accused of being one of the leading instigators. He was named an "enemy of the people" and finally executed by firing squad.

On the novel's integrity

Looking back on Cold War spy fiction over the years, it's easy to see how the East-West adversaries have been simplified to an almost ludicrous extent. By contrast, I have attempted to portray the various intelligence agencies in true relation to each other.

Contrary to current perception, the Soviet intelligence apparatus under Stalin was far from monolithic. We tend to remember the KGB but this only came into being after his death. During the last years of Stalin's regime, the functions were divided between the MGB and MVD. Both were both led by ministers of the Politburo and were therefore highly political and extremely competitive.

In the Soviet puppet state of East Germany, the MfS, or Stasi, was little more than an MGB surrogate. Only later did it grow more self-sufficient under the direction of the wily Markus Wolf.

The West, too, was more disorganized than it ever appeared, the Gehlen Organization being a good example. Set up and sponsored by the CIA, it became the American "eyes and ears" on the ground in Central Europe, even as it contained elements of ODESSA, the post-war, ex-SS escape group.

Meanwhile, the British clandestine services, which had been so heavily infiltrated by Communist sympathizers, were still trying to maintain the illusion of global capability, despite the new reality of US dominance. Indeed, some critics have claimed that the early success of Ian Fleming's James Bond was partly due to a national desire to regain some pride in the field of intelligence, after a decade of such well-publicized failures.

To add to the realism, I've also drawn inspiration from historical personalities. Among them: Joseph Stalin and his daughter, Svetlana; Politburo members Khrushchev, Malenkov, Bulganin and Ignatyev; Commission Control Chairman Chuikov; Admiral Kuznetsov; US Presidents Truman and Eisenhower; Secretary of State Acheson; CIA Director Bedell "Beetle" Smith; Ambassador Gifford; and West German Chancellor, Konrad Adenauer.

In particular, careful attention has been paid to Lavrenti Pavlovich Beria, the deceptively ordinary Minister for Internal Affairs whose duplicity, insecurity and pedophilia have been corroborated by many sources. Even his depraved "flower arrangement" has been documented.

Another of the leading characters drawn from life is the ever-controversial Lina von Osten, widow of the assassinated Reinhard Heydrich, chief of Third Reich security and prime instigator of the Holocaust, as well as a potential successor to Adolf Hitler. After the war, she converted her family home on the rural Baltic island of Fehmarn into a guesthouse, where she continued to receive journalists and defend her husband's motives.

Then, of course, there's the charismatic ex-Nazi, Reinhard Gehlen, who really did talk his way out of an American POW camp in order to set up the freelance organization that bore his name. Eventually, he used that self-same ability to become the official head of West German intelligence.

Others from the field of espionage include: the legendary Yuri Modin, who later confessed his role as a Soviet case officer in his auto-biography; and Kim Philby, the notorious British "mole," who finally found refuge in Moscow. Also mentioned in passing are the names of Rosenberg, Sarant, Barr, Fuchs, Burgess, Maclean and Cairncross, all of whom became infamous in the annals of Cold War treason.

By the way, Guy the gorilla was real, too, a favourite inhabitant of the Regent's Park Zoo in London for over thirty years.

I've also drawn on historical fact, as well as personal experience, for countless descriptive details. For example: the cities of London, Berlin, Moscow, Beijing, Paris and Monte Carlo; branded locations like Kardomah, Selfridges, Fortnum & Mason, The Lanesborough, The Queen's, Le Raphaël, Les Galeries Lafayette, and Rules restaurant; vessels such as the Soviet S-80 submarine, the Danish frigate "Holder Danske," and the luxury motor launch "Guinevere," which exists under another name; the British train, "Flying Scotsman," which is today powered by diesel but still makes a daily run; the old Quarry Hill tenement, now torn down, in the northern English city of Leeds, which really was marked on SS invasion plans; the Nazi propaganda magazine *Signal*, which was published in English specially for the occupied British Channel Islands; plus all the automobiles, armaments and other equipment, as used in various chapters - including, surprisingly, the MGB chemical compound that caused death by means of a simple touch, which was a genuine development of Laboratory 12, a covert department of the Soviet technological institute.

It should be noted, too, that Berlin, Ontario, where the protagonist was born, is now the vibrant city of Kitchener, named after Lord Kitchener, commander of British forces during the 1914-18 War. It has a German immigrant heritage and the change was made to prove loyalty to the Crown.

As a plot catalyst, the concept of the manuscript is based on the notorious, all-too-real tract, *The Protocols of the Elders of Zion*, which is still being shamelessly used for anti-Semitic propaganda in many parts of the world, even though academic experts have unanimously concluded that it was originated, not by a cadre of rabbis, but by the Tsar's secret police, the Okhranka, in the late 19th century.

Lastly, there's the idea of the letter, the peace initiative from Stalin to Hitler during the vital battle for Stalingrad in the winter of 1942. While there's no record of any such missive, this remains an intriguing and plausible scenario.

It must be remembered this was a desperate time for the Soviet Red Army. Its officer class had been depleted as a result of Stalin's purges, its military options were restricted due to a lack of resources and the number of casualties was already horrendous. By recalling the Nazi-Soviet pre-war pact, Stalin might well have thought that a personal appeal had a chance of extricating him from the expected disaster. Like Hitler, he already had a system of concentration camps, the infamous gulags, and he never much cared for the large Jewish population he inherited. From his perspective, making an offer to build a Soviet version of Auschwitz might therefore have been a valid option.

Leon Berger

★

THE
BERLIN
DOSSIER

Leon Berger

A novel

"Evocative"
"Smart"
"Spell-binding"

If you liked THE KREMLIN BETRAYAL, you'll also enjoy
THE BERLIN DOSSIER, another "Ed Schaeffer" novel by
LEON BERGER from LOON IN BALLOON.

**"THE BERLIN DOSSIER is evocative with haunting
undertones. It's also smart, tight and a solid read."
Sheila Kindellan-Sheehan, author of the best-selling
thriller *Cutting Corners*.**

**"THE BERLIN DOSSIER takes us on a spine-chilling ride
through one of the most dangerous periods in human history.
Berger makes us believe we are there. A spellbinding read." Hugh
MacDonald, author of *Cold Against The Heart* and *Murder at
Mussel Cove*.**

Set in Berlin 1938 and impeccably researched, THE BERLIN
DOSSIER richly evokes the atmosphere of a continent about to go
up in flames.

Once again, our protagonist is Edmund Albert Schaeffer, a
German-Canadian émigré who struggles to make a living as a small-
time freelance journalist. When he happens to meet the beautiful,
high-born Katharina Vollbrecht, he's drawn into a deadly plot involving
key members of the Nazi hierarchy, each conspiring to be Hitler's
successor. Himmler and Göring, Heydrich and Canaris... they're all
here, with their true-life personalities and ruthless machinations.

A gripping novel of love and loss, of sex and violence, of friendship and betrayal, THE BERLIN DOSSIER will have you flipping
the pages to its pulse-pounding climax.